Agatha Christie is known throughout the world as the Queen ... me. Her books have sold over a billion copies in English with another billion in foreign languages. She is the most widely published author of all time and in any language, outsold only by the Bible and Shakespeare. She is the author of 80 crime novels and short story collections, 20 plays, and six novels written under the name of Mary Westmacott.

Agatha Christie's first novel, *The Mysterious Affair at Styles*, was written towards the end of the First World War, in which she served as a VAD. In it she created Hercule Poirot, the little Belgian detective who was destined to become the most popular detective in crime fiction since Sherlock Holmes. It was eventually published by The Bodley Head in 1920.

In 1926, after averaging a book a year, Agatha Christie wrote her masterpiece. *The Murder of Roger Ackroyd* was the first of her books to be published by Collins and marked the beginning of an author–publisher relationship which lasted for 50 years and well over 70 books. *The Murder of Roger Ackroyd* was also the first of Agatha Christie's books to be dramatized – under the name *Alibi* – and to have a successful run in London's West End. *The Mousetrap*, her most famous play of all, opened in 1952 and is the longest-running play in history.

Agatha Christie was made a Dame in 1971. She died in 1976, since when a number of books have been published posthumously: the bestselling novel *Sleeping Murder* appeared later that year, followed by her autobiography and the short story collections *Miss Marple's Final Cases*, *Problem at Pollensa Bay* and *While the Light Lasts*. In 1998 *Black Coffee* was the first of her plays to be novelized by another author, Charles Osborne.

CHRISTIE COLLECTION

Brown Suit
Chimneys
The Seven Dials Mystery
The Mysterious Mr Quin
The Sittaford Mystery
The Hound of Death
The Listerdale Mystery
Why Didn't They Ask Evans?
Parker Pyne Investigates
Murder is Easy
And Then There Were None
Towards Zero
Death Comes as the End
Sparkling Cyanide
Crooked House
They Came to Baghdad
Destination Unknown
Ordeal by Innocence
The Pale Horse
Endless Night
Passenger to Frankfurt
Problem at Pollensa Bay
While the Light Lasts

Poirot
The Mysterious Affair at Styles
The Murder on the Links
Poirot Investigates
The Murder of Roger Ackroyd
The Big Four
The Mystery of the Blue Train
Peril at End House
Lord Edgware Dies
Murder on the Orient Express
Three-Act Tragedy
Death in the Clouds
The ABC Murders
Murder in Mesopotamia
Cards on the Table
Murder in the Mews
Dumb Witness
Death on the Nile
Appointment With Death
Hercule Poirot's Christmas
Sad Cypress
One, Two, Buckle My Shoe
Evil Under the Sun
Five Little Pigs
The Hollow
The Labours of Hercules
Taken at the Flood
Mrs McGinty's Dead
After the Funeral
Hickory Dickory Dock

Dead Man's Folly
Cat Among the Pigeons
The Adventure of the Christmas Pudding
The Clocks
Third Girl
Hallowe'en Party
Elephants Can Remember
Poirot's Early Cases
Curtain: Poirot's Last Case

Marple
The Murder at the Vicarage
The Thirteen Problems
The Body in the Library
The Moving Finger
A Murder is Announced
They Do It With Mirrors
A Pocket Full of Rye
4.50 from Paddington
The Mirror Crack'd from Side to Side
A Caribbean Mystery
At Bertram's Hotel
Nemesis
Sleeping Murder
Miss Marple's Final Cases

Tommy & Tuppence
The Secret Adversary
Partners in Crime
N or M?
By the Pricking of My Thumbs
Postern of Fate

Published as Mary Westmacott
Giant's Bread
Unfinished Portrait
Absent in the Spring
The Rose and the Yew Tree
A Daughter's a Daughter
The Burden

Memoirs
An Autobiography
Come, Tell Me How You Live

Play Collections
The Mousetrap and Selected Plays
Witness for the Prosecution
and Selected Plays

Play Adaptations by Charles Osborne
Black Coffee (Poirot)
Spider's Web
The Unexpected Guest

Agatha Christie

MURDER IN THREE STAGES

•

BLACK COFFEE

•

SPIDER'S WEB

•

THE UNEXPECTED GUEST

•

novelised by Charles Osborne

HARPER

An imprint of HarperCollins*Publishers*
77–85 Fulham Palace Road,
Hammersmith, London W6 8JB
www.harpercollins.co.uk

This edition first published 2007
3

This collection copyright © 2007 Agatha Christie Limited,
a Chorion company. All rights reserved.
www.agathachristie.com

Black Coffee © Agatha Christie Limited 1997
Spider's Web © Agatha Christie Limited 2000
The Unexpected Guest © Agatha Christie Limited 1999

ISBN-10 0-00-724579-3
ISBN-13 978-0-00-724579-6

Typeset in Plantin Light and Gill Sans by
Palimpsest Book Production Limited,
Grangemouth, Stirlingshire

Printed and bound in Great Britain by
Clays Ltd, St Ives plc

CONTENTS

Foreword by Mathew Prichard 1

•

BLACK COFFEE 3

•

SPIDER'S WEB 181

•

THE UNEXPECTED GUEST 369

•

The Plays of Agatha Christie 525

•

It was almost certainly because of her dissatisfaction with *Alibi*, someone else's stage adaption in 1928 of her novel, *The Murder of Roger Ackroyd*, that my grandmother Agatha Christie decided to write a play of her own, which is something she had not previously attempted. *Black Coffee*, featuring her favourite detective, Hercule Poirot, was finished by the summer of 1929. But when Agatha showed it to her agent, he advised her not to bother submitting it to any theatre as, in his opinion, it was not good enough to be staged. Fortunately, a friend who was connected with theatrical management persuaded her to ignore such a negative advice, and the play was accepted for production in 1930 at the Embassy Theatre in Swiss Cottage, London.

Black Coffee was favourable received, and in April of the following year transferred to the West End, where it had a successful run of several months at the St Martin's Theatre (where a later Christie play, *The Mousetrap*, began a much longer run in 1952). In 1930, Poirot had been played by a popular actor of the time, Francis L. Sullivan, with John Boxer as his associate Captain Hastings; Joyce Bland played

Lucia Amory, and Shakespearian actor Donald Wolfit was Dr Carelli. In the West End production, Francis L. Sullivan was still Poirot, but Hastings was now played by Roland Culver, and Dr Carelli by Dino Galvani.

Some months later, *Black Coffee* was filmed in England at the Twickenham Studios, directed by Leslie Hiscott and starring Austin Trevor, who had already played Poirot in the film version of *Alibi*. The play remained a favourite with repertory companies for some years, and in 1956 Charles Osborne, then earning his living as a young actor, found himself playing Dr Carelli in *Black Coffee* in a summer season at Tunbridge Wells.

Nearly forty years later, after he had in the intervening years not only become a world authority on opera but had also written a splendid book entitled *The Life and Crimes of Agatha Christie*, Osborne remembered the play. He suggested to Agatha Christie Limited (who control the copyright of her works) that, twenty years after the author's death, it would be marvellous to give the world a new Agatha Christie crime novel. We agreed enthusiastically, and the result is this Hercule Poirot murder mystery, which to me reads like authentic, vintage Christie. I feel sure Agatha would be proud to have written it.

Mathew Prichard

BLACK COFFEE

CHAPTER I

Hercule Poirot sat at breakfast in his small but agreeably cosy flat in Whitehall Mansions. He had enjoyed his brioche and his cup of hot chocolate. Unusually, for he was a creature of habit and rarely varied his breakfast routine, he had asked his valet, George, to make him a second cup of chocolate. While he was awaiting it, he glanced again at the morning's post which lay on his breakfast table.

Meticulously tidy as always, he had placed the discarded envelopes in one neat pile. They had been opened very carefully, with the paper-knife in the form of a miniature sword which his old friend Hastings had given him for a birthday many years ago. A second pile contained those communications he found of no interest – circulars, mostly – which in a moment he would ask George to dispose of. The third pile consisted of those letters which would require an answer of some kind, or at least an acknowledgement. These would be dealt with after breakfast, and in any case not before ten o'clock. Poirot thought it not quite professional to begin a routine working day before ten. When he was on a case – ah, well, of course that was different. He remembered that once he and Hastings had set out well before dawn in order to –

But, no, Poirot did not want his thoughts to dwell on the past. The happy past. Their last case, involving an international crime organization known as 'The Big Four', had been brought to a satisfactory conclusion, and Hastings had returned to the Argentine, his wife and his ranch. Though his old friend was temporarily back in London on business connected with the ranch, it was highly unlikely that Poirot and he would find themselves working together again to solve a crime. Was that why Hercule Poirot was feeling restless on this fine spring morning in May 1934? Ostensibly retired, he had been lured out of that retirement more than once when an especially interesting problem had been presented to him. He had enjoyed being on the scent again, with Hastings by his side to act as a kind of sounding board for his ideas and theories. But nothing of professional interest had presented itself to Poirot for several months. Were there no imaginative crimes and criminals any more? Was it all violence and brutality, the kind of sordid murder or robbery which it was beneath his, Poirot's, dignity to investigate?

His thoughts were interrupted by the arrival, silently at his elbow, of George with that second and welcome cup of chocolate. Welcome not only because Poirot would enjoy the rich, sweet taste, but also because it would enable him to postpone, for a few more minutes, the realization that the day, a fine sunny morning, stretched before him with nothing more exciting in prospect than a constitutional in the park and a walk through Mayfair to his favourite restaurant in Soho where he would lunch alone on – what, now? – perhaps a little pâté to begin, and then the sole *bonne femme*, followed by –

He became aware that George, having placed the chocolate on the table, was addressing him. The impeccable and imperturbable George, an intensely English, rather wooden-faced individual, had been with Poirot for some time now, and was all that he wished in the way of a valet. Completely incurious, and extraordinarily reluctant to express a personal opinion on any subject, George was a mine of information about the English aristocracy, and as fanatically neat as the great detective himself. Poirot had more than once said to him, 'You press admirably the trousers, George, but the imagination, you possess it not.' Imagination, however, Hercule Poirot possessed in abundance. The ability to press a pair of trousers properly was, in his opinion, a rare accomplishment. Yes, he was indeed fortunate in having George to look after him.

'– and so I took the liberty, sir, of promising that you would return the call this morning,' George was saying.

'I do beg your pardon, my dear George,' replied Poirot. 'My attention was wandering. Someone has telephoned, you say?'

'Yes, sir. It was last night, sir, while you were out at the theatre with Mrs Oliver. I had retired to bed before you arrived home, and thought it unnecessary to leave a message for you at that late hour.'

'Who was it who called?'

'The gentleman said he was Sir Claud Amory, sir. He left his telephone number, which would appear to be somewhere in Surrey. The matter, he said, was a somewhat delicate one, and when you rang you were not to give your name to anyone else, but were to insist on speaking to Sir Claud himself.'

'Thank you, George. Leave the telephone number on my desk,' said Poirot. 'I shall ring Sir Claud after I have perused this morning's *Times*. It is still a trifle early in the morning for telephoning, even on somewhat delicate matters.'

George bowed and departed, while Poirot slowly finished his cup of chocolate and then repaired to the balcony with that morning's newspaper.

A few minutes later, *The Times* had been laid aside. The international news was, as usual, depressing. That terrible Hitler had turned the German courts into branches of the Nazi party, the Fascists had seized power in Bulgaria and, worst of all, in Poirot's own country, Belgium, forty-two miners were feared dead after an explosion at a mine near Mons. The home news was little better. Despite the misgivings of officials, women competitors at Wimbledon were to be allowed to wear shorts this summer. Nor was there much comfort in the obituaries, for people Poirot's age and younger seemed intent on dying.

His newspaper abandoned, Poirot lay back in his comfortable wicker chair, his feet on a small stool. Sir Claud Amory, he thought to himself. The name struck a chord, surely? He had heard it somewhere. Yes, this Sir Claud was well-known in some sphere or other. But what was it? Was he a politician? A barrister? A retired civil servant? Sir Claud Amory. Amory.

The balcony faced the morning sun, and Poirot found it warm enough to bask in for a moment or two. Soon it would become too warm for him, for he was no sun-worshipper. 'When the sun drives me inside,' he mused, 'then I will exert myself and consult the *Who's Who*. If this Sir Claud is a person of some distinction, he will surely be included in that so admirable volume. If he is not –?' The little detective gave an expressive shrug of his shoulders. An inveterate snob, he was already predisposed in Sir Claud's favour by virtue of his title. If he were to be found in *Who's Who*, a volume in which the details of Poirot's own career could also be discovered, then perhaps this Sir Claud was someone with a valid claim on his, Hercule Poirot's, time and attention.

A quickening of curiosity and a sudden cool breeze combined to send Poirot indoors. Entering his library, he went to a shelf of reference books and took down the thick red volume whose title, *Who's Who*, was embossed in gold on its spine. Turning the pages, he came to the entry he sought, and read aloud.

AMORY, Sir Claud (Herbert); Kt. 1927; *b.* 24 Nov. 1878. *m.* 1907, Helen Graham (*d.* 1929); one *s. Educ*: Weymouth Gram. Sch.; King's Coll., London. Research Physicist GEC Laboratories, 1905; RAE Farnborough (Radio Dept.), 1916; Air Min. Research Establishment, Swanage, 1921; demonstrated a new Principle for accelerating particles: the travelling wave linear accelerator, 1924. Awarded Monroe Medal of Physical Soc. *Publications*: papers in learned journals. *Address*: Abbot's Cleve, nr. Market Cleve, Surrey. *T*: Market Cleve 314. *Club*: Athenaeum.

'Ah, yes,' Poirot mused. 'The famous scientist.' He remembered a conversation he had had some months previously with a member of His Majesty's government, after Poirot had retrieved some missing documents whose contents could have proved embarrassing to the government. They had talked of security, and the politician had admitted that security measures in general were not sufficiently stringent. 'For instance,' he had said, 'what Sir Claud Amory is working on now is of such fantastic importance in any future war – but he refuses to work under laboratory conditions where he and his invention can be properly guarded. Insists on working alone at his house in the country. No security at all. Frightening.'

'I wonder,' Poirot thought to himself as he replaced *Who's Who* on the bookshelf, 'I wonder – can Sir Claud want to engage Hercule Poirot to be a tired old watchdog? The inventions of war, the secret weapons, they are not for me. If Sir Claud –'

The telephone in the next room rang, and Poirot could hear George answering it. A moment later, the valet appeared. 'It's Sir Claud Amory again, sir,' he said.

Poirot went to the phone. ''Allo. It is Hercule Poirot who speaks,' he announced into the mouthpiece.

'Poirot? We've not met, though we have acquaintances in common. My name is Amory, Claud Amory –'

'I have heard of you, of course, Sir Claud,' Poirot responded.

'Look here, Poirot. I've got a devilishly tricky problem on my hands. Or rather, I might have. I can't be certain. I've been working on a formula to bombard the atom – I won't go into details, but the Ministry of Defence regards it as of the utmost importance. My work is now complete, and I've produced a formula from which a new and deadly explosive can be made. I have reason to suspect that a member of my household is attempting to steal the formula. I can't say any more now, but I should be greatly obliged if you would come down to Abbot's Cleve for the weekend, as my house-guest. I want you to take the formula back with you to London, and hand it over to a certain person at the Ministry. There are good reasons why a Ministry courier can't do the job. I need someone who is ostensibly an unobtrusive, unscientific member of the public but who is also astute enough –'

Sir Claud talked on. Hercule Poirot, glancing across at the reflection in the mirror of his bald, egg-shaped head and his elaborately waxed moustache, told himself that he had never before, in a long career, been considered unobtrusive, nor did he so consider himself. But a weekend in the country and a chance to meet the distinguished scientist could be agreeable, as, no doubt, could the suitably expressed thanks of a grateful government – and merely for carrying in his pocket from Surrey to Whitehall an obscure, if deadly, scientific formula.

'I shall be delighted to oblige you, my dear Sir Claud,' he interrupted. 'I shall arrange to arrive on Saturday afternoon, if that is convenient to you, and return to London with whatever you wish me to take with me, on Monday morning. I look forward greatly to making your acquaintance.'

Curious, he thought, as he replaced the receiver. Foreign agents might well be interested in Sir Claud's formula, but could it really be the case that someone in the scientist's own household –? Ah well, doubtless more would be revealed during the course of the weekend.

'George,' he called, 'please take my heavy tweed suit and my dinner jacket and trousers to the cleaners. I must have them back by Friday, as I am going to the Country for the Weekend.' He made it sound like the Steppes of Central Asia and for a lifetime.

Then, turning to the phone, he dialled a number and waited for a few moments before speaking. 'My dear Hastings,' he began, 'would you not like to have a few days away from your business concerns in London? Surrey is very pleasant at this time of the year . . .'

CHAPTER 2

I

Sir Claud Amory's house, Abbot's Cleve, stood just on the outskirts of the small town – or rather overgrown village – of Market Cleve, about twenty-five miles south-east of London. The house itself, a large but architecturally non-descript Victorian mansion, was set amid an attractive few acres of gently undulating countryside, here and there heavily wooded. The gravel drive, from the gatehouse up to the front door of Abbot's Cleve, twisted its way through trees and dense shrubbery. A terrace ran along the back of the house, with a lawn sloping down to a somewhat neglected formal garden.

On the Friday evening two days after his telephone conversation with Hercule Poirot, Sir Claud sat in his study, a small but comfortably furnished room on the ground floor of the house, on the east side. Outside, the light was beginning to fade. Sir Claud's butler, Tredwell, a tall, lugubrious-looking individual with an impeccably correct manner, had sounded the gong for dinner two or three minutes earlier, and no doubt the family was now assembling in the dining-room on the other side of the hall.

Sir Claud drummed on the desk with his fingers, his habit when forcing himself to a quick decision. A man in his fifties, of medium height and build, with greying hair brushed straight back from a high forehead, and eyes of a piercingly cold blue, he now wore an expression in which anxiety was mixed with puzzlement.

There was a discreet knock on the study door, and Tredwell appeared in the doorway. 'Excuse me, Sir Claud. I wondered if perhaps you had not heard the gong –'

'Yes, yes, Tredwell, that's all right. Would you tell them I shall be in very shortly? Say I'm caught on the phone. In fact, I am about to make a quick phone call. You may as well begin serving.'

Tredwell withdrew silently, and Sir Claud, taking a deep breath, pulled the telephone towards himself. Extracting a small address-book from a drawer of his desk, he consulted it briefly and then picked up the receiver. He listened for a moment and then spoke.

'This is Market Cleve three-one-four. I want you to get me a London number.' He gave the number, then sat back, waiting. The fingers of his right hand began to drum nervously on the desk.

II

Several minutes later, Sir Claud Amory joined the dinner-party, taking his place at the head of the table around which the six others were already seated. On Sir Claud's right sat his niece, Barbara Amory, with Richard, her cousin and the only son of Sir Claud, next to her. On Richard Amory's right was a house-guest, Dr Carelli, an Italian. Continuing round, at the opposite end of the table to Sir Claud, sat Caroline

Amory, his sister. A middle-aged spinster, she had run Sir
Claud's house for him ever since his wife died some years
earlier. Edward Raynor, Sir Claud's secretary, sat on Miss
Amory's right, with Lucia, Richard Amory's wife, between
him and the head of the household.

Dinner, on this occasion, was not at all festive. Caroline
Amory made several attempts at small-talk with Dr Carelli,
who answered her politely enough without offering much
in the way of conversation himself. When she turned to
address a remark to Edward Raynor, that normally polite
and socially suave young man gave a nervous start, mumbled
an apology and looked embarrassed. Sir Claud was as taciturn
as he normally was at meal-times, or perhaps even more so.
Richard Amory cast an occasional anxious glance across the
table at his wife, Lucia. Barbara Amory alone seemed in good
spirits, and made spasmodic light conversation with her Aunt
Caroline.

It was while Tredwell was serving the dessert course that Sir
Claud suddenly addressed the butler, speaking loudly enough
for all at the dinner-table to hear his words.

'Tredwell,' he said, 'would you ring Jackson's garage in
Market Cleve, and ask them to send a car and driver to the
station to meet the eight-fifty from London? A gentleman
who is visiting us after dinner will be coming by that train.'

'Very well, Sir Claud,' replied Tredwell as he left. He
was barely out of the room when Lucia, with a murmured
apology, got up abruptly from the table and hurried out,
almost colliding with the butler as he was about to close the
door behind him.

Crossing the hall, she hurried along the corridor and proceeded to the large room at the back of the house. The library –

as it was generally called – served normally as a drawing-room as well. It was a comfortable room rather than an elegant one. French windows opened from it on to the terrace, and another door led to Sir Claud's study. On the mantelpiece, above a large open fireplace, stood an old-fashioned clock and some ornaments, as well as a vase of spills for use in lighting the fire.

The library furniture consisted of a tall bookcase with a tin box on the top of it, a desk with a telephone on it, a stool, a small table with a gramophone and records, a settee, a coffee table, an occasional table with book-ends and books on it, two upright chairs, an arm-chair, and another table on which stood a plant in a brass pot. The furniture in general was old-fashioned, but not sufficiently old or distinguished to be admired as antique.

Lucia, a beautiful young woman of twenty-five, had luxuriant dark hair which flowed to her shoulders, and brown eyes which could flash excitingly but were now smouldering with a suppressed emotion not easy to define. She hesitated in the middle of the room, then crossed to the french windows and, parting the curtains slightly, looked out at the night. Uttering a barely audible sigh, she pressed her brow to the cool glass of the window, and stood lost in thought.

Miss Amory's voice could be heard outside in the hall, calling, 'Lucia – Lucia – where are you?' A moment later, Miss Amory, a somewhat fussy elderly lady a few years older than her brother, entered the room. Going across to Lucia, she took the younger woman by the arm and propelled her towards the settee.

'There, my dear. You sit down here,' she said, pointing to a corner of the settee. 'You'll be all right in a minute or two.'

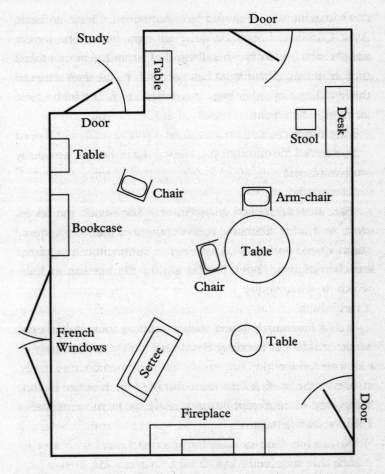

As she sat, Lucia gave a wan smile of gratitude to Caroline Amory. 'Yes, of course,' she agreed. 'It's passing already, in fact.' Though she spoke English impeccably, perhaps too impeccably, an occasional inflection betrayed that English was not her native tongue.

'I just came over all faint, that's all,' she continued. 'How ridiculous of me. I've never done such a thing before. I can't imagine why it should have happened. Please go back, Aunt Caroline. I shall be quite all right here.' She took a handkerchief from her handbag, as Caroline Amory looked on solicitously. Dabbing at her eyes with it, she then returned the handkerchief to her bag, and smiled again. 'I shall be quite all right,' she repeated. 'Really, I shall.'

Miss Amory looked unconvinced. 'You've really not looked well, dear, all the evening, you know,' she remarked, anxiously studying Lucia.

'Haven't I?'

'No, indeed,' replied Miss Amory. She sat on the settee, close to Lucia. 'Perhaps you've caught a little chill, dear,' she twittered anxiously. 'Our English summers can be rather treacherous, you know. Not at all like the hot sun in Italy, which is what you're more used to. So delightful, Italy, I always think.'

'Italy,' murmured Lucia with a faraway look in her eyes, as she placed her handbag beside her on the settee. 'Italy –'

'I know, my child. You must miss your own country badly. It must seem such a dreadful contrast – the weather for one thing, and the different customs. And we must seem such a cold lot. Now, Italians –'

'No, never. I never miss Italy,' cried Lucia, with a vehemence that surprised Miss Amory. 'Never.'

'Oh, come now, child, there's no disgrace in feeling a little homesick for –'

'Never!' Lucia repeated. 'I hate Italy. I always hated it. It is like heaven for me to be here in England with all you kind people. Absolute heaven!'

'It's really very sweet of you to say that, my dear,' said Caroline Amory, 'though I'm sure you're only being polite.

It's true we've all tried to make you feel happy and at home here, but it would be only natural for you to yearn for Italy sometimes. And then, not having any mother –'

'Please – *please* –', Lucia interrupted her, 'do not speak of my mother.'

'No, of course not, dear, if you'd rather I didn't. I didn't mean to upset you. Shall I get you some smelling-salts? I've got some in my room.'

'No, thank you,' Lucia replied. 'Really, I'm perfectly all right now.'

'It's no trouble at all, you know,' Caroline Amory persisted. 'I've got some very nice smelling-salts, a lovely pink colour, and in the most charming little bottle. And very pungent. Sal ammoniac, you know. Or is it spirits of salts? I can never remember. But anyway it's not the one you clean the bath with.'

Lucia smiled gently, but made no reply. Miss Amory had risen, and apparently could not decide whether to go in search of smelling-salts or not. She moved indecisively to the back of the settee, and rearranged the cushions. 'Yes, I think it must be a sudden chill,' she continued. 'You were looking the absolute picture of health this morning. Perhaps it was the excitement of seeing this Italian friend of yours, Dr Carelli? He turned up so suddenly and unexpectedly, didn't he? It must have given you quite a shock.'

Lucia's husband, Richard, had entered the library while Caroline Amory was speaking. Evidently Miss Amory did not notice him, for she could not understand why her words appeared to have upset Lucia, who leaned back, closed her eyes and shivered. 'Oh, my dear, what is it?' asked Miss Amory. 'Are you coming over faint again?'

Richard Amory closed the door and approached the two women. A conventionally handsome young Englishman of about thirty, with sandy hair, he was of medium height, with a somewhat thick-set, muscular figure. 'Do go and finish your dinner, Aunt Caroline,' he said to Miss Amory. 'Lucia will be all right with me. I'll look after her.'

Miss Amory still appeared irresolute. 'Oh, it's you, Richard. Well, perhaps I'd better go back,' she said, taking a reluctant step or two in the direction of the door leading to the hall. 'You know how your father does hate a disturbance of any kind. And particularly with a guest here. It's not as though it was someone who was a close friend of the family.'

She turned back to Lucia. 'I was just saying, dear, wasn't I, what a very strange thing it was that Dr Carelli should turn up in the way he did, with no idea that you were living in this part of the world. You simply ran into him in the village, and invited him here. It must have been a great surprise for you, my dear, mustn't it?'

'It was,' replied Lucia.

'The world really is such a very small place, I've always said so,' Miss Amory continued. 'Your friend is a very good-looking man, Lucia.'

'Do you think so?'

'Foreign-looking, of course,' Miss Amory conceded, 'but distinctly handsome. And he speaks English very well.'

'Yes, I suppose he does.'

Miss Amory seemed disinclined to let the topic go. 'Did you really have no idea,' she asked, 'that he was in this part of the world?'

'None whatsoever,' replied Lucia emphatically.

Richard Amory had been watching his wife intently. Now he spoke again. 'What a delightful surprise it must have been for you, Lucia,' he said.

His wife looked up at him quickly, but made no reply. Miss Amory beamed. 'Yes, indeed,' she continued. 'Did you know him well in Italy, my dear? Was he a great friend of yours? I suppose he must have been.'

There was a sudden bitterness in Lucia's voice. 'He was never a friend,' she said.

'Oh, I see. Merely an acquaintance. But he accepted your generous invitation to stay. I often think foreigners are inclined to be a little pushy. Oh, I don't mean you, of course, dear –' Miss Amory had the grace to pause and blush. 'I mean, well, you're half English in any case.' She looked archly at her nephew, and continued, 'In fact, she's quite English now, isn't she, Richard?'

Richard Amory did not respond to his aunt's archness, but moved towards the door and opened it, as though in invitation to Miss Amory to return to the others.

'Well,' said that lady as she moved reluctantly to the door, 'if you're sure I can't do anything more –'

'No, no.' Richard's tone was as abrupt as his words, as he held the door open for her. With an uncertain gesture, and a last nervous smile at Lucia, Miss Amory left.

Emitting a sigh of relief, Richard shut the door after her, and came back to his wife. 'Natter, natter, natter,' he complained. 'I thought she'd never go.'

'She was only trying to be kind, Richard.'

'Oh, I dare say she was. But she tries a damn sight too hard.'

'I think she's fond of me,' murmured Lucia.

'What? Oh, of course.' Richard Amory's tone was abstracted. He stood, observing his wife closely. For a few moments there was a constrained silence. Then, moving nearer to her, Richard looked down at Lucia. 'You're sure there's nothing I can get you?'

Lucia looked up at him, forcing a smile. 'Nothing, really, thank you, Richard. Do go back to the dining-room. I really am perfectly all right now.'

'No,' replied her husband. 'I'll stay with you.'

'But I'd rather be alone.'

There was a pause. Then Richard spoke again, as he moved behind the settee. 'Cushions all right? Would you like another one under your head?'

'I am quite comfortable as I am,' Lucia protested. 'It would be nice to have some air, though. Could you open the window?'

Richard moved to the french windows and fumbled with the catch. 'Damn!' he exclaimed. 'The old boy's locked it with one of those patent catches of his. You can't open it without the key.'

Lucia shrugged her shoulders. 'Oh, well,' she murmured, 'it really doesn't matter.'

Richard came back from the french windows, and sat in one of the chairs by the table. He leaned forward, resting his elbows on his thighs. 'Wonderful fellow, the old man. Always inventing something or other.'

'Yes,' replied Lucia. 'He must have made a lot of money out of his inventions.'

'Pots of it,' said Richard, gloomily. 'But it isn't the money that appeals to him. They're all the same, these scientists. Always on the track of something utterly impracticable that can be of no earthly interest to anyone other than themselves. Bombarding the atom, for heaven's sake!'

'But all the same, he is a great man, your father.'

'I suppose he's one of the leading scientists of the day,' said Richard grudgingly. 'But he can't see any point of view except his own.' He spoke with increasing irritation. 'He's treated me damned badly.'

'I know,' Lucia agreed. 'He keeps you here, chained to this house, almost as though you were a prisoner. Why did he make you give up the army and come to live here?'

'I suppose,' said Richard, 'that he thought I could help him in his work. But he ought to have known that I should be of no earthly use to him in that way. I simply haven't got the brains for it.' He moved his chair a little closer to Lucia, and leaned forward again. 'My God, Lucia, it makes me feel pretty desperate, sometimes. There he is, rolling in money, and he spends every penny on those damned experiments of his. You'd think he'd let me have something of what will be mine some day, in any case, and allow me to get free of this place.'

Lucia sat upright. 'Money!' she exclaimed bitterly. 'Everything comes round to that. Money!'

'I'm like a fly caught in a spider's web,' Richard continued. 'Helpless. Absolutely helpless.'

Lucia looked at him with an imploring eagerness. 'Oh, Richard,' she exclaimed. 'So am I.'

Her husband looked at her with alarm. He was about to speak when Lucia continued, 'So am I. Helpless. And I want to get out.' She rose suddenly, and moved towards him, speaking excitedly. 'Richard, for God's sake, before it's too late, take me away!'

'Away?' Richard's voice was empty and despairing. 'Away where?'

'Anywhere,' replied Lucia, with growing excitement. 'Anywhere in the world! But away from this house. That's the important thing, away from this house! I am afraid, Richard, I tell you I'm afraid. There are shadows –' she looked over her shoulder as though she could see them, 'shadows everywhere.'

Richard remained seated. 'How can we go away without money?' he asked. He looked up at Lucia, and continued, bitterly, 'A man's not much good to a woman without money, is he, Lucia? Is he?'

She backed away from him. 'Why do you say that?' she asked. 'What do you mean?'

Richard continued to look at her in silence, his face tense yet curiously expressionless.

'What's the matter with you tonight, Richard?' Lucia asked him. 'You're different, somehow –'

Richard rose from his chair. 'Am I?'

'Yes – what is it?'

'Well –' Richard began, and then stopped. 'Nothing. It's nothing.'

He started to turn away from her, but Lucia pulled him back and placed her hands on his shoulders. 'Richard, my dear –' she began. He took her hands from his shoulders. 'Richard,' she said again.

Putting his hands behind his back, Richard looked down at her. 'Do you think I'm a complete fool?' he asked. 'Do you think I didn't see this *old friend* of yours slip a note into your hand tonight?'

'Do you mean you thought that –'

He interrupted her fiercely. 'Why did you come out from dinner? You weren't feeling faint. That was all a pretence. You wanted to be alone to read your precious note. You couldn't wait. You were nearly mad with impatience because you couldn't get rid of us. First Aunt Caroline, then me.' His eyes were cold with hurt and anger as he looked at her.

'Richard,' said Lucia, 'you're mad. Oh, it's absurd. You can't think I care for Carelli! Can you? Can you, really? My dear, Richard, my dear – it's *you*. It's nobody but you. You must know that.'

Richard kept his eyes fixed on her. 'What is in that note?' he asked quietly.

'Nothing – nothing at all.'

'Then show it to me.'

'I – I can't,' said Lucia. 'I've destroyed it.'

A frigid smile appeared and disappeared on Richard's face. 'No, you haven't,' he said. 'Show it to me.'

Lucia was silent for a moment. She looked at him imploringly. Then, 'Richard,' she asked, 'can't you trust me?'

'I could take it from you by force,' he muttered through clenched teeth, as he advanced a step towards her. 'I've half a mind –'

Lucia backed away with a faint cry, her eyes still on Richard's face as though willing him to believe her. Suddenly he turned away. 'No,' he said, as though to himself. 'I suppose there are some things one can't do.' He turned back to face his wife. 'But, by God, I'll have it out with Carelli.'

Lucia caught his arm, with a cry of alarm. 'No, Richard, you mustn't. You mustn't. Don't do that, I beg you. Don't do that.'

'You're afraid for your lover, are you?' sneered Richard.

'He's not my lover,' Lucia retorted, fiercely.

Richard took her by the shoulders. 'Perhaps he isn't – yet,' he said. 'Perhaps he –'

Hearing voices outside in the hall, he stopped speaking. Making an effort to control himself, he moved to the fireplace, took out a cigarette-case and lighter, and lit a cigarette. As the door from the hall opened, and the voices grew louder, Lucia moved to the chair Richard had recently vacated, and sat. Her face was white, her hands clasped together in tension.

Miss Amory entered, accompanied by her niece Barbara, an extremely modern young woman of twenty-one. Swinging her handbag, Barbara crossed the room towards her. 'Hello, Lucia, are you all right now?' she asked.

Lucia forced a smile as Barbara Amory approached her. 'Yes, thank you, darling,' she replied. 'I'm perfectly all right. Really.'

Barbara looked down at her cousin's beautiful, black-haired wife. 'Not broken any glad tidings to Richard, have you?' she asked. 'Is that what it's all about?'

'Glad tidings? What glad tidings? I don't know what you mean,' protested Lucia.

Barbara clasped her arms together, and made a rocking motion as though cradling a baby. Lucia's reaction to this pantomime was a sad smile and a shake of the head. Miss Amory, however, collapsed in horror onto a chair. 'Really, Barbara!' she admonished.

'Well,' said Barbara, 'accidents will happen, you know.'

Her aunt shook her head vigorously. 'I cannot think what young girls are coming to, nowadays,' she announced to no one in particular. 'In my young days we did not speak flippantly of motherhood, and I would never have allowed –' She broke off at the sound of the door opening, and looked around in time to see Richard leave the room. 'You've embarrassed Richard,' she continued, addressing Barbara, 'and I can't say I'm at all surprised.'

'Well, Aunt Caroline,' Barbara replied, 'you are a Victorian, you know, born when the old Queen still had a good twenty years of life ahead of her. You're thoroughly representative of *your* generation, and I dare say I am of mine.'

'I'm in no doubt as to which I prefer –', her aunt began, only to be interrupted by Barbara, who chuckled and said, 'I think the Victorians were too marvellous. Fancy telling children that babies were found under gooseberry bushes! I think it's sweet.'

She fumbled in her handbag, found a cigarette and a lighter, and lit the cigarette. She was about to begin speaking again when Miss Amory silenced her with a gesture. 'Oh, do stop being silly, Barbara. I'm really very worried about this poor child here, and I wish you wouldn't make fun of me.'

Lucia suddenly broke down and began to weep. Trying to wipe the tears from her eyes, she said between sobs, 'You are all so good to me. No one was ever kind to me until I came here, until I married Richard. It's been wonderful to be here with you. I can't help it, I –'

'There, there,' murmured Miss Amory, rising and going to Lucia. She patted her on the shoulder. 'There, there, my dear. I know what you mean – living abroad all your life – most unsuitable for a young girl. Not a proper kind of upbringing at all, and of course the continentals have some very peculiar ideas about education. There, there.'

Lucia stood up, and looked about her, uncertainly. She allowed Miss Amory to lead her to the settee, and sat at one end while Miss Amory patted cushions around her and then sat next to her. 'Of course you're upset, my dear. But you must try to forget about Italy. Although, of course, the dear Italian lakes are quite delightful in the spring, I always think. Very suitable for holidays, but one wouldn't want to live there, naturally. Now, now, don't cry, my dear.'

'I think she needs a good stiff drink,' suggested Barbara, sitting on the coffee table and peering critically but not unsympathetically into Lucia's face. 'This is an awful house, Aunt Caroline. It's years behind the times. You never see the ghost of a cocktail in it. Nothing but sherry or whisky before dinner, and brandy afterwards. Richard can't make a decent Manhattan, and just try asking Edward Raynor for a Whisky Sour. Now what would *really* pull Lucia around in no time would be a Satan's Whisker.'

Miss Amory turned a shocked countenance upon her niece. 'What,' she enquired in horrified tones, 'might a Satan's Whisker be?'

'It's quite simple to make, if you have the ingredients,' replied Barbara. 'It's merely equal parts of brandy and crème de menthe, but you mustn't forget a shake of red pepper. That's most important. It's absolutely super, and guaranteed to put some pep into you.'

'Barbara, you know I disapprove of these alcoholic stimulants,' Miss Amory exclaimed with a shudder. 'My dear father always said –'

'I don't know what he *said*,' replied Barbara, 'but absolutely everyone in the family knows that dear old Great-Uncle Algernon had the reputation of being a three-bottle man.'

At first, Miss Amory looked as if she might explode, but then the slight twitch of a smile appeared on her lips, and all she said was, 'Gentlemen are different.'

Barbara was having none of this. 'They're not in the least

different,' she said. 'Or at any rate I can't imagine why they should be allowed to be different. They simply got away with it in those days.' She produced from her handbag a small mirror, a powder-puff and lipstick. 'Well, how do we look?' she asked herself. 'Oh, my God!' And she began vigorously to apply lipstick.

'Really, Barbara,' said her aunt, 'I do wish you wouldn't put quite so much of that red stuff on your lips. It's such a very bright colour.'

'I hope so,' replied Barbara, still completing her make-up. 'After all, it cost seven and sixpence.'

'Seven shillings and sixpence! What a disgraceful waste of money, just for – for –'

'For "Kissproof", Aunt Caroline.'

'I beg your pardon?'

'The lipstick. It's called "Kissproof".'

Her aunt sniffed disapprovingly. 'I know, of course,' she said, 'that one's lips are inclined to chap if one has been out in a high wind, and that a little grease is advisable. Lanoline, for instance. I always use –'

Barbara interrupted her. 'My dear Aunt Caroline, take it from me, a girl simply can't have too much lipstick on. After all, she never knows how much of it she's going to lose in the taxi coming home.' As she spoke, she replaced the mirror, powder-puff and lipstick in her handbag.

Miss Amory looked puzzled. 'What do you mean, "in the taxi coming home"?' she asked. 'I don't understand.'

Barbara rose and, moving behind the settee, leaned over to Lucia. 'Never mind. Lucia understands, don't you, my love?' she asked, giving Lucia's chin a little tickle.

Lucia Amory looked around, blankly. 'I'm so sorry,' she

said to Barbara, 'I haven't been listening. What did you say?'

Focusing her attention on Lucia again, Caroline Amory returned to the subject of that young lady's health. 'You know, my dear,' she said, 'I really am worried about you.' She looked from Lucia to Barbara. 'She ought to have something, Barbara. What have we got now? Sal volatile, of course, that would be the very thing. Unfortunately, that careless Ellen broke my bottle this morning when she was dusting in my room.'

Pursing her lips, Barbara considered for a moment. 'I know,' she exclaimed. 'The hospital stores!'

'Hospital stores? What do you mean? What hospital stores?' Miss Amory asked.

Barbara came and sat in a chair close to her aunt. 'You remember,' she reminded her. 'All of Edna's things.'

Miss Amory's face brightened. 'Ah, yes, of course!' Turning to Lucia, she said, 'I wish you had met Edna, my elder niece, Barbara's sister. She went to India with her husband – oh, it must have been about three months before you came here with Richard. Such a capable girl, Edna was.'

'Most capable,' Barbara confirmed. 'She's just had twins. As there are no gooseberry bushes in India, I think she must have found them under a double mango tree.'

Miss Amory allowed herself a smile. 'Hush, Barbara,' she said. Then, turning back to Lucia, she continued, 'As I was saying, dear, Edna trained as a dispenser during the war. She worked at our hospital here. We turned the Town Hall into a hospital, you know, during the war. And then for some years after the war, until she was married, Edna continued to work in the dispensary at the County Hospital. She was very knowledgable about drugs and pills and that sort of thing. I dare say she still is. That knowledge must be invaluable to her in India. But what was I saying? Oh, yes – when she left. Now what did we do with all those bottles of hers?'

'I remember perfectly well,' said Barbara. 'A lot of old things of Edna's from the dispensary were bundled into a box. They were supposed to be sorted out and sent to hospitals, but everyone forgot, or at least no one did anything about it. They were put away in the attic, and they only came to light again when Edna was packing to go to India. They're up there –' she gestured towards the bookcase – 'and they still haven't been looked through and sorted out.'

She rose and, taking her chair across to the bookcase, stood on it and, reaching up, lifted the black tin box down from the top.

Ignoring Lucia's murmured 'Please don't bother, darling, I really don't need anything', Barbara carried the box over to the table and put it down.

'Well,' she said, 'at least we might as well have a look at the things now that I've got them down.' She opened the box. 'Oh dear, it's a motley collection,' she said, taking out various bottles as she spoke. 'Iodine, Friar's balsam, something called "Tinct.Card.Co", castor oil.' She grimaced. 'Ah, now we're coming to the hot stuff,' she exclaimed, as she took out of the box some small brown glass tubes. 'Atropine, morphine, strychnine,' she read from the labels. 'Be careful, Aunt Caroline. If you arouse my furious temper, I'll poison your coffee with strychnine, and you'll die in the most awful agony.' Barbara made a mock-menacing gesture at her aunt, who waved her away with a snort.

'Well, there's nothing here we could possibly try out on Lucia as a tonic, that's for certain,' she laughed, as she began to pack the bottles and phials back into the tin box. She was holding a tube of morphine aloft in her right hand as the door to the hall opened, and Tredwell ushered in Edward Raynor, Dr Carelli, and Sir Claud Amory. Sir Claud's secretary, Edward Raynor, entered first, an unremarkable-looking young man in his late twenties. He moved across to Barbara, and stood looking at the box. 'Hello, Mr Raynor. Interested in poisons?' she asked him as she continued to pack up the bottles.

Dr Carelli, too, approached the table. A very dark, swarthy individual of about forty, Carelli wore perfectly fitting evening clothes. His manner was suave, and when he spoke it was with the slightest Italian accent. 'What have we here, my dear Miss Amory?' he queried.

Sir Claud paused at the door to speak to Tredwell. 'You understand my instructions?' he asked, and was satisfied by the reply, 'Perfectly, Sir Claud.' Tredwell left the room, and Sir Claud moved across to his guest.

'I hope you will excuse me, Dr Carelli,' he said, 'if I go straight to my study? I have several important letters which must go off tonight. Raynor, will you come with me?' The secretary joined his employer, and they went into Sir Claud's study by the connecting door. As the door closed behind them, Barbara suddenly dropped the tube she had been holding.

CHAPTER 4

Dr Carelli stepped forward quickly, and picked up the tube Barbara had dropped. Glancing at it before handing it back to her with a polite bow, he exclaimed, 'Hello, what's this? Morphine!' He picked up another one from the table. 'And strychnine! May I ask, my dear young lady, where you got hold of these lethal little tubes?' He began to examine the contents of the tin box.

Barbara looked at the suave Italian with distaste. 'The spoils of war,' she replied shortly, with a tight little smile.

Rising anxiously, Caroline Amory approached Dr Carelli. 'They're not really poison, are they, doctor? I mean, they couldn't harm anyone, could they?' she asked. 'That box has been in the house for years. Surely it's harmless, isn't it?'

'I should say,' replied Carelli dryly, 'that, with the little lot you have here, you could kill, roughly, twelve strong men. I don't know what *you* regard as harmful.'

'Oh, good gracious,' Miss Amory gasped with horror as she moved back to her chair, and sat heavily.

'Here, for instance,' continued Carelli, addressing the assembled company. He picked up a tube and read slowly from the label. '"Strychnine hydrochloride; one sixteenth of a grain." Seven or eight of these little tablets, and you would die a very unpleasant death indeed. An extremely painful way out of the world.' He picked up another tube. '"Atropine sulphate." Now, atropine poisoning is sometimes very hard to tell from ptomaine poisoning. It is also a very painful death.'

Replacing the two tubes he had handled, he picked up another. 'Now here –' he continued, now speaking very slowly and deliberately, 'here we have hyoscine hydrobromide, one hundredth of a grain. That doesn't sound very potent, does it? Yet I assure you, you would only have to swallow half of the little white tablets in this tube, and –' he made a graphic gesture. 'There would be no pain – no pain at all. Just a swift and completely dreamless sleep, but a sleep from which there would be no awakening.' He moved towards Lucia, and held out the tube to her, as though inviting her to examine it. There was a smile on his face, but not in his eyes.

Lucia stared at the tube as though she were fascinated by it. Stretching out a hand, she spoke in a voice that sounded almost as though it were hypnotized. 'A swift and completely dreamless sleep –' she murmured, reaching for the tube.

Instead of giving it to her, Dr Carelli glanced at Caroline Amory with an almost questioning look. That lady shuddered and looked distressed, but said nothing. With a shrug of the shoulders, Carelli turned away from Lucia, still holding the tube of hyoscine hydrobromide.

The door to the hallway opened, and Richard Amory entered. Without speaking, he strolled across to the stool by the desk, and sat down. He was followed into the room by Tredwell, who carried a tray containing a jug of coffee with cups and saucers. Placing the tray on the coffee table, Tredwell left the room as Lucia moved to pour out the coffee.

Barbara went across to Lucia, took two cups of coffee from the tray, and then moved over to Richard to give him one of them, keeping the other for herself. Dr Carelli, meanwhile, was busy replacing the tubes in the tin box on the centre table.

'You know,' said Miss Amory to Carelli, 'you make my flesh creep, doctor, with your talk of swift, dreamless sleep and unpleasant deaths. I suppose that, being Italian as you are, you know a lot about poisons?'

'My dear lady,' laughed Carelli, 'is that not an extremely unjust – what do you say – *non sequitur*? Why should an Italian know any more about poisons than an Englishman? I have heard it said,' he continued playfully, 'that poison is a woman's weapon, rather than a man's. Perhaps I should ask you –? Ah, but perhaps, dear lady, it is an Italian woman you were thinking of? Perhaps you were about to mention a certain Borgia. Is that it, eh?' He took a cup of coffee from Lucia at the coffee table, and handed it to Miss Amory, returning to take another cup for himself.

'Lucrezia Borgia – that dreadful creature! Yes, I suppose that's what I was thinking of,' admitted Miss Amory. 'I used to have nightmares about her when I was a child, you know. I imagined her as very pale, but tall, and with jet-black hair just like our own dear Lucia.'

Dr Carelli approached Miss Amory with the sugar bowl. She shook her head in refusal, and he took the bowl back to the coffee tray. Richard Amory put his coffee down, took a magazine from the desk and began to browse through it, as his aunt developed her Borgia theme. 'Yes, dreadful nightmares I used to have,' Miss Amory was saying. 'I would be the only child in a room full of adults, all of them drinking out of very elaborate goblets. Then this glamorous woman – now I come to think of it, she did look remarkably like you, Lucia dear – would approach me and force a goblet upon me. I could tell by the way she smiled, somehow, that I ought not to drink, but I knew I wasn't going to be able to refuse. Somehow, she hypnotized me into drinking, and then I would begin to feel a dreadful burning sensation in my throat, and I would find myself fighting for breath. And then, of course, I woke up.'

Dr Carelli had moved close to Lucia. Standing in front of her, he gave an ironic bow. 'My dear Lucrezia Borgia,' he implored, 'have mercy on us all.'

Lucia did not react to Carelli's joke. She appeared not to have heard him. There was a pause. Smiling to himself, Dr Carelli turned away from Lucia, drank his coffee, and placed his cup on the centre table. Finishing her coffee rapidly, Barbara seemed to realize that a change of mood was called for. 'What about a little tune?' she suggested, moving across to the gramophone. 'Now, what shall we have? There's a marvellous record here that I bought up in town the other day.' She began to sing, accompanying her words with a jazzy little dance. '"Ikey – oh, crikey – what *have* you got on?" Or what else is there?'

'Oh, Barbara dear, not that vulgar song,' implored Miss Amory, moving across to her, and helping to look through the gramophone records. 'There are some much nicer records here. If we must have popular music, there are some lovely songs by John McCormack here, somewhere. Or what about "The Holy City"? – I can't remember the soprano's name. Or why not that nice Melba record? Oh – ah, yes – here's Handel's *Largo*.'

'Oh, come on, Aunt Caroline. We're not likely to be cheered up by Handel's *Largo*,' Barbara protested. 'There's some Italian opera here, if we must have classical music. Come on, Dr Carelli, this ought to be your province. Come and help us choose.'

Carelli joined Barbara and Miss Amory around the gramophone, and all three of them began to sort through the pile of records. Richard now seemed engrossed in his magazine.

Lucia rose, moved slowly and apparently aimlessly across to the centre table, and glanced at the tin box. Then, taking care to establish that the others were not observing her, she took a tube from the box and read the label. 'Hyoscine hydrobromide.' Opening the tube, Lucia poured nearly all of the tablets into the palm of her hand. As she did so, the door to Sir Claud's study opened, and Sir Claud's secretary, Edward Raynor, appeared in the doorway. Unknown to Lucia, Raynor watched her as she put the tube back into the tin box before moving over to the coffee table.

At that moment, Sir Claud's voice was heard to call from the study. His words were indistinct, but Raynor, turning to answer him, said, 'Yes, of course, Sir Claud. I'll bring you your coffee now.'

The secretary was about to enter the library when Sir Claud's voice arrested him. 'And what about that letter to Marshall's?'

'It went off by the afternoon post, Sir Claud,' replied the secretary.

'But Raynor, I told you – oh, come back here, man,' Sir Claud boomed from his study.

'I'm sorry, sir,' Raynor was heard to say as he retreated from the doorway to rejoin Sir Claud Amory in his study.

Lucia, who had turned to watch the secretary at the sound of his voice, seemed not to realize that he had been observing her movements. Turning, so that her back was to Richard, she dropped the tablets she had been holding into one of the coffee cups on the coffee table, and moved to the front of the settee.

The gramophone suddenly burst into life with a quick foxtrot. Richard Amory put down the magazine he had been reading, finished his coffee quickly, placed the cup on the centre table, and moved across to his wife. 'I'll take you at your word. I've decided. We'll go away together.'

Lucia looked up at him in surprise. 'Richard,' she said faintly, 'do you really mean it? We can get away from here? But I thought you said – what about? – where will the money come from?'

'There are always ways of acquiring money,' said Richard, grimly.

There was alarm in Lucia's voice as she asked, 'What do you mean?'

'I mean,' said her husband, 'that when a man cares about a woman as much as I care about you, he'll do anything. Anything!'

'It does not flatter me to hear you say that,' Lucia responded. 'It only tells me that you still do not trust me – that you think you must buy my love with –'

She broke off, and looked around as the door to the study opened and Edward Raynor returned. Raynor walked over to the coffee table and picked up a cup of coffee, as Lucia changed her position on the settee, moving down to one end of it. Richard had wandered moodily across to the fireplace, and was staring into the unlit fire.

Barbara, beginning a tentative foxtrot alone, looked at her cousin Richard as though considering whether to invite him to dance. But, apparently put off by his stony countenance, she turned to Raynor. 'Care to dance, Mr Raynor?' she asked.

'I'd love to, Miss Amory,' the secretary replied. 'Just a moment, while I take Sir Claud his coffee.'

Lucia suddenly rose from the settee. 'Mr Raynor,' she said hurriedly, 'that isn't Sir Claud's coffee. You've taken the wrong cup.'

'Have I?' said Raynor. 'I'm so sorry.'

Lucia picked up another cup from the coffee table, and held it out to Raynor. They exchanged cups. 'That,' said Lucia, as she handed her cup to Raynor, 'is Sir Claud's coffee.' She smiled enigmatically to herself, placed the cup Raynor had given her on the coffee table, and returned to the settee.

Turning his back to Lucia, the secretary took some tablets from his pocket and dropped them into the cup he was holding. As he was walking with it towards the study door, Barbara intercepted him. 'Do come and dance with me, Mr Raynor,' she pleaded, with one of her most engaging smiles. 'I'd force Dr Carelli to, except that I can tell he's simply dying to dance with Lucia.'

As Raynor hovered indecisively, Richard Amory approached. 'You may as well give in to her, Raynor,' he advised. 'Everyone does, eventually. Here, give the coffee to me. I'll take it to my father.'

Reluctantly, Raynor allowed the coffee cup to be taken from him. Turning away, Richard paused momentarily and then went through into Sir Claud's study. Barbara and Edward Raynor, having first turned over the gramophone record on the machine, were now slowly waltzing in each other's arms. Dr Carelli watched them for a moment or two with an indulgent smile, before approaching Lucia who, wearing a look of utter dejection, was still seated on the settee.

Carelli addressed her. 'It was most kind of Miss Amory to allow me to join you for the weekend,' he said.

Lucia looked up at him. For a few seconds she did not speak, but then said, finally, 'She is the kindest of people.'

'And this is such a charming house,' continued Carelli, moving behind the settee. 'You must show me over it some time. I am extremely interested in the domestic architecture of this period.'

While he was speaking, Richard Amory had returned from the study. Ignoring his wife and Carelli, he went across to the box of drugs on the centre table, and began to tidy its contents.

'Miss Amory can tell you much more about this house than I can,' Lucia told Dr Carelli. 'I know very little of these things.'

Looking around first, to confirm that Richard Amory was busying himself with the drugs, that Edward Raynor and Barbara Amory were still waltzing at the far end of the room, and that Caroline Amory appeared to be dozing, Carelli moved to the front of the settee, and sat next to Lucia. In low, urgent tones, he muttered, 'Have you done what I asked?'

Her voice even lower, almost a whisper, Lucia said desperately, 'Have you no pity?'

'Have you done what I told you to?' Carelli asked more insistently.

'I – I –' Lucia began, but then, faltering, rose, turned abruptly, and walked swiftly to the door which led into the hall. Turning the handle, she discovered that the door would not open.

'There's something wrong with this door,' she exclaimed, turning to face the others. 'I can't get it open.'

'What's that?' called Barbara, still waltzing with Raynor.

'I can't get this door open,' Lucia repeated.

Barbara and Raynor stopped dancing and went across to Lucia at the door. Richard Amory moved to the gramophone to switch it off before joining them. They took it in turns to attempt to get the door open, but without success, observed by Miss Amory, who was awake but still seated, and by Dr Carelli, who stood by the bookcase.

Unnoticed by any of the company, Sir Claud emerged from his study, coffee cup in hand, and stood for a moment or two observing the group clustered around the door to the hall.

'What an extraordinary thing,' Raynor exclaimed, abandoning his attempt to open the door, and turning to face the others. 'It seems to have got stuck, somehow.'

Sir Claud's voice rang across the room, startling them all. 'Oh, no, it's not stuck. It's locked. Locked from the outside.'

His sister rose and approached Sir Claud. She was about to speak, but he forestalled her. 'It was locked by my orders, Caroline,' he told her.

With all eyes upon him, Sir Claud walked across to the coffee table, took a lump of sugar from the bowl, and dropped it into his cup. 'I have something to say to you all,' he announced to the assembled company. 'Richard, would you be so kind as to ring for Tredwell?'

His son looked as though he were about to make some reply. However, after a pause he went to the fireplace and pressed a bell in the wall nearby.

'I suggest that you all sit down,' Sir Claud continued, with a gesture towards the chairs.

Dr Carelli, with raised eyebrows, crossed the room to sit on the stool. Edward Raynor and Lucia Amory found chairs for themselves, while Richard Amory chose to stand in front of the fireplace, looking puzzled. Caroline Amory and her niece Barbara occupied the settee.

When all were comfortably seated, Sir Claud moved the arm-chair to a position where he could most easily observe all the others. He sat.

The door on the left opened, and Tredwell entered.

'You rang, Sir Claud?'

'Yes, Tredwell. Did you call the number I gave you?'

'Yes, sir.'

'Was the answer satisfactory?'

'Perfectly satisfactory, sir.'

'And a car has gone to the station?'

'Yes, sir. A car has been ordered to meet the train.'

'Very well, Tredwell,' said Sir Claud. 'You may lock up now.'

'Yes, sir,' replied Tredwell, as he withdrew.

After the butler had closed the door behind him, the sound of a key turning in the lock could be heard.

'Claud,' Miss Amory exclaimed, 'what on earth does Tredwell think –?'

'Tredwell is acting on my instructions, Caroline,' Sir Claud interrupted sharply.

Richard Amory addressed his father. 'May we ask the meaning of all this?' he enquired, coldly.

'I am about to explain,' replied Sir Claud. 'Please listen to me calmly, all of you. To begin with, as you now realize, those two doors' – he gestured towards the two doors on the hall side of the library – 'are locked on the outside. From my study next door, there is no way out except through this room. The french windows in this room are locked.' Swivelling around in his seat to Carelli, he explained, as though in parenthesis, 'Locked, in fact, by a patent device of my own, which my family knows of, but which they do not know how to immobilize.' Again addressing everyone, Sir Claud continued, 'This place is a rat-trap.' He looked at his watch. 'It is now ten minutes to nine. At a few minutes past nine, the rat-catcher will arrive.'

'The *rat-catcher*?' Richard Amory's face was a study in perplexity. 'What rat-catcher?'

'A detective,' explained the famous scientist dryly, as he sipped his coffee.

Consternation greeted Sir Claud's announcement. Lucia uttered a low cry, and her husband stared at her intently. Miss Amory gave a shriek, Barbara exclaimed, 'Crikey!' and Edward Raynor contributed an ineffectual, 'Oh, I say, Sir Claud!' Only Dr Carelli seemed unaffected.

Sir Claud settled in his arm-chair, holding his coffee cup in his right hand and the saucer in his left. 'I seem to have achieved my little effect,' he observed with satisfaction. Finishing his coffee, he set the cup and saucer down on the table with a grimace. 'The coffee is unusually bitter this evening,' he complained.

His sister's countenance registered a certain annoyance at the aspersion cast on the coffee, which she took as a direct criticism of her housekeeping. She was about to say something, when Richard Amory spoke. 'What detective?' he asked his father.

'His name is Hercule Poirot,' replied Sir Claud. 'He is a Belgian.'

'But why?' Richard persisted. 'Why did you send for him?'

'A leading question,' said his father, with an unpleasantly

grim smile. 'Now we come to the point. For some time past, as most of you know, I have been engaged in atomic research. I have made a discovery of a new explosive. Its force is such that everything hitherto attempted in that line will be mere child's play beside it. Most of this you know already –'

Carelli got to his feet quickly. 'I did not know,' he exclaimed eagerly. 'I am much interested to hear of this.'

'Indeed, Dr Carelli?' Sir Claud invested the conventionally meaningless phrase with a curious significance, and Carelli, in some embarrassment, resumed his seat.

'As I was saying,' Sir Claud continued, 'the force of Amorite, as I call it, is such that where we have hitherto killed by thousands, we can now kill by hundreds of thousands.'

'How horrible,' exclaimed Lucia, with a shudder.

'My dear Lucia,' her father-in-law smiled thinly at her as he spoke, 'the truth is never horrible, only interesting.'

'But why –' asked Richard, 'are you telling us all this?'

'Because I have had occasion for some time to believe that a member of this household was attempting to steal the Amorite formula. I had asked Monsieur Poirot to join us tomorrow for the weekend, so that he could take the formula back to London with him on Monday, and deliver it personally to an official at the Ministry of Defence.'

'But, Claud, that's absurd. Indeed, it's highly offensive to all of us,' Caroline Amory expostulated. 'You can't seriously suspect –'

'I have not finished, Caroline,' her brother interrupted. 'And I assure you there is nothing absurd about what I am saying. I repeat, I *had* invited Hercule Poirot to join us tomorrow, but I have had to change my plans and ask Monsieur Poirot to hurry down here from London this evening. I have taken this step because –'

Sir Claud paused. When he resumed speaking, it was more slowly, and with a much more deliberate emphasis. 'Because,' he repeated, as his glance swept around the assembled company, 'the formula, written on an ordinary sheet of notepaper and enclosed in a long envelope, was stolen from the safe in my study some time before dinner this evening. It was stolen by someone in this room!'

A chorus of shocked exclamations greeted the eminent scientist's announcement. Then everyone began to speak at once. 'Stolen formula?' Caroline Amory began.

'What? From the safe? Impossible!' Edward Raynor exclaimed.

The babble of voices did not include that of Dr Carelli, who remained seated, with a thoughtful expression on his face. The others, however, were silenced only when Sir Claud raised his voice and continued.

'I am in the habit of being certain of my facts,' he assured his hearers. 'At twenty minutes past seven exactly, I placed the formula in the safe. As I left the study, Raynor here entered it.'

Blushing either from embarrassment or from anger, the secretary began, 'Sir Claud, really, I must protest –'

Sir Claud raised a hand to silence him. 'Raynor remained in the study,' he went on, 'and was still there, working, when Dr Carelli appeared at the door. After greeting him, Raynor left Carelli alone in the study while he went to let Lucia know –'

'I protest – I –' Carelli began, but again Sir Claud raised his hand for silence, and continued his narrative. 'Raynor, however,' he said, 'did not get further than the door of this room where he met my sister Caroline, with Barbara. The three of them remained in this room, and Dr Carelli joined them. Caroline and Barbara were the only two members of the party who did not enter the study.'

Barbara glanced at her aunt, and then addressed Sir Claud. 'I'm afraid your information about our movements isn't quite correct, Uncle Claud,' she said. 'I can't be excluded from your list of suspects. Do you remember, Aunt Caroline? You sent me into the study to look for a knitting needle you said you'd mislaid. You wondered if it might be in there.'

Ignoring his niece's interruption, the scientist continued. 'Richard came down next. He strolled into the study by himself and remained there for some minutes.'

'My God!' Richard exclaimed. 'Really, father, you surely don't suspect that I'd steal your wretched formula, do you?'

Looking directly at his son, Sir Claud replied, meaningfully, 'That piece of paper was worth a great deal of money.'

'I see.' His son regarded him steadily. 'And I'm in debt. That's what you mean, isn't it?'

Sir Claud made no reply to him. His gaze sweeping over the others, he continued. 'As I was saying, Richard remained in the study for some minutes. He reappeared in this room just as Lucia came in. When dinner was announced, a few minutes later, Lucia was no longer with us. I found her in the study, standing by the safe.'

'Father!' exclaimed Richard, moving to his wife and putting an arm protectively about her.

'I repeat, standing by the safe,' Sir Claud insisted. 'She seemed very much agitated, and when I asked what was the matter she told me she felt unwell. I suggested that a glass of wine might be good for her. She assured me, however, that she was quite all right again, and then left me to join the others. Instead of following Lucia immediately to the dining-room, I remained behind in my study. I don't know why, but some instinct urged me to look in the safe. The envelope with the formula in it had disappeared.'

There was a pause. No one spoke. The immense seriousness of the situation appeared to be dawning on everyone. Then Richard asked, 'How have you assembled this information about our movements, father?'

'By taking thought, of course,' Sir Claud replied. 'By observation and deduction. By the evidence of my own eyes, and by what I learned from questioning Tredwell.'

'I notice you don't include Tredwell or any of the other servants among your suspects, Claud,' Caroline Amory observed tartly. 'Only your family.'

'My family – and our guest,' her brother corrected her. 'That is so, Caroline. I have established to my own satisfaction that neither Tredwell nor any of the domestics were in the study between the time I placed the formula in the safe and the time I opened the safe again to find it missing.'

He looked at each of them in turn, before adding, 'I hope the position is clear to you all. Whoever took the formula must still have it. Since we returned here from dinner, the dining-room has been thoroughly searched. Tredwell would have informed me if the piece of paper had been found hidden there. And, as you now realize, I have seen to it that no one has had the opportunity to leave this room.'

For some moments there was a tense silence, broken only when Dr Carelli asked, politely, 'Is it your suggestion, then, Sir Claud, that we should all be searched?'

'That is not my suggestion,' replied Sir Claud, consulting

his watch. 'It is now two minutes to nine. Hercule Poirot will have arrived at Market Cleve, where he is being met. At nine o'clock precisely, Tredwell has orders to switch off the lights from the main switch in the basement. We shall be in complete darkness in this room, for one minute, and one minute only. When the lights go on again, matters will be out of my hands. Hercule Poirot will be here shortly, and he will be in charge of the case. But if, under cover of darkness, the formula is placed here,' and Sir Claud slapped his hand down on the table, 'then I shall inform Monsieur Poirot that I had made a mistake and that I have no need of his services.'

'That's an outrageous suggestion,' Richard declared heatedly. He looked around at the others. 'I say we should all be searched. I'm certainly willing.'

'So am I, of course,' Edward Raynor made haste to announce.

Richard Amory looked pointedly at Dr Carelli. The Italian smiled and shrugged his shoulders. 'And I.'

Richard's glance moved to his aunt. 'Very well, if we must, we must,' Miss Amory grumbled.

'Lucia?' Richard asked, turning to his wife.

'No, no, Richard,' Lucia replied breathily. 'Your father's plan is best.'

Richard looked at her in silence for a moment.

'Well, Richard?' queried Sir Claud.

A heavy sigh was at first his only reply, and then, 'Very well, I agree.' He looked at his cousin Barbara who gave a gesture of assent.

Sir Claud leaned back in his chair, wearily, and spoke in a slow, dragging voice. 'The taste of that coffee is still in my mouth,' he said, and then yawned.

The clock on the mantelpiece began to strike, and there

was complete silence as all turned to listen. Sir Claud turned slowly in his chair and looked steadily at his son Richard. On the last stroke of nine, the lights suddenly went out and the room was plunged into darkness.

There were a few gasps, and some stifled exclamations from the women, and then Miss Amory's voice rang out clearly. 'I don't care for this at all.'

'Do be quiet, Aunt Caroline,' Barbara ordered her. 'I'm trying to listen.'

For a few seconds there was absolute silence, followed by the sounds of heavy breathing, and then a rustling of paper. Silence again, before they all heard a kind of metallic clink, the sound of something tearing, and a loud bang, which must surely have been a chair being knocked over.

Suddenly, Lucia screamed. 'Sir Claud! Sir Claud! I can't bear it. I must have light. Somebody, please!'

The room remained in darkness. There was a sharp intake of breath, and then a loud knock at the door leading to the hall. Lucia screamed again. As though in response, the lights suddenly came on again.

Richard was now standing by the door, apparently unable to decide whether or not to attempt to open it. Edward Raynor was on his feet by his chair, which had overturned. Lucia lay back in her chair, as though about to faint.

Sir Claud sat absolutely still in his arm-chair, with his eyes closed. His secretary suddenly pointed to the table beside his employer. 'Look,' he exclaimed. 'The formula.'

On the table beside Sir Claud was a long envelope, of the type he had earlier described.

'Thank God!' cried Lucia. 'Thank God!'

There was another knock at the door, which now opened

slowly. Everyone's attention was fixed on the doorway, as Tredwell ushered in a stranger, and then withdrew.

The assembled company stared at the stranger. What they saw was an extraordinary-looking little man, hardly more than five feet four inches in height, who carried himself with great dignity. His head was exactly the shape of an egg, and he carried it at a slight angle, like an enquiring terrier. His moustache was distinctly stiff and military. He was very neatly dressed.

'Hercule Poirot, at your service,' said the stranger, and bowed.

Richard Amory held out a hand. 'Monsieur Poirot,' he said as they shook hands.

'Sir Claud?' asked Poirot. 'Ah, no, you are too young, of course. You are his son, perhaps?' He moved past Richard into the centre of the room. Behind him, another man, tall, middle-aged and of military bearing, had unobtrusively entered. As he moved to Poirot's side, the detective announced, 'My colleague, Captain Hastings.'

'What a delightful room,' Hastings observed as he shook hands with Richard Amory.

Richard turned back to Poirot. 'I'm sorry, Monsieur Poirot,' he said, 'but I fear we have brought you down here under a misapprehension. The need for your services has passed.'

'Indeed?' replied Poirot.

'Yes, I'm sorry,' Richard continued. 'It's too bad, dragging you all the way down here from London. Of course, your fee – and expenses – I mean – er, that'll be all right, of course –'

'I comprehend perfectly,' said Poirot, 'but for the moment it is neither my fee nor my expenses which interests me.'

'No? Then what – er –?'

'What does interest me, Mr Amory? I will tell you. It is just a little point, of no consequence, of course. But it was your father who sent for me to come. Why is it not he who tells me to go?'

'Oh, of course. I'm sorry,' said Richard, turning towards Sir Claud. 'Father, would you please tell Monsieur Poirot that we no longer have any need of his services?'

Sir Claud did not answer.

'Father!' Richard exclaimed, moving quickly to Sir Claud's arm-chair. He bent over his father, and then turned around wildly. 'Dr Carelli,' he called.

Miss Amory rose, white-faced. Carelli swiftly crossed to Sir Claud, and felt his pulse. Frowning, he placed his hand over Sir Claud's heart, and then shook his head.

Poirot moved slowly to the arm-chair, and stood looking down at the motionless body of the scientist. 'Ye-es – I fear –,' he murmured, as though to himself, 'I very much fear –'

'What do you fear?' asked Barbara, moving towards him.

Poirot looked at her. 'I fear that Sir Claud has sent for me too late, mademoiselle.'

Stunned silence followed Hercule Poirot's statement. Dr Carelli continued his examination of Sir Claud for a few moments before straightening himself and turning to the others. Addressing Richard Amory, 'I am afraid your father is dead,' he confirmed.

Richard stared at him in disbelief, as though he were unable to take in the Italian doctor's words. Then, 'My God – what was it? Heart failure?' he asked.

'I – I suppose so,' replied Carelli somewhat doubtfully.

Barbara moved to her aunt to comfort her, for Miss Amory seemed about to faint. Edward Raynor joined them, helping to support Miss Amory, and whispering to Barbara as he did so, 'I suppose that fellow *is* a real doctor?'

'Yes, but only an Italian one,' Barbara murmured in reply, as between them they settled Miss Amory into a chair. Overhearing Barbara's remark, Poirot shook his head energetically. Then, stroking his luxuriant moustache with exquisite care, he smiled as he commented, softly, 'Me, I am a detective – but only a Belgian one. Nevertheless, mademoiselle, we foreigners do arrive at the correct answer occasionally.'

Barbara had the grace to look at least a trifle embarrassed. She and Raynor remained in conversation for a few moments, but then Lucia approached Poirot, taking his arm and drawing him aside from the others.

'Monsieur Poirot,' she urged him breathlessly, 'you must stay! You must not let them send you away.'

Poirot regarded her steadily. His face remained quite impassive as he asked her, 'Is it that you wish me to stay, madame?'

'Yes, yes,' replied Lucia, glancing anxiously towards the body of Sir Claud still seated in its upright position in the armchair. 'There's something wrong about all this. My father-in-law's heart was perfectly all right. Perfectly, I tell you. Please, Monsieur Poirot, you must find out what has happened.'

Dr Carelli and Richard Amory continued to hover near the body of Sir Claud. Richard, in an agony of indecision, appeared to be almost petrified into immobility. 'I would suggest, Mr Amory,' Dr Carelli urged him, 'that you send for your father's own physician. I assume he had one?'

Richard roused himself with an effort. 'What? Oh yes,' he responded. 'Dr Graham. Young Kenneth Graham. He has a practice in the village. In fact, he's rather keen on my cousin Barbara. I mean – sorry, that's irrelevant, isn't it?' Glancing across the room at Barbara, he called to her. 'What's Kenneth Graham's phone number?'

'Market Cleve five,' Barbara told him. Richard moved to the phone, lifted the receiver and asked for the number. While he was waiting to be connected, Edward Raynor, recalling his secretarial duties, asked Richard, 'Do you think I should order the car for Monsieur Poirot?'

Poirot spread out his hands apologetically. He was about

to speak when Lucia forestalled him. 'Monsieur Poirot is remaining – at my request,' she announced to the company in general.

Still holding the telephone receiver to his ear, Richard turned, startled. 'What do you mean?' he asked his wife tersely.

'Yes, yes, Richard, he must stay,' Lucia insisted. Her voice sounded almost hysterical.

Miss Amory looked up in consternation, Barbara and Edward Raynor exchanged worried glances, Dr Carelli stood looking down thoughtfully at the lifeless body of the great scientist, while Hastings, who had been absent-mindedly examining the books on the library shelves, turned to survey the gathering.

Richard was about to respond to Lucia's outburst when his attention was claimed by the telephone he was holding. 'Oh what . . . Is that Dr Graham?' he asked. 'Kenneth, it's Richard Amory speaking. My father has had a heart attack. Can you come up at once? . . . Well, actually, I'm afraid there's nothing to be done . . . Yes, he's dead . . . No . . . I'm afraid so . . . Thank you.' Replacing the receiver, he crossed the room to his wife and, in a low, agitated voice, muttered, 'Lucia, are you mad? What have you done? Don't you realize we must get rid of this detective?'

Astonished, Lucia rose from her chair. 'What do you mean?' she asked Richard.

Their exchange continued quietly but urgently. 'Didn't you hear what father said?' His tone fraught with meaning, he murmured, '"The coffee is very bitter."'

At first, Lucia seemed not to understand. 'The coffee is very bitter?' she repeated. She looked at Richard uncomprehendingly for a moment, and then suddenly uttered a cry of horror which she quickly stifled.

'You see? Do you understand now?' Richard asked. Lowering his voice to a whisper, he added, 'He's been poisoned. And obviously by a member of the family. You don't want a ghastly scandal, do you?'

'Oh, my God,' murmured Lucia, staring straight in front of her. 'Oh, merciful God.'

Turning away from her, Richard approached Poirot. 'Monsieur Poirot –' he began, and then hesitated.

'M'sieur?' Poirot queried, politely.

Summoning up his determination, Richard continued, 'Monsieur Poirot, I'm afraid I do not quite understand what it is that my wife has asked you to investigate.'

Poirot considered for a moment before replying. Then, smiling pleasantly, he answered, 'Shall we say, the theft of a document? That, mademoiselle tells me,' he continued, gesturing towards Barbara, 'is what I was called down for.'

Casting a glance of reproach at Barbara, Richard told Poirot, 'The document in question has been – returned.'

'Has it?' asked Poirot, his smile becoming rather enigmatic. The little detective suddenly had the attention of everyone present, as he moved to the table in the centre of the room and looked at the envelope still lying on it, which had been generally forgotten in the excitement and commotion caused by the discovery of Sir Claud's death.

'What do you mean?' Richard Amory asked Hercule Poirot.

Poirot gave a flamboyant twist to his moustache, and carefully brushed an imaginary speck of dust from his sleeve. Then, 'It is just a – no doubt foolish – idea of mine,' the little detective finally replied. 'You see, someone told me the

other day a most amusing story. The story of the empty bottle
– there was nothing in it.'

'I'm sorry, I don't understand you,' Richard Amory declared.

Picking up the envelope from the table, Poirot murmured,
'I just wondered . . .' He glanced at Richard, who took the
envelope from him, and looked inside.

'It's empty!' Richard exclaimed. Screwing up the envelope,
he threw it on the table and looked searchingly at Lucia, who
moved away from him. 'Then,' he continued uncertainly, 'I
suppose we must be searched – we . . .'

Richard's voice trailed away, and he looked around the
room as though seeking guidance. He was met with looks
of confusion from Barbara and her aunt, indignation from
Edward Raynor and blandness from Dr Carelli. Lucia continued to avoid his eye.

'Why do you not take my advice, monsieur?' Poirot suggested. 'Do nothing until the doctor comes. Tell me,' he
asked, pointing towards the study, 'that doorway, where does
he go?'

'That's my father's study in there,' Richard told him. Poirot
crossed the room to the door, put his head around it to look
into the study, and then turned back into the library, nodding
as though satisfied.

'I see,' he murmured. Then, addressing Richard, he added,
'*Eh bien*, monsieur. I see no need why any of you should remain
in this room if you would prefer not to.'

There was a general stir of relief. Dr Carelli was the first to
move. 'It is understood, of course,' Poirot announced, looking
at the Italian doctor, 'that no one should leave the house.'

'I will hold myself responsible for that,' Richard declared
as Barbara and Raynor left together, followed by Carelli.

Caroline Amory lingered by her brother's chair. 'Poor dear Claud,' she murmured to herself. 'Poor dear Claud.'

Poirot approached her. 'You must have courage, mademoiselle,' he told her. 'The shock to you has been great, I know.'

Miss Amory looked at him with tears in her eyes. 'I'm so glad that I ordered the cook to prepare fried sole tonight,' she said. 'It was one of my brother's favourite dishes.'

With a brave attempt to look serious and to match the solemnity of her delivery, Poirot answered, 'Yes, yes, that must be a real comfort to you, I am sure.' He shepherded Miss Amory out of the room. Richard followed his aunt out and, after a moment's hesitation, Lucia made a brisk exit. Poirot and Hastings were left alone in the room with the body of Sir Claud.

CHAPTER 7

As soon as the room was empty, Hastings addressed Poirot eagerly. 'Well, what do you think?' he asked.

'Shut the door, please, Hastings,' was the only reply he received. As his friend complied, Poirot shook his head slowly and looked around the room. He moved about, casting an eye over the furniture and occasionally looking down at the floor. Suddenly, he stooped down to examine the overturned chair, the chair in which the secretary Edward Raynor had been sitting when the lights had gone out. From beneath the chair Poirot picked up a small object.

'What have you found?' Hastings asked him.

'A key,' Poirot replied. 'It looks to me as though it might be the key to a safe. I observed a safe in Sir Claud's study. Will you have the goodness, Hastings, to try this key and tell me if it fits?'

Hastings took the key from Poirot, and went into the study with it. Meanwhile, Poirot approached the body of the scientist and, feeling in the trouser pocket, removed from it a bunch of keys, each of which he examined closely. Hastings returned, informing Poirot that, indeed, the key fitted the safe in the study. 'I think I can guess what happened,' Hastings continued. 'I imagine Sir Claud must have dropped it, and – er –'

He broke off, and Poirot slowly shook his head, doubtfully. 'No, no, *mon ami*, give me the key, please,' he requested, frowning to himself as though perplexed. He took the key from Hastings and compared it with one of the keys on the bunch. Then, putting them back in the dead scientist's pocket, he held up the single key. 'This,' he told Hastings, 'is a duplicate. It is, indeed, clumsily made, but no doubt it served its purpose.'

In great excitement, Hastings exclaimed, 'Then that means –'

He was stopped by a warning gesture from Poirot. The sound of a key being turned in the lock of the door which led to the front hall and the staircase to the upper floors of the house was heard. As the two men turned, it opened slowly, and Tredwell, the butler, stood in the doorway.

'I beg your pardon, sir,' said Tredwell as he came into the room and shut the door behind him. 'The master told me to lock this door, as well as the other one leading from this room, until you arrived. The master . . .' He stopped, on seeing the motionless figure of Sir Claud in the chair.

'I am afraid your master is dead,' Poirot told him. 'May I ask your name?'

'Tredwell, sir.' The servant moved to the front of the desk, looking at the body of his master. 'Oh dear. Poor Sir Claud!' he murmured. Turning to Poirot, he added, 'Do please forgive me, sir, but it's such a shock. May I ask what happened? Is it – murder?'

'Why should you ask that?' said Poirot.

Lowering his voice, the butler replied, 'There have been strange things happening this evening, sir.'

'Oh?' exclaimed Poirot, as he exchanged glances with Hastings. 'Tell me about these strange things.'

'Well, I hardly know where to begin, sir,' Tredwell replied. 'I – I think I first felt that something was wrong when the Italian gentleman came to tea.'

'The Italian gentleman?'

'Dr Carelli, sir.'

'He came to tea unexpectedly?' asked Poirot.

'Yes, sir, and Miss Amory asked him to stay, seeing as how he was a friend of Mrs Richard's. But if you ask me, sir –'

He stopped, and Poirot gently prompted him. 'Yes?'

'I hope you will understand, sir,' said Tredwell, 'that it is not my custom to gossip about the family. But seeing that the master is dead . . .'

He paused again, and Poirot murmured sympathetically, 'Yes, yes, I understand. I am sure you were very attached to your master.' Tredwell nodded, and Poirot continued, 'Sir Claud sent for me in order to tell me something. You must tell me all you can.'

'Well, then,' Tredwell responded, 'in my opinion, sir, Mrs Richard Amory did not want the Italian gentleman asked to dinner. I observed her face when Miss Amory gave the invitation.'

'What is your own impression of Dr Carelli?' asked Poirot.

'Dr Carelli, sir,' replied the butler rather haughtily, 'is not one of us.'

Not quite understanding Tredwell's remark, Poirot looked enquiringly at Hastings who turned away to hide a smile. Throwing his colleague a glance of mild reproof, Poirot turned again to Tredwell. The butler's countenance remained perfectly serious.

'Did you feel,' Poirot queried, 'that there was something odd about Dr Carelli's coming to the house in the way that he did?'

'Precisely, sir. It wasn't natural, somehow. And it was after he arrived that the trouble began, with the master telling me earlier this evening to send for you, and giving orders about the doors being locked. Mrs Richard, too, hasn't been herself all the evening. She had to leave the dinner-table. Mr Richard, he was very upset about it.'

'Ah,' said Poirot, 'she had to leave the table? Did she come into this room?'

'Yes, sir,' Tredwell replied.

Poirot looked around the room. His eye alighted on the handbag which Lucia had left on the table. 'One of the ladies has left her bag, I see,' he observed, as he picked it up.

Moving closer to him to look at the handbag, Tredwell told Poirot, 'That is Mrs Richard's, sir.'

'Yes,' Hastings confirmed. 'I noticed her laying it down there just before she left the room.'

'Just before she left the room, eh?' said Poirot. 'How curious.' He put the bag down on the settee, frowned perplexedly, and stood apparently lost in thought.

'About locking the doors, sir,' Tredwell continued after a brief pause. 'The master told me –'

Suddenly starting out of his reverie, Poirot interrupted the butler. 'Yes, yes, I must hear all about that. Let us go through here,' he suggested, indicating the door to the front of the house.

Tredwell went to the door, followed by Poirot. Hastings, however, declared rather importantly, 'I think I'll stay here.'

Poirot turned, and regarded Hastings quizzically. 'No, no, please come with us,' he requested his colleague.

'But don't you think it better –' Hastings began, when Poirot interrupted him, now speaking solemnly and meaningfully. 'I need your co-operation, my friend,' he said.

'Oh, well, of course, in that case –'

The three men left the room together, closing the door behind them. No more than a few seconds later, the door leading to the hallway was opened cautiously and Lucia entered surreptitiously. After a hurried glance around the room as though to assure herself that there was no one there, she approached the round table in the centre of the room, and picked up Sir Claud's coffee cup. A shrewd, hard look came into her eyes which belied their customary innocent appearance, and she suddenly looked a good deal older.

Lucia was still standing with the cup in her hand, as though undecided what to do, when the other door leading to the front of the house opened and Poirot entered the library alone.

'Permit me, madame,' said Poirot, causing Lucia to start violently. He moved across to her, and took the cup from her hand with the air of one indulging in a gesture of simple politeness.

'I – I – came back for my bag,' Lucia gasped.

'Ah, yes,' said Poirot. 'Now, let me see, where did I observe a lady's handbag? Ah yes, over here.' He went to the settee, picked up the bag, and handed it to Lucia. 'Thank you so much,' she said, glancing around distractedly as she spoke.

'Not at all, madame.'

After a brief nervous smile at Poirot, Lucia quickly left the room. When she had gone, Poirot stood quite still for a moment or two, and then picked up the coffee cup. After smelling it cautiously, he took from his pocket a test tube, poured some of the dregs from Sir Claud's cup into it, and sealed the tube. Replacing it in his pocket, he then proceeded to look around the room, counting the cups aloud. 'One, two, three, four, five, six. Yes, six coffee cups.'

A perplexed frown was beginning to gather between Poirot's brows, when suddenly his eyes shone with that green light that always betokened inward excitement. Moving swiftly to the door through which he had recently entered, he opened it and slammed it noisily shut again, and then darted to the french windows, concealing himself behind the curtains. After a few moments the other door, the one to the hallway, opened, and Lucia entered again, this time even more cautiously than before, appearing to be very much on her guard. Looking about her in an attempt to keep both doors in her sight, she snatched up the coffee cup from which Sir Claud had drunk, and surveyed the entire room.

Her eye alighted on the small table near the door to the hall, on which there stood a large bowl containing a house plant. Moving to the table, Lucia thrust the coffee cup upside down into the bowl. Then, still watching the door, she took one of the other coffee cups and placed it near Sir Claud's body. She then moved quickly to the door, but as she reached it, the door opened and her husband Richard entered with a very tall, sandy-haired man in his early thirties, whose countenance, though amiable, had an air of authority about it. The newcomer was carrying a Gladstone bag.

'Lucia!' Richard exclaimed, startled. 'What are you doing here?'

'I – I – came to get my handbag,' Lucia explained. 'Hello, Dr Graham. Excuse me, please,' she added, hurrying past them. As Richard watched her go, Poirot emerged from behind the curtains, approaching the two men as though he had just entered the room by the other door.

'Ah, here is Monsieur Poirot. Let me introduce you. Poirot, this is Dr Graham. Kenneth Graham.' Poirot and the doctor bowed to each other, and Dr Graham went immediately to the body of the dead scientist to examine it, watched by Richard. Hercule Poirot, to whom they paid no further attention, moved about the room, counting the coffee cups again with a smile. 'One, two, three, four, five,' he murmured. 'Five, indeed.' A light of pure enjoyment lit up Poirot's face, and he smiled in his most inscrutable fashion. Taking the test tube out of his pocket, he looked at it, and slowly shook his head.

Meanwhile, Dr Graham had concluded a cursory examination of Sir Claud Amory's body. 'I'm afraid,' he said to Richard, 'that I shan't be able to sign a death certificate. Sir Claud was in a perfectly healthy condition, and it seems extremely unlikely to me that he could have suffered a sudden heart attack. I fear we shall have to find out what he had eaten or drunk in his last hours.'

'Good heavens, man, is that really necessary?' asked Richard, with a note of alarm in his voice. 'He hadn't eaten or drunk anything that the rest of us didn't. It's absurd to suggest –'

'I'm not suggesting anything,' Dr Graham interrupted, speaking firmly and with authority. 'I'm telling you that there will have to be an inquest, by law, and that the coroner will certainly want to know the cause of death. At present I simply do not know what caused Sir Claud's death. I'll have his body removed, and I'll arrange for an autopsy to be done first thing tomorrow morning as a matter of urgency. I should be able to get back to you later tomorrow with some hard facts.'

He left the room swiftly, followed by a still expostulating Richard. Poirot looked after them, and then assumed a puzzled expression as he turned to look again at the body of the man who had called him away from London with such urgency in his voice. 'What was it you wanted to tell me, my friend? I wonder. What did you fear?' he thought to himself. 'Was it simply the theft of your formula, or did you fear for your life as well? You relied on Hercule Poirot for help. You called for help too late, but I shall try to discover the truth.'

Shaking his head thoughtfully, Poirot was about to leave the room when Tredwell entered. 'I've shown the other gentleman to his room, sir,' he told Poirot. 'May I take you to yours, which is the adjoining one at the top of the stairs? I've also taken the liberty of providing a little cold supper for you both, after your journey. On the way upstairs I'll show you where the dining-room is.'

Poirot inclined his head in polite acceptance. 'Thank you very much, Tredwell,' he said. 'Incidentally, I am going to advise Mr Amory most strongly that this room should be kept locked until tomorrow, when we should have further information about this evening's distressing occurrence. Would you be so kind as to make it secure after we leave it now?'

'Most certainly, sir, if that is your wish,' replied Tredwell as Poirot preceded him out of the library.

CHAPTER 8

I

When Hastings came down to breakfast late the following morning, after having slept long and well, he found himself eating alone. From Tredwell he learned that Edward Raynor had breakfasted much earlier, and had gone back to his room to put some of Sir Claud's papers in order, that Mr and Mrs Amory had had breakfast in their suite of rooms and had not yet appeared, and that Barbara Amory had taken a cup of coffee out into the garden where she was presumably still sunning herself. Miss Caroline Amory had ordered breakfast in her room, pleading a slight headache, and Tredwell had not seen her subsequently.

'Have you caught sight of Monsieur Poirot at all this morning, Tredwell?' Hastings asked, and was told that his friend had risen early and had decided to take a walk to the village. 'I understood Monsieur Poirot to say that he had some business to conduct there,' Tredwell added.

After finishing a lavish breakfast of bacon, sausage and eggs, toast and coffee, Hastings returned to his comfortable room on the first floor, which offered a splendid view of part of the garden and, for a few minutes which Hastings found rewarding, of the sun-bathing Barbara Amory as well. It was not until Barbara had come indoors that Hastings settled down in an arm-chair with that morning's *Times*, which had of course gone to press too early to contain any mention of Sir Claud Amory's death the previous evening.

Hastings turned to the editorial page and began to read. A good half-hour later, he awakened from a light slumber to find Hercule Poirot standing over him.

'Ah, *mon cher*, you are hard at work on the case, I see,' Poirot chuckled.

'As a matter of fact, Poirot, I was thinking about last night's events for quite some time,' Hastings asserted. 'I must have dozed off.'

'And why not, my friend?' Poirot assured him. 'Me, I have been thinking about the death of Sir Claud as well, and, of course, the theft of his so important formula. I have, in fact, already taken some action, and I am expecting at any minute a telephone message to tell me if a certain suspicion of mine is correct or not.'

'What or whom do you suspect, Poirot?' Hastings asked eagerly.

Poirot looked out of the window before replying. 'No, I do not think I can reveal that to you at this stage of the game, my friend,' he replied mischievously. 'Let us just say that, as the magicians on the stage like to assure us, the quickness of the hand deceives the eye.'

'Really, Poirot,' Hastings exclaimed, 'you can be extremely irritating at times. I do think you ought to at least let me know whom you suspect of having stolen the formula. After all, I might be able to help you by –'

Poirot stopped his colleague with an airy gesture of his hand. The little detective was now wearing his most innocent expression, and gazing out of the window, meditatively, into the far distance. 'You are puzzled, Hastings?' he asked. 'You are wondering to yourself why I do not launch myself in pursuit of a suspect?'

'Well – something of the kind,' Hastings admitted.

'It is no doubt what you would do, if you were in my place,' observed Poirot complacently. 'I understand that. But I am not of those who enjoy rushing about, seeking a needle in a hay-stack, as you English say. For the moment, I am content to wait. As to why I wait – *eh bien*, to the intelligence of Hercule Poirot things are sometimes perfectly clear which are not at all clear to those who are not so greatly gifted.'

'Good Lord, Poirot!' Hastings exclaimed. 'Do you know, I'd give a considerable sum of money to see you make a thorough ass of yourself – just for once. You're so confoundedly conceited!'

'Do not enrage yourself, my dear Hastings,' Poirot replied soothingly. 'In verity, I observe that there are times when you seem almost to detest me! Alas, I suffer the penalties of greatness!'

The little man puffed out his chest, and sighed so comically that Hastings was forced to laugh. 'Poirot, you really have the best opinion of yourself of anyone I've ever known,' he declared.

'What will you? When one is unique, one knows it. But now to serious matters, my dear Hastings. Let me tell you that I have asked Sir Claud's son, Mr Richard Amory, to meet us in the library at noon. I say "us", Hastings, for I need you to be there, my friend, to observe closely.'

'As always, I shall be delighted to assist you, Poirot,' his friend assured him.

II

At noon, Poirot, Hastings and Richard Amory met in the library, from which the body of Sir Claud had been removed late the previous evening. While Hastings listened and observed from a comfortable position on the settee, the detective asked Richard Amory to recount in detail the events of the evening, prior to his, Poirot's, arrival. When he had concluded his recital of events, Richard, sitting in the chair which his father had occupied the previous evening, added, 'Well, that's about everything, I think. I hope I've made myself clear?'

'But perfectly, Monsieur Amory, perfectly,' Poirot replied, leaning against an arm of the only arm-chair in the room. 'I now have a clear *tableau*.' Shutting his eyes, he attempted to conjure up the scene. 'There is Sir Claud in his chair, dominating the situation. Then the darkness, the knocking on the door. Yes, indeed, a dramatic little scene.'

'Well,' said Richard, making as if to rise, 'if that is all –'

'Just one little minute,' said Poirot, with a gesture as though to detain him.

Lowering himself to his chair again with an air of reluctance, Richard asked, 'Yes?'

'What about earlier in the evening, Monsieur Amory?'

'Earlier in the evening?'

'Yes,' Poirot reminded him. 'After dinner.'

'Oh, that!' said Richard. 'There's really nothing more to tell. My father and his secretary, Raynor – Edward Raynor – went straight into my father's study. The rest of us were in here.'

Poirot beamed at Richard encouragingly. 'And you did – what?'

'Oh, we just talked. We had the gramophone on for most of the time.'

Poirot thought for a moment. Then, 'Nothing took place that strikes you as worth recalling?' he asked.

'Nothing whatever,' Richard affirmed very quickly.

Watching him closely, Poirot pressed on. 'When was the coffee served?'

'Immediately after dinner,' was Richard's reply.

Poirot made a circular motion with his hand. 'Did the butler hand it around, or did he leave it here to be poured out?'

'I really can't remember,' said Richard.

Poirot gave a slight sigh. He thought for a moment, and then asked, 'Did you all take coffee?'

'Yes, I think so. All except Raynor, that is. He doesn't drink coffee.'

'And Sir Claud's coffee was taken to him in the study?'

'I suppose so,' replied Richard with some irritation beginning to show in his voice. 'Are all these details really necessary?'

Poirot lifted his arms in a gesture of apology. 'I am so sorry,' he said. 'It is just that I am very anxious to get the whole picture straight in my mind's eye. And, after all, we do want to get this precious formula back, do we not?'

'I suppose so,' was again Richard's rather sullen rejoinder, at which Poirot's eyebrows shot up exaggeratedly and he uttered an exclamation of surprise. 'No, of course, of course, we do,' Richard hastened to add.

Poirot, looking away from Richard Amory, asked, 'Now, when did Sir Claud come from the study into this room?'

'Just as they were trying to get that door open,' Amory told him.

'They?' queried Poirot, rounding on him.

'Yes. Raynor and the others.'

'May I ask who wanted it opened?'

'My wife, Lucia,' said Richard. 'She hadn't been feeling well all the evening.'

Poirot's tone was sympathetic as he replied, '*La pauvre dame!* I hope she finds herself better this morning? There are one or two things I urgently desire to ask her.'

'I'm afraid that's quite impossible,' said Richard. 'She's not up to seeing anyone, or answering any questions. In any case, there's nothing she could tell you that I couldn't.'

'Quite so, quite so,' Poirot assured him. 'But women, Monsieur Amory, have a great capacity for observing things in detail. Still, doubtless your aunt, Miss Amory, will do as well.'

'She's in bed,' said Richard hastily. 'My father's death was a great shock to her.'

'Yes, I see,' murmured Poirot thoughtfully. There was a pause. Richard, looking distinctly uncomfortable, rose and turned to the french windows. 'Let's have some air,' he announced. 'It's very hot in here.'

'Ah, you are like all the English,' Poirot declared, smiling. 'The good open air, you will not leave it in the open. No! It must be brought inside the house.'

'You don't mind, I hope?' Richard asked.

'Me?' said Poirot. 'No, of course not. I have adopted all the English habits. Everywhere, I am taken for an Englishman.' On the settee, Hastings could not help but smile to himself. 'But, pardon me, Monsieur Amory, is not that window locked by some ingenious device?'

'Yes, it is,' replied Richard, 'but the key to it is on my father's bunch of keys which I have here.' Taking a bunch of keys from his pocket, he moved to the french windows and undid the catch, flinging the windows open wide.

Moving away from him, Poirot sat on the stool, well away from the french windows and the fresh air, and shivered, while Richard took a deep breath of air and then stood for a moment, looking out at the garden, before coming back to Poirot with the air of someone who has arrived at a decision.

'Monsieur Poirot,' Richard Amory declared, 'I won't beat about the bush. I know my wife begged you last night to remain, but she was upset and hysterical, and hardly knew what she was doing. I'm the person concerned, and I tell you frankly that I don't care a damn about the formula. My father was a rich man. This discovery of his was worth a great deal of money, but I don't need more than I've got, and I can't pretend to share his enthusiasm in the matter. There are explosives enough in the world already.'

'I see,' murmured Poirot thoughtfully.

'What I say,' continued Richard, 'is that we should let the whole thing drop.'

Poirot's eyebrows shot up, as he made his familiar gesture of surprise. 'You prefer that I should depart?' he asked. 'That I should make no further investigations?'

'Yes, that's it.' Richard Amory sounded uncomfortable, as he half turned away from Poirot.

'But,' the detective persisted, 'whoever stole the formula would not do so in order to make no use of it.'

'No,' Richard admitted. He turned back to Poirot. 'But still –'

Slowly and meaningfully, Poirot continued, 'Then you do not object to the – how shall I put it – the stigma?'

'Stigma?' exclaimed Richard sharply.

'Five people –' Poirot explained to him, 'five people had the opportunity of stealing the formula. Until one is proved guilty, the other four cannot be proved innocent.'

Tredwell had entered the room while Poirot was speaking. As Richard began to stammer irresolutely, 'I – that is –' the butler interrupted him.

'I beg your pardon, sir,' he said to his employer, 'but Dr Graham is here, and would like to see you.'

Clearly glad of the opportunity to escape further questioning from Poirot, Richard replied, 'I'll come at once,' moving to the door as he spoke. Turning to Poirot, he asked, formally, 'Would you excuse me, please?' as he left with Tredwell.

When the two men had departed, Hastings rose from the settee and approached Poirot, bursting with suppressed excitement. 'I say!' he exclaimed. 'Poison, eh?'

'What, my dear Hastings?' asked Poirot.

'Poison, surely!' Hastings repeated, nodding his head vigorously.

CHAPTER 9

Poirot surveyed his friend with an amused twinkle in his eye. 'How dramatic you are, my dear Hastings!' he exclaimed. 'With what swiftness and brilliance you leap to conclusions!'

'Now then, Poirot,' Hastings protested, 'you can't put me off that way. You're not going to pretend that you think the old fellow died of heart disease. What happened last night positively leaps to the eye. But I must say Richard Amory can't be a very bright sort of chap. The possibility of poison doesn't seem to have occurred to him.'

'You think not, my friend?' asked Poirot.

'I spotted it last night, when Dr Graham announced that he couldn't issue a death certificate and said that there would have to be an autopsy.'

Poirot gave a slight sigh. 'Yes, yes,' he murmured placatingly. 'It is the result of the autopsy that Dr Graham comes to announce this morning. We shall know whether you are right or not in a very few minutes.' Poirot seemed to be about to say something further, but then checked himself. He moved to the mantelpiece, and began to adjust the vase containing the spills used for lighting the fire.

Hastings watched him affectionately. 'I say, Poirot,' he laughed, 'what a fellow you are for neatness.'

'Is not the effect more pleasing now?' asked Poirot, as he surveyed the mantelpiece with his head on one side.

Hastings snorted. 'I can't say it worried me greatly before.'

'Beware!' said Poirot, shaking an admonishing finger at him. 'The symmetry, it is everything. Everywhere there should be neatness and order, especially in the little grey cells of the brain.' He tapped his head as he spoke.

'Oh, come on, don't leap onto your hobby horse,' Hastings begged him. 'Just tell me what your precious little grey cells make of this business.'

Poirot moved to the settee, and sat before replying. He regarded Hastings steadily, his eyes narrowing like a cat's until they showed only a gleam of green. 'If you would use your grey cells, and attempt to see the whole case clearly – as I attempt to do – you would perhaps perceive the truth, my friend,' he announced smugly. 'However,' he continued, in a tone which suggested that he considered he was behaving with great magnanimity, 'before Dr Graham arrives, let us first hear the ideas of my friend Hastings.'

'Well,' Hastings began, eagerly, 'the key being found under the secretary's chair is suspicious.'

'You think so, do you, Hastings?'

'Of course,' his friend replied. 'Highly suspicious. But, on the whole, I plump for the Italian.'

'Ah!' Poirot murmured. 'The mysterious Dr Carelli.'

'Mysterious, exactly,' Hastings continued. 'That's precisely the right word for him. What is he doing, down here in the country? I'll tell you. He was after Sir Claud Amory's formula. He's almost certainly the emissary of a foreign government. You know the kind of thing I mean.'

'I do, indeed, Hastings,' Poirot responded with a smile. 'After all, I do occasionally go to the cinema, you know.'

'And if it turns out that Sir Claud was indeed poisoned' – Hastings was now well into his stride – 'it makes Dr Carelli more than ever the prime suspect. Remember the Borgias? Poison is a very Italian sort of crime. But what I'm afraid of is that Carelli will get away with the formula in his possession.'

'He will not do that, my friend,' said Poirot, shaking his head.

'How on earth can you be so sure?' Hastings enquired.

Poirot leaned back in his chair, and brought the tips of his fingers together in his familiar manner. 'I do not exactly know, Hastings,' he admitted. 'I cannot be sure, of course. But I have a little idea.'

'What do you mean?'

'Where do you think that formula is now, my clever collaborator?' Poirot asked.

'How should I know?'

Poirot looked at Hastings for a moment, as though giving his friend a chance to consider the question. Then, 'Think, my friend,' he said encouragingly. 'Arrange your ideas. Be methodical. Be orderly. That is the secret of success.' When Hastings merely shook his head with a perplexed air, the detective attempted to give his colleague a clue. 'There is only one place where it can be,' Poirot told him.

'And where is that, for heaven's sake?' Hastings asked, with a distinct note of irritation in his voice.

'In this room, of course,' Poirot announced, a triumphant Cheshire cat-like grin appearing on his face.

'What on earth do you mean?'

'But yes, Hastings. Just consider the facts. We know from the good Tredwell that Sir Claud took certain precautions to prevent the formula from being removed from this room. When he sprang his little surprise and announced our imminent arrival, it is quite certain, therefore, that the thief still had the formula on his person. What must he do? He dare not risk having it found on him when I arrived. He can do only two things. He can return it, in the manner suggested by Sir Claud, or else he can hide it somewhere, under cover of that one minute of total darkness. Since he did not do the first, he must have done the second. *Voilà!* It is obvious to me that the formula is hidden in this room.'

'By God, Poirot,' Hastings exclaimed in great excitement, 'I believe you're right! Let's look for it.' He rose quickly, and moved to the desk.

'By all means, if it amuses you,' Poirot responded. 'But there is someone who will be able to find it more easily than you can.'

'Oh, and who is that?' asked Hastings.

Poirot twirled his moustache with enormous energy. 'Why, the person who hid it, *parbleu!*' he exclaimed, accompanying his words with the kind of gesture more suitably employed by a magician pulling a rabbit out of a hat.

'You mean that –'

'I mean,' Poirot explained patiently to his colleague, 'that sooner or later the thief will try to recapture his booty. One or the other of us, therefore, must constantly remain on guard –' Hearing the door being opened slowly and cautiously, he broke off, and beckoned Hastings to join him by the gramophone, out of the immediate sight of anyone entering the room.

CHAPTER 10

The door opened, and Barbara Amory entered the room cautiously. Taking a chair from near the wall, she placed it in front of the bookcase, climbed on it, and reached for the tin box containing the drugs. At that moment, Hastings suddenly sneezed, and Barbara, with a start, dropped the box. 'Oh!' she exclaimed in some confusion. 'I didn't know there was anyone here.'

Hastings rushed forward and retrieved the box, which Poirot then took from him. 'Permit me, mademoiselle,' said the detective. 'I am sure that is too heavy for you.' He moved to the table and placed the tin box upon it. 'It is a little collection of yours?' he asked. 'The birds' eggs? The sea shells, perhaps?'

'I'm afraid it's much more prosaic, Monsieur Poirot,' replied Barbara, with a nervous laugh. 'Nothing but pills and powders!'

'But surely,' said Poirot, 'one so young, so full of health and vigour, has no need of these bagatelles?'

'Oh, it's not for me,' Barbara assured him. 'It's for Lucia. She's got such an awful headache this morning.'

'*La pauvre dame*,' murmured Poirot, his voice dripping with sympathy. 'She sent you for these pills, then?'

'Yes,' replied Barbara. 'I gave her a couple of aspirin, but she wanted some real dope. I said I'd bring up the whole outfit – that is, if no one were here.'

Poirot, leaning his hands on the box, spoke thoughtfully. 'If no one were here. Why would that matter, mademoiselle?'

'Well, you know what it is in a place like this,' Barbara explained. 'Fuss, fuss, fuss! I mean, Aunt Caroline for instance is like a clucky old hen! And Richard's a damned nuisance and completely useless into the bargain, as men always are when you're ill.'

Poirot nodded in comprehension. 'I understand, I understand,' he told Barbara, bowing his head as a sign that he accepted her explanation. He rubbed his fingers along the lid of the case containing the drugs, and then looked quickly at his hands. Pausing for a moment, he cleared his throat with a slightly affected sound, and then went on, 'Do you know, mademoiselle, that you are very fortunate in your domestic servants?'

'What do you mean?' asked Barbara.

Poirot showed her the tin box. 'See –' he pointed out, 'on this box there is no speck of dust. To mount on a chair and bother to dust so high up there – not all domestics would be so conscientious.'

'Yes,' Barbara agreed. 'I thought it odd last night that it wasn't dusty.'

'You had this case of drugs down last night?' Poirot asked her.

'Yes, after dinner. It's full of old hospital stuff, you know.'

'Let us have a look at these hospital drugs,' suggested Poirot as he opened the box. Taking out some phials and holding them up, he raised his eyebrows exaggeratedly. 'Strychnine – atropine – a very pretty little collection! Ah! Here is a tube of hyoscine, nearly empty!'

'What?' exclaimed Barbara. 'Why, they were all full last night. I'm sure they were.'

'*Voilà!*' Poirot held out a tube to her, and then replaced it in the box. 'This is very curious. You say that all these little – what do you call them – phials – were full? Where exactly was this case of drugs last night, mademoiselle?'

'Well, when we took it down, we placed it on this table,' Barbara informed him. 'And Dr Carelli was looking through the drugs, commenting on them and –'

She broke off as Lucia entered the room. Richard Amory's wife looked surprised to see the two men. Her pale, proud face seemed careworn in the daylight, and there was something wistful in the curve of her mouth. Barbara hastened to her. 'Oh, darling, you shouldn't have got up,' she told Lucia. 'I was just coming up to you.'

'My headache is much better, Barbara dear,' Lucia replied, her eyes fixed on Poirot. 'I came down because I want to speak to Monsieur Poirot.'

'But, my pet, don't you think you should –'

'Please, Barbara.'

'Oh, very well, you know best,' said Barbara as she moved to the door, which Hastings rushed to open for her. When she had gone, Lucia moved to a chair and sat down. 'Monsieur Poirot –' she began.

'I am at your service, madame,' Poirot responded politely.

Lucia spoke hesitantly, and her voice trembled a little. 'Monsieur Poirot,' she began again, 'last night I made a request to you. I asked you to stay on here. I – I begged you to do so. This morning I see that I made a mistake.'

'Are you sure, madame?' Poirot asked her quietly.

'Quite sure. I was nervous last night, and overwrought. I am most grateful to you for doing what I asked, but now it is better that you should go.'

'Ah, *c'est comme ça!*' Poirot murmured beneath his breath. Aloud, his response was merely a non-committal, 'I see, madame.'

Rising, Lucia glanced at him nervously as she asked, 'That is settled, then?'

'Not quite, madame,' replied Poirot, taking a step towards her. 'If you remember, you expressed a doubt that your father-in-law had died a natural death.'

'I was hysterical last night,' Lucia insisted. 'I did not know what I was saying.'

'Then you are now convinced,' Poirot persisted, 'that his death was, after all, natural?'

'Absolutely,' Lucia declared.

Poirot's eyebrows rose a trifle. He looked at her in silence.

'Why do you look at me like that?' Lucia asked with alarm in her voice.

'Because, madame, it is sometimes difficult to set a dog on the scent. But once he has found it, nothing on earth will make him leave it. Not if he is a good dog. And I, madame, I, Hercule Poirot, am a very good dog!'

In great agitation, Lucia declared, 'Oh! But you must, you really must go. I beg you, I implore you. You don't know what harm you may do by remaining!'

'Harm?' asked Poirot. 'To you, madame?'

'To all of us, Monsieur Poirot. I can't explain further, but I beg you to accept my word that it is so. From the first moment I saw you, I trusted you. Please –'

She broke off as the door opened, and Richard, looking shocked, entered with Dr Graham. 'Lucia!' her husband exclaimed as he caught sight of her.

'Richard, what is it?' asked Lucia anxiously as she rushed to his side. 'What has happened? Something new has happened, I can see it in your face. What is it?'

'Nothing, my dear,' replied Richard with an attempt at reassurance in his tone. 'Do you mind leaving us for a moment?'

Lucia's eyes searched his face. 'Can't I –' she began, but hesitated as Richard moved to the door and opened it. 'Please,' he repeated.

With a final backward glance in which there was a distinct element of fear, Lucia left the room.

Putting his Gladstone bag on the coffee table, Dr Graham crossed to the settee and sat down. 'I'm afraid this is a bad business, Monsieur Poirot,' he announced to the detective.

'A bad business, you say? Yes? You have discovered what caused the death of Sir Claud?' asked Poirot.

'His death was due to poisoning by a powerful vegetable alkaloid,' Graham declared.

'Such as hyoscine, perhaps?' Poirot suggested, picking up the tin box of drugs from the table.

'Why, yes, exactly.' Dr Graham sounded surprised at the detective's accurate surmise. Poirot took the case to the other side of the room, placing it on the gramophone table, and Hastings followed him there. Meanwhile, Richard Amory joined the doctor on the settee. 'What does this mean, actually?' Richard asked Dr Graham.

'For one thing, it means the involvement of the police,' was Graham's prompt reply.

'My God!' exclaimed Richard. 'This is terrible. Can't you possibly hush it up?'

Dr Graham looked at Richard Amory steadily before he

spoke, slowly and deliberately. 'My dear Richard,' he said. 'Believe me, nobody could be more pained and grieved at this horrible calamity than I am. Especially since, under the circumstances, it does not seem likely that the poison could have been self-administered.'

Richard paused for several seconds before he spoke. 'Are you saying it was murder?' he asked in an unsteady voice.

Dr Graham did not speak, but nodded solemnly.

'Murder!' exclaimed Richard. 'What on earth are we going to do?'

Adopting a brisker, more business-like manner, Graham explained the procedure to be followed. 'I have notified the coroner. The inquest will be held tomorrow at the King's Arms.'

'And – you mean – the police will have to be involved? There's no way out of it?'

'There is not. Surely you must realize that, Richard?' said Dr Graham.

Richard's tone was frantic as he began to exclaim, 'But why didn't you warn me that –'

'Come on, Richard. Take a hold of yourself. I'm sure you understand that I have only taken such steps as I thought absolutely necessary,' Graham interrupted him. 'After all, no time should be lost in matters of this kind.'

'My God!' exclaimed Richard.

Dr Graham addressed Amory in a kindlier tone. 'Richard, I know. I do understand. This has been a terrible shock to you. But there are things I must ask you about. Do you feel equal to answering a few questions?'

Richard made a visible effort to pull himself together. 'What do you want to know?' he asked.

'First of all,' said Graham, 'what food and drink did your father have at dinner last night?'

'Let's see, we all had the same. Soup, fried sole, cutlets, and we finished off with a fruit salad.'

'Now, what about drink?' continued Dr Graham.

Richard considered for a moment before replying. 'My father and my aunt drank burgundy. So did Raynor, I think. I stuck with whisky and soda, and Dr Carelli – yes, Dr Carelli drank white wine throughout the meal.'

'Ah, yes, the mysterious Dr Carelli,' Graham murmured. 'You'll excuse me, Richard, but how much precisely do you know about this man?'

Interested to hear Richard Amory's reply to this, Hastings moved closer to the two men. In answer to Dr Graham, Richard declared, 'I know nothing about him. I'd never met him, or even heard of him, until yesterday.'

'But he is a friend of your wife?' asked the doctor.

'Apparently he is.'

'Does she know him intimately?'

'Oh, no, he is a mere acquaintance, I gather.'

Graham made a little clicking sound with his tongue, and shook his head. 'You've not allowed him to leave the house, I hope?' he asked.

'No, no,' Richard assured him. 'I pointed out to him last night that, until this matter was cleared up – the business of the formula being stolen, I mean – it would be best for him to remain here at the house. In fact, I sent down to the inn where he had a room, and had his things brought up here.'

'Didn't he make any protest at all?' Graham asked in some surprise.

'Oh, no, in fact he agreed quite eagerly.'

'H'm,' was Graham's only response to this. Then, looking about him, he asked, 'Well now, what about this room?'

Poirot approached the two men. 'The doors were locked last night by Tredwell, the butler,' he assured Dr Graham, 'and the keys were given to me. Everything is exactly as it was, except that we have moved the chairs, as you see.'

Dr Graham looked at the coffee cup on the table. Pointing to it, he asked, 'Is that the cup?' He went across to the table, picked up the cup and sniffed at it. 'Richard,' he asked, 'is this the cup your father drank from? I'd better take it. It will have to be analysed.' Carrying the cup over to the coffee table, he opened his bag.

Richard sprang to his feet. 'Surely you don't think –' he began, but then broke off.

'It seems highly unlikely,' Graham told him, 'that the poison could have been administered at dinner. The most likely explanation is that the hyoscine was added to Sir Claud's coffee.'

'I – I –' Richard tried to utter as he rose and took a step towards the doctor, but then broke off with a despairing gesture, and left the room abruptly through the french windows into the garden.

Dr Graham took a small cardboard box of cotton wool from his bag, and carefully packed the cup in it, talking to Poirot as he did so. 'A nasty business,' he confided. 'I'm not at all surprised that Richard Amory is upset. The newspapers will make the most of this Italian doctor's friendship with his wife. And mud tends to stick, Monsieur Poirot. Mud tends to stick. Poor lady! She was probably wholly innocent. The man obviously made her acquaintance in some plausible way. They're astonishingly clever, these foreigners. Of course, I suppose I shouldn't be talking this way, as though the thing were a foregone conclusion, but what else is one to imagine?'

'You think it leaps to the eye, yes?' Poirot asked him, exchanging glances with Hastings.

'Well, after all,' Dr Graham explained, 'Sir Claud's invention was valuable. This foreigner comes along, of whom nobody knows anything. An Italian. Sir Claud is mysteriously poisoned –'

'Ah, yes! The Borgias,' exclaimed Poirot.

'I beg your pardon?' asked the doctor.

'Nothing, nothing.'

Dr Graham picked up his bag and prepared to leave, holding out his hand to Poirot. 'Well, I'd best be off.'

'Goodbye – for the present, Monsieur le docteur,' said Poirot as they shook hands.

At the door, Graham paused and looked back. 'Goodbye, Monsieur Poirot. You will see that nobody disturbs anything in this room until the police arrive, won't you? That's extremely important.'

'Most certainly, I shall make myself responsible for it,' Poirot assured him.

As Graham left, closing the door behind him, Hastings observed dryly, 'You know, Poirot, I shouldn't like to be ill in this house. For one thing, there appears to be a poisoner at loose in the place – and, for another, I'm not at all sure I trust that young doctor.'

Poirot gave Hastings a quizzical look. 'Let us hope that we will not be in this house long enough to become ill,' he said, moving to the fireplace and pressing the bell. 'And now, my dear Hastings, to work,' he announced as he rejoined his colleague who was contemplating the coffee table with a puzzled expression.

'What are you going to do?' Hastings asked.

'You and I, my friend,' replied Poirot with a twinkle in his eye, 'are going to interview Cesare Borgia.'

Tredwell entered in response to Poirot's call. 'You rang, sir?' the butler asked.

'Yes, Tredwell. Will you please ask the Italian gentleman, Dr Carelli, if he would be kind enough to come here?'

'Certainly, sir,' Tredwell replied. He left the room, and Poirot went to the table to pick up the case of drugs. 'It would be well, I think,' he confided to Hastings, 'if we were to put this box of so very dangerous drugs back in its proper place. Let us, above all things, be neat and orderly.'

Handing the tin box to Hastings, Poirot took a chair to the bookcase and climbed onto it. 'The old cry for neatness and symmetry, eh?' Hastings exclaimed. 'But there's more to it than that, I imagine.'

'What do you mean, my friend?' asked Poirot.

'I know what it is. You don't want to scare Carelli. After all, who handled those drugs last night? Amongst others, he did. If he saw them down on the table, it might put him on his guard, eh, Poirot?'

Poirot tapped Hastings on the head. 'How astute is my friend Hastings,' he declared, taking the case from him.

'I know you too well,' Hastings insisted. 'You can't throw dust in my eyes.'

As Hastings spoke, Poirot drew a finger along the top of the bookshelf, sweeping dust down into his friend's upturned face. 'It seems to me, my dear Hastings, that that is precisely what I have done,' Poirot exclaimed as he gingerly drew a finger along the shelf again, making a grimace as he did so. 'It appears that I have praised the domestics too soon. This shelf is thick with dust. I wish I had a good wet duster in my hand to clean it up!'

'My dear Poirot,' Hastings laughed, 'you're not a house-maid.'

'Alas, no,' observed Poirot sadly. 'I am only a detective!'

'Well, there's nothing to detect up there,' Hastings declared, 'so get down.'

'As you say, there is nothing –' Poirot began, and then stopped dead, standing quite still on the chair as though turned to stone.

'What is it?' Hastings asked him impatiently, adding, 'Do get down, Poirot. Dr Carelli will be here at any minute. You don't want him to find you up there, do you?'

'You are right, my friend,' Poirot agreed as he got down slowly from the chair. His face wore a solemn expression.

'What on earth is the matter?' asked Hastings.

'It is that I am thinking of something,' Poirot replied with a faraway look in his eyes.

'What are you thinking of?'

'Dust, Hastings. Dust,' said Poirot in an odd voice.

The door opened, and Dr Carelli entered the room. He and Poirot greeted each other with the greatest of ceremony, each politely speaking the other's native tongue. 'Ah, Monsieur Poirot,' Carelli began. '*Vous voulez me questionner?*'

'*Si, signor dottore, si lei permette,*' Poirot replied.

'*Ah, lei parla Italiano?*'

'*Si, ma preferisco parlare in Francese.*'

'*Alors,*' said Carelli, '*qu'est-ce que vous voulez me demander?*'

'I say,' Hastings interjected with a certain irritation in his voice. 'What the devil is all this?'

'Ah, the poor Hastings is not a linguist. I had forgotten,' Poirot smiled. 'We had better speak English.'

'I beg your pardon. Of course,' Carelli agreed. He addressed Poirot with an air of great frankness. 'I am glad that you have sent for me, Monsieur Poirot,' he declared. 'Had you not done so, I should myself have requested an interview.'

'Indeed?' remarked Poirot, indicating a chair by the table.

Carelli sat, while Poirot seated himself in the arm-chair, and Hastings made himself comfortable on the settee. 'Yes,' the Italian doctor continued. 'As it happens, I have business in London of an urgent nature.'

'Pray, continue,' Poirot encouraged him.

'Yes. Of course, I quite appreciated the position last night. A valuable document had been stolen. I was the only stranger present. Naturally, I was only too willing to remain, to permit myself to be searched, in fact to insist on being searched. As a man of honour, I could do nothing else.'

'Quite so,' Poirot agreed. 'But today?'

'Today is different,' replied Carelli. 'I have, as I say, urgent business in London.'

'And you wish to take your departure?'

'Exactly.'

'It seems most reasonable,' Poirot declared. 'Do you not think so, Hastings?'

Hastings made no reply, but looked as though he did not think it at all reasonable.

'Perhaps a word from you, Monsieur Poirot, to Mr Amory, would be in order,' Carelli suggested. 'I should like to avoid any unpleasantness.'

'My good offices are at your disposal, Monsieur le docteur,' Poirot assured him. 'And now, perhaps you can assist me with one or two details.'

'I should be only too happy to do so,' Carelli replied.

Poirot considered for a moment, before asking, 'Is Madame Richard Amory an old friend of yours?'

'A very old friend,' said Carelli. He sighed. 'It was a delightful surprise, running across her so unexpectedly in this out-of-the-way spot.'

'Unexpectedly, you say?' Poirot asked.

'Quite unexpectedly,' Carelli replied, with a quick glance at the detective.

'Quite unexpectedly,' Poirot repeated. 'Fancy that!'

A certain tension had crept into the atmosphere. Carelli looked at Poirot sharply, but said nothing.

'You are interested in the latest discoveries of science?' Poirot asked him.

'Certainly. I am a doctor.'

'Ah! But that does not quite follow, surely,' Poirot observed. 'A new vaccine, a new ray, a new germ – all this, yes. But a new explosive, surely that is not quite the province of a doctor of medicine?'

'Science should be of interest to all of us,' Carelli insisted. 'It represents the triumph of man over nature. Man wrings secrets from nature in spite of her bitter opposition.'

Poirot nodded his head in agreement. 'It is indeed admirable, what you say there. It is poetic! But, as my friend Hastings reminded me just now, I am only a detective. I appreciate things from a more practical standpoint. This discovery of Sir Claud's – it was worth a great amount of money, eh?'

'Possibly,' Carelli's tone was dismissive. 'I have not given that side of the matter much thought.'

'You are evidently a man of lofty principles,' observed Poirot, 'and also, no doubt, a man of means. Travelling, for instance, is an expensive hobby.'

'One should see the world one lives in,' said Carelli dryly.

'Indeed,' Poirot agreed. 'And the people who live in it. Curious people, some of them. The thief, for instance – what a curious mentality he must have!'

'As you say,' Carelli agreed, 'most curious.'

'And the blackmailer,' Poirot continued.

'What do you mean?' Carelli asked sharply.

'I said, the blackmailer,' Poirot repeated. There was an awkward pause, before he continued, 'but we are wandering from our subject – the death of Sir Claud Amory.'

'The death of Sir Claud Amory? Why is that our subject?'

'Ah, of course,' Poirot recalled. 'You do not yet know. I am afraid that Sir Claud did not die as the result of a heart attack. He was poisoned.' He watched the Italian closely for his reaction.

'Ah!' murmured Carelli, with a nod of the head.

'That does not surprise you?' asked Poirot.

'Frankly, no,' Carelli replied. 'I suspected as much last night.'

'You see, then,' Poirot continued, 'that the matter has become much more serious.' His tone changed. 'You will not be able to leave the house today, Dr Carelli.'

Leaning forward to Poirot, Carelli asked, 'Do you connect Sir Claud's death with the stealing of the formula?'

'Certainly,' Poirot replied. 'Do not you?'

Carelli spoke quickly and urgently. 'Is there no one in this house, no member of his family, who desired the death of Sir Claud, quite apart from any question of the formula? What does his death mean to most of the people in this house? I will tell you. It means freedom, Monsieur Poirot. Freedom, and what you mentioned just now – money. That old man was a tyrant, and apart from his beloved work he was a miser.'

'Did you observe all this last night, Monsieur le docteur?' asked Poirot, innocently.

'What if I did?' replied Carelli. 'I have eyes. I can see. At least three of the people in this house wanted Sir Claud out of the way.' He rose, and looked at the clock on the mantelpiece. 'But that does not concern me now.'

Hastings leaned forward, looking very interested, as Carelli continued, 'I am vexed that I cannot keep my appointment in London.'

'I am desolated, Monsieur le docteur,' said Poirot. 'But what can I do?'

'Well, then, you have no further need of me?' asked Carelli.

'For the moment, no,' Poirot told him.

Dr Carelli moved to the door. 'I will tell you one thing more, Monsieur Poirot,' he announced, opening the door and turning back to face the detective. 'There are some women whom it is dangerous to drive too far.'

Poirot bowed to him politely, and Carelli returned his bow somewhat more ironically before making his exit.

When Carelli had left the room, Hastings stared after him for a few moments. 'I say, Poirot,' he asked finally, 'what do you think he meant by that?'

Poirot shrugged his shoulders. 'It was a remark of no consequence,' he declared.

'But Poirot,' Hastings persisted, 'I'm sure Carelli was trying to tell you something.'

'Ring the bell once more, Hastings,' was the little detective's only response. Hastings did as he was bidden, but could not refrain from a further enquiry. 'What are you going to do now?'

Poirot's reply was in his most enigmatic vein. 'You will see, my dear Hastings. Patience is a great virtue.'

Tredwell entered the room again with his usual respectful enquiry of 'Yes, sir?' Poirot beamed at him genially. 'Ah, Tredwell. Will you present my compliments to Miss Caroline Amory, and ask her if she will be good enough to allow me a few minutes of her time?'

'Certainly, sir.'

'I thank you, Tredwell.'

When the butler had left, Hastings exclaimed, 'But the old soul's in bed. Surely you're not going to make her get up, if she isn't feeling well.'

'My friend Hastings knows everything! So she is in bed, yes?'

'Well, isn't she?'

Poirot patted his friend's shoulder affectionately. 'That is just what I want to find out.'

'But, surely –' Hastings elaborated. 'Don't you remember? Richard Amory said so.'

The detective regarded his friend steadily. 'Hastings,' he declared, 'here is a man killed. And how does his family react? With lies, lies, lies everywhere! Why does Madame Amory want me to go? Why does Monsieur Amory want me to go? Why does he wish to prevent me from seeing his aunt? What can she tell me that he does not want me to hear? I tell you, Hastings, what we have here is drama! Not a simple, sordid crime, but drama. Poignant, human drama!'

He looked as though he would have expanded on this theme had not Miss Amory entered at that moment. 'Monsieur Poirot,' she addressed him as she closed the door, 'Tredwell tells me you wanted to see me.'

'Ah yes, mademoiselle,' Poirot declared as he went to her. 'It is just that I would like to ask you a few questions. Will you not sit down?' He led her to a chair by the table, and she sat, looking at him nervously. 'But I understood that you were prostrated, ill?' Poirot continued as he sat on the other side of the table, and regarded her with an expression of anxious solicitude.

'It's all been a terrible shock, of course,' Caroline Amory sighed. 'Really terrible! But what I always say is, somebody must keep their head. The servants, you know, are in a turmoil. Well,' she continued, speaking more quickly, 'you know what servants are, Monsieur Poirot. They positively delight in funerals! They prefer a death to a wedding, I do believe. Now, dear Dr Graham! He is so kind – such a comfort. A really clever doctor, and of course he's so fond of Barbara. I think it's a pity that Richard doesn't seem to care for him, but – what was I saying? Oh yes, Dr Graham. So young. And he quite cured my neuritis last year. Not that I am often ill. Now, this rising generation doesn't seem to me to be at all strong. There was poor Lucia last night, having to come out from dinner feeling faint. Of course, poor child, she's a mass of nerves, and what else can you expect with Italian blood in her veins? Though she was not so bad, I remember, when her diamond necklace was stolen –'

Miss Amory paused for breath. Poirot, while she was speaking, had taken out his cigarette-case and was about to light a cigarette, but he paused and took the opportunity to ask her, 'Madame Amory's diamond necklace was stolen? When was this, mademoiselle?'

Miss Amory assumed a thoughtful expression. 'Let me see, it must have been – yes, it was two months ago – just about the same time that Richard had such a quarrel with his father.'

Poirot looked at the cigarette in his hand. 'You permit that I smoke, mademoiselle?' he asked, and on receiving a smile and a gracious nod of assent, he took a box of matches from his pocket, lit his cigarette, and looked at Miss Amory encouragingly. When that lady made no effort to resume speaking, Poirot prompted her. 'I think you were saying that Monsieur Amory quarrelled with his father,' he suggested.

'Oh, it was nothing serious,' Miss Amory told him. 'It was

only over Richard's debts. Of course, all young men have debts! Although, indeed, Claud himself was never like that. He was always so studious, even when he was a lad. Later, of course, his experiments always used up a lot of money. I used to tell him he was keeping Richard too short of money, you know. But, yes, about two months ago they had quite a scene, and what with that, and Lucia's necklace missing, and her refusing to call in the police, it was a very upsetting time. And so absurd, too! Nerves, all nerves!'

'You are sure that my smoke is not deranging you, mademoiselle?' asked Poirot, holding up his cigarette.

'Oh, no, not at all,' Miss Amory assured him. 'I think gentlemen *ought* to smoke.'

Only now noticing that his cigarette had failed to light properly, Poirot retrieved his box of matches from the table in front of him. 'Surely, it is a very unusual thing for a young and beautiful woman to take the loss of her jewels so calmly?' he asked, as he lit his cigarette again, carefully replacing two dead matches in the box which he then returned to his pocket.

'Yes, it is odd. That's what I call it,' Miss Amory agreed. 'Distinctly odd! But there, she didn't seem to care a bit. Oh dear, here I am gossiping on about things which can't possibly interest you, Monsieur Poirot.'

'But you interest me enormously, mademoiselle,' Poirot assured her. 'Tell me, when Madame Amory came out from dinner last night, feeling faint, did she go upstairs?'

'Oh, no,' replied Caroline Amory. 'She came into this room. I settled her here on the sofa, and then I went back to the dining-room, leaving Richard with her. Young husbands and wives, you know, Monsieur Poirot! Not that young men are nearly so romantic as they used to be when I was a girl! Oh dear! I remember a young fellow called Aloysius Jones. We used to play croquet together. Foolish fellow – foolish fellow! But there, I'm wandering from the point again. We were talking about Richard and Lucia. A very handsome couple they make, don't you think so, Monsieur Poirot? He met her in Italy, you know – on the Italian lakes – last November. It was love at first sight. They were married within a week. She was an orphan, alone in the world. Very sad, although I sometimes wonder whether it wasn't a blessing in disguise. If she'd had a lot of foreign relations – that would be a bit trying, don't you think? After all, you know what foreigners are! They – oh!' She suddenly broke off, turning in her chair to look at Poirot in embarrassed dismay. 'Oh, I do beg your pardon!'

'Not at all, not at all,' murmured Poirot, with an amused glance at Hastings.

'So stupid of me,' Miss Amory apologized, highly flustered. 'I didn't mean – of course, it's so different in your case. "*Les braves Belges*", as we used to say during the war.'

'Please, do not concern yourself,' Poirot assured her. After a pause, he continued, as though her mention of the war had reminded him, 'I believe – that is – I understand that the box of drugs above the bookcase is a relic of the war. You were all examining it last night, were you not?'

'Yes, that's right. So we were.'

'Now, how did that come about?' enquired Poirot.

Miss Amory considered for a moment, before replying. 'Now, how did it happen? Ah, yes, I remember. I said I wished I had some sal volatile, and Barbara got the box down to look through it, and then the gentlemen came in, and Dr Carelli frightened me to death with the things he said.'

Hastings began to show great interest in the turn being taken by the discussion, and Poirot prompted Miss Amory to continue. 'You mean the things Dr Carelli said about the drugs? He looked through them and examined them thoroughly, I suppose?'

'Yes,' Miss Amory confirmed, 'and he held one glass tube up, something with a most innocent name – bromide, I think – which I have often taken for sea-sickness – and he said it would kill twelve strong men!'

'Hyoscine hydrobromide?' asked Poirot.

'I beg your pardon?'

'Was it hyoscine hydrobromide that Dr Carelli was referring to?'

'Yes, yes, that was it,' Miss Amory exclaimed. 'How clever of you! And then Lucia took it from him, and repeated something he had said – about a dreamless sleep. I detest this modern neurotic poetry. I always say that, ever since dear Lord Tennyson died, no one has written poetry of any –'

'Oh dear,' muttered Poirot.

'I beg your pardon?' asked Miss Amory.

'Ah, I was just thinking of the dear Lord Tennyson. But please go on. What happened next?'

'Next?'

'You were telling us about last night. Here, in this room –'

'Ah, yes. Well, Barbara wanted to put on an extremely vulgar song. On the gramophone, I mean. Fortunately, I stopped her.'

'I see,' murmured Poirot. 'And this little tube that the doctor held up – was it full?'

'Oh, yes,' Miss Amory replied without hesitation. 'Because, when the doctor made his quotation about dreamless sleep, he said that half the tablets in the tube would be sufficient.'

Miss Amory got up from her chair, and moved away from the table. 'You know, Monsieur Poirot,' she continued as Poirot rose to join her, 'I've said all along that I didn't like that man. That Dr Carelli. There's something about him – not sincere – and so oily in manner. Of course, I couldn't say anything in front of Lucia, since he is supposed to be a friend of hers, but I did not like him. You see, Lucia is so trusting! I'm certain that the man must have wormed his way into her confidence with a view to getting asked to the house and stealing the formula.'

Poirot regarded Miss Amory quizzically before he asked, 'You have no doubt, then, that it was Dr Carelli who stole Sir Claud's formula?'

Miss Amory looked at the detective in surprise. 'Dear Monsieur Poirot!' she exclaimed. 'Who else could have done so? He was the only stranger present. Naturally, my brother would not have liked to accuse a guest, so he made an opportunity for the document to be returned. I thought it was very delicately done. Very delicately indeed!'

'Quite so,' Poirot agreed tactfully, putting a friendly arm around Miss Amory's shoulder, to that lady's evident displeasure. 'Now, mademoiselle, I am going to try a little experiment in which I would like your co-operation.' He removed his arm from her. 'Where were you sitting last night when the lights went out?'

'There!' Miss Amory declared, indicating the settee.

'Then, would you be so good as to sit there once again?'

Miss Amory moved to the settee, and sat. 'Now, mademoiselle,' announced Poirot, 'I want you to make a strong effort of the imagination! Shut your eyes, if you please.'

Miss Amory did as she was asked. 'That is right,' Poirot continued. 'Now, imagine that you are back again where you were last night. It is dark. You can see nothing. But you can hear. Throw yourself back.'

Interpreting his words literally, Miss Amory flung herself backwards on the settee. 'No, no,' said Poirot. 'I mean, throw your mind back. What can you hear? That is right, cast your mind back. Now, tell me what you hear in the darkness.'

Impressed by the detective's evident earnestness, Miss Amory made an effort to do as he requested. Pausing for a moment, she then began to speak, slowly and in jerks. 'Gasps,' she said. 'A lot of little gasps – and then the noise of a chair falling – and a metallic kind of clink –'

'Was it like this?' asked Poirot, taking a key from his pocket and throwing it down on the floor. It made no sound, and Miss Amory, after waiting for a few seconds, declared that she could hear nothing. 'Well, like this, perhaps?' Poirot tried again, retrieving the key from the floor and hitting it sharply against the coffee table.

'Why, that's exactly the sound I heard last night!' Miss Amory exclaimed. 'How curious!'

'Continue, I pray you, mademoiselle,' Poirot encouraged her.

'Well, I heard Lucia scream and call out to Sir Claud. And then the knocking came on the door.'

'That was all? You are sure?'

'Yes, I think so – oh, wait a minute! Right at the beginning, there was a curious noise, like the tearing of silk. Somebody's dress, I suppose.'

'Whose dress, do you think?' asked Poirot.

'It must have been Lucia's. It wouldn't have been Barbara's, because she was sitting right next to me, here.'

'That is curious,' murmured Poirot thoughtfully.

'And that really is all,' Miss Amory concluded. 'May I open my eyes now?'

'Oh yes, certainly, mademoiselle.' As she did so, Poirot asked her, 'Who poured out Sir Claud's coffee? Was it you?'

'No,' Miss Amory told him. 'Lucia poured out the coffee.'

'When was that, exactly?'

'It must have been just after we were talking about those dreadful drugs.'

'Did Mrs Amory take the coffee to Sir Claud herself?'

Caroline Amory paused for thought. 'No –', she finally decided.

'No?' asked Poirot. 'Then, who did?'

'I don't know – I'm not sure – let me see, now. Oh yes, I remember! Sir Claud's coffee cup was on the table beside Lucia's own cup. I remember that, because Mr Raynor was carrying the cup to Sir Claud in the study, and Lucia called him back and said he had taken the wrong cup – which really was very silly, because they were both exactly the same – black, without sugar.'

'So,' Poirot observed, 'Monsieur Raynor took the coffee to Sir Claud?'

'Yes – or, at least – no, that's right, Richard took it from him, because Barbara wanted to dance with Mr Raynor.'

'Oh! So Monsieur Amory took the coffee to his father.'

'Yes, that's correct,' Miss Amory confirmed.

'Ah!' exclaimed Poirot. 'Tell me, what had Monsieur Amory been doing just before that? Dancing?'

'Oh, no,' Miss Amory replied. 'He had been packing away the drugs. Putting them all back in the box tidily, you know.'

'I see, I see. Sir Claud, then, drank his coffee in his study?'

'I suppose he began to do so,' Miss Amory remembered. 'But he came back in here with the cup in his hand. I remember his complaining about the taste, saying that it was bitter. And I assure you, Monsieur Poirot, it was the very best coffee. A special mixture that I had ordered myself from the Army and Navy Stores in London. You know, that wonderful department store in Victoria Street. It's so convenient, not far from the railway station. And I –'

She broke off as the door opened and Edward Raynor entered. 'Am I interrupting?' the secretary asked. 'I am so sorry. I wanted to speak to Monsieur Poirot, but I can come back later.'

'No, no,' declared Poirot. 'I have finished putting this poor lady upon the rack!'

Miss Amory rose. 'I'm afraid I haven't been able to tell you anything useful,' she apologized, as she went to the door.

Poirot rose, and walked ahead of her. 'You have told me a great deal, mademoiselle. More than you realize, perhaps,' he assured Miss Amory as he opened the door for her.

CHAPTER 13

After seeing Miss Amory out, Poirot turned his attention to Edward Raynor. 'Now, Monsieur Raynor,' he said as he gestured the secretary to a chair, 'let me hear what you have to tell me.'

Raynor sat, and regarded Poirot earnestly. 'Mr Amory has just told me the news about Sir Claud. The cause of his death, I mean. This is a most extraordinary business, monsieur.'

'It has come as a shock to you?' asked Poirot.

'Certainly. I never suspected such a thing.'

Approaching him, Poirot handed Raynor the key that he had found, watching the secretary keenly as he did so. 'Have you ever seen this key before, Monsieur Raynor?' he asked.

Raynor took the key, and turned it about in his hands with a puzzled air. 'It looks rather like the key to Sir Claud's safe,' he observed. 'But I understand from Mr Amory that Sir Claud's key was in its proper place on his chain.' He handed the key back to Poirot.

'Yes, this is a key to the safe in Sir Claud's study, but it is a duplicate key,' Poirot told him, adding slowly and with emphasis, 'a duplicate which was lying on the floor beside the chair you occupied last night.'

Raynor looked at the detective unflinchingly. 'If you think it was I who dropped it, you are mistaken,' he declared.

Poirot regarded him searchingly for a moment, and then nodded his head as if satisfied. 'I believe you,' he said. Moving briskly to the settee, he sat down and rubbed his hands together. 'Now, let us get to work, Monsieur Raynor. You were Sir Claud's confidential secretary, were you not?'

'That is correct.'

'Then you knew a lot about his work?'

'Yes. I have a certain amount of scientific training, and I occasionally helped him with his experiments.'

'Do you know anything,' asked Poirot, 'that can throw light upon this unfortunate affair?'

Raynor took a letter from his pocket. 'Only this,' he replied, as he rose, moved across to Poirot and handed him the letter. 'One of my tasks was to open and sort out all of Sir Claud's correspondence. This came two days ago.'

Poirot took the letter and read it aloud. '"You are nourishing a viper in your bosom." Bosom?' he queried, turning to Hastings before continuing, '"Beware of Selma Goetz and her brood. Your secret is known. Be on your guard." It is signed "Watcher". H'm, very picturesque and dramatic. Hastings, you will enjoy this,' Poirot remarked, passing the letter to his friend.

'What I would like to know,' declared Edward Raynor, 'is this. Who is Selma Goetz?'

Leaning back and putting his finger-tips together, Poirot announced, 'I think I can satisfy your curiosity, monsieur. Selma Goetz was the most successful international spy ever known. She was also a very beautiful woman. She worked for Italy, for France, for Germany, and eventually, I believe, for Russia. Yes, she was an extraordinary woman, Selma Goetz.'

Raynor stepped back a pace, and spoke sharply. 'Was?'

'She is dead,' Poirot declared. 'She died in Genoa, last November.' He retrieved the letter from Hastings, who had been shaking his head over it with a perplexed expression.

'Then this letter must be a hoax,' Raynor exclaimed.

'I wonder,' Poirot murmured. '"Selma Goetz and her brood," it says. Selma Goetz left a daughter, Monsieur Raynor, a very beautiful girl. Since her mother's death she has disappeared completely.' He put the letter in his pocket.

'Could it be possible that –?' Raynor began, then paused.

'Yes? You were going to say something, monsieur?' Poirot prompted him.

Moving to the detective, Raynor spoke eagerly. 'Mrs Amory's Italian maid. She brought her from Italy with her, a very pretty girl. Vittoria Muzio, her name is. Could she possibly be this daughter of Selma Goetz?'

'Ah, it is an idea, that.' Poirot sounded impressed.

'Let me send her to you,' Raynor suggested, turning to go.

Poirot rose. 'No, no, a little minute. Above all, we must not alarm her. Let me speak to Madame Amory first. She will be able to tell me something about this girl.'

'Perhaps you are right,' Raynor agreed. 'I'll tell Mrs Amory at once.'

The secretary left the room with the air of a determined man, and Hastings approached Poirot in great excitement. 'That's it, Poirot! Carelli and the Italian maid in collusion, working for a foreign government. Don't you agree?'

Deep in thought, Poirot paid his colleague no heed.

'Poirot? Don't you think so? I said, it must be Carelli and the maid working together.'

'Ah, yes, that is exactly what you would say, my friend.'

Hastings looked affronted. 'Well, what is your idea?' he asked Poirot in an injured tone.

'There are several questions to be answered, my dear Hastings. Why was Madame Amory's necklace stolen two months ago? Why did she refuse to call in the police on that occasion? Why –?'

He broke off as Lucia Amory entered the room, carrying her handbag. 'I understand you wanted to see me, Monsieur Poirot. Is that correct?' she asked.

'Yes, madame. I would like simply to ask you a few questions.' He indicated a chair by the table. 'Won't you sit down?'

Lucia moved to the chair and sat, as Poirot turned to Hastings. 'My friend, the garden outside that window is very fine,' Poirot observed, taking Hastings by the arm and propelling him gently towards the french windows. Hastings looked distinctly reluctant to leave, but Poirot's insistence, though gentle, was firm. 'Yes, my friend. Observe the beauties of nature. Do not ever lose a chance of observing the beauties of nature.'

Somewhat unwillingly, Hastings allowed himself to be bundled out of doors. Then, the day being warm and sunny, he decided to make the best of his present situation and explore the Amorys' garden. Ambling across the lawn, he made his way towards a hedge beyond which a formal garden looked extremely inviting.

As he walked along the length of the hedge, Hastings

became aware of voices quite close by, voices which, as he approached, he recognized as those of Barbara Amory and Dr Graham, who were, it seemed, enjoying a *tête à tête* on a bench, just the other side of the hedge. In the hope that he might overhear something relevant to Sir Claud Amory's death or the disappearance of the formula that it would be useful for Poirot to know, Hastings stopped to listen.

'– perfectly clear that he thinks his beautiful young cousin can do better for herself than a country doctor. That seems to be the basis of his lack of enthusiasm for our seeing each other,' Kenneth Graham was saying.

'Oh, I know Richard can be an old stick-in-the-mud at times, and carry on like someone twice his age,' Barbara's voice replied. 'But I don't think you ought to allow yourself to be affected by it, Kenny. I certainly don't take any notice of him.'

'Well, I shan't either,' said Dr Graham. 'But, look here, Barbara, I asked you to meet me out here because I wanted to talk to you privately, without being seen or heard by the family. First of all, I ought to tell you that there can be no doubt about it, your uncle was poisoned last night.'

'Oh, yes?' Barbara sounded bored.

'You don't seem at all surprised to hear that.'

'Oh I suppose I'm surprised. After all, members of one's family don't get poisoned every day, do they? But I have to admit that I'm not particularly upset that he's dead. In fact, I think I'm glad.'

'Barbara!'

'Now, don't you start pretending you're surprised to hear that, Kenny. You've listened to me going on about the mean old so-and-so on countless occasions. He didn't really care for any of us, he was only interested in his mouldy old experiments. He treated Richard very badly, and he wasn't particularly welcoming to Lucia when Richard brought her back from Italy as his bride. And Lucia is so sweet, and so absolutely right for Richard.'

'Barbara, darling, I have to ask you this. Now, I promise that anything you say to me will go no further. I'll protect you if necessary. But, tell me, do you know something – anything at all – about your uncle's death? Have you any reason to suspect that Richard, for example, might have felt so desperate about his financial situation that he would think of killing his father in order to get his hands now on what would eventually be his inheritance?'

'I don't want to continue this conversation, Kenny. I thought you asked me out here to whisper sweet nothings to me, not to accuse my cousin of murder.'

'Darling, I'm not accusing Richard of anything. But you must admit there's something wrong here. Richard doesn't seem to want a police investigation into his uncle's death. It's almost as though he were afraid of what it might reveal. There's no way he can stop the police from taking over, of course, but he's made it perfectly clear that he's furious with me for having instigated an official investigation. I was only doing my duty as a doctor, after all. How could I possibly have signed a death certificate stating that Sir Claud had died of a heart attack? For heaven's sake, there was absolutely nothing wrong with his heart when I last gave him a regular check-up only a few weeks ago.'

'Kenny, I don't want to hear any more. I'm going indoors. You'll make your own way out through the garden, won't you? I'll see you another time.'

'Barbara, I only want –' But she had already gone, and Dr Graham emitted a deep sigh that was almost a groan. At that moment, Hastings thought it expedient to retrace his steps quickly back to the house without being seen by either of them.

Back in the library, it was only after Hastings, propelled by Hercule Poirot, had made his unwilling exit into the garden that the little detective turned his attention again to Lucia Amory, first taking care to close the french windows.

Lucia looked at Poirot anxiously. 'You want to ask me about my maid, I understand, Monsieur Poirot. That is what Mr Raynor told me. But she is a very good girl. I am sure there is nothing wrong with her.'

'Madame,' Poirot replied, 'it is not about your maid that I wish to speak to you.'

Lucia sounded startled as she began, 'But Mr Raynor said –'

Poirot interrupted her. 'I am afraid I allowed Mr Raynor to think so for reasons of my own.'

'Well, what is it then?' Lucia's voice was guarded now.

'Madame,' Poirot observed, 'you paid me a very pretty compliment yesterday. You said, when you first saw me – you said – that you trusted me.'

'Well?'

'Well, madame, I ask you to trust me now!'

'What do you mean?'

Poirot observed her solemnly. 'You have youth, beauty, admiration, love – all the things a woman wants and craves. But there is one thing, madame, that you lack – a father confessor! Let Papa Poirot offer himself for the post.'

Lucia was about to speak, when Poirot interrupted her. 'Now, think well before you refuse, madame. It was at your request that I remained here. I stayed to serve you. I still wish to serve you.'

With a sudden flash of temperament, Lucia replied, 'You can serve me best now by going, monsieur.'

'Madame,' Poirot continued imperturbably, 'do you know that the police have been called in?'

'The police?'

'Yes.'

'But by whom? And why?'

'Dr Graham and the other doctors, his colleagues,' Poirot told her, 'have discovered that Sir Claud Amory was poisoned.'

'Ah, no! No! Not that!' Lucia sounded more horrified than surprised.

'Yes. So you see, madame, there is very little time for you to decide on the most prudent course of action. At present, I serve you. Later, I may have to serve justice.'

Lucia's eyes searched Poirot's face as though trying to decide whether to confide in him. At last, 'What do you want me to do?' she asked, falteringly.

Poirot sat and faced her. 'What will you?' he murmured to himself, and then, addressing Lucia, he suggested gently, 'Why not simply tell me the truth, madame?'

Lucia paused. Stretching out her hand towards him, she

began, 'I – I –' She paused again, irresolutely, and then her expression hardened. 'Really, Monsieur Poirot, I am at a loss to understand you.'

Poirot eyed her keenly. 'Ah! It is to be like that, is it? I am very sorry.'

Her composure somewhat regained, Lucia spoke coldly. 'If you will tell me what you want with me, I will answer any questions you wish to ask.'

'So!' the little detective exclaimed. 'You pit your wits against Hercule Poirot, do you? Very well, then. Be assured however, madame, that we shall get at the truth just the same.' He tapped the table. 'But by a less pleasant process.'

'I have nothing to conceal,' Lucia told him defiantly.

Taking from his pocket the letter Edward Raynor had given him, Poirot handed it to Lucia. 'A few days ago, Sir Claud received this anonymous letter,' he revealed.

Lucia glanced through the letter, apparently unmoved. 'Well, what of it?' she commented as she handed it back to Poirot.

'Have you ever heard the name Selma Goetz before?'

'Never! Who is she?' asked Lucia.

'She died – in Genoa – last November,' Poirot informed her.

'Indeed?'

'Perhaps you met her there,' Poirot remarked, replacing the letter in his pocket. 'In fact, I think you did.'

'I was never in Genoa in my life,' Lucia insisted, sharply.

'Then, if anyone were to say that they had seen you there?'

'They would – they would be mistaken.'

Poirot persisted. 'But I understand, madame, that you first met your husband in Genoa?'

'Did Richard say that? How stupid of him! We met first in Milan.'

'Then the woman you were with in Genoa –'

Lucia interrupted him angrily. 'I tell you I was never in Genoa!'

'Ah, pardon!' exclaimed Poirot. 'Of course, you said so just now. Yet it is odd!'

'What is odd?'

Poirot closed his eyes and leaned back in his chair. His voice came purringly from between his lips. 'I will tell you a little story, madame,' he announced, taking out a pocket book. 'I have a friend who does the photography for certain London journals. He takes – how do you say? – the snapshots of contessas and other fashionable ladies who bathe themselves on the Lido. That sort of thing.' Poirot searched in the pocket book before continuing, 'Last November, this friend of mine, he finds himself in Genoa, and he recognizes a very notorious lady. The Baronne de Giers, she calls herself at this time, and she is the *chère amie* of a very noted French diplomat. The world talks, but that does not matter to the lady, because the diplomat, he talks also, and that is what she wants. He is more amorous than discreet, you understand –' Poirot broke off with an innocent air. 'I do not bore you, I hope, madame?'

'Not at all, but I hardly see the point of this story.'

Looking through the contents of his pocket book, Poirot continued. 'I am arriving at the point, I assure you, madame. My friend, he shows me a snapshot he has taken. We agree with each other that the Baronne de Giers is *une très belle femme*, and we are not at all surprised at the behaviour of the diplomat.'

'Is that all?'

'No, madame. You see, the lady was not alone. She was photographed walking with her daughter, and that daughter, madame, had a very beautiful face, and one, moreover, that it would not be at all easy to forget.' Poirot rose, made his most gallant bow, and closed his pocket book. 'Of course, I recognized that face as soon as I arrived here.'

Lucia looked at Poirot, and drew her breath in, sharply. 'Oh!' she exclaimed. After a moment, she pulled herself together, and laughed. 'My dear Monsieur Poirot, what a curious mistake. Of course, I see the point of all your questions now. I remember the Baronne de Giers perfectly, and her daughter as well. The daughter was rather a dull girl, but the mother fascinated me. I was quite romantic about her, and went out walking with her on several occasions. I think my devotion amused her. That was doubtless how the mistake arose. That is how someone thought that I must be the woman's daughter.' Lucia sank back in her chair.

Poirot nodded slow appreciation, at which Lucia appeared visibly to relax. Then suddenly, leaning over the table towards her, the detective remarked, 'But I thought you had never been to Genoa.'

Taken unawares, Lucia gasped. She stared at Poirot as he put his pocket book back in an inner pocket of his jacket. 'You have no photograph,' she said. It was half question, half statement.

'No,' Poirot confessed. 'I have no photograph, madame. I knew the name that Selma Goetz passed under in Genoa. The rest – my friend and his photography – all of that was a harmless little invention of mine!'

Lucia leapt to her feet, her eyes blazing with anger. 'You set a trap for me!' she exclaimed furiously.

Poirot shrugged his shoulders. 'Yes, madame,' he affirmed. 'I fear I had no alternative.'

'What has all this to do with Sir Claud's death?' Lucia muttered as though to herself, looking wildly about the room.

Poirot affected a tone of indifference as, instead of answering, he posed another question. 'Madame,' he asked, brushing an imaginary speck of dust from his jacket as he spoke, 'is it true that you lost a valuable diamond necklace a little time ago?'

Lucia glared at him. 'Again I ask,' her words emerging as though through clenched teeth, 'what has that to do with Sir Claud's death?'

Poirot spoke slowly and deliberately. 'First a stolen necklace – then a stolen formula. Both would bring in a very large sum of money.'

'What do you mean?' Lucia gasped.

'I mean, madame, that I would like you to answer this question. How much did Dr Carelli want – this time?'

Lucia turned away from Poirot. 'I – I – I will not answer any more questions,' she whispered.

'Because you are afraid?' asked Poirot, moving to her.

Lucia turned to face him again, flinging her head back in a gesture of defiance. 'No,' she asserted, 'I'm not afraid. I simply don't know what you are talking about! Why should Dr Carelli ask me for money?'

'To buy his silence,' Poirot replied. 'The Amorys are a proud family, and you would not have wanted them to know that you are – the daughter of Selma Goetz!'

Lucia glared at Poirot for a moment without replying, and then, her shoulders sagging, she collapsed onto a stool, resting her head in her hands. At least a minute elapsed before she looked up with a sigh. 'Does Richard know?' she murmured.

'He does not know yet, madame,' Poirot replied slowly.

Lucia sounded desperate as she pleaded, 'Don't tell him, Monsieur Poirot! Please don't tell him! He is so proud of his family name, so proud of his honour! I was wicked to have married him! But I was so miserable. I hated that life, that awful life I was forced to live with my mother. I felt degraded by it. But what could I do? And then, when Mama died, I was at last free! Free to be honest! Free to get away from that life of lies and intrigue. I met Richard. That was the most wonderful thing that had ever happened to me. Richard came into my life. I loved him, and he wanted to marry me. How could I tell him who I was? Why should I tell him?'

'And then,' Poirot prompted her gently, 'Carelli recognized you somewhere with Monsieur Amory, and began to black-mail you?'

'Yes, but I had no money of my own,' Lucia gasped. 'I sold the necklace and paid him. I thought that was the end of it all. But yesterday he turned up here. He had heard of this formula that Sir Claud had invented.'

'He wanted you to steal it for him?'

Lucia sighed. 'Yes.'

'And did you?' asked Poirot, moving closer to her.

'You won't believe me – now,' murmured Lucia, shaking her head sorrowfully.

Poirot contemplated the beautiful young woman with a look of sympathy. 'Yes, yes, my child,' he assured her. 'I will still believe you. Have courage, and trust Papa Poirot, yes? Just tell me the truth. Did you take Sir Claud's secret formula?'

'No, no, I didn't, I didn't!' Lucia declared vehemently. 'But it's true that I meant to. Carelli made a key to Sir Claud's safe from an impression I took.'

Taking a key from his pocket and showing it to her, Poirot asked, 'Is this it?'

Lucia looked at the key. 'Yes, it was all quite easy. Carelli gave me that key. I was in the study, just steeling myself to open the safe when Sir Claud came in and found me. That's the truth, I swear it!'

'I believe you, madame,' said Poirot. He returned the key to his pocket, moved to the arm-chair and sat, placing the tips of his fingers together, and pondering for a moment. 'And yet you acquiesced eagerly in Sir Claud's scheme of plunging the room into darkness?'

'I didn't want to be searched,' Lucia explained. 'Carelli had passed me a note at the same time as the key, and they were both in my dress.'

'What did you do with them?' Poirot asked her.

'When the lights went out, I threw the key as far from me as I could. Over there.' She pointed in the direction of the chair in which Edward Raynor had sat on the previous evening.

'And the note that Carelli had passed to you?' Poirot continued.

'I didn't know what to do with the note.' Lucia rose and went to the table. 'So I slipped it between the leaves of a book.' Taking a book from the table, she searched in it. 'Yes, it is still here,' she declared as she removed a piece of paper from the book. 'Do you wish to see it?'

'No, madame, it is yours,' Poirot assured her.

Sitting in a chair by the table, Lucia tore the note into small pieces which she put in her handbag. Poirot watched her, but paused before asking, 'One little thing more, madame. Did you, by any chance, tear your dress last night?'

'I? No!' Lucia sounded surprised.

'During those moments of darkness,' asked Poirot, 'did you hear the sound of a dress tearing?'

Lucia considered for a few seconds. Then, 'Yes, now that you mention it,' she said, 'I believe I did. But it was not mine. It must have been Miss Amory's or Barbara's.'

'Well, we will not worry about that,' remarked Poirot dismissively. 'Now, let us pass on to something else. Who poured out Sir Claud's coffee last night?'

'I did.'

'And you put it down on that table, beside your own cup?'

'Yes.'

Poirot rose, leaned forward over the table towards Lucia, and suddenly shot his next question at her. 'Into which cup did you put the hyoscine?'

Lucia looked at him wildly. 'How did you know?' she gasped.

'It is my business to know things. Into which cup, madame?'

Lucia sighed. 'My own.'

'Why?'

'Because I wanted – I wanted to die. Richard suspected that there was something between Carelli and me – that we were having an affair. He could not have been further from the truth. I hated Carelli! I hate him now. But, as I had failed to obtain the formula for him, I was sure he would expose me to Richard. To kill myself was a way out – the only way. A swift, dreamless sleep – and no awakening – that's what he said.'

'Who said that to you?'

'Dr Carelli.'

'I begin to see – I begin to see,' said Poirot slowly. He pointed to the cup on the table. 'This is your cup, then? A full cup, untasted?'

'Yes.'

'What made you change your mind about drinking it?'

'Richard came over to me. He said that he would take me away – abroad – that he would get the money to do so, somehow. He gave me back – hope.'

'Now, listen to me carefully, madame,' said Poirot gravely. 'This morning, Dr Graham took away the cup that was beside Sir Claud's chair.'

'Yes?'

'His fellow-doctors will have found nothing but the dregs of coffee in it –' He paused.

Without looking at him, Lucia answered, 'Of – of course.'

'That is correct, yes?' Poirot persisted.

Lucia looked straight ahead of her without replying. Then, looking up at Poirot, she exclaimed, 'Why are you staring at me like that? You frighten me!'

'I said,' Poirot repeated, 'that they took away the cup that was beside Sir Claud's chair this morning. Let us suppose instead that they had taken away the cup that was by his chair last night?' He moved to the table near the door and took a coffee cup from the plant bowl. 'Let us suppose that they had taken this cup!'

Lucia rose quickly, putting her hands up to her face. 'You know!' she gasped.

Poirot moved to her. 'Madame!' His voice now was stern. 'They will test their cup, if they have not already done so, and they will find – nothing. But last night I took some of the dregs from the original cup. What would you say if I were to tell you that there was hyoscine in Sir Claud's cup?'

Lucia looked stricken. She swayed, but then recovered herself. For a moment she said nothing. Then, 'You are right,' she whispered. 'You are quite right. I killed him.' Her voice rang out suddenly. 'I killed him! I put the hyoscine in *his* cup.' Going to the table, she grasped the full cup of coffee. 'This one – is only coffee!'

She raised the full cup to her lips, but Poirot sprang forward, interposing his hand between the cup and her lips. They looked at each other intently for a time, then Lucia burst into sobs. Poirot took the cup from her, and placed it on the table. 'Madame!' he exclaimed.

'Why did you stop me?' Lucia murmured.

'Madame,' Poirot told her, 'the world is very beautiful. Why should you wish to leave it?'

'I – Oh!' Lucia collapsed onto the settee, sobbing bitterly.

When Poirot spoke, his voice was warm and gentle. 'You told me the truth. You put the hyoscine in your own cup. I believe you. But there was hyoscine in the other cup as well. Now, speak the truth to me again. Who put the hyoscine in Sir Claud's cup?'

Lucia stared at Poirot in terror. 'No, no, you're wrong. He didn't. I killed him,' she cried hysterically.

'Who didn't? Whom are you shielding, madame? Tell me,' Poirot demanded.

'He didn't, I tell you,' Lucia sobbed.

There was a knock at the door. 'That will be the police!' declared Poirot. 'We have very little time. I will make you two promises, madame. Promise number one is that I will save you –'

'But I killed him, I tell you.' Lucia's voice was almost at screaming pitch.

'Promise number two,' Poirot continued imperturbably, 'is that I will save your husband!'

'Oh!' Lucia gasped, gazing at him in bewilderment.

The butler, Tredwell, entered the room. Addressing Poirot, he announced, 'Inspector Japp, from Scotland Yard.'

CHAPTER 15

Fifteen minutes later, Inspector Japp, accompanied by Johnson, a young constable, had finished his initial inspection of the library. Japp, a bluff, hearty, middle-aged man with a thick-set figure and a ruddy complexion, was reminiscing with Poirot and Hastings, who had returned from his exile in the garden.

'Yes,' Japp told his constable, 'Mr Poirot and I go back a long way. You've heard me speak often of him. He was still a member of the Belgian police force when we first worked together. It was the Abercrombie forgery case, wasn't it, Poirot? We ran him down in Brussels. Ah, those were great days. And do you remember "Baron" Altara? There was a pretty rogue for you! He eluded the clutches of half the police in Europe. But we nailed him in Antwerp – thanks to Mr Poirot here.'

Japp turned from Johnson to Poirot. 'And then we met again in this country, didn't we, Poirot?' he exclaimed. 'You'd retired by then, of course. You solved that mysterious affair at Styles, remember? The last time we collaborated on a case was about two years ago, wasn't it? That affair of the Italian nobleman in

London. Well it's really good to see you again, Poirot. You could have knocked me down with a feather when I came in a few minutes ago and saw your funny old mug.'

'My mug?' asked Poirot, looking puzzled. English slang never failed to mystify him.

'Your face, I mean, old chap,' Japp explained, with a grin. 'Well, shall we work together on this?'

Poirot smiled. 'My good Japp, you know my little weaknesses!'

'Secretive old beggar, aren't you?' remarked Japp, smacking Poirot on the shoulder. 'I say, that Mrs Amory you were talking to when I came in, she's a good looker. Richard Amory's wife, I suppose? I'll bet you were enjoying yourself, you old dog!'

The inspector gave a rather coarse laugh, and seated himself on a chair by the table. 'Anyway,' he continued, 'this is just the sort of case that suits you down to the ground. It pleases your tortuous mind. Now, I loathe a poisoning case. Nothing to go on. You have to find out what they ate and drank, and who handled it, and who so much as breathed on it! I admit Dr Graham seems pretty clear on the case. He says the dope must have been in the coffee. According to him, such a large dose would have had an almost instantaneous effect. Of course, we shall know for certain when we get the analyst's report, but we've got enough to go on.'

Japp rose to his feet. 'Well, I've finished with this room,' he declared. 'I'd better have a few words with Mr Richard Amory, I suppose, and then I'll see this Dr Carelli. It looks as though he's our man. But keep an open mind, that's what I always say, keep an open mind.' He moved to the door. 'Coming, Poirot?'

'But certainly, I will accompany you,' said Poirot, joining him.

'Captain Hastings too, I've no doubt,' Japp laughed. 'Sticks as close to you as your shadow, doesn't he, Poirot?'

Poirot threw a meaningful glance at his friend. 'Perhaps Hastings would prefer to remain here,' he remarked.

Taking his cue in a somewhat obvious manner, Hastings replied, 'Yes, yes, I think I'll stay here.'

'Well, as you please.' Japp sounded surprised. He and Poirot left, followed by the young constable, and a moment later Barbara Amory entered from the garden through the french windows, wearing a pink blouse and light-coloured slacks. 'Ah! There you are, my pet. I say, what's this that's just blown in upon us?' she asked Hastings, as she moved across to the settee and sat down. 'Is it the police?'

'Yes,' Hastings told her. He joined her on the settee. 'It's Inspector Japp of Scotland Yard. He's gone to see your cousin now, to ask him a few questions.'

'Will he want to ask me questions, do you think?'

'I don't imagine so. But even if he does,' Hastings assured her, 'there's nothing to be alarmed about.'

'Oh, I'm not alarmed,' Barbara declared. 'In fact, I think it would be absolutely wizard! But it would be so tempting to embroider a bit, just to make a sensation. I adore sensation, don't you?'

Hastings looked puzzled. 'I – I really don't know. No, I don't think I adore sensation.'

Barbara Amory regarded him quizzically. 'You know, you intrigue me,' she declared. 'Where have you been all your life?'

'Well, I've spent several years in South America.'

'I knew it!' Barbara exclaimed. She gestured, with her hand over her eyes. 'The wide open spaces. That's why you're so deliciously old-fashioned.'

Hastings now looked offended. 'I'm sorry,' he said stiffly.

'Oh, but I adore it,' Barbara hastened to explain. 'I think you're a pet, an absolute pet.'

'What exactly do you mean by old-fashioned?'

'Well,' Barbara continued, 'I'm sure you believe in all sorts of stuffy old things, like decency, and not telling lies except for a very good reason, and putting a good face on things.'

'Quite,' agreed Hastings in some surprise. 'Don't you?'

'Me? Well, for example, do you expect me to keep up the fiction that Uncle Claud's death is a regrettable incident?'

'Isn't it?' Hastings sounded shocked.

'My dear!' exclaimed Barbara. She rose, and perched herself on the edge of the coffee table. 'As far as I'm concerned, it's the most marvellous thing that ever happened. You don't know what an old skinflint he was. You don't know how he ground us all down!' She stopped, overcome by the strength of her feelings.

Embarrassed, Hastings began, 'I – I – wish you wouldn't –' but was interrupted by Barbara. 'You don't like honesty?' she asked. 'That's just what I thought you'd be like. You'd prefer me to be wearing black instead of this, and to be talking in a hushed voice about "Poor Uncle Claud! So good to us all."'

'Really!' Hastings exclaimed.

'Oh, you needn't pretend,' Barbara went on, 'I knew that's what you'd turn out to be like, if I got to know you properly. But what I say is that life isn't long enough for all that lying and pretence. Uncle Claud wasn't good to us at all. I'm certain we're all glad he's dead, really, in our heart of hearts. Yes, even Aunt Caroline. Poor dear, she's stood him longer than any of us.'

Barbara suddenly calmed down. When she spoke again, it was in a milder tone. 'You know, I've been thinking. Scientifically speaking, Aunt Caroline might have poisoned Uncle Claud. That heart attack last night was really very queer. I don't believe it was a heart attack at all. Just suppose that suppressing her feelings all these years had led to Aunt Caroline developing some powerful complex –'

'I suppose it's theoretically possible,' Hastings murmured guardedly.

'I wonder who pinched the formula, though,' Barbara continued. 'Everyone says it was the Italian, but personally I suspect Tredwell.'

'Your butler? Good heavens! Why?'

'Because he never went near the study!'

Hastings looked perplexed. 'But then –'

'I'm very orthodox in some ways,' Barbara remarked. 'I've been brought up to suspect the least likely person. That's who it is in all the best murder mysteries. And Tredwell is certainly the least likely person.'

'Except you, perhaps,' Hastings suggested with a laugh.

'Oh, me!' Barbara smiled uncertainly as she rose and moved away from him. 'How curious –' she murmured to herself.

'What's curious?' Hastings asked, rising to his feet.

'Something I've just thought of. Let's go out in the garden. I hate it in here.' She moved towards the french windows.

'I'm afraid I have to stay here,' Hastings told her.

'Why?'

'I mustn't leave this room.'

'You know,' Barbara observed, 'you've got a complex about this room. Do you remember last night? There we all were, completely shattered by the disappearance of the formula, and in you strode, and produced the most marvellous anti-climax by saying in your best conversational manner, "What a delightful room, Mr Amory." It was so funny when the two of you walked in. There was this extraordinary little man with you, no more than five feet four, but with an air of immense dignity. And you, being oh, so polite.'

'Poirot is rather odd at first sight, I admit,' Hastings agreed. 'And he has all kinds of little foibles. For instance, he has an absolute passion for neatness of any kind. If he sees an ornament set crookedly, or a speck of dust, or even a slight disarray in someone's attire, it's absolute torture to him.'

'You make such a wonderful contrast to each other,' Barbara said, laughing.

'Poirot's methods of detection are very much his own, you know,' Hastings continued. 'Order and method are his gods. He has a great disdain for tangible evidence, things like footprints and cigarette ash, you know what I mean. In fact he maintains that, taken by themselves, they would never enable a detective to solve a problem. The true work, he says, is done from within. And then he taps that egg-shaped head of his, and remarks with great satisfaction, "The little grey cells of the brain – always remember the little grey cells, *mon ami.*"'

'Oh, I think he's a poppet,' Barbara declared. 'But not as sweet as you, with your "What a delightful room"!'

'But it *is* a delightful room,' Hastings insisted, sounding rather nettled.

'Personally, I don't agree with you,' said Barbara. She took his hand and tried to pull him towards the open french windows. 'Anyway, you've had quite enough of it for now. Come along.'

'You don't understand,' Hastings declared, taking his hand away from her. 'I promised Poirot.'

Barbara spoke slowly. 'You promised Monsieur Poirot that you would not leave this room? But why?'

'I can't tell you that.'

'Oh!' Barbara was silent for a moment or two, and then her manner changed. She moved behind Hastings and began to recite, in an exaggerated dramatic voice, '"The boy stood on the burning deck –"'

'I beg your pardon?'

'"Whence all but he had fled." Well, my pet?'

'I simply cannot understand you,' Hastings declared in exasperation.

'Why should you understand me? Oh, you really are a delight,' declared Barbara, slipping her arm through his. 'Come and be vamped. Really, you know, I think you're adorable.'

'You're pulling my leg.'

'Not at all,' Barbara insisted. 'I'm crazy about you. You're positively pre-war.'

She pulled him to the french windows, and this time Hastings allowed himself to yield to the pressure of her arm. 'You really are an extraordinary person,' he told her. 'You're quite different from any girl I've ever met.'

'I'm delighted to hear it. That's a very good sign,' said Barbara, as they now stood, face to face, framed in the open windows.

'A good sign?'

'Yes, it makes a girl feel hopeful.'

Hastings blushed, and Barbara laughed light-heartedly as she dragged him out into the garden.

After Barbara's exit with Hastings into the garden, the library remained unoccupied for no longer than a moment or two. Then the door to the hall opened, and Miss Amory entered, carrying a small work-bag. She went over to the settee, put the bag down, knelt, and began to feel at the back of the seat. As she did so, Dr Carelli entered by the other door, carrying a hat and a small suitcase. Seeing Miss Amory, Carelli stopped and murmured a word of apology at having intruded upon her.

Miss Amory rose from the settee, looking a trifle flustered. 'I was searching for a knitting needle,' she explained unnecessarily, brandishing her discovery as she spoke. 'It had slipped down behind the seat.' Then, taking in the significance of his suitcase, she asked, 'Are you leaving us, Dr Carelli?'

Carelli put his hat and suitcase on a chair. 'I feel I can no longer trespass on your hospitality,' he announced.

Obviously delighted, Miss Amory was polite enough to murmur, 'Well, of course, if you feel like that –' Then, remembering the situation in which the occupants of the house currently found themselves, she added, 'But I thought there were some tiresome formalities –' Her voice trailed off indecisively.

'Oh, that is all arranged,' Carelli assured her.

'Well, if you feel you must go –'

'I do, indeed.'

'Then I will order the car,' Miss Amory declared briskly, moving to the bell above the fireplace.

'No, no,' Carelli insisted. 'That, too, is all arranged.'

'But you've even had to carry your suitcase down yourself. Really, the servants! They're all demoralized, completely demoralized!' She returned to the settee, and took her knitting from her bag. 'They can't concentrate, Dr Carelli. They cannot keep their heads. So curious, is it not?'

Looking distinctly on edge, Carelli replied off-handedly, 'Very curious.' He glanced at the telephone.

Miss Amory began to knit, keeping up a flow of aimless conversation as she did so. 'I suppose you are catching the twelve-fifteen. You mustn't run it too fine. Not that I want to fuss, of course. I always say that fussing over –'

'Yes, indeed,' Dr Carelli interrupted peremptorily, 'but there is plenty of time, I think. I – I wondered if I might use the telephone?'

Miss Amory looked up momentarily. 'Oh, yes, of course,' she said, as she continued to knit. It seemed not to have occurred to her that Dr Carelli might have wanted to make his telephone call in private.

'Thank you,' murmured Carelli, moving to the desk and making a pretence of looking up a number in the telephone directory. He glanced across impatiently at Miss Amory. 'I think your niece was looking for you,' he remarked.

Miss Amory's only reaction to this information was to talk about her niece while continuing with her knitting undisturbed. 'Dear Barbara!' she exclaimed. 'Such a sweet creature. You know, she leads rather a sad life here, far too dull for a young girl. Well, well, things will be different now, I dare say.' She dwelt pleasurably on this thought for a moment, before continuing, 'Not that I haven't done all I could. But what a girl needs is a little gaiety. All the Beeswax in the world won't make up for that.'

Dr Carelli's face was a study in incomprehension, mixed with more than a little irritation. 'Beeswax?' he felt obliged to ask.

'Yes, Beeswax – or is it Bemax? Vitamins, you know, or at least that's what it says on the tin. A and B and C and D. All of them, except the one that keeps you from having beri-beri. And I really think there's no need for that, if one is living in England. It's not a disease one encounters here. It comes, I believe, from polishing the rice in native countries. So interesting. I made Mr Raynor take it – Beeswax, I mean – after breakfast every day. He was looking pale, poor young fellow. I tried to make Lucia take it too, but she wouldn't.' Miss Amory shook her head disapprovingly. 'And to think, when I was a girl, I was strictly forbidden to eat caramels because of the Beeswax – I mean Bemax. Times change, you know. Times do change.'

Though he attempted to disguise the fact, by now Dr Carelli was positively fuming. 'Yes, yes, Miss Amory,' he replied as politely as he could manage. Moving towards her, he tried a somewhat more direct approach. 'I think your niece is calling you.'

'Calling me?'

'Yes. Do you not hear?'

Miss Amory listened. 'No – no,' she confessed. 'How curious.' She rolled up her knitting. 'You must have keen ears, Dr Carelli. Not that my hearing is bad. Indeed, I've been told that –'

She dropped her ball of wool, and Carelli picked it up for her. 'Thank you so much,' she said. 'All the Amorys have keen hearing, you know.' She rose from the settee. 'My father kept his faculties in the most remarkable way. He could read without glasses when he was eighty.' She dropped the ball of wool again, and again Carelli stooped to retrieve it for her.

'Oh, thank you so much,' Miss Amory continued. 'A remarkable man, Dr Carelli. My father, I mean. Such a remarkable man. He always slept in a four-poster feather bed; and the windows of his bedroom were never opened. The night air, he used to say, was most injurious. Unfortunately, when he had an attack of gout he was nursed by a young woman who insisted on the window being opened at the top, and my poor father died of it.'

She dropped the ball of wool yet again. This time, after picking it up, Carelli planted it firmly in her hand and led her to the door. Miss Amory moved slowly, talking all the time. 'I do not care at all for hospital nurses, Dr Carelli,' she informed him. 'They gossip about their cases, they drink far too much tea, and they always upset the servants.'

'Very true, dear lady, very true,' Carelli agreed hastily, opening the door for her.

'Thank you so much,' Miss Amory said as he propelled her out of the room. Shutting the door after her, Carelli moved quickly to the desk and lifted the telephone receiver. After a pause, he spoke into it softly but urgently. 'This is Market Cleve three-one-four. I want London . . . Soho double eight-five-three . . . no, five-three, that's right . . . Eh? . . . Will you call me? . . . Right.'

He replaced the receiver, and then stood, biting his nails impatiently. After a moment, he crossed to the door of the study, opened it, and entered the room. Hardly had he done so, when Edward Raynor came into the library from the hall. Glancing around, Raynor strolled casually to the fireplace. He touched the vase of spills on the mantelpiece and, as he did so, Carelli came back into the room from the study. As Carelli closed the study door, Raynor turned and saw him.

'I didn't know you were in here,' said the secretary.

'I'm waiting for a phone call,' Carelli explained.

'Oh!'

After a pause, Carelli spoke again. 'When did the police inspector come?'

'About twenty minutes ago, I believe. Have you seen him?'

'Only in the distance,' replied Carelli.

'He's a Scotland Yard man,' Raynor informed him. 'Apparently, he happened to be down in the neighbourhood clearing up some other case, so he was called in by the local police.'

'That was a piece of luck, eh?' observed Carelli.

'Wasn't it?' The telephone rang, and Raynor moved towards it. Walking quickly ahead of him to the phone, Carelli said, 'I think that will be my call.' He looked at Raynor. 'I wonder if you'd mind –'

'Certainly, my dear fellow,' the secretary assured him. 'I'll clear out.'

Raynor left the room, and Carelli lifted the receiver. He spoke quietly. 'Hello? . . . Is that Miguel? . . . Yes? . . . No, damn it, I haven't. It's been impossible . . . No, you don't understand, the old gentleman died last night . . . I'm leaving at once . . . Japp's here . . . Japp. You know, the Scotland

Yard man . . . No, I've not met him yet . . . I hope so, too
. . . At the usual place, nine-thirty tonight . . . Right.'

Replacing the receiver, Carelli moved to the recess, picked
up his suitcase, put on his hat, and went towards the french
windows. At that moment, Hercule Poirot entered from the
garden, and he and Carelli collided. 'I beg your pardon,' said
the Italian.

'Not at all,' replied Poirot politely, continuing to block the
way out.

'If you would allow me to pass –'

'Impossible,' said Poirot, mildly. 'Quite impossible.'

'I insist.'

'I shouldn't,' murmured Poirot, with a friendly smile.

Suddenly, Carelli charged at Poirot. The little detective
stepped briskly aside, tripping Carelli up neatly with an
unexpected movement, and taking the Italian doctor's suitcase from him at the same time. At that moment, Japp
slid into the room behind Poirot, and Carelli fell into the
Inspector's arms.

'Hello, what's all this?' exclaimed Inspector Japp. 'Why,
bless me if it isn't Tonio!'

'Ah!' Poirot gave a little laugh as he moved away from them
both. 'I thought, my dear Japp, that you would probably be
able to give a name to this gentleman.'

'Oh, I know all about *him*,' Japp affirmed. 'Tonio's quite a
public character. Aren't you, Tonio? I'll bet you were surprised
at Monsieur Poirot's move just then. What do you call that
stuff, Poirot? *Ju-jitsu* or suchlike, isn't it? Poor old Tonio!'

As Poirot placed the Italian's suitcase on the table and
opened it, Carelli growled at Japp, 'You've got nothing against
me. You can't hold me.'

'I wonder,' said the Inspector. 'I'll bet we won't have far to look for the man who stole that formula, and did in the old gentleman.' Turning to Poirot, he added, 'That formula is absolutely bang in Tonio's line, and, since we've found him trying to make a getaway, I shouldn't be surprised if he's got the goods on him this minute.'

'I agree with you,' declared Poirot.

Japp ran his hands over Carelli, while Poirot went through the suitcase.

'Well?' Japp asked Poirot.

'Nothing,' the detective replied, closing the suitcase. 'Nothing. I am disappointed.'

'You think yourselves very clever, do you not?' snarled Carelli. 'But I could tell you –'

Poirot interrupted him, speaking quietly and significantly. 'You could, perhaps, but it would be very unwise.'

Startled, Carelli exclaimed, 'What do you mean?'

'Monsieur Poirot's quite right,' Japp declared. 'You'd better keep your mouth shut.' Moving to the hall door, he opened it and called, 'Johnson!' The young constable put his head around the door. 'Get the whole family together for me, will you?' Japp asked him. 'I want them all here.'

'Yes, sir,' said Johnson as he left the room.

'I protest! I –' Carelli gasped. Suddenly, he grabbed his suitcase and made a dash towards the french windows. Japp rushed after him, grabbed him, and threw him on to the settee, taking the suitcase from him as he did so. 'No one's hurt you yet, so don't squeal,' Japp barked at the now thoroughly cowed Italian.

Poirot strolled towards the french windows. 'Please don't go away now, Monsieur Poirot,' Japp called after him, putting

Carelli's suitcase down by the coffee table. 'This should be very interesting.'

'No, no, my dear Japp, I am not leaving,' Poirot assured him. 'I shall be right here. This family gathering, as you say, will be most interesting indeed.'

A few minutes later, when the Amory family began to assemble in the library, Carelli was still seated on the settee, looking rather sullen, while Poirot continued to hover by the french windows. Barbara Amory, with Hastings in tow, returned from the garden through the french windows, and Barbara moved to share the settee with Carelli while Hastings went to stand by Poirot's side. Poirot whispered to his colleague, 'It would be helpful, Hastings, if you would make a note – a mental note, you understand – of where they all choose to sit.'

'Helpful? How?' asked Hastings.

'Psychologically, my friend,' was Poirot's only reply.

When Lucia entered the room, Hastings watched her as she sat in the chair to the right of the table. Richard arrived with his aunt, Miss Amory, who sat on the stool as Richard moved behind the table to keep a protective eye on his wife. Edward Raynor was the last to arrive, taking up a position behind the arm-chair. He was followed into the room by the constable, Johnson, who shut the door and stood close to it.

Richard Amory introduced Inspector Japp to those two members of the family whom Japp had not already met.

'My aunt, Miss Amory,' he announced, 'and my cousin, Miss Barbara Amory.'

Acknowledging the introduction, Barbara asked, 'What's all the excitement, Inspector?'

Japp avoided her question. 'Now, I think we're all here, are we not?' he remarked, moving to the fireplace.

Miss Amory looked bewildered and a little apprehensive. 'I don't quite understand,' she said to Richard. 'What is this – this gentleman doing here?'

'I think perhaps I ought to tell you something,' Richard answered her. 'You see, Aunt Caroline – and all of you,' he added, glancing around the room, 'Dr Graham has discovered that my father was – poisoned.'

'What?' exclaimed Raynor sharply. Miss Amory gave a cry of horror.

'He was poisoned with hyoscine,' Richard continued.

Raynor gave a start. 'With hyoscine? Why, I saw –' He stopped dead, looking at Lucia.

Taking a step towards him, Inspector Japp asked, 'What did you see, Mr Raynor?'

The secretary looked embarrassed. 'Nothing – at least –' he began uncertainly. His voice trailed off into silence.

'I'm sorry, Mr Raynor,' Japp insisted, 'but I've got to have the truth. Come now, everyone realizes you're keeping something back.'

'It's nothing, really,' said the secretary. 'I mean, there's obviously some quite reasonable explanation.'

'Explanation for what, Mr Raynor?' asked Japp.

Raynor still hesitated.

'Well?' Japp prompted him.

'It was only that –' Raynor paused again, and then made

up his mind to continue. 'It was only that I saw Mrs Amory emptying out some of those little tablets into her hand.'

'When was this?' Japp asked him.

'Last night. I was coming out of Sir Claud's study. The others were busy with the gramophone. They were all clustered around it. I noticed her pick up a tube of tablets – I thought it was the hyoscine – and pour most of them out into the palm of her hand. Then Sir Claud called me back into the study for something.'

'Why didn't you mention this before?' asked Japp.

Lucia began to speak, but the Inspector silenced her. 'One minute, please, Mrs Amory,' he insisted. 'I'd like to hear from Mr Raynor first.'

'I never thought of it again,' Raynor told him. 'It was only when Mr Amory said just now that Sir Claud had been poisoned with hyoscine that it came back to me. Of course, I realize it's perfectly all right. It was just the coincidence that startled me. The tablets might not have been hyoscine at all. It could have been one of the other tubes that she was handling.'

Japp now turned to Lucia. 'Well, ma'am,' he asked, 'what have you got to say about it?'

Lucia seemed quite composed as she answered, 'I wanted something to make me sleep.'

Addressing Raynor again, Japp asked, 'You say she pretty well emptied the tube?'

'It seemed so to me,' said Raynor.

Japp turned again to Lucia. 'You wouldn't have needed so many tablets to make you sleep. One or two would have been sufficient. What did you do with the rest?'

Lucia thought for a moment, before replying, 'I can't

remember.' She was about to continue, when Carelli rose to his feet and burst out venomously, 'You see, Inspector? There's your murderess.'

Barbara rose quickly from the settee and moved away from Carelli, while Hastings hurried to her side. The Italian continued, 'You shall have the truth, Inspector. I came down here especially to see that woman. She had sent for me. She said she would get Sir Claud's formula, and she offered to sell it to me. I'll admit that I've dealt with such things in the past.'

'That's not much of an admission,' Japp advised him, moving between Carelli and Lucia. 'We know as much already.' He turned to Lucia. 'What have you to say to all this, ma'am?'

Lucia rose, her face drained of colour, and Richard went to her. 'I'm not going to allow –' he began, when Japp stopped him.

'If you please, sir.'

Carelli spoke again. 'Just look at that woman! None of you know who she is. But I do! She's the daughter of Selma Goetz. The daughter of one of the most infamous women the world has ever known.'

'It's not true, Richard,' Lucia cried. 'It's not true! Don't listen to him –'

'I'll break every bone in your body!' Richard Amory growled at Carelli.

Japp took a pace towards Richard. 'Keep calm, sir, do keep calm, please,' he admonished. 'We've got to get to the bottom of this.' Japp turned to Lucia. 'Now then, Mrs Amory.'

There was a pause. Then Lucia tried to speak. 'I – I –' she began. She looked at her husband and then at Poirot, holding out her hand helplessly to the detective.

'Have courage, madame,' Poirot advised her. 'Trust in me. Tell them. Tell them the truth. We have come to the point where lies will serve no longer. The truth will have to come out.'

Lucia looked pleadingly at Poirot, but he merely repeated, 'Have courage, madame. *Si, si*. Be brave and speak.' He returned to his position by the french windows.

After a long pause, Lucia began to speak, her voice low and stifled. 'It is true that I am Selma Goetz's daughter. It is *not* true that I asked that man to come here, or that I offered to sell him Sir Claud's formula. He came here to blackmail me!'

'Blackmail!' gasped Richard, moving to her.

Lucia turned to Richard. There was an urgency in her tone as she spoke. 'He threatened to tell you about my mother unless I got the formula for him, but I didn't do it. I think he must have stolen it. He had the chance. He was alone in there – in the study. And I see now that he wanted me to take the hyoscine and kill myself, so that everyone would think that it was I who had stolen the formula. He almost hypnotized me into –' She broke down and sobbed on Richard's shoulder.

With a cry of 'Lucia, my darling!' Richard embraced her. Then, passing his wife over to Miss Amory, who had risen and who now embraced the distressed young woman consolingly, Richard addressed Japp. 'Inspector, I want to speak to you alone.'

Japp looked at Richard Amory for a moment, and then gave a brief nod to Johnson. 'Very well,' he agreed, as the constable opened the door for Miss Amory and Lucia. Barbara and Hastings took the opportunity of returning to the garden through the french windows, while Edward Raynor, as he left, murmured to Richard, 'I'm sorry, Mr Amory, very sorry.'

As Carelli picked up his suitcase and followed Raynor out, Japp instructed his constable, 'Keep your eye on Mrs Amory – and also on Dr Carelli.' Carelli turned at the door, and Japp continued, to the constable, 'There's to be no funny business from anyone, you understand?'

'I understand, sir,' replied Johnson as he followed Carelli out of the room.

'I'm sorry, Mr Amory,' said Japp to Richard Amory, 'but after what Mr Raynor has told us, I'm bound to take every precaution. And I want Mr Poirot to remain here, as a witness to whatever you tell me.'

Richard approached Japp with the air of a man who has come to a momentous decision. Taking a deep breath, he spoke with determination. 'Inspector!'

'Well, sir, what is it?' asked Japp.

Very deliberately and slowly, Richard replied, 'I think it's time I confessed. I killed my father.'

Japp smiled. 'I'm afraid that won't wash, sir.'

Richard looked astonished. 'What do you mean?'

'No, sir,' Japp continued. 'Or, to put it differently, that cat won't jump. You're very set on your good lady, I realize. Newly married and all that. But, to speak plainly to you, it's no manner of use putting your neck in a halter for the sake of a bad woman. Though she's a good looker, and no mistake, I'll admit.'

'Inspector Japp!' exclaimed Richard, angrily.

'There's no point in getting upset with me, sir,' Japp continued imperturbably. 'I've told you the plain truth without beating about the bush, and I've no doubt that Mr Poirot here will tell you the same. I'm sorry, sir, but duty is duty, and murder is murder. That's all there is to it.' Japp nodded decisively, and left the room.

Turning to Poirot, who had been observing the scene from the settee, Richard asked coldly, 'Well, *are* you going to tell me the same, Monsieur Poirot?'

Rising, Poirot took a cigarette-case from his pocket and extracted a cigarette. Instead of answering Richard's question, he posed one of his own. 'Monsieur Amory, when did you first suspect your wife?' he asked.

'I never –' Richard began, but Poirot interrupted him, picking up a box of matches from the table as he spoke.

'Please, I beg of you, Monsieur Amory, nothing but the truth! You did suspect her, I know it. You suspected her before I arrived. That is why you were so anxious to get me away from this house. Do not deny it. It is impossible to deceive Hercule Poirot.' He lit his cigarette, replaced the box of matches on the table, and smiled up at the much taller man who towered over him. They made a ridiculous contrast.

'You are mistaken,' Richard told Poirot stiffly. 'Utterly mistaken. How could I suspect Lucia?'

'And yet, of course, there is an equally good case to be made against you,' Poirot continued reflectively, as he resumed his seat. 'You handled the drugs, you handled the coffee, you were short of money and desperate to acquire some. Oh, yes, anyone might be excused for suspecting you.'

'Inspector Japp doesn't seem to agree with you,' Richard observed.

'Ah, Japp! He has the common sense,' Poirot smiled. 'He is not a woman in love.'

'A woman in love?' Richard sounded puzzled.

'Let me give you a lesson in psychology, monsieur,' Poirot offered. 'When I first arrived, your wife came up to me and begged me to stay here and discover the murderer. Would a guilty woman have done that?'

'You mean –' Richard began quickly.

'I mean,' Poirot interrupted him, 'that before the sun sets tonight, you will be asking her pardon upon your knees.'

'What are you saying?'

'I am saying too much, perhaps,' Poirot admitted, rising. 'Now, monsieur, place yourself in my hands. In the hands of Hercule Poirot.'

'You can save her?' Richard asked with desperation in his voice.

Poirot regarded him solemnly. 'I have pledged my word – although, when I did so, I did not realize how difficult it was going to be. You see, the time it is very short, and something must be done quickly. You must promise me that you will do exactly as I tell you, without asking questions or making difficulties. Do you promise me that?'

'Very well,' replied Richard rather unwillingly.

'That is good. And now, listen to me. What I suggest is neither difficult nor impossible. It is, in fact, the common sense. This house will shortly be given over to the police. They will swarm all over it. They will make their investigations everywhere. For yourself and your family it could be very unpleasant. I suggest that you leave.'

'Give the house over to the police?' Richard asked, incredulously.

'That is my suggestion,' Poirot repeated. 'Of course, you will have to remain in the neighbourhood. But they say the local hotel is fairly comfortable. Engage rooms there. Then you will be close at hand when the police wish to question you all.'

'But when do you suggest that this should take place?'

Poirot beamed at him. 'My idea was – immediately.'

'Surely it will all look very odd?'

'Not at all, not at all,' the little detective assured Richard, smiling again. 'It will appear to be a move of the utmost – how do you say? – the utmost sensitivity. The associations here are hateful to you – you cannot bear to remain another hour. I assure you, it will sound very well.'

'But how about the Inspector?'

'I myself will fix it up with Inspector Japp.'

'I still can't see what good this is going to achieve,' Richard persisted.

'No, of course you do not see.' Poirot sounded more than a trifle smug. He shrugged his shoulders. 'It is not necessary that you should see. But I see. I, Hercule Poirot. That is enough.' He took Richard by the shoulders. 'Go, and make the arrangements. Or, if you cannot give your mind to it, let Raynor make them for you. Go! Go!' He almost pushed Richard to the door.

With a final anxious look back at Poirot, Richard left the room. 'Oh, these English! How obstinate,' muttered Poirot. He moved to the french windows and called, 'Mademoiselle Barbara!'

In answer to Poirot's call, Barbara Amory appeared outside the french windows. 'What is it? Has something else happened?' she asked.

Poirot gave her his most winning smile. 'Ah, mademoiselle,' he said. 'I wonder if you might be able to spare my colleague Hastings for just a little minute or two, perhaps?'

Barbara's reply was accompanied by a skittish glance. 'So! You want to take my little pet away from me, do you?'

'Just for a very short time, mademoiselle, I promise you.'

'Then you shall, Monsieur Poirot.' Turning back into the garden, Barbara called, 'My pet, you're wanted.'

'I thank you,' Poirot smiled again with a polite bow. Barbara returned to the garden, and a few moments later Hastings entered the library through the french windows, looking somewhat ashamed.

'And what have you to say for yourself?' Poirot asked in a tone of mock annoyance.

Hastings attempted an apologetic smile. 'It is all very well to put on the grin of the sheep,' Poirot admonished him. 'I leave you here, on guard, and the next thing I know you are promenading yourself with that very charming young lady in the garden. You are generally the most reliable of men, *mon cher*, but as soon as a pretty young woman appears upon the scene, your judgement flies out of the window. *Zut alors!*'

Hastings' sheepish grin faded, to be replaced by a blush of embarrassment. 'I say, I'm awfully sorry, Poirot,' he exclaimed. 'I just stepped outside for a second, and then I saw you through the window, coming into the room, so I thought it didn't matter.'

'You mean you thought it better not to return to face me,' declared Poirot. 'Well, my dear Hastings, you may have done the most irreparable damage. I found Carelli in here. The good Lord alone knows what he was doing, or what evidence he was tampering with.'

'I say, Poirot, I really am sorry,' Hastings apologized again. 'I'm most awfully sorry.'

'If you have not done the damage irreparable, it is more by good luck than for any other reason. But now, *mon ami*, the moment has come when we must employ our little grey cells.' Pretending to smack Hastings on the cheek, Poirot in fact gave his colleague an affectionate pat.

'Ah, good! Let's get to work,' Hastings exclaimed.

'No, it is not good, my friend,' Poirot told him. 'It is bad. It is obscure.' His face wore a troubled look as he continued, 'It is dark, as dark as it was last night.' He thought for a moment, and then added, 'But – yes – I think there is perhaps an idea. The germ of an idea. Yes, we will start there!'

Looking completely mystified, Hastings asked, 'What on earth are you talking about?'

The tone of Poirot's voice changed. He spoke gravely and

thoughtfully. 'Why did Sir Claud die, Hastings? Answer me that. Why did Sir Claud die?'

Hastings stared at him. 'But we know that,' he exclaimed.

'Do we?' asked Poirot. 'Are you so very sure?'

'Er – yes,' Hastings responded, though somewhat uncertainly. 'He died – he died because he was poisoned.'

Poirot made an impatient gesture. 'Yes, but *why* was he poisoned?'

Hastings thought carefully before replying. Then, 'Surely it must have been because the thief suspected –' he began.

Poirot slowly shook his head as Hastings continued, 'because the thief suspected – that he had been discovered –' He broke off again as he observed Poirot continuing to shake his head.

'Suppose, Hastings –' Poirot murmured, 'just suppose that the thief did not suspect?'

'I don't quite see,' Hastings confessed.

Poirot moved away, and then turned back with his arm raised in a gesture that seemed intended to hold his friend's attention. He paused and cleared his throat. 'Let me recount to you, Hastings,' he declared, 'the sequence of events as they might have gone, or rather as I think they were meant to go.'

Hastings sat in the chair by the table as Poirot continued.

'Sir Claud dies in his chair one night.' Poirot moved to the arm-chair, sat, and paused for a moment before repeating thoughtfully, 'Yes, Sir Claud dies in his chair. There are no suspicious circumstances attending that death. In all probability it will be put down to heart failure. It will be some days before his private papers are examined. His will is the only document that will be searched for. After the funeral, in due course, it will be discovered that his notes on the new explosive are incomplete. It may never be known that the exact formula existed. You see what that gives to our thief, Hastings?'

'Yes.'

'What?' asked Poirot.

Hastings looked puzzled. 'What?' he repeated.

'Security. That is what it gives the thief. He can dispose of his booty quite safely, whenever he wishes to. There is no pressure upon him. Even if the existence of the formula is known, he will have had plenty of time to cover his tracks.'

'Well, it's an idea – yes, I suppose so,' Hastings commented in a dubious tone.

'But naturally it is an idea!' Poirot cried. 'Am I not Hercule Poirot? But see now where this idea leads us. It tells us that the murder of Sir Claud was not a chance manoeuvre executed on the spur of the moment. It was planned beforehand. Beforehand. You see now where we are?'

'No,' Hastings admitted with an engaging candour. 'You know very well I never see these things. I know that we're in the library of Sir Claud's house, and that's all.'

'Yes, my friend, you are right,' Poirot told him. 'We are in the library of Sir Claud Amory's house. It is not morning but evening. The lights have just gone out. The thief's plans have gone awry.'

Poirot sat very upright, and wagged his forefinger emphatically to emphasize his points. 'Sir Claud, who, in the normal course of things, would not have gone to that safe until the following day, has discovered his loss by a mere chance. And, as the old gentleman himself said, the thief is caught like a rat in a trap. Yes, but the thief, who is also the murderer, knows something, too, that Sir Claud does not. The thief knows that in a very few minutes Sir Claud will be silenced for ever. He – or she – has one problem that has to be solved, and one only – to hide the paper safely during those few moments of darkness. Shut your eyes, Hastings, as I shut mine. The lights have gone out, and we can see nothing. But we can hear. Repeat to me, Hastings, as accurately as you can, the words of Miss Amory when she described this scene for us.'

Hastings shut his eyes. Then he began to speak, slowly, with an effort of memory and several pauses. 'Gasps,' he uttered.

Poirot nodded. 'A lot of little gasps,' Hastings went on, and Poirot nodded again.

Hastings concentrated for a time, and then continued, 'The noise of a chair falling – a metallic clink – that must have been the key, I imagine.'

'Quite right,' said Poirot. 'The key. Continue.'

'A scream. That was Lucia screaming. She called out to Sir Claud – Then the knocking came at the door – Oh! Wait a moment – right at the beginning, the noise of tearing silk.' Hastings opened his eyes.

'Yes, tearing silk,' Poirot exclaimed. He rose, moved to the desk, and then crossed to the fireplace. 'It is all there, Hastings, in those few moments of darkness. All there. And yet our ears tell us – nothing.' He stopped at the mantelpiece and mechanically straightened the vase of spills.

'Oh, do stop straightening those damned things, Poirot,' Hastings complained. 'You're always at it.'

His attention arrested, Poirot removed his hand from the vase. 'What is that you say?' he asked. 'Yes, it is true.' He stared at the vase of spills. 'I remember straightening them but a little hour ago. And now – it is necessary that I straighten them again.' He spoke excitedly. 'Why, Hastings – why is that?'

'Because they're crooked, I suppose,' Hastings replied in a bored tone. 'It's just your little mania for neatness.'

'Tearing silk!' exclaimed Poirot. 'No, Hastings! The sound is the same.' He stared at the paper spills, and snatched up the vase that contained them. 'Tearing paper –' he continued as he moved away from the mantelpiece.

His excitement communicated itself to his friend. 'What is it?' Hastings asked, springing up and moving to him.

Poirot stood, tumbling out the spills onto the settee, and examining them. Every now and then he handed one to Hastings, muttering, 'Here is one. Ah, another, and yet another.'

Hastings unfolded the spills and scrutinized them. 'C19 N23 –' he began to read aloud from one of them.

'Yes, yes!' exclaimed Poirot. 'It is the formula!'

'I say, that's wonderful!'

'Quick! Fold them up again!' Poirot ordered, and Hastings began to do so. 'Oh, you are so slow!' Poirot admonished him. 'Quick! Quick!' Snatching the spills from Hastings, he put them back into the vase and hastened to return it to the mantelpiece.

Looking dumbfounded, Hastings joined him there.

Poirot beamed. 'It intrigues you what I do there, yes? Tell me, Hastings, what is it that I have here in this vase?'

'Why, spills, of course,' Hastings replied in a tone of tremendous irony.

'No, *mon ami*, it is cheese.'

'*Cheese?*'

'Precisely, my friend, cheese.'

'I say, Poirot,' Hastings enquired sarcastically, 'you're all right, aren't you? I mean, you haven't got a headache or anything?'

Poirot's reply ignored his friend's frivolous question. 'For what do you use cheese, Hastings? I will tell you, *mon ami*. You use it to bait a mousetrap. We wait now for one thing only – the mouse.'

'And the mouse –'

'The mouse will come, my friend,' Poirot assured Hastings. 'Rest assured of that. I have sent him a message. He will not fail to respond.'

Before Hastings had time to react to Poirot's cryptic announcement, the door opened and Edward Raynor entered the room. 'Oh, you're here, Monsieur Poirot,' the secretary observed. 'And Captain Hastings also. Inspector Japp would like to speak to you both upstairs.'

'We will come at once,' Poirot replied. Followed by Hastings, he walked to the door, as Raynor entered the library and crossed to the fireplace. At the door, Poirot suddenly wheeled round to look at the secretary. 'By the way, Mr Raynor,' the detective asked, as he moved back to the centre of the room, 'do you by any chance know whether Dr Carelli was here in the library at all this morning?'

'Yes, he was,' Raynor told the detective. 'I found him here.'

'Ah!' Poirot seemed pleased at this. 'And what was he doing?'

'He was telephoning, I believe.'

'Was he telephoning when you came in?'

'No, he was just coming back into the room. He had been in Sir Claud's study.'

Poirot considered this for a moment, and then asked Raynor, 'Where exactly were you then? Can you remember?'

Still standing by the fireplace, Raynor replied, 'Oh, somewhere about here, I think.'

'Did you hear any of Dr Carelli's conversation on the phone?'

'No,' said the secretary. 'He made it perfectly clear that he wanted to be alone, so I cleared out.'

'I see.' Poirot hesitated, and then took a notebook and pencil from his pocket. Writing a few words on a page, he tore it out. 'Hastings!' he called.

Hastings, who had been hovering by the door, came to him, and Poirot gave his friend the folded page. 'Would you be so kind as to take that up to Inspector Japp?'

Raynor watched Hastings leave the room on his errand, and then asked, 'What was that all about?'

Putting the notebook and pencil back in his pocket, Poirot replied, 'I told Japp that I would be with him in a few minutes, and that I might be able to tell him the name of the murderer.'

'Really? You know who it is?' asked Raynor in a state of some excitement.

There was a momentary pause. Hercule Poirot seemed to hold the secretary under the spell of his personality. Raynor watched the detective, fascinated, as he slowly began to speak. 'Yes, I think I know who the murderer is – at last,' Poirot announced. 'I am reminded of another case, not so long ago. Never shall I forget the killing of Lord Edgware. I was nearly defeated – yes, I, Hercule Poirot! – by the extremely simple cunning of a vacant brain. You see, Monsieur Raynor, the very simple-minded have often the genius to commit an uncomplicated crime and then leave it alone. Let us hope that the murderer of Sir Claud, on the other hand, is intelligent and superior and thoroughly pleased with himself and unable to resist – how do you say? – painting the lily.' Poirot's eyes lit up in vivid animation.

'I'm not sure that I understand you,' said Raynor. 'Do you mean that it's *not* Mrs Amory?'

'No, it is not Mrs Amory,' Poirot told him. 'That is why I wrote my little note. That poor lady has suffered enough. She must be spared any further questioning.'

Raynor looked thoughtful, and then exclaimed, 'Then I'll bet it's Carelli. Yes?'

Poirot wagged a finger at him playfully. 'Monsieur Raynor, you must permit me to keep my little secrets until the last moment.' Taking out a handkerchief, he mopped his brow. '*Mon Dieu*, how hot it is today!' he complained.

'Would you like a drink?' asked Raynor. 'I'm forgetting my manners. I should have offered you one earlier.'

Poirot beamed. 'You are very kind. I will have a whisky, please, if I may.'

'Certainly. Just a moment.' Raynor left the room, while Poirot wandered across to the french windows and looked out into the garden for a moment. Then, moving to the settee, he shook the cushions, before drifting across to the mantelpiece to examine the ornaments. In a few moments Raynor returned with two whiskies and sodas on a tray. He watched as Poirot lifted a hand to an ornament on the mantelpiece.

'This is a valuable antique, I fancy,' Poirot remarked, picking up a jug.

'Is it?' was Raynor's uninterested comment. 'I don't know much about that kind of thing. Come and have a drink,' he suggested as he set his tray down on the coffee table.

'Thank you,' murmured Poirot, joining him there.

'Well, here's luck,' said Raynor, taking a glass and drinking.

With a bow, Poirot raised the other glass to his lips. 'To you, my friend. And now let me tell you of my suspicions. I first realized that –'

He broke off suddenly, jerking his head over his shoulder as though some sound had caught his ear. Looking first at the door and then at Raynor, he put his finger to his lips, indicating that he thought someone might be eavesdropping.

Raynor nodded in comprehension. The two men crept stealthily up to the door, and Poirot gestured to the secretary to remain in the room. Poirot opened the door sharply and bounced outside, but returned immediately looking extremely crestfallen. 'Surprising,' he admitted to Raynor. 'I could have sworn I heard something. Ah well, I made a mistake. It does not happen very often. *A votre santé*, my friend.' He drained the contents of his glass.

'Ah!' exclaimed Raynor, as he also drank.

'I beg your pardon?' asked Poirot.

'Nothing. A load off my mind, that is all.'

Poirot moved to the table and put his glass down. 'Do you know, Monsieur Raynor,' he confided, 'to be absolutely honest with you, I have never become quite used to your English national drink, the whisky. The taste, it pleases me not. It is bitter.' He moved to the arm-chair and sat.

'Really? I'm so sorry. Mine didn't taste at all bitter.' Raynor put his glass down on the coffee table, and continued, 'I think you were about to tell me something just now, were you not?'

Poirot looked surprised. 'Was I? What can it have been? Can I have forgotten already? I think that perhaps I wanted to explain to you how I proceed in an investigation. *Voyons!* One fact leads to another, so we continue. Does the next one fit in with that? *A merveille!* Good! We can proceed. This next little fact – no! Ah, that is curious! There is something missing – a link in the chain that is not there. We examine. We search. And that little curious fact, that perhaps paltry little detail that will not tally, we put it here!' Poirot made an extravagant gesture to his head with his hand. 'It is significant! It is tremendous!'

'Y-es, I see,' Raynor murmured dubiously.

Poirot shook his forefinger so fiercely in Raynor's face that the secretary almost quailed before it. 'Ah, beware! Peril to the detective who says, "It is so small – it does not matter. It will not agree. I will forget it." That way lies confusion! Everything matters.' Poirot suddenly stopped, and tapped his head. 'Ah! Now I remember what I wanted to talk to you about. It was one of those small, unimportant little facts. I wanted to talk to you, Monsieur Raynor, about dust.'

Raynor smiled politely. 'Dust?'

'Precisely. Dust,' Poirot repeated. 'My friend Hastings, he reminded me just now that I am a detective and not a housemaid. He thought himself very clever to make such a remark, but I am not so sure. The housemaid and the detective, after all, have something in common. The housemaid, what does she do? She explores all the dark corners with her broom. She brings into the light of day all the hidden things that have rolled conveniently out of sight. Does not the detective do much the same?'

Raynor looked bored, but murmured, 'Very interesting, Monsieur Poirot.' He moved to the chair by the table and sat, before asking, 'But – is that all you were intending to say?'

'No, not quite,' replied Poirot. He leaned forward. 'You did not throw dust in my eyes, Monsieur Raynor, because there was no dust. Do you understand?'

The secretary stared at him intently. 'No, I'm afraid I don't.'

'There was no dust on that box of drugs. Mademoiselle

Barbara commented on the fact. But there should have been dust. That shelf on which it stands' – and Poirot gestured towards it as he spoke – 'is thick with dust. It was then that I knew –'

'Knew what?'

'I knew,' Poirot continued, 'that someone had taken that box down recently. That the person who poisoned Sir Claud Amory would not need to go near the box last night, since he had on some earlier occasion helped himself to all the poison he needed, choosing a time when he knew he would not be disturbed. You did not go near the box of drugs last night, because you had already taken from it the hyoscine you needed. But you did handle the coffee, Monsieur Raynor.'

Raynor smiled patiently. 'Dear me! Do you accuse me of murdering Sir Claud?'

'Do you deny it?' asked Poirot.

Raynor paused before replying. When he spoke again, a harsher tone had entered his voice. 'Oh no,' he declared, 'I don't deny it. Why should I? I'm really rather proud of the whole thing. It ought to have gone off without a hitch. It was sheer bad luck that made Sir Claud open the safe again last night. He's never done such a thing before.'

Poirot sounded rather drowsy as he asked, 'Why are you telling me all this?'

'Why not? You're so sympathetic. It's a pleasure to talk to you.' Raynor laughed, and continued. 'Yes, things very nearly went wrong. But that's what I really pride myself on, turning a failure into a success.' A triumphant expression appeared on his face. 'To devise a hiding place on the spur of the moment was really rather creditable. Would you like me to tell you where the formula is now?'

His drowsiness now accentuated, Poirot seemed to find difficulty in speaking clearly. 'I – I do not understand you,' he whispered.

'You made one little mistake, Monsieur Poirot,' Raynor told him with a sneer. 'You underestimated my intelligence. I wasn't really taken in just now by your ingenious red herring about poor old Carelli. A man with your brains couldn't seriously have believed that Carelli – why, it won't bear thinking about. You see, I'm playing for big stakes. That piece of paper, delivered in the right quarters, means fifty thousand pounds to me.' He leaned back. 'Just think what a man of my ability can do with fifty thousand pounds.'

In a voice of increasing drowsiness, Poirot managed to reply, 'I – I do not – like to think of it.'

'Well, perhaps not. I appreciate that,' Raynor conceded. 'One has to allow for a different point of view.'

Poirot leaned forward, and appeared to be making an effort to pull himself together. 'And it will not be so,' he exclaimed. 'I will denounce you. I, Hercule Poirot –' He broke off suddenly.

'Hercule Poirot will do nothing,' declared Raynor, as the detective sank back in his seat. With a laugh which was close to a sneer, the secretary continued, 'You never guessed, did you, even when you said that the whisky was bitter? You see, my dear Monsieur Poirot, I took not just one but several tubes of hyoscine from that box. If anything, you have had slightly more than I gave Sir Claud.'

'Ah, *mon Dieu*,' Poirot gasped, struggling to rise. In a weak voice he tried to call, 'Hastings! Hast –' His voice faded away, and he sank back into his chair. His eyelids closed.

Raynor got to his feet, pushed his chair aside, and moved to stand over Poirot. 'Try to keep awake, Monsieur Poirot,' he said. 'Surely you'd like to see where the formula was hidden, wouldn't you?'

He waited for a moment, but Poirot's eyes remained closed. 'A swift, dreamless sleep, and no awakening, as our dear friend Carelli puts it,' Raynor commented dryly as he went to the mantelpiece, took the spills, folded them, and put them in his pocket. He moved towards the french windows, pausing only to call over his shoulder, 'Goodbye, my dear Monsieur Poirot.'

He was about to step out into the garden when he was halted by the sound of Poirot's voice, speaking cheerfully and naturally. 'Would you not like the envelope as well?'

Raynor spun around, and at the same moment Inspector Japp entered the library from the garden. Moving back a few steps, Raynor paused irresolutely, and then decided to bolt. He rushed to the french windows, only to be seized by Japp and by Constable Johnson, who also suddenly appeared from the garden.

Poirot rose from his chair, stretching himself. 'Well, my dear Japp,' he asked. 'Did you get it all?'

Dragging Raynor back to the centre of the room with the aid of his constable, Japp replied, 'Every word, thanks to your note, Poirot. You can hear everything perfectly from the terrace there, just outside the window. Now, let's go over him and see what we can find.' He pulled the spills from Raynor's pocket, and threw them onto the coffee table. He next pulled out a small tube. 'Aha! Hyoscine! Empty.'

'Ah, Hastings,' Poirot greeted his friend, as he entered from the hall carrying a glass of whisky and soda which he handed to the detective.

'You see?' Poirot addressed Raynor in his kindliest manner. 'I refused to play in your comedy. Instead, I made you play in mine. In my note, I gave instructions to Japp and also to Hastings. Then I make things easy for you by complaining of the heat. I know you will suggest a drink. It is, after all, the opening that you need. After that, it is all so straightforward. When I go to the door, the good Hastings he is ready outside with another whisky and soda. I change glasses and I am back again. And so – on with the comedy.'

Poirot gave the glass back to Hastings. 'Myself, I think I play my part rather well,' he declared.

There was a pause while Poirot and Raynor surveyed each other. Then Raynor spoke. 'I've been afraid of you ever since you came into this house. My scheme could have worked. I could have set myself up for life with the fifty thousand pounds – perhaps even more – that I would have got for that wretched formula. But, from the moment you arrived, I stopped feeling absolutely confident that I'd get away with killing that pompous old fool and stealing his precious scrap of paper.'

'I have observed already that you are intelligent,' Poirot replied. He sat again in the arm-chair, looking distinctly pleased with himself, as Japp began to speak rapidly.

'Edward Raynor, I arrest you for the wilful murder of Sir Claud Amory, and I warn you that anything you say may be used in evidence.' Japp made a gesture to the constable to take Raynor away.

As Raynor made his exit in the custody of Constable Johnson, the two men passed Miss Amory, who was entering the library at the same moment. She looked back at them anxiously, and then hastened to Poirot. 'Monsieur Poirot,' she gasped as Poirot rose to greet her, 'is this true? Was it Mr Raynor who murdered my poor brother?'

'I am afraid so, mademoiselle,' said Poirot.

Miss Amory looked dumbfounded. 'Oh! Oh!' she exclaimed. 'I can't believe it! What wickedness! We've always treated him like one of the family. And the Beeswax and everything –' She turned abruptly, and was about to leave when Richard entered and held the door open for her. As she almost ran from the room, her niece Barbara entered from the garden.

'This is simply too shattering for words,' Barbara exclaimed. 'Edward Raynor, of all people. Who would have believed it? Somebody has been frightfully clever to have found out. I wonder who!'

She looked meaningfully at Poirot who, however, gave a bow in the direction of the police inspector as he murmured, 'It was Inspector Japp who solved the case, mademoiselle.'

Japp beamed. 'I will say for you, Monsieur Poirot, you're the goods. And a gentleman as well.' With a nod to the assembled company, Japp made a brisk exit, snatching the whisky glass from a bemused Hastings as he did so, with the words, 'I'll take charge of the evidence, if you please, Captain Hastings!'

'Yes, but was it really Inspector Japp who found out who killed Uncle Claud? Or,' Barbara asked Poirot coyly as she approached him, 'was it you, Monsieur Hercule Poirot?'

Poirot moved to Hastings, putting an arm around his old friend. 'Mademoiselle,' he informed Barbara, 'the real credit belongs to Hastings here. He made a remark of surpassing brilliance which put me on the right track. Take him into the garden and make him tell you about it.'

He pushed Hastings towards Barbara and shepherded them both towards the french windows. 'Ah, my pet,' Barbara sighed comically to Hastings as they went out into the garden.

Richard Amory was about to address Poirot, when the door to the hall opened and Lucia entered. Giving a start when she saw her husband, Lucia murmured uncertainly, 'Richard –'

Richard turned to look at her. 'Lucia!'

Lucia moved a few steps into the room. 'I –,' she began, and then broke off.

Richard approached her, and then stopped. 'You –'

They both looked extremely nervous, and ill at ease with each other. Then Lucia suddenly caught sight of Poirot and went to him with outstretched hands. 'Monsieur Poirot! How can we ever thank you?'

Poirot took both her hands in his. 'So, madame, your troubles are over!' he announced.

'A murderer has been caught. But my troubles, are they really over?' Lucia asked wistfully.

'It is true that you do not look quite happy yet, my child,' Poirot observed.

'Shall I ever be happy again, I wonder?'

'I think so,' said Poirot with a twinkle in his eye. 'Trust in your old Poirot.' Guiding Lucia to the chair by the table in the centre of the room, he picked up the spills from the coffee table, went across to Richard, and handed them to him. 'Monsieur,' he declared, 'I have pleasure in restoring to you Sir Claud's formula! It can be pieced together – what is the expression you use? – it will be as good as new.'

'My God, the formula!' Richard exclaimed. 'I'd almost forgotten it. I can hardly bear to look at it again. Think what it has done to us all. It's cost my father his life, and it's all but ruined the lives of all of us as well.'

'What are you going to do with it, Richard?' Lucia asked him.

'I don't know. What would you do with it?'

Rising and moving to him, Lucia whispered, 'Would you let me?'

'It's yours,' her husband told her, handing her the spills. 'Do as you like with the wretched thing.'

'Thank you, Richard,' murmured Lucia. She went to the fireplace, took a match from the box on the mantelpiece, and set fire to the spills, dropping the pieces one by one into the fireplace. 'There is so much suffering already in the world. I cannot bear to think of any more.'

'Madame,' said Poirot, 'I admire the manner in which you burn many thousands of pounds with as little emotion as though they were just a few pence.'

'They are nothing but ashes,' Lucia sighed. 'Like my life.'

Poirot gave a snort. '*Oh, là, là!* Let us all order our coffins,' he remarked in a tone of mock gloom. 'No! Me, I like to be happy, to rejoice, to dance, to sing. See you, my children,' he continued, turning to address Richard as well, 'I am about to take a liberty with you both. Madame looks down her nose and thinks, "I have deceived my husband." Monsieur looks down his nose and thinks, "I have suspected my wife." And yet what you really want, both of you, is to be in each other's arms, is it not?'

Lucia took a step towards her husband. 'Richard –' she began in a low voice.

'Madame,' Poirot interrupted her, 'I fear that Sir Claud may have suspected you of planning to steal his formula because, a few weeks ago, someone – no doubt an ex-colleague of Carelli, for people of that kind are continually falling out with one another – someone, I say, sent Sir Claud an anonymous letter about your mother. But, do you know, my foolish child, that your husband tried to accuse himself to Inspector Japp – that he actually confessed to the murder of Sir Claud – in order to save you?'

Lucia gave a little cry, and looked adoringly at Richard.

'And you, monsieur,' Poirot continued. 'Figure to yourself that, not more than half an hour ago, your wife was shouting in my ear that she had killed your father, all because she feared that you might have done so.'

'Lucia,' Richard murmured tenderly, going to her.

'Being English,' Poirot remarked as he moved away from them, 'you will not embrace in my presence, I suppose?'

Lucia went to him, and took his hand. 'Monsieur Poirot, I do not think I shall ever forget you – ever.'

'Neither shall I forget you, madame,' Poirot declared gallantly as he kissed her hand.

'Poirot,' Richard Amory declared, 'I don't know what to say, except that you've saved my life and my marriage. I can't express what I feel —'

'Do not derange yourself, my friend,' replied Poirot. 'I am happy to have been of service to you.'

Lucia and Richard went out into the garden together, looking into each other's eyes, his arm around her shoulders. Following them to the window, Poirot called after them, 'Bless you, *mes enfants*! Oh, and if you encounter Miss Barbara in the garden, please ask her to return Captain Hastings to me. We must shortly begin our journey to London.' Turning back into the room, his glance fell on the fireplace.

'Ah!' he exclaimed as he went to the mantelpiece over the fireplace and straightened the spill vase. '*Voilà!* Now, order and neatness are restored.' With that, Poirot walked towards the door with an air of immense satisfaction.

SPIDER'S WEB

Copplestone Court, the elegant, eighteenth-century country home of Henry and Clarissa Hailsham-Brown, set in gently undulating hilly country in Kent, looked handsome even at the close of a rainy March afternoon. In the tastefully furnished ground-floor drawing-room, with French windows onto the garden, two men stood near a console table on which there was a tray with three glasses of port, each marked with a sticky label, one, two and three. Also on the table was a pencil and sheet of paper.

Sir Rowland Delahaye, a distinguished-looking man in his early fifties with a charming and cultivated manner, seated himself on the arm of a comfortable chair and allowed his companion to blindfold him. Hugo Birch, a man of about sixty and inclined to be somewhat irascible in manner, then placed in Sir Rowland's hand one of the glasses from the table. Sir Rowland sipped, considered for a moment, and then said, 'I should think – yes – definitely – yes, this is the Dow 'forty-two.'

Hugo replaced the glass on the table, murmuring 'Dow 'forty-two', made a note on the paper, and handed over the next glass. Again Sir Rowland sipped the wine. He paused, took another sip, and then nodded affirmatively. 'Ah, yes,' he declared with conviction. 'Now, this is a very fine port indeed.' He took another sip. 'No doubt about it. Cockburn 'twenty-seven.'

He handed the glass back to Hugo as he continued, 'Fancy Clarissa wasting a bottle of Cockburn 'twenty-seven on a silly experiment like this. It's positively sacrilegious. But then women just don't understand port at all.'

Hugo took the glass from him, noted his verdict on the piece of paper on the table, and handed him the third glass. After a quick sip, Sir Rowland's reaction was immediate and violent. 'Ugh!' he exclaimed in disgust. 'Rich Ruby port-type wine. I can't imagine why Clarissa has such a thing in the house.'

His opinion duly noted, he removed the blindfold. 'Now it's your turn,' he told Hugo.

Taking off his horn-rimmed spectacles, Hugo allowed Sir Rowland to blindfold him. 'Well, I imagine she uses the cheap port for jugged hare or for flavouring soup,' he suggested. 'I don't imagine Henry would allow her to offer it to guests.'

'There you are, Hugo,' Sir Rowland declared as he finished tying the blindfold over his companion's eyes. 'Perhaps I ought to turn you around three times like they do in Blind Man's Buff,' he added as he led Hugo to the armchair and turned him around to sit in it.

'Here, steady on,' Hugo protested. He felt behind him for the chair.

'Got it?' asked Sir Rowland.

'Yes.'

'Then I'll swivel the glasses around instead,' Sir Rowland said as he moved the glasses on the table slightly.

'There's no need to,' Hugo told him. 'Do you think I'm likely to be influenced by what you said? I'm as good a judge of port as you are any day, Roly, my boy.'

'Don't be too sure of that. In any case, one can't be too careful,' Sir Rowland insisted.

Just as he was about to take one of the glasses across to Hugo, the third of the Hailsham-Browns' guests came in from the garden. Jeremy Warrender, an attractive young man in his twenties, was wearing a raincoat over his suit. Panting, and obviously out of breath, he headed for the sofa and was about to flop into it when he noticed what was going on. 'What on earth are you two up to?' he asked, as he removed his raincoat and jacket. 'The three-card trick with glasses?'

'What's that?' the blindfolded Hugo wanted to know. 'It sounds as though someone's brought a dog into the room.'

'It's only young Warrender,' Sir Rowland assured him. 'Behave yourself.'

'Oh, I thought it sounded like a dog that's been chasing a rabbit,' Hugo declared.

'I've been three times to the lodge gates and back, wearing a mackintosh over my clothes,' Jeremy explained as he fell heavily onto the sofa. 'Apparently the Herzoslovakian Minister did it in four minutes fifty-three seconds, weighed down by his mackintosh. I went all out, but I couldn't do any better than six minutes ten seconds. And I don't believe he did, either. Only Chris Chataway himself could do it in that time, with or without a mackintosh.'

'Who told you that about the Herzoslovakian Minister?' Sir Rowland enquired.

'Clarissa.'

'Clarissa!' exclaimed Sir Rowland, chuckling.

'Oh, Clarissa.' Hugo snorted. 'You shouldn't pay any attention to what Clarissa tells you.'

Still chuckling, Sir Rowland continued, 'I'm afraid you don't know your hostess very well, Warrender. She's a young lady with a very vivid imagination.'

Jeremy rose to his feet. 'Do you mean she made the whole thing up?' he asked, indignantly.

'Well, I wouldn't put it past her,' Sir Rowland answered as he handed one of the three glasses to the still blindfolded Hugo. 'And it certainly sounds like her idea of a joke.'

'Does it, indeed? You just wait till I see that young woman,' Jeremy promised. 'I'll certainly have something to say to her. Gosh, I'm exhausted.' He stalked out to the hall carrying his raincoat.

'Stop puffing like a walrus,' Hugo complained. 'I'm trying to concentrate. There's a fiver at stake. Roly and I have got a bet on.'

'Oh, what is it?' Jeremy enquired, returning to perch on an arm of the sofa.

'It's to decide who's the best judge of port,' Hugo told him. 'We've got Cockburn 'twenty-seven, Dow 'forty-two, and the local grocer's special. Quiet now. This is important.' He sipped from the glass he was holding, and then murmured rather non-committally, 'Mmm-ah.'

'Well?' Sir Roland queried. 'Have you decided what the first one is?'

'Don't hustle me, Roly,' Hugo exclaimed. 'I'm not going to rush my fences. Where's the next one?'

He held on to the glass as he was handed another. He sipped and then announced, 'Yes, I'm pretty sure about those two.' He sniffed at both glasses again. 'This first one's the Dow,' he decided as he held out one glass. 'The second was the Cockburn,' he continued, handing the other glass back as Sir Rowland repeated, 'Number three glass the Dow, number one the Cockburn', writing as he spoke.

'Well, it's hardly necessary to taste the third,' Hugo declared, 'but I suppose I'd better go through with it.'

'Here you are,' said Sir Rowland, handing over the final glass.

After sipping from it, Hugo made an exclamation of extreme distaste. 'Tschah! Ugh! What unspeakable muck.' He returned the glass to Sir Rowland, then took a handkerchief from his pocket and wiped his lips to get rid of the offending taste. 'It'll take me an hour to get the taste of that stuff out of my mouth,' he complained. 'Get me out of this, Roly.'

'Here, I'll do it,' Jeremy offered, rising and moving behind Hugo to remove his blindfold while Sir Rowland thoughtfully sipped the last of the three glasses before putting it back on the table.

'So that's what you think, Hugo, is it? Glass number two, grocer's special?' He shook his head. 'Rubbish! That's the Dow 'forty-two, not a doubt of it.'

Hugo put the blindfold in his pocket. 'Pah! You've lost your palate, Roly,' he declared.

'Let me try,' Jeremy suggested. Going to the table, he took a quick sip from each glass. He paused for a moment, sipped each of them again, and then admitted, 'Well, they all taste the same to me.'

'You young people!' Hugo admonished him. 'It's all this confounded gin you keep on drinking. Completely ruins your palate. It's not just women who don't appreciate port. Nowadays, no man under forty does, either.'

Before Jeremy had a chance to reply to this, the door leading to the library opened, and Clarissa Hailsham-Brown, a beautiful dark-haired woman in her late twenties, entered. 'Hello, my darlings,' she greeted Sir Rowland and Hugo. 'Have you settled it yet?'

'Yes, Clarissa,' Sir Rowland assured her. 'We're ready for you.'

'I know I'm right,' said Hugo. 'Number one's the Cockburn, number two's the port-type stuff, and three's the Dow. Right?'

'Nonsense,' Sir Rowland exclaimed before Clarissa could answer. 'Number one's the Dow, two's the Cockburn, and three's the port-type stuff. I'm right, aren't I?'

'Darlings!' was Clarissa's only immediate response. She kissed first Hugo and then Sir Rowland, and continued, 'Now one of you take the tray back to the dining-room. You'll find the decanter on the sideboard.' Smiling to herself, she selected a chocolate from a box on an occasional table.

Sir Rowland had picked up the tray with the glasses on it, and was about to leave with them. He stopped. 'The decanter?' he asked, warily.

Clarissa sat on the sofa, tucking her feet up under her. 'Yes,' she replied. 'Just one decanter.' She giggled. 'It's all the same port, you know.'

CHAPTER 2

Clarissa's announcement produced a different reaction from each of her hearers. Jeremy burst into hoots of laughter, went across to his hostess and kissed her, while Sir Rowland stood gaping with astonishment, and Hugo seemed undecided what attitude to adopt to her having made fools of them both.

When Sir Rowland finally found words, they were, 'Clarissa, you unprincipled humbug.' But his tone was affectionate.

'Well,' Clarissa responded, 'it's been such a wet afternoon, and you weren't able to play golf. You must have some fun, and you have had fun over this, darlings, haven't you?'

'Upon my soul,' Sir Rowland exclaimed as he carried the tray to the door. 'You ought to be ashamed of yourself, showing up your elders and betters. It turns out that only young Warrender here guessed they were all the same.'

Hugo, who by now was laughing, accompanied him to the door. 'Who was it?' he asked, putting an arm around Sir Rowland's shoulder, 'Who was it who said that he'd know Cockburn 'twenty-seven anywhere?'

'Never mind, Hugo,' Sir Rowland replied resignedly, 'let's

have some more of it later, whatever it is.' Talking as they went, the two men left by the door leading to the hall, Hugo closing the door behind them.

Jeremy confronted Clarissa on her sofa. 'Now then, Clarissa,' he said accusingly, 'what's all this about the Herzoslovakian Minister?'

Clarissa looked at him innocently. 'What about him?' she asked.

Pointing a finger at her, Jeremy spoke clearly and slowly. 'Did he ever run to the lodge gates and back, in a mackintosh, three times in four minutes fifty-three seconds?'

Clarissa smiled sweetly as she replied, 'The Herzoslovakian Minister is a dear, but he's well over sixty, and I doubt very much if he's run anywhere for years.'

'So you did make the whole thing up. They told me you probably did. But why?'

'Well,' Clarissa suggested, her smile even sweeter than before, 'you'd been complaining all day about not getting enough exercise. So I thought the only friendly thing to do was to help you get some. It would have been no good ordering you to go for a brisk run through the woods, but I knew you'd respond to a challenge. So I invented someone for you to challenge.'

Jeremy gave a comical groan of exasperation. 'Clarissa,' he asked her, 'do you ever speak the truth?'

'Of course I do – sometimes,' Clarissa admitted. 'But when I am speaking the truth, nobody ever seems to believe me. It's very odd.' She thought for a moment, and then continued. 'I suppose when you're making things up, you get carried away and that makes it sound more convincing.' She drifted over to the French windows.

'I might have broken a blood vessel,' Jeremy complained. 'A fat lot you'd have cared about that.'

Clarissa laughed. Opening the window she observed, 'I do believe it's cleared up. It's going to be a lovely evening. How delicious the garden smells after rain.' She leaned out and sniffed. 'Narcissus.'

As she closed the window again, Jeremy came over to join her. 'Do you really like living down here in the country?' he asked.

'I love it.'

'But you must get bored to death,' he exclaimed. 'It's all so incongruous for you, Clarissa. You must miss the theatre terribly. I hear you were passionate about it when you were younger.'

'Yes, I was. But I manage to create my own theatre right here,' said Clarissa with a laugh.

'But you ought to be leading an exciting life in London.'

Clarissa laughed again. 'What – parties and night clubs?' she asked.

'Parties, yes. You'd make a brilliant hostess,' Jeremy told her, laughing.

She turned to face him. 'It sounds like an Edwardian novel,' she said. 'Anyway, diplomatic parties are terribly dull.'

'But it's such a waste, your being tucked away down here,' he persisted, moving close to her and attempting to take her hand.

'A waste – of me?' asked Clarissa, withdrawing her hand.

'Yes,' Jeremy responded fervently. 'Then there's Henry.'

'What about Henry?' Clarissa busied herself patting a cushion on an easy chair.

Jeremy looked at her steadily. 'I can't imagine why you ever married him,' he replied, plucking up his courage. 'He's years older than you, with a daughter who's a school-kid.' He leaned on the armchair, still observing her closely. 'He's an excellent man, I have no doubt, but really, of all the pompous stuffed shirts. Going about looking like a boiled owl.' He paused, waiting for a reaction. When none came, he continued, 'He's as dull as ditchwater.'

Still she said nothing. Jeremy tried again. 'And he has no sense of humour,' he muttered somewhat petulantly.

Clarissa looked at him, smiled, but said nothing.

'I suppose you think I oughtn't to say these things,' Jeremy exclaimed.

Clarissa sat on one end of a long stool. 'Oh, I don't mind,' she told him. 'Say anything you like.'

Jeremy went over to sit beside her. 'So you do realize that you've made a mistake?' he asked, eagerly.

'But I haven't made a mistake,' was Clarissa's softly uttered response. Then, teasingly, she added, 'Are you making immoral advances to me, Jeremy?'

'Definitely,' was his prompt reply.

'How lovely,' exclaimed Clarissa. She nudged him with her elbow. 'Do go on.'

'I think you know how I feel about you, Clarissa,' Jeremy responded somewhat moodily. 'But you're just playing with me, aren't you? Flirting. It's another one of your games. Darling, can't you be serious just for once?'

'Serious? What's so good about "serious"?' Clarissa replied. 'There's enough seriousness in the world already. I like to enjoy myself, and I like everyone around me to enjoy themselves as well.'

Jeremy smiled ruefully. 'I'd be enjoying myself a great

deal more at this moment if you were serious about me,' he observed.

'Oh, come on,' she ordered him playfully. 'Of course you're enjoying yourself. Here you are, our house-guest for the weekend, along with my lovely godfather Roly. And sweet old Hugo's here for drinks this evening as well. He and Roly are so funny together. You can't say you're not enjoying yourself.'

'Of course I'm enjoying myself,' Jeremy admitted. 'But you won't let me say what I really want to say to you.'

'Don't be silly, darling,' she replied. 'You know you can say anything you like to me.'

'Really? You mean that?' he asked her.

'Of course.'

'Very well, then,' said Jeremy. He rose from the stool and turned to face her. 'I love you,' he declared.

'I'm so glad,' replied Clarissa, cheerfully.

'That's entirely the wrong answer,' Jeremy complained. 'You ought to say, "I'm so sorry" in a deep, sympathetic voice.'

'But I'm not sorry,' Clarissa insisted. 'I'm delighted. I like people to be in love with me.'

Jeremy sat down beside her again, but turned away from her. Now he seemed deeply upset. Looking at him for a moment, Clarissa asked, 'Would you do anything in the world for me?'

Turning to her, Jeremy responded eagerly. 'You know I would. Anything. Anything in the world,' he declared.

'Really?' said Clarissa. 'Supposing, for instance, that I murdered someone, would you help – no, I must stop.' She rose and walked away a few paces.

Jeremy turned to face Clarissa. 'No, go on,' he urged her.

She paused for a moment and then began to speak. 'You asked me just now if I ever got bored, down here in the country.'

'Yes.'

'Well, I suppose in a way, I do,' she admitted. 'Or, rather, I might, if it wasn't for my private hobby.'

Jeremy looked puzzled. 'Private hobby? What is that?' he asked her.

Clarissa took a deep breath. 'You see, Jeremy,' she said, 'my life has always been peaceful and happy. Nothing exciting ever happened to me, so I began to play my little game. I call it "supposing".'

Jeremy looked perplexed. 'Supposing?'

'Yes,' said Clarissa, beginning to pace about the room. 'For example, I might say to myself, "Supposing I were to come down one morning and find a dead body in the library, what should I do?" Or "Supposing a woman were to be shown in here one day and told me that she and Henry had been secretly married in Constantinople, and that our marriage was bigamous, what should I say to her?" Or "Supposing I'd followed my instincts and become a famous actress." Or "Supposing I had to choose between betraying my country and seeing Henry shot before my eyes?" Do you see what I mean?' She smiled suddenly at Jeremy. 'Or even –' She settled into the armchair. '"Supposing I were to run away with Jeremy, what would happen next?"'

Jeremy went and knelt beside her. 'I feel flattered,' he told her. 'But have you ever really imagined that particular situation?'

'Oh yes,' Clarissa replied with a smile.

'Well? What did happen?' He clasped her hand.

Again she withdrew it. 'Well, the last time I played, we were on the Riviera at Juan les Pins, and Henry came after us. He had a revolver with him.'

Jeremy looked startled. 'My God!' he exclaimed. 'Did he shoot me?'

Clarissa smiled reminiscently. 'I seem to remember,' she told Jeremy, 'that he said –' She paused, and then, adopting a highly dramatic delivery, continued, '"Clarissa, either you come back with me, or I kill myself."'

Jeremy rose and moved away. 'Jolly decent of him,' he said, sounding unconvinced. 'I can't imagine anything more unlike Henry. But, anyway, what did you say to that?'

Clarissa was still smiling complacently. 'Actually, I've played it both ways,' she admitted. 'On one occasion I told Henry that I was terribly sorry. I didn't really want him to kill himself, but I was very deeply in love with Jeremy, and there was nothing I could do about it. Henry flung himself at my feet, sobbing, but I was adamant. "I am fond of you, Henry," I told him, "but I can't live without Jeremy. This is goodbye." Then I rushed out of the house and into the garden where you were waiting for me. As we ran down the garden path to the front gate, we heard a shot ring out in the house, but we went on running.'

'Good heavens!' Jeremy gasped. 'Well, that was certainly telling him, wasn't it? Poor Henry.' He thought for a moment, and then continued, 'But you say you've played it both ways. What happened the other time?'

'Oh, Henry was so miserable, and pleaded so pitifully that I didn't have the heart to leave him. I decided to give you up, and devote my life to making Henry happy.'

Jeremy now looked absolutely desolate. 'Well, darling,' he declared ruefully, 'you certainly do have fun. But please, please be serious for a moment. I'm very serious when I say I love you. I've loved you for a long time. You must have realized that. Are you sure there's no hope for me? Do you really want to spend the rest of your life with boring old Henry?'

Clarissa was spared from answering by the arrival of a thin, tallish child of twelve, wearing school uniform and carrying a satchel. She called out, 'Hello, Clarissa' by way of greeting as she came into the room.

'Hullo, Pippa,' her stepmother replied. 'You're late.'

Pippa put her hat and satchel on an easy chair. 'Music lesson,' she explained, laconically.

'Oh, yes,' Clarissa remembered. 'It's your piano day, isn't it? Was it interesting?'

'No. Ghastly. Awful exercises I had to repeat and repeat. Miss Farrow said it was to improve my fingering. She wouldn't let me play the nice solo piece I'd been practising. Is there any food about? I'm starving.'

Clarissa got to her feet. 'Didn't you get the usual buns to eat in the bus?' she asked.

'Oh yes,' Pippa admitted, 'but that was half an hour ago.' She gave Clarissa a pleading look that was almost comical. 'Can't I have some cake or something to last me till supper?'

Taking her hand, Clarissa led Pippa to the hall door, laughing. 'We'll see what we can find,' she promised. As they left, Pippa asked excitedly, 'Is there any of that cake left – the one with the cherries on top?'

'No,' Clarissa told her. 'You finished that off yesterday.'

Jeremy shook his head, smiling, as he heard their voices trailing away down the hall. As soon as they were out of earshot, he moved quickly to the desk and hurriedly opened one or two of the drawers. But suddenly hearing a hearty female voice calling from the garden, 'Ahoy there!', he gave a start, and hastily closed the drawers. He turned towards the French windows in time to see a big, jolly-looking woman of about forty, in tweeds and gumboots, opening the French windows. She paused as she saw Jeremy. Standing on the window step, she asked, brusquely, 'Mrs Hailsham-Brown about?'

Jeremy moved casually away from the desk, and ambled across to the sofa as he replied, 'Yes, Miss Peake. She's just gone to the kitchen with Pippa to get her something to eat. You know what a ravenous appetite Pippa always has.'

'Children shouldn't eat between meals,' was the response, delivered in ringing, almost masculine tones.

'Will you come in, Miss Peake?' Jeremy asked.

'No, I won't come in because of my boots,' she explained, with a hearty laugh. 'I'd bring half the garden with me if I did.' Again she laughed. 'I was just going to ask her what veggies she wanted for tomorrow's lunch.'

'Well, I'm afraid I –' Jeremy began, when Miss Peake interrupted him. 'Tell you what,' she boomed, 'I'll come back.'

She began to go, but then turned back to Jeremy. 'Oh, you will be careful of that desk, won't you, Mr Warrender?' she said, peremptorily.

'Yes, of course I will,' replied Jeremy.

'It's a valuable antique, you see,' Miss Peake explained. 'You really shouldn't wrench the drawers out like that.'

Jeremy looked bemused. 'I'm terribly sorry,' he apologized. 'I was only looking for notepaper.'

'Middle pigeon-hole,' Miss Peake barked, pointing at it as she spoke.

Jeremy turned to the desk, opened the middle pigeon-hole, and extracted a sheet of writing-paper.

'That's right,' Miss Peake continued brusquely. 'Curious how often people can't see what's right in front of their eyes.' She chortled heartily as she strode away, back to the garden. Jeremy joined in her laughter, but stopped abruptly as soon as she had gone. He was about to return to the desk when Pippa came back munching a bun.

'Hmm. Smashing bun,' said Pippa with her mouth full, as she closed the door behind her and wiped her sticky fingers on her skirt.

'Hello, there,' Jeremy greeted her. 'How was school today?'

'Pretty foul,' Pippa responded cheerfully as she put what was left of the bun on the table. 'It was World Affairs today.' She opened her satchel. 'Miss Wilkinson loves World Affairs. But she's terribly wet. She can't keep the class in order.'

As Pippa took a book out of her satchel, Jeremy asked her, 'What's your favourite subject?'

'Biology,' was Pippa's immediate and enthusiastic answer. 'It's heaven. Yesterday we dissected a frog's leg.' She pushed her book in his face. 'Look what I got at the second-hand book-stall. It's awfully rare, I'm sure. Over a hundred years old.'

'What is it, exactly?'

'It's a kind of recipe book,' Pippa explained. She opened the book. 'It's thrilling, absolutely thrilling.'

'But what's it all about?' Jeremy wanted to know.

Pippa was already enthralled by her book. 'What?' she murmured as she turned its pages.

'It certainly seems very absorbing,' he observed.

'What?' Pippa repeated, still engrossed in the book. To herself she murmured, 'Gosh!' as she turned another page.

'Evidently a good tuppenny-worth,' Jeremy commented, and picked up a newspaper.

Apparently puzzled by what she was reading in the book, Pippa asked him, 'What's the difference between a wax candle and a tallow candle?'

Jeremy considered for a moment before replying. 'I should imagine that a tallow candle is markedly inferior,' he said. 'But surely you can't eat it? What a strange recipe book.'

Much amused, Pippa got to her feet. '"Can you eat it?"' she declaimed. 'Sounds like "Twenty Questions".' She laughed, threw the book onto the easy chair, and fetched a pack of cards from the bookcase. 'Do you know how to play Demon Patience?' she asked.

By now Jeremy was totally occupied with his newspaper. 'Um' was his only response.

Pippa tried again to engage his attention. 'I suppose you wouldn't like to play Beggar-my-neighbour?'

'No,' Jeremy replied firmly. He replaced the newspaper on the stool, then sat at the desk and addressed an envelope.

'No, I thought you probably wouldn't,' Pippa murmured wistfully. Kneeling on the floor in the middle of the room, she spread out her cards and began to play Demon Patience. 'I wish we could have a fine day for a change,' she complained. 'It's such a waste being in the country when it's wet.'

Jeremy looked across at her. 'Do you like living in the country, Pippa?' he asked.

'Rather,' she replied enthusiastically. 'I like it much better than living in London. This is an absolutely wizard house, with a tennis court and everything. We've even got a priest's hole.'

'A priest's hole?' Jeremy queried, smiling. 'In this house?'

'Yes, we have,' said Pippa.

'I don't believe you,' Jeremy told her. 'It's the wrong period.'

'Well, I call it a priest's hole,' she insisted. 'Look, I'll show you.'

She went to the right-hand side of the bookshelves, took out a couple of books, and pulled down a small lever in the wall behind the books. A section of wall to the right of the shelves swung open, revealing itself to be a concealed door. Behind it was a good-sized recess, with another concealed door in its back wall.

'I know it isn't really a priest's hole, of course,' Pippa admitted. 'But it's certainly a secret passage-way. Actually, that door goes through into the library.'

'Oh, does it?' said Jeremy as he went to investigate. He opened the door at the back of the recess, glanced into the library and then closed it and came back into the room. 'So it does.'

'But it's all rather secret, and you'd never guess it was there unless you knew,' Pippa said as she lifted the lever to close the panel. 'I'm using it all the time,' she continued. 'It's the sort of place that would be very convenient for putting a dead body, don't you think?'

Jeremy smiled. 'Absolutely made for it,' he agreed.

Pippa went back to her card game on the floor, as Clarissa came in.

Jeremy looked up. 'The Amazon is looking for you,' he informed her.

'Miss Peake? Oh, what a bore,' Clarissa exclaimed as she picked up Pippa's bun from the table and took a bite.

Pippa immediately got to her feet. 'Hey, that's mine!' she protested.

'Greedy thing,' Clarissa murmured as she handed over what was left of the bun. Pippa put it back on the table and returned to her game.

'First she hailed me as though I were a ship,' Jeremy told Clarissa, 'and then she ticked me off for manhandling this desk.'

'She's a terrible pest,' Clarissa admitted, leaning over one end of the sofa to peer down at Pippa's cards. 'But we're only renting the house, and she goes with it, so –' She broke off to say to Pippa, 'Black ten on the red Jack,' before continuing, '– so we have to keep her on. And in any case she's really a very good gardener.'

'I know,' Jeremy agreed, putting his arm around her. 'I saw her out of my bedroom window this morning. I heard these sounds of exertion, so I stuck my head out of the window, and there was the Amazon, in the garden, digging something that looked like an enormous grave.'

'That's called deep trenching,' Clarissa explained. 'I think you plant cabbages in it, or something.'

Jeremy leaned over to study the card game on the floor. 'Red three on the black four,' he advised Pippa, who responded with a furious glare.

Emerging from the library with Hugo, Sir Rowland gave Jeremy a meaningful look. He tactfully dropped his arm and moved away from Clarissa.

'The weather seems to have cleared at last,' Sir Rowland announced. 'Too late for golf, though. Only about twenty minutes of daylight left.' Looking down at Pippa's card game, he pointed with his foot. 'Look, that goes on there,' he told her. Crossing to the French windows, he failed to notice the fierce glare Pippa shot his way. 'Well,' he said, glancing out at the garden, 'I suppose we might as well go across to the club house now, if we're going to eat there.'

'I'll go and get my coat,' Hugo announced, leaning over Pippa to point out a card as he passed her. Pippa, really furious by now, leaned forward and covered the cards with her body, as Hugo turned back to address Jeremy. 'What about you, my boy?' he asked. 'Coming with us?'

'Yes,' Jeremy answered. 'I'll just go and get my jacket.' He and Hugo went out into the hall together, leaving the door open.

'You're sure you don't mind dining at the club house this evening, darling?' Clarissa asked Sir Rowland.

'Not a bit,' he assured her. 'Very sensible arrangement, since the servants are having the night off.'

The Hailsham-Browns' middle-aged butler, Elgin, came into the room from the hall and went across to Pippa. 'Your supper is ready in the schoolroom, Miss Pippa,' he told her. 'There's some milk, and fruit, and your favourite biscuits.'

'Oh, good!' Pippa shouted, springing to her feet. 'I'm ravenous.'

She darted towards the hall door but was stopped by Clarissa, who told her sharply to pick up her cards first and put them away.

'Oh, bother,' Pippa exclaimed. She went back to the cards, knelt, and slowly began to shovel them into a heap against one end of the sofa.

Elgin now addressed Clarissa. 'Excuse me, madam,' he murmured respectfully.

'Yes, Elgin, what is it?' Clarissa asked.

The butler looked uncomfortable. 'There has been a little – er – unpleasantness, over the vegetables,' he told her.

'Oh, dear,' said Clarissa. 'You mean with Miss Peake?'

'Yes, madam,' the butler continued. 'My wife finds Miss Peake most difficult, madam. She is continually coming into the kitchen and criticizing and making remarks, and my wife doesn't like it, she doesn't like it at all. Wherever we have been, Mrs Elgin and myself have always had very pleasant relations with the garden.'

'I'm really sorry about that,' Clarissa replied, suppressing a smile. 'I'll – er – I'll try to do something about it. I'll speak to Miss Peake.'

'Thank you, madam,' said Elgin. He bowed and left the room, closing the hall door behind him.

'How tiresome they are, servants,' Clarissa observed to Sir Rowland. 'And what curious things they say. How can one have pleasant relations with the garden? It sounds improper, in a pagan kind of way.'

'I think you're lucky, however, with this couple – the Elgins,' Sir Rowland advised her. 'Where did you get them?'

'Oh, the local Registry office,' Clarissa replied.

Sir Rowland frowned. 'I hope not that what's-its-name one where they always send you crooks,' he observed.

'Cooks?' asked Pippa, looking up from the floor where she was still sorting out cards.

'No, dear. Crooks,' Sir Rowland repeated. 'Do you remember,' he continued, now addressing Clarissa, 'that agency with the Italian or Spanish name – de Botello, wasn't it? – who kept sending you people to interview, most of whom turned out to be illegal aliens? Andy Hulme was virtually cleaned out by a couple he and his wife took on. They used Andy's horsebox to move out half the house. And they've never caught up with them yet.'

'Oh, yes,' Clarissa laughed. 'I do remember. Come on, Pippa, hurry up,' she ordered the child.

Pippa picked up the cards, and got to her feet. 'There!' she exclaimed petulantly as she replaced the cards on the bookshelves. 'I wish one didn't always have to do clearing up.' She went towards the door, but was stopped by Clarissa who, picking up what was left of Pippa's bun from the table, called to her, 'Here, take your bun with you,' and handed it to her.

Pippa started to go again. 'And your satchel,' Clarissa continued.

Pippa ran to the easy chair, snatched up her satchel, and turned again towards the hall door.

'Hat!' Clarissa shouted.

Pippa put the bun on the table, picked up her hat, and ran to the hall door.

'Here!' Clarissa called her back again, picked up the piece of bun, stuffed it in Pippa's mouth, took the hat, jammed it on the child's head, and pushed her into the hall. 'And shut the door, Pippa,' she called after her.

Pippa finally made her exit, closing the door behind her. Sir Rowland laughed, and Clarissa, joining in, took a cigarette from a box on the table. Outside, the daylight was now beginning to fade, and the room was becoming a little darker.

'You know, it's wonderful!' Sir Rowland exclaimed. 'Pippa's a different child, now. You've done a remarkably good job there, Clarissa.'

Clarissa sank down on the sofa. 'I think she really likes me now and trusts me,' she said. 'And I quite enjoy being a stepmother.'

Sir Rowland took a lighter from the occasional table by the sofa to light Clarissa's cigarette. 'Well,' he observed, 'she certainly seems a normal, happy child again.'

Clarissa nodded in agreement. 'I think living in the country has made all the difference,' she suggested. 'And she goes to a very nice school and is making lots of friends there. Yes, I think she's happy, and, as you say, normal.'

Sir Rowland frowned. 'It's a shocking thing,' he exclaimed, 'to see a kid get into the state she was in. I'd like to wring Miranda's neck. What a dreadful mother she was.'

'Yes,' Clarissa agreed. 'Pippa was absolutely terrified of her mother.'

He joined her on the sofa. 'It was a shocking business,' he murmured.

Clarissa clenched her fists and made an angry gesture. 'I feel furious every time I think of Miranda,' she said. 'What she made Henry suffer, and what she made that child go through. I still can't understand how any woman could.'

'Taking drugs is a nasty business,' Sir Rowland went on. 'It alters your whole character.'

They sat for a moment in silence, then Clarissa asked, 'What do you think started her on drugs in the first place?'

'I think it was her friend, that swine Oliver Costello,' Sir Rowland declared. 'I believe he's in on the drug racket.'

'He's a horrible man,' Clarissa agreed. 'Really evil, I always think.'

'She's married him now, hasn't she?'

'Yes, they married about a month ago.'

Sir Rowland shook his head. 'Well, there's no doubt Henry's well rid of Miranda,' he said. 'He's a nice fellow, Henry.' He repeated, emphatically, 'A really nice fellow.'

Clarissa smiled, and murmured gently, 'Do you think you need to tell me that?'

'I know he doesn't say much,' Sir Rowland went on. 'He's what you might call undemonstrative – but he's sound all the way through.' He paused, and then added, 'That young fellow, Jeremy. What do you know about him?'

Clarissa smiled again. 'Jeremy? He's very amusing,' she replied.

'Ptscha!' Sir Rowland snorted. 'That's all people seem to care about these days.' He gave Clarissa a serious look, and continued, 'You won't – you won't do anything foolish, will you?'

Clarissa laughed. 'Don't fall in love with Jeremy Warrender,' she answered him. 'That's what you mean, isn't it?'

Sir Rowland still regarded her seriously. 'Yes,' he told her, 'that's precisely what I mean. He's obviously very fond of you. Indeed, he seems unable to keep his hands off you. But you have a very happy marriage with Henry, and I wouldn't want you to do anything to put that in jeopardy.'

Clarissa gave him an affectionate smile. 'Do you really think I would do anything so foolish?' she asked, playfully.

'That would certainly be extremely foolish,' Sir Rowland advised. He paused before continuing, 'You know, Clarissa darling, I've watched you grow up. You really mean a great deal to me. If ever you're in trouble of any kind, you would come to your old guardian, wouldn't you?'

'Of course, Roly darling,' Clarissa replied. She kissed him on the cheek. 'And you needn't worry about Jeremy. Really, you needn't. I know he's very engaging, and attractive and all that. But you know me, I'm only enjoying myself. Just having fun. It's nothing serious.'

Sir Rowland was about to speak again when Miss Peake suddenly appeared at the French windows.

Miss Peake had by now discarded her boots, and was in her stockinged feet. She was carrying a head of broccoli.

'I hope you don't mind my coming in this way, Mrs Hailsham-Brown,' she boomed, as she strode across to the sofa. 'I shan't make the room dirty, I've left my boots outside. I'd just like you to look at this broccoli.' She thrust it belligerently over the back of the sofa and under Clarissa's nose.

'It – er – it looks very nice,' was all Clarissa could think of by way of reply.

Miss Peake pushed the broccoli at Sir Rowland. 'Take a look,' she ordered him.

Sir Rowland did as he was told and pronounced his verdict. 'I can't see anything wrong with it,' he declared. But he took the broccoli from her in order to give it a closer investigation.

'Of course there's nothing wrong with it,' Miss Peake barked at him. 'I took another one just like this into the kitchen yesterday, and that woman in the kitchen –' She broke off to add, by way of parenthesis, 'Of course, I don't want to say anything against your servants, Mrs Hailsham-Brown, though I could say a great deal.' Returning to her main theme, she continued, 'But that Mrs Elgin actually had the nerve to tell me that it was such a poor specimen she wasn't going to cook it. She said something about, "If you can't do better than that in the kitchen garden, you'd better take up some other job." I was so angry I could have killed her.'

Clarissa began to speak, but Miss Peake ploughed on regardless. 'Now you know I never want to make trouble,' she insisted, 'but I'm not going into that kitchen to be insulted.' After a brief pause for breath, she resumed her tirade. 'In future,' she announced, 'I shall dump the vegetables outside the back door, and Mrs Elgin can leave a list there –'

Sir Rowland at this point attempted to hand the broccoli back to her, but Miss Peake ignored him, and continued, 'She can leave a list there of what is required.' She nodded her head emphatically.

Neither Clarissa nor Sir Rowland could think of anything to say in reply, and just as the gardener opened her mouth to speak again the telephone rang. 'I'll answer it,' she bellowed. She crossed to the phone and lifted the receiver. 'Hello – yes,' she barked into the mouthpiece, wiping the top of the table with a corner of her overall as she spoke. 'This is Copplestone Court – You want Mrs Brown? – Yes, she's here.'

Miss Peake held out the receiver, and Clarissa stubbed out her cigarette, went over to the phone, and took the receiver from her.

'Hello,' said Clarissa, 'This is Mrs Hailsham-Brown. – Hello – hello.' She looked at Miss Peake. 'How odd,' she exclaimed. 'They seem to have rung off.'

As Clarissa replaced the receiver, Miss Peake suddenly

darted to the console table and set it back against the wall. 'Excuse me,' she boomed, 'but Mr Sellon always liked this table flat against the wall.'

Clarissa surreptitiously pulled a face at Sir Rowland, but hastened nevertheless to assist Miss Peake with the table. 'Thank you,' said the gardener. 'And,' she added, 'you will be careful about marks made with glasses on the furniture, won't you, Mrs Brown-Hailsham.' Clarissa looked anxiously at the table as the gardener corrected herself. 'I'm sorry – I mean Mrs Hailsham-Brown.' She laughed in a hearty fashion. 'Oh well, Brown-Hailsham, Hailsham-Brown,' she continued. 'It's really all the same thing, isn't it?'

'No, it's not, Miss Peake,' Sir Rowland declared, with very distinct enunciation. 'After all, a horse chestnut is hardly the same thing as a chestnut horse.'

While Miss Peake was laughing jovially at this, Hugo came into the room. 'Hello, there,' she greeted him. 'I'm getting a regular ticking off. Quite sarcastic, they're being.' Going across to Hugo, she thumped him on the back, and then turned to the others. 'Well, good night, all,' she shouted. 'I must be toddling back. Give me the broccoli.'

Sir Rowland handed it over. 'Horse chestnut – chestnut horse,' she boomed at him. 'Jolly good – I must remember that.' With another boisterous laugh she disappeared through the French windows.

Hugo watched her leave, and then turned to Clarissa and Sir Rowland. 'How on earth does Henry bear that woman?' he wondered aloud.

'He does actually find her very hard to take,' Clarissa replied. She picked up Pippa's book from the easy chair, put it on the table and collapsed into the chair as Hugo responded, 'I should think so. She's so damned arch! All that hearty schoolgirl manner.'

'A case of arrested development, I'm afraid,' Sir Rowland added, shaking his head.

Clarissa smiled. 'I agree she's maddening,' she said, 'but she's a very good gardener and, as I keep telling everyone, she goes with the house, and since the house is so wonderfully cheap –'

'Cheap? Is it?' Hugo interrupted her. 'You surprise me.'

'Marvellously cheap,' Clarissa told him. 'It was advertised. We came down and saw it a couple of months ago, and took it then and there for six months, furnished.'

'Whom does it belong to?' Sir Rowland asked.

'It used to belong to a Mr Sellon,' Clarissa replied. 'But he died. He was an antique dealer in Maidstone.'

'Ah, yes!' Hugo exclaimed. 'That's right. Sellon and Brown. I once bought a very nice Chippendale mirror from their shop in Maidstone. Sellon lived out here in the country, and used to go into Maidstone every day, but I believe he sometimes brought customers out here to see things that he kept in the house.'

'Mind you,' Clarissa told them both, 'there are one or two disadvantages about this house. Only yesterday, a man in a violent check suit drove up in a sports car and wanted to buy that desk.' She pointed to the desk. 'I told him that it wasn't ours and therefore we couldn't sell it, but he simply wouldn't believe me and kept on raising the price. He went up to five hundred pounds in the end.'

'Five hundred pounds!' exclaimed Sir Rowland, sounding really startled. He went across to the desk. 'Good Lord!' he continued. 'Why, even at the Antique Dealers' Fair I wouldn't have thought it would fetch anything near to that. It's a pleasant enough object, but surely not especially valuable.'

Hugo joined him at the desk, as Pippa came back into the room. 'I'm still hungry,' she complained.

'You can't be,' Clarissa told her firmly.

'I am,' Pippa insisted. 'Milk and chocolate biscuits and a banana aren't really filling.' She made for the armchair and flung herself into it.

Sir Rowland and Hugo were still contemplating the desk. 'It's certainly a nice desk,' Sir Rowland observed. 'Quite genuine, I imagine, but not what I'd call a collector's piece. Don't you agree, Hugo?'

'Yes, but perhaps it's got a secret drawer with a diamond necklace in it,' Hugo suggested facetiously.

'It has got a secret drawer,' Pippa chimed in.

'What?' Clarissa exclaimed.

'I found a book in the market, all about secret drawers in old furniture,' Pippa explained. 'So I tried looking at desks and things all over the house. But this is the only one that's got a secret drawer.' She got up from the armchair. 'Look,' she invited them. 'I'll show you.'

She went over to the desk and opened one of its pigeon-holes. While Clarissa came and leaned over the sofa to watch, Pippa slid her hand into the pigeon-hole. 'See,' she said as she did so, 'you slide this out, and there's a sort of little catch thing underneath.'

'Humph!' Hugo grunted. 'I don't call that very secret.'

'Ah, but that's not all,' Pippa went on. 'You press this thing underneath – and a little drawer flies out.' Again she demonstrated, and a small drawer shot out of the desk. 'See?'

Hugo took the drawer and picked a small piece of paper

out of it. 'Hello,' he said, 'what's this, I wonder?' He read aloud. '"Sucks to you".'

'What!' Sir Rowland exclaimed, and Pippa went off into a gale of laughter. The others joined in, and Sir Rowland playfully shook Pippa, who pretended to punch him in return as she boasted, 'I put that there!'

'You little villain!' said Sir Rowland, ruffling her hair. 'You're getting as bad as Clarissa with your silly tricks.'

'Actually,' Pippa told them, 'there was an envelope with an autograph of Queen Victoria in it. Look, I'll show you.' She dashed to the bookshelves, while Clarissa went to the desk, replaced the drawers, and closed the pigeon-hole.

At the bookshelves, Pippa opened a small box on one of the lower shelves, took out an old envelope containing three scraps of paper, and displayed them to the assembled company.

'Do you collect autographs, Pippa?' Sir Rowland asked her.

'Not really,' replied Pippa. 'Only as a side-line.' She handed one of the pieces of paper to Hugo, who glanced at it and passed it on to Sir Rowland.

'A girl at school collects stamps, and her brother's got a smashing collection himself,' Pippa told them. 'Last autumn he thought he'd got one like the one he saw in the paper – a Swedish something or other which was worth hundreds of pounds.' As she spoke, she handed the two remaining autographs and the envelope to Hugo, who passed them on to Sir Rowland.

'My friend's brother was awfully excited,' Pippa continued, 'and he took the stamp to a dealer. But the dealer said it wasn't what he thought it was, though it was quite a good stamp. Anyway, he gave him five pounds for it.'

Sir Rowland handed two of the autographs back to Hugo, who passed them on to Pippa. 'Five pounds is pretty good, isn't it?' Pippa asked him, and Hugo grunted his agreement.

Pippa looked down at the autographs. 'How much do you think Queen Victoria's autograph would be worth?' she wondered aloud.

'About five to ten shillings, I should think,' Sir Rowland told her, as he looked at the envelope he was still holding.

'There's John Ruskin's here too, and Robert Browning's,' Pippa told them.

'They're not worth much either, I'm afraid,' said Sir Rowland, handing the remaining autograph and the envelope to Hugo, who passed them on to Pippa, murmuring sympathetically as he did so, 'Sorry, my dear. You're not doing very well, are you?'

'I wish I had Neville Duke's and Roger Bannister's,' Pippa murmured wistfully. 'These historical ones are rather mouldy, I think.' She replaced the envelope and autographs in the box, placed the box back on the shelf, and then began to back towards the hall door. 'Can I see if there are any more chocolate biscuits in the larder, Clarissa?' she asked, hopefully.

'Yes, if you like,' Clarissa told her, smiling.

'We must be off,' said Hugo, following Pippa towards the door and calling up the staircase, 'Jeremy! Hi! Jeremy!'

'Coming,' Jeremy shouted back as he hurried down the stairs carrying a golf club.

'Henry ought to be home soon,' Clarissa murmured, to herself as much as to the others.

Hugo went across to the French windows, calling to Jeremy, 'Better go out this way. It's nearer.' He turned back to Clarissa.

'Goodnight, Clarissa dear,' he said. 'Thank you for putting up with us. I'll probably go straight home from the club, but I promise to send your weekend guests back to you in one piece.'

'Goodnight, Clarissa,' Jeremy joined in, as he followed Hugo out into the garden.

Clarissa waved them goodbye, as Sir Rowland came across and put his arm around her. 'Goodnight, my dear,' he said. 'Warrender and I will probably not be in until about midnight.'

Clarissa accompanied him to the French windows. 'It's really a lovely evening,' she observed. 'I'll come with you as far as the gate onto the golf course.'

They strolled across the garden together, making no attempt to catch up with Hugo and Jeremy. 'What time do you expect Henry home?' Sir Rowland asked.

'Oh, I'm not sure. It varies. Quite soon, I imagine. Anyway, we'll have a quiet evening together and some cold food, and we'll probably have retired to bed by the time you and Jeremy get back.'

'Yes, don't wait up for us, for heaven's sake,' Sir Rowland told her.

They walked on in companionable silence until they reached the garden gate. Then, 'All right, my dear, I'll see you later, or probably at breakfast tomorrow,' said Clarissa.

Sir Rowland gave her an affectionate peck on the cheek, and walked on briskly to catch up with his companions, while Clarissa made her way back to the house. It was a pleasant evening, and she walked slowly, stopping to enjoy the sights and smells of the garden, and allowing her thoughts to wander. She laughed to herself as the image of Miss Peake with her broccoli came into her mind, then found herself smiling when she thought of Jeremy and his clumsy attempt to make love to her. She wondered idly whether he had really been serious about it. As she approached the house, she began to contemplate with pleasure the prospect of a quiet evening at home with her husband.

CHAPTER 5

Clarissa and Sir Rowland had hardly been gone more than a few minutes when Elgin, the butler, entered the room from the hall, carrying a tray of drinks which he placed on a table. When the door bell rang, he went to the front door. A theatrically handsome, dark-haired man was standing outside.

'Good evening, sir,' Elgin greeted him.

'Good evening. I've come to see Mrs Brown,' the man told him, rather brusquely.

'Oh yes, sir, do come in,' said Elgin. Closing the door behind the man, he asked, 'What name, sir?'

'Mr Costello.'

'This way, sir.' Elgin led the way along the hall. He stood aside to allow the newcomer to enter the drawing-room, and then said, 'Would you wait here, sir. Madam is at home. I'll see if I can find her.' He started to go, then stopped and turned back to the man. 'Mr Costello, did you say?'

'That's right,' the stranger replied. 'Oliver Costello.'

'Very good, sir,' murmured Elgin as he left the room, closing the door behind him.

Left alone, Oliver Costello looked around the room, walked

across to listen first at the library door and next at the hall door, and then approached the desk, bent over it, and looked closely at the drawers. Hearing a sound, he quickly moved away from the desk, and was standing in the centre of the room when Clarissa came in through the French windows.

Costello turned. When he saw who it was, he looked amazed.

It was Clarissa who spoke first. Sounding intensely surprised, she gasped, 'You?'

'Clarissa! What are you doing here?' exclaimed Costello. He sounded equally surprised.

'That's a rather silly question, isn't it?' Clarissa replied. 'It's my house.'

'This is your house?' His tone was one of disbelief.

'Don't pretend you don't know,' said Clarissa, sharply.

Costello stared at her without speaking for a moment or two. Then, adopting a complete change of manner, he observed, 'What a charming house this is. It used to belong to old what's-his-name, the antique dealer, didn't it? I remember he brought me out here once to show me some Louis Quinze chairs.' He took a cigarette case from his pocket. 'Cigarette?' he offered.

'No, thank you,' replied Clarissa abruptly. 'And,' she added, 'I think you'd better go. My husband will be home quite soon, and I don't think he'd be very pleased to see you.'

Costello responded with rather insolent amusement, 'But I particularly do want to see him. That's why I've come here, really, to discuss suitable arrangements.'

'Arrangements?' Clarissa asked, her tone one of puzzlement.

'Arrangements for Pippa,' Costello explained. 'Miranda's

quite agreeable to Pippa's spending part of the summer holidays with Henry, and perhaps a week at Christmas. 'But otherwise –'

Clarissa interrupted him sharply. 'What do you mean?' she asked. 'Pippa's home is here.'

Costello wandered casually over to the table with the drinks on it. 'But my dear Clarissa,' he exclaimed, 'you're surely aware that the court gave Miranda the custody of the child?' He picked up a bottle of whisky. 'May I?' he asked, and without waiting for a reply poured a drink for himself. 'The case was undefended, remember?'

Clarissa faced him belligerently. 'Henry allowed Miranda to divorce him,' she declared, speaking clearly and concisely, 'only after it was agreed between them privately that Pippa should live with her father. If Miranda had not agreed to that, Henry would have divorced her.'

Costello gave a laugh which bordered on a sneer. 'You don't know Miranda very well, do you?' he asked. 'She so often changes her mind.'

Clarissa turned away from him. 'I don't believe for one moment,' she said contemptuously, 'that Miranda wants that child or even cares twopence about her.'

'But you're not a mother, my dear Clarissa,' was Costello's impertinent response. 'You don't mind my calling you Clarissa, do you?' he went on, with another unpleasant smile. 'After all, now that I'm married to Miranda, we're practically relations-in-law.'

He swallowed his drink in one gulp and put his glass down. 'Yes, I can assure you,' he continued, 'Miranda is now feeling violently maternal. She feels she must have Pippa to live with us for most of the time.'

'I don't believe it,' Clarissa snapped.

'Please yourself.' Costello made himself comfortable in the armchair. 'But there's no point in your trying to contest it. After all, there was no arrangement in writing, you know.'

'You're not going to have Pippa,' Clarissa told him firmly. 'The child was a nervous wreck when she came to us. She's much better now, and she's happy at school, and that's the way she's going to remain.'

'How will you manage that, my dear?' Costello sneered. 'The law is on our side.'

'What's behind all this?' Clarissa asked him, sounding bewildered. 'You don't care about Pippa. What do you really want?' She paused, and then struck her forehead. 'Oh! What a fool I am. Of course, it's blackmail.'

Costello was about to reply, when Elgin appeared. 'I was looking for you, madam,' the butler told Clarissa. 'Will it be quite all right for Mrs Elgin and myself to leave now for the evening, madam?'

'Yes, quite all right, Elgin,' Clarissa replied.

'The taxi has come for us,' the butler explained. 'Supper is laid all ready in the dining-room.' He was about to go, but then turned back to Clarissa. 'Do you want me to shut up in here, madam?' he asked, keeping an eye on Costello as he spoke.

'No, I'll see to it,' Clarissa assured him. 'You and Mrs Elgin can go off for the evening now.'

'Thank you, madam,' said Elgin. He turned at the hall door to say, 'Goodnight, madam.'

'Goodnight, Elgin,' Clarissa responded.

Costello waited until the butler had closed the door behind him before he spoke again. 'Blackmail is a very ugly word, Clarissa,' he pointed out to her somewhat unoriginally. 'You should take a little more care before you accuse people wrongfully. Now, have I mentioned money at all?'

'Not yet,' replied Clarissa. 'But that's what you mean, isn't it?'

Costello shrugged his shoulders and held his hands out in an expressive gesture. 'It's true that we're not very well off,' he admitted. 'Miranda has always been very extravagant, as you no doubt know. I think she feels that Henry might be able to reinstate her allowance. After all, he's a rich man.'

Clarissa went up to Costello and faced him squarely. 'Now listen,' she ordered him. 'I don't know about Henry, but I do know about myself. You try to get Pippa away from here, and I'll fight you tooth and nail.' She paused, then added, 'And I don't care what weapons I use.'

Apparently unmoved by her outburst, Costello chuckled, but Clarissa continued, 'It shouldn't be difficult to get medical evidence proving Miranda's a drug addict. I'd even go to Scotland Yard and talk to the Narcotic Squad, and I'd suggest that they kept an eye on you as well.'

Costello gave a start at this. 'The upright Henry will hardly care for your methods,' he warned Clarissa.

'Then Henry will have to lump them,' she retorted fiercely. 'It's the child that matters. I'm not going to have Pippa bullied or frightened.'

At this point, Pippa came into the room. Seeing Costello, she stopped short, looking terrified.

'Why, hello, Pippa,' Costello greeted her. 'How you've grown.'

Pippa backed away as he moved towards her. 'I've just come to make some arrangements about you,' he told her. 'Your mother is looking forward to having you with her again. She and I are married now, and –'

'I won't come,' Pippa cried hysterically, running to Clarissa for protection. 'I won't come. Clarissa, they can't make me, can they? They wouldn't –'

'Don't worry, Pippa darling,' Clarissa said soothingly, putting her arm around the child. 'Your home is here with your father and with me, and you're not leaving it.'

'But I assure you –' Costello began, only to be interrupted angrily by Clarissa. 'Get out of here at once,' she ordered him.

Mockingly pretending to be afraid of her, Costello put his hands above his head, and backed away.

'At once!' Clarissa repeated. She advanced upon him. 'I won't have you in my house, do you hear?'

Miss Peake appeared at the French windows, carrying a large garden-fork. 'Oh, Mrs Hailsham-Brown,' she began, 'I –'

'Miss Peake,' Clarissa interrupted her. 'Will you show Mr Costello the way through the garden to the back gate?'

Costello looked at Miss Peake, who lifted her garden-fork as she returned his gaze.

'Miss – Peake?' he queried.

'Pleased to meet you,' she replied, robustly. 'I'm the gardener here.'

'Indeed, yes,' said Costello. 'I came here once before, you may remember, to look at some antique furniture.'

'Oh, yes,' Miss Peake replied. 'In Mr Sellon's time. But you can't see him today, you know. He's dead.'

'No, I didn't come to see him,' Costello declared. 'I came to see – Mrs Brown.' He gave the name a certain emphasis.

'Oh, yes? Is that so? Well, now you've seen her,' Miss Peake told him. She seemed to realize that the visitor had outstayed his welcome.

Costello turned to Clarissa. 'Goodbye, Clarissa,' he said. 'You will hear from me, you know.' He sounded almost menacing.

'This way,' Miss Peake showed him, gesturing to the French windows. She followed him out, asking as they went, 'Do you want the bus, or did you bring your own car?'

'I left my car round by the stables,' Costello informed her as they made their way across the garden.

CHAPTER 6

As soon as Oliver Costello had left with Miss Peake, Pippa burst into tears. 'He'll take me away from here,' she cried, sobbing bitterly as she clung to Clarissa.

'No, he won't,' Clarissa assured her, but Pippa's only response was to shout, 'I hate him. I always hated him.'

Fearing that the girl was on the verge of hysteria, Clarissa addressed her sharply, 'Pippa!'

Pippa backed away from her. 'I don't want to go back to my mother, I'd rather die,' she screamed. 'I'd much rather die. I'll kill him.'

'Pippa!' Clarissa admonished her.

Pippa now seemed completely uncontrollable. 'I'll kill myself,' she cried. 'I'll cut my wrists and bleed to death.'

Clarissa seized her by the shoulders. 'Pippa, control yourself,' she ordered the child. 'It's all right, I tell you. I'm here.'

'But I don't want to go back to Mother, and I hate Oliver,' Pippa exclaimed desperately. 'He's wicked, wicked, wicked.'

'Yes, dear, I know. I know,' Clarissa murmured soothingly.

'But you don't know.' Pippa now sounded even more desperate. 'I didn't tell you everything before – when I came to live here. I just couldn't bear to mention it. But it wasn't only Miranda being so nasty and drunk or something, all the time. One night, when she was out somewhere or other, and Oliver was at home with me – I think he'd been drinking a lot – I don't know – but –' She stopped, and for a moment seemed unable to continue. Then, forcing herself to go on, she looked down at the floor and muttered indistinctly, 'He tried to do things to me.'

Clarissa looked aghast. 'Pippa, what do you mean?' she asked. 'What are you trying to say?'

Pippa looked desperately about her, as though seeking someone else who would say the words for her. 'He – he tried to kiss me, and when I pushed him away, he grabbed me, and started to tear my dress off. Then he –' She stopped suddenly, and burst into a fit of sobbing.

'Oh, my poor darling,' Clarissa murmured, as she hugged the child to her. 'Try not to think about it. It's all over, and nothing like that will ever happen to you again. I'll make sure that Oliver is punished for that. The disgusting beast. He won't get away with it.'

Pippa's mood suddenly changed. Her tone now had a hopeful note, as a new thought apparently came to her. 'Perhaps he'll be struck by lightning,' she wondered aloud.

'Very likely,' Clarissa agreed, 'very likely.' Her face wore a look of grim determination. 'Now pull yourself together, Pippa,' she urged the child. 'Everything's quite all right.' She took a handkerchief from her pocket. 'Here, blow your nose.'

Pippa did as she was told, and then used the handkerchief to wipe her tears off Clarissa's dress.

Clarissa managed to summon up a laugh at this. 'Now, you go upstairs and have your bath,' she ordered, turning Pippa around to face the hall door. 'Mind you have a really good wash – your neck is absolutely filthy.'

Pippa seemed to be returning to normal. 'It always is,' she replied as she went to the door. But, as she was about to leave, she turned suddenly and ran to Clarissa. 'You won't let him take me away, will you?' she pleaded.

'Over my dead body,' Clarissa replied with determination. Then she corrected herself. 'No – over *his* dead body. There! Does that satisfy you?'

Pippa nodded, and Clarissa kissed her forehead. 'Now, run along,' she ordered.

Pippa gave her stepmother a final hug, and left. Clarissa stood for a moment in thought, and then, noticing that the room had become rather dark, switched on the concealed lighting. She went to the French windows and closed them, then sat on the sofa, staring ahead of her, apparently lost in thought.

Only a minute or two had passed when, hearing the front door of the house slam, she looked expectantly towards the hall door through which, a moment later, her husband Henry Hailsham-Brown entered. He was a quite good-looking man of about forty with a rather expressionless face, wearing horn-rimmed spectacles and carrying a brief-case.

'Hello, darling,' Henry greeted his wife, as he switched on the wall-bracket lights and put his briefcase on the armchair.

'Hello, Henry,' Clarissa replied. 'Hasn't it been an absolutely awful day?'

'Has it?' He came across to lean over the back of the sofa and kiss her.

'I hardly know where to begin,' she told him. 'Have a drink first.'

'Not just now,' Henry replied, going to the French windows and closing the curtains. 'Who's in the house?'

Slightly surprised at the question, Clarissa answered, 'Nobody. It's the Elgins' night off. Black Thursday, you know. We'll dine on cold ham, chocolate mousse, and the coffee will be really good because I shall make it.'

A questioning 'Um?' was Henry's only response to this.

Struck by his manner, Clarissa asked, 'Henry, is anything the matter?'

'Well, yes, in a way,' he told her.

'Something wrong?' she queried. 'Is it Miranda?'

'No, no, there's nothing wrong, really,' Henry assured her. 'I should say quite the contrary. Yes, quite the contrary.'

'Darling,' said Clarissa, speaking with affection and only a very faint note of ridicule, 'do I perceive behind that impenetrable Foreign Office façade a certain human excitement?'

Henry wore an air of pleasured anticipation. 'Well,' he admitted, 'it is rather exciting in a way.' He paused, then added, 'As it happens, there's a slight fog in London.'

'Is that very exciting?' Clarissa asked.

'No, no, not the fog, of course.'

'Well?' Clarissa urged him.

Henry looked quickly around, as though to assure himself that he could not be overheard, and then went across to the sofa to sit beside Clarissa. 'You'll have to keep this to yourself,' he impressed upon her, his voice very grave.

'Yes?' Clarissa prompted him, hopefully.

'It's really very secret,' Henry reiterated. 'Nobody's supposed to know. But, actually, you'll have to know.'

'Well, come on, tell me,' she urged him.

Henry looked around again, and then turned to Clarissa. 'It's all very hush-hush,' he insisted. He paused for effect, and then announced, 'The Soviet Premier, Kalendorff, is flying to London for an important conference with the Prime Minister tomorrow.'

Clarissa was unimpressed. 'Yes, I know,' she replied.

Henry looked startled. 'What do you mean, you know?' he demanded.

'I read it in the paper last Sunday,' Clarissa informed him casually.

'I can't think why you want to read these low-class papers,' Henry expostulated. He sounded really put out. 'Anyway,' he continued, 'the papers couldn't possibly know that Kalendorff was coming over. It's top secret.'

'My poor sweet,' Clarissa murmured. Then, in a voice in which compassion was mixed with incredulity, she continued, 'But top secret? Really! The things you high-ups believe.'

Henry rose and began to stride around the room, looking distinctly worried. 'Oh dear, there must have been some leak,' he muttered.

'I should have thought,' Clarissa observed tartly, 'that by now you'd know there always is a leak. In fact I should have thought that you'd all be prepared for it.'

Henry looked somewhat affronted. 'The news was only released officially tonight,' he told her. 'Kalendorff's plane is due at Heathrow at eight-forty, but actually –' He leaned over the sofa and looked doubtfully at his wife. 'Now, Clarissa,' he asked her very solemnly, 'can I really trust you to be discreet?'

'I'm much more discreet than any Sunday newspaper,' Clarissa protested, swinging her feet off the sofa and sitting up.

Henry sat on an arm of the sofa and leaned towards Clarissa conspiratorially. 'The conference will be at Whitehall tomorrow,' he informed her, 'but it would be a great advantage if a conversation could take place first between Sir John himself and Kalendorff. Now, naturally the reporters are all waiting at Heathrow, and the moment the plane arrives Kalendorff's movements are more or less public property.'

He looked around again, as though expecting to find gentlemen of the press peering over his shoulder, and continued, in a tone of increasing excitement, 'Fortunately, this incipient fog has played into our hands.'

'Go on,' Clarissa encouraged him. 'I'm thrilled, so far.'

'At the last moment,' Henry informed her, 'the plane will find it inadvisable to land at Heathrow. It will be diverted, as is usual on these occasions –'

'To Bindley Heath,' Clarissa interrupted him. 'That's just fifteen miles from here. I see.'

'You're always very quick, Clarissa dear,' Henry commented somewhat disapprovingly. 'But yes, I shall go off there now to the aerodrome in the car, meet Kalendorff, and bring him here. The Prime Minister is motoring down here direct from Downing Street. Half an hour will be ample for what they have to discuss, and then Kalendorff will travel up to London with Sir John.'

Henry paused. He got up and took a few paces away, before turning to say to her, disarmingly, 'You know,

Clarissa, this may be of very great value to me in my career. I mean, they're reposing a lot of trust in me, having this meeting here.'

'So they should,' Clarissa replied firmly, going to her husband and flinging her arms around him. 'Henry, darling,' she exclaimed, 'I think it's all wonderful.'

'By the way,' Henry informed her solemnly, 'Kalendorff will be referred to only as Mr Jones.'

'Mr Jones?' Clarissa attempted, not altogether successfully, to keep a note of amused incredulity out of her voice.

'That's right,' Henry explained, 'one can't be too careful about using real names.'

'Yes – but – Mr Jones?' Clarissa queried. 'Couldn't they have thought of something better than that?' She shook her head doubtfully, and continued, 'Incidentally, what about me? Do I retire to the harem, as it were, or do I bring in the drinks, utter greetings to them both and then discreetly fade away?'

Henry regarded his wife somewhat uneasily as he admonished her, 'You must take this seriously, dear.'

'But Henry, darling,' Clarissa insisted, 'can't I take it seriously and still enjoy it a little?'

Henry gave her question a moment's consideration, before replying, gravely, 'I think it would be better, perhaps, Clarissa, if you didn't appear.'

Clarissa seemed not to mind this. 'All right,' she agreed, 'but what about food? Will they want something?'

'Oh no,' said Henry. 'There need be no question of a meal.'

'A few sandwiches, I think,' Clarissa suggested. She sat on an arm of the sofa, and continued, 'Ham sandwiches would be best. In a napkin to keep them moist. And hot coffee, in a Thermos jug. Yes, that'll do very well. The chocolate mousse I shall take up to my bedroom to console me for being excluded from the conference.'

'Now, Clarissa –' Henry began, disapprovingly, only to be interrupted by his wife as she rose and flung her arms around his neck. 'Darling, I am being serious, really,' she assured him. 'Nothing will go wrong. I shan't let it.' She kissed him affectionately.

Henry gently disentangled himself from her embrace. 'What about old Roly?' he asked.

'He and Jeremy are dining at the club house with Hugo,' Clarissa told him. 'They're going to play bridge afterwards, so Roly and Jeremy won't be back here until about midnight.'

'And the Elgins are out?' Hugo asked her.

'Darling, you know they always go to the cinema on Thursdays,' Clarissa reminded him. 'They won't be back until well after eleven.'

Henry looked pleased. 'Good,' he exclaimed. 'That's all quite satisfactory. Sir John and Mr – er –'

'Jones,' Clarissa prompted him.

'Quite right, darling. Mr Jones and the Prime Minister will have left long before then.' Henry consulted his watch. 'Well, I'd better have a quick shower before I start off for Bindley Heath,' he announced.

'And I'd better go and make the ham sandwiches,' Clarissa said, dashing out of the room.

Picking up his briefcase, Henry called after her, 'You must remember about the lights, Clarissa.' He went to the door and switched off the concealed lighting. 'We're making our own electricity here, and it costs money.' He switched off the wall-brackets as well. 'It's not like London, you know.'

After a final glance around the room, which was now in darkness except for a faint glow of light from the hall door, Henry nodded and left, closing the door behind him.

At the golf club, Hugo was busily complaining about Clarissa's behaviour in making them test the port. 'Really, she ought to stop playing these games, you know,' he said as they made their way to the bar. 'Do you remember, Roly, the time I received that telegram from Whitehall telling me that I was going to be offered a knighthood in the next Honours List? It was only when I mentioned it in confidence to Henry one evening when I was dining with them both, and Henry was perplexed but Clarissa started giggling – it was only then that I discovered she'd sent the bloody thing. She can be so childish sometimes.'

Sir Rowland chuckled. 'Yes, she can indeed. And she loves play-acting. You know, she was actually a damned good actress in her school's drama club. At one time I thought she'd take it up seriously and go on the stage professionally. She's so convincing, even when she's telling the most dreadful lies. And that's what actors are, surely. Convincing liars.'

He was lost in reminiscence for a moment, and then continued, 'Clarissa's best friend at school was a girl called Jeanette Collins, whose father had been a famous footballer.

And Jeanette herself was a mad football fan. Well, one day Clarissa rang Jeanette in an assumed voice, claiming to be the public relations officer for some football team or other, and told her that she'd been chosen to be the team's new mascot, but that it all depended on her dressing in a funny costume as a rabbit, and standing outside the Chelsea Stadium that afternoon as the customers were queuing up to get in. Somehow Jeanette managed to hire a costume in time, and got to the stadium dressed as a bunny rabbit, where she was laughed at by hundreds of people and photographed by Clarissa who was waiting there for her. Jeanette was furious. I don't think the friendship survived.'

'Oh, well,' Hugo growled resignedly, as he picked up a menu and began to devote his attention to the serious business of choosing what they would eat later.

Meanwhile, back in the Hailsham-Browns' drawing-room, only minutes after Henry had gone off to have his shower, Oliver Costello entered the empty room stealthily through the French windows, leaving the curtains open so that moonlight streamed in. He shone a torch carefully around the room, then went to the desk and switched on the lamp that was on it. After lifting the flap of the secret drawer, he suddenly switched off the lamp and stood motionless for a moment as though he had heard something. Apparently reassured, he switched the desk lamp on again, and opened the secret drawer.

Behind Costello, the panel beside the bookshelf slowly and quietly opened. He shut the secret drawer in the desk, switched the lamp off again, and then turned sharply as he was struck a fierce blow on the head by someone standing at the recess. Costello collapsed immediately, falling behind the sofa, and the panel closed again, this time more quickly.

The room remained in darkness for a moment, until Henry Hailsham-Brown entered from the hall, switched on the wall-brackets, and shouted 'Clarissa!' Putting his spectacles on, he filled his cigarette-case from the box on a table near the sofa as Clarissa came in, calling, 'Here I am, darling. Do you want a sandwich before you go?'

'No, I think I'd better start,' Henry replied, patting his jacket nervously.

'But you'll be hours too early,' Clarissa told him. 'It can't take you more than twenty minutes to drive there.'

Henry shook his head. 'One never knows,' he declared. 'I might have a puncture, or something might go wrong with the car.'

'Don't fuss, darling,' Clarissa admonished him, straightening his tie as she spoke. 'It's all going to go very smoothly.'

'Now, what about Pippa?' Henry asked, anxiously. 'You're sure she won't come down or barge in while Sir John and Kalen – I mean, Mr Jones, are talking privately?'

'No, there's no danger of that,' Clarissa assured him. 'I'll go up to her room and we'll have a feast together. We'll toast tomorrow's breakfast sausages and share the chocolate mousse between us.'

Henry smiled affectionately at his wife. 'You're very good to Pippa, my dear,' he told her. 'It's one of the things I'm most grateful to you for.' He paused, embarrassed, then went on. 'I can never express myself very well – I – you know – so much misery – and now, everything's so different. You –' Taking Clarissa in his arms, he kissed her.

For some moments they remained locked in a loving embrace. Then Clarissa gently broke away, but continued to hold his hands. 'You've made me very happy, Henry,' she told him. 'And Pippa is going to be fine. She's a lovely child.'

Henry smiled affectionately at her. 'Now, you go and meet your Mr Jones,' she ordered him, pushing him towards the hall door. 'Mr Jones,' she repeated. 'I still think that's a ridiculous name to have chosen.'

Henry was about to leave the room when Clarissa asked him, 'Are you going to come in by the front door? Shall I leave it unlatched?'

He paused in the doorway to consider. Then, 'No,' he said. 'I think we'll come in through the French windows.'

'You'd better put on your overcoat, Henry. It's quite chilly,' Clarissa advised, pushing him into the hall as she spoke. 'And perhaps your muffler as well.' He took his coat obediently from a rack in the hall, and she followed him to the front door with a final word of advice. 'Drive carefully, darling, won't you?'

'Yes, yes,' Henry called back. 'You know I always do.'

Clarissa shut the door behind him, and went off to the kitchen to finish making the sandwiches. As she put them on a plate, wrapping a damp napkin around it to keep them fresh, she could not help thinking of her recent unnerving encounter with Oliver Costello. She was frowning as she carried the sandwiches back to the drawing-room, where she put them on the small table.

Suddenly fearful of incurring Miss Peake's wrath for having marked the table, she snatched the plate up again, rubbed unsuccessfully at the mark it had made, and compromised by covering it with a nearby vase of flowers. She transferred the plate of sandwiches to the stool, then carefully shook the cushions on the sofa. Singing quietly to herself, she picked up Pippa's book and took it across to replace it on the bookshelves.

'Can a body meet a body, coming through the –' She suddenly stopped singing and uttered a scream as she stumbled and nearly fell over Oliver Costello.

Bending over the body, Clarissa recognized who it was. 'Oliver!' she gasped. She stared at him in horror for what seemed an age. Then, convinced that he was dead, she straightened up quickly and ran towards the door to call Henry, but immediately realized that he had gone. She turned back to the body, and then ran to the telephone, and lifted the receiver. She began to dial, but then stopped and replaced the receiver again. She stood thinking for a moment, and looked at the panel in the wall. Making up her mind quickly, she glanced at the panel again, and then reluctantly bent down and began to drag the body across to it.

While she was engaged in doing this, the panel slowly opened and Pippa emerged from the recess, wearing a dressing-gown over her pyjamas. 'Clarissa!' she wailed, rushing to her stepmother.

Trying to stand between her and the body of Costello, Clarissa gave Pippa a little shove, in an attempt to turn her away. 'Pippa,' she begged, 'don't look, darling. Don't look.'

In a strangled voice, Pippa cried, 'I didn't mean to. Oh, really, I didn't mean to do it.'

Horrified, Clarissa seized the child by her arms. 'Pippa! Was it – you?' she gasped.

'He's dead, isn't he? He's quite dead?' Pippa asked. Sobbing hysterically, she cried, 'I didn't – mean to kill him. I didn't mean to.'

'Quiet now, quiet,' Clarissa murmured soothingly. 'It's all right. Come on, sit down.' She led Pippa to the armchair and sat her in it.

'I didn't mean to. I didn't mean to kill him,' Pippa went on crying.

Clarissa knelt beside her. 'Of course you didn't mean to,' she agreed. 'Now listen, Pippa –'

When Pippa continued to cry even more hysterically, Clarissa shouted at her. 'Pippa, listen to me. Everything's going to be all right. You've got to forget about this. Forget all about it, do you hear?'

'Yes,' Pippa sobbed, 'but – but I –'

'Pippa,' Clarissa continued more forcefully, 'you must trust me and believe what I'm telling you. Everything is going to be all right. But you've got to be brave and do exactly what I tell you.'

Still sobbing hysterically, Pippa tried to turn away from her.

'Pippa!' Clarissa shouted. 'Will you do as I tell you?' She pulled the child around to face her. 'Will you?'

'Yes, yes, I will,' Pippa cried, putting her head on Clarissa's bosom.

'That's right.' Clarissa adopted a consoling tone as she helped Pippa out of the chair. 'Now, I want you to go upstairs and get into bed.'

'You come with me, please,' the child pleaded.

'Yes, yes,' Clarissa assured her, 'I'll come up very soon, as soon as I can, and I'll give you a nice little white tablet. Then you'll go to sleep, and in the morning everything will seem quite different.' She looked down at the body, and added, 'There may be nothing to worry about.'

'But he is dead – isn't he?' Pippa asked.

'No, no, he may not be dead,' Clarissa replied evasively. 'I'll see. Now go on, Pippa. Do as I tell you.'

Pippa, still sobbing, left the room and ran upstairs. Clarissa watched her go, and then turned back to the body on the floor. 'Supposing I were to find a dead body in the drawing-room, what should I do?' she murmured to herself. After standing for a moment in thought, she exclaimed more emphatically, 'Oh, my God, what *am* I going to do?'

CHAPTER 8

Fifteen minutes later, Clarissa was still in the drawing-room and murmuring to herself. But she had been busy in the meantime. All the lights were now on, the panel in the wall was closed, and the curtains had been drawn across the open French windows. Oliver Costello's body was still behind the sofa, but Clarissa had been moving the furniture about, and had set up a folding bridge-table in the centre of the room, with cards and markers for bridge, and four upright chairs around the table.

Standing at the table, Clarissa scribbled figures on one of the markers. 'Three spades, four hearts, four no trumps, pass,' she muttered, pointing at each hand as she made its call. 'Five diamonds, pass, six spades – double – and I think they go down.' She paused for a moment, looking down at the table, and then continued, 'Let me see, doubled vulnerable, two tricks, five hundred – or shall I let them make it? No.'

She was interrupted by the arrival of Sir Rowland, Hugo, and young Jeremy, who entered through the French windows. Hugo paused a moment before coming into the room, to close one half of the windows.

Putting her pad and pencil on the bridge table, Clarissa rushed to meet them. 'Thank God you've come,' she told Sir Rowland, sounding extremely distraught.

'What is all this, my dear?' Sir Rowland asked her, with concern in his voice.

Clarissa turned to address them all. 'Darlings,' she cried, 'you've got to help me.'

Jeremy noticed the table with the playing cards spread out on it. 'Looks like a bridge party,' he observed gaily.

'You're being very melodramatic, Clarissa,' Hugo contributed. 'What are you up to, young woman?'

Clarissa clutched Sir Rowland. 'It's serious,' she insisted. 'Terribly serious. You will help me, won't you?'

'Of course we'll help you, Clarissa,' Sir Rowland assured her, 'but what's it all about?'

'Yes, come on, what is it this time?' Hugo asked, somewhat wearily.

Jeremy, too, sounded unimpressed. 'You're up to something, Clarissa,' he insisted. 'What is it? Found a body or something?'

'That's just it,' Clarissa told him. 'I have – found a body.'

'What do you mean – found a body?' Hugo asked. He sounded puzzled, but not all that interested.

'It's just as Jeremy said,' Clarissa answered him. 'I came in here, and I found a body.'

Hugo gave a cursory glance around the room. 'I don't know what you're talking about,' he complained. 'What body? Where?'

'I'm not playing games. I'm serious,' Clarissa shouted angrily. 'It's there. Go and look. Behind the sofa.' She pushed Sir Rowland towards the sofa, and moved away.

Hugo went quickly to the sofa. Jeremy followed him, and leaned over the back of it. 'My God, she's right,' Jeremy murmured.

Sir Rowland joined them. He and Hugo bent down to examine the body. 'Why, it's Oliver Costello,' Sir Rowland exclaimed.

'God almighty!' Jeremy went quickly to the French windows and drew the curtains.

'Yes,' said Clarissa. 'It's Oliver Costello.'

'What was he doing here?' Sir Rowland asked her.

'He came this evening to talk about Pippa,' Clarissa replied. 'It was just after you'd gone to the club.'

Sir Rowland looked puzzled. 'What did he want with Pippa?'

'He and Miranda were threatening to take her away,' Clarissa told him. 'But all that doesn't matter now. I'll tell you about it later. We have to hurry. We've got very little time.'

Sir Rowland held up a hand in warning. 'Just a moment,' he instructed, coming closer to Clarissa. 'We must have the facts clear. What happened when he arrived?'

Clarissa shook her head impatiently. 'I told him that he and Miranda were not going to get Pippa, and he went away.'

'But he came back?'

'Obviously,' said Clarissa.

'How?' Sir Rowland asked her. 'When?'

'I don't know,' Clarissa answered. 'I just came into the room, as I said, and I found him – like that.' She gestured towards the sofa.

'I see,' said Sir Rowland, moving back to the body on the floor and leaning over it. 'I see. Well, he's dead all right. He's been hit over the head with something heavy and sharp.' He looked around at the others. 'I'm afraid this isn't going to be a very pleasant business,' he continued, 'but there's only one thing to be done.' He went across to the telephone as he spoke. 'We must ring up the police and –'

'No,' Clarissa exclaimed sharply.

Sir Rowland was already lifting the receiver. 'You ought to have done it at once, Clarissa,' he advised her. 'Still, I don't suppose they'll blame you much for that.'

'No, Roly, stop,' Clarissa insisted. She ran across the room, took the receiver from him, and replaced it on its rest.

'My dear child –' Sir Rowland expostulated, but Clarissa would not let him continue. 'I could have rung up the police myself if I'd wanted to,' she admitted. 'I knew perfectly well that it was the proper thing to do. I even started dialling. Then, instead, I rang you up at the club and asked you to come back here immediately, all three of you.' She turned to Jeremy and Hugo. 'You haven't even asked me why, yet.'

'You can leave it all to us,' Sir Rowland assured her. 'We will –'

Clarissa interrupted him vehemently. 'You haven't begun to understand,' she insisted. 'I want you to help me. You said you would if I was ever in trouble.' She turned to include the other two men. 'Darlings, you've got to help me.'

Jeremy moved to position himself so that he hid the body from her sight. 'What do you want us to do, Clarissa?' he asked gently.

'Get rid of the body,' was her abrupt reply.

'My dear, don't talk nonsense,' Sir Rowland ordered her. 'This is murder.'

'That's the whole point,' Clarissa told him. 'The body mustn't be found in this house.'

Hugo gave a snort of impatience. 'You don't know what

you're talking about, my dear girl,' he exclaimed. 'You've been reading too many murder mysteries. In real life you can't go monkeying about, moving dead bodies.'

'But I've already moved it,' Clarissa explained. 'I turned it over to see if he was dead, and then I started dragging it into that recess, and then I realized I was going to need help, and so I rang you up at the club, and while I was waiting for you I made a plan.'

'Including the bridge table, I assume,' Jeremy observed, gesturing towards the table.

Clarissa picked up the bridge marker. 'Yes,' she replied. 'That's going to be our alibi.'

'What on earth –' Hugo began, but Clarissa gave him no chance to continue. 'Two and a half rubbers,' she announced. 'I've imagined all the hands, and put down the scores on this marker. You three must fill up the others in your own handwriting, of course.'

Sir Rowland stared at her in amazement. 'You're mad, Clarissa. Quite mad,' he declared.

Clarissa paid no attention to him. 'I've worked it out beautifully,' she went on. 'The body has to be taken away from here.' She looked at Jeremy. 'It will take two of you to do that,' she instructed him. 'A dead body is very difficult to manage – I've found that out already.'

'Where the hell do you expect us to take it to?' Hugo asked in exasperation.

Clarissa had already given this some thought. 'The best place, I think, would be Marsden Wood,' she advised. 'That's only two miles from here.' She gestured away to the left. 'You turn off into that side road, just a few yards after you've passed the front gate. It's a narrow road, and there's hardly ever any traffic on it.' She turned to Sir Rowland. 'Just leave the car by the side of the road when you get into the wood,' she instructed him. 'Then you walk back here.'

Jeremy looked perplexed. 'Do you mean you want us to dump the body in the wood?' he asked.

'No, you leave it in the car,' Clarissa explained. 'It's his car, don't you see? He left it here, round by the stables.'

All three men now wore puzzled expressions. 'It's really all quite easy,' Clarissa assured them. 'If anybody does happen to see you walking back, it's quite a dark night and they won't know who you are. And you've got an alibi. All four of us have been playing bridge here.' She replaced the marker on the bridge table, looking almost pleased with herself, while the men, stupefied, stared at her.

Hugo walked about in a complete circle. 'I – I –' he spluttered, waving his hands in the air.

Clarissa went on issuing her instructions. 'You wear gloves, of course,' she told them, 'so as not to leave fingerprints on anything. I've got them here all ready for you.' Pushing past Jeremy to the sofa, she took three pairs of gloves from under one of the cushions, and laid them out on an arm of the sofa.

Sir Rowland continued to stare at Clarissa. 'Your natural talent for crime leaves me speechless,' he informed her.

Jeremy gazed at her admiringly. 'She's got it all worked out, hasn't she?' he declared.

'Yes,' Hugo admitted, 'but it's all damned foolish nonsense just the same.'

'Now, you must hurry,' Clarissa ordered them vehemently. 'At nine o'clock Henry and Mr Jones will be here.'

'Mr Jones? Who on earth is Mr Jones?' Sir Rowland asked her.

Clarissa put a hand to her head. 'Oh dear,' she exclaimed, 'I never realized what a terrible lot of explaining one has to do in a murder. I thought I'd simply ask you to help me and you would, and that is all there'd be to it.' She looked around at all three of them. 'Oh, darlings, you must.' She stroked Hugo's hair. 'Darling, darling Hugo –'

'This play-acting is all very well, my dear,' said Hugo, sounding distinctly annoyed, 'but a dead body is a nasty, serious business, and monkeying about with it could land you in a real mess. You can't go carting bodies about at dead of night.'

Clarissa went to Jeremy and placed her hand on his arm. 'Jeremy, darling, you'll help me, surely. Won't you?' she asked, with urgent appeal in her voice.

Jeremy gazed at her adoringly. 'All right, I'm game,' he replied cheerfully. 'What's a dead body or two among friends?'

'Stop, young man,' Sir Rowland ordered. 'I'm not going to allow this.' He turned to Clarissa. 'Now, you must be guided by me, Clarissa. I insist. After all, there's Henry to consider, too.'

Clarissa gave him a look of exasperation. 'But it's Henry I *am* considering,' she declared.

....

The three men greeted Clarissa's announcement in silence. Sir Rowland shook his head gravely, Hugo continued to look puzzled, while Jeremy simply shrugged his shoulders as though giving up all hope of understanding the situation.

Taking a deep breath, Clarissa addressed all three of them. 'Something terribly important is happening tonight,' she told them. 'Henry's gone to – to meet someone and bring him back here. It's very important and secret. A top political secret. No one is supposed to know about it. There was to be absolutely no publicity.'

'Henry's gone to meet a Mr Jones?' Sir Rowland queried, dubiously.

'It's a silly name, I agree,' said Clarissa, 'but that's what they're calling him. I can't tell you his real name. I can't tell you any more about it. I promised Henry I wouldn't say a word to anybody, but I have to make you see that I'm not just –' she turned to look at Hugo as she continued, '– not just being an idiot and play-acting as Hugo called it.'

She turned back to Sir Rowland. 'What sort of effect do you think it will have on Henry's career,' she asked him, 'if he has to walk in here with this distinguished person – and another very distinguished person travelling down from London for this meeting – only to find the police investigating a murder – the murder of a man who has just married Henry's former wife?'

'Good Lord!' Sir Rowland exclaimed. Then, looking Clarissa straight in the eye, he added, suspiciously, 'You're not making all this up now, are you? This isn't just another of your complicated games, intended to make fools of us all?'

Clarissa shook her head mournfully. 'Nobody ever believes me when I'm speaking the truth,' she protested.

'Sorry, my dear,' said Sir Rowland. 'Yes, I can see it's a more difficult problem than I thought.'

'You see?' Clarissa urged him. 'So it's absolutely vital that we get the body away from here.'

'Where's his car, did you say?' Jeremy asked.

'Round by the stables.'

'And the servants are out, I gather?'

Clarissa nodded. 'Yes.'

Jeremy picked up a pair of gloves from the sofa. 'Right,' he exclaimed decisively. 'Do I take the body to the car, or bring the car to the body?'

Sir Rowland held out a hand in a restraining gesture. 'Wait a moment,' he advised. 'We mustn't rush it like this.'

Jeremy put the gloves down again, but Clarissa turned to Sir Rowland, crying desperately, 'But we must hurry.'

Sir Rowland regarded her gravely. 'I'm not sure that this plan of yours is the best one, Clarissa,' he declared. 'Now, if we could just delay finding the body until tomorrow morning – that would meet the case, I think, and it would be very much simpler. If, for now, we merely moved the body to another room, for instance, I think that might be just excusable.'

Clarissa turned to address him directly. 'It's you I've got to convince, isn't it?' she told him. Looking at Jeremy, she continued, 'Jeremy's ready enough.' She glanced at Hugo. 'And Hugo will grunt and shake his head, but he'd do it all the same. It's you . . .'

She went to the library door and opened it. 'Will you both excuse us for a short time?' she asked Jeremy and Hugo. 'I want to speak to Roly alone.'

'Don't you let her talk you into any tomfoolery, Roly,' Hugo warned as they left the room. Jeremy gave Clarissa a reassuring smile and a murmured 'Good luck!'

Sir Rowland, looking grave, took a seat at the library table.

'Now!' Clarissa exclaimed, as she sat and faced him on the other side of the table.

'My dear,' Sir Rowland warned her, 'I love you, and I will always love you dearly. But, before you ask, in this case the answer simply has to be no.'

Clarissa began to speak seriously and with emphasis. 'That man's body mustn't be found in this house,' she insisted. 'If he's found in Marsden Wood, I can say that he was here today for a short time, and I can also tell the police exactly when he left. Actually, Miss Peake saw him off, which turns out to be very fortunate. There need be no question of his ever having come back here.'

She took a deep breath. 'But if his body is found here,' she continued, 'then we shall all be questioned.' She paused before adding, with great deliberation, 'And Pippa won't be able to stand it.'

'Pippa?' Sir Rowland was obviously puzzled.

Clarissa's face was grim. 'Yes, Pippa. She'll break down and confess that she did it.'

'Pippa!' Sir Rowland repeated, as he slowly took in what he was hearing.

Clarissa nodded.

'My God!' Sir Rowland exclaimed.

'She was terrified when he came here today,' Clarissa told him. 'I tried to reassure her that I wouldn't let him take her away, but I don't think she believed me. You know what she's been through – the nervous breakdown she's had? Well, I don't think she could have survived being made to go back and live with Oliver and Miranda. Pippa was here when I found Oliver's body. She told me she never meant to do it, I'm sure she was telling the truth. It was sheer panic. She got hold of that stick, and struck out blindly.'

'What stick?' Sir Rowland asked.

'The one from the hall stand. It's in the recess. I left it there, I didn't touch it.'

Sir Rowland thought for a moment, and then asked sharply, 'Where is Pippa now?'

'In bed,' said Clarissa. 'I've given her a sleeping pill. She ought not to wake up till morning. Tomorrow I'll take her up to London, and my old nanny will look after her for a while.'

Sir Rowland got up and walked over to look down at Oliver Costello's body behind the sofa. Returning to Clarissa, he kissed her. 'You win, my dear,' he said. 'I apologize. That child musn't be asked to face the music. Get the others back.'

He went across to the window and closed it, while Clarissa opened the library door, calling, 'Hugo, Jeremy. Would you come back, please?'

The two men came back into the room. 'That butler of yours doesn't lock up very carefully,' Hugo announced. 'The window in the library was open. I've shut it now.'

Addressing Sir Rowland, he asked abruptly, 'Well?'

'I'm converted,' was the equally terse reply.

'Well done,' was Jeremy's comment.

'There's no time to lose,' Sir Rowland declared. 'Now, those gloves.' He picked up a pair and put them on. Jeremy picked up the others, handed one pair to Hugo, and they both put them on. Sir Rowland went over to the panel. 'How does this thing open?' he asked.

Jeremy went across to join him. 'Like this, sir,' he said. 'Pippa showed me.' He moved the lever and opened the panel.

Sir Rowland looked into the recess, reached in, and brought out the walking stick. 'Yes, it's heavy enough,' he commented. 'Weighted in the head. All the same, I shouldn't have thought –' He paused.

'What wouldn't you have thought?' Hugo wanted to know.

Sir Rowland shook his head. 'I should have thought,' he replied, 'that it would have to have been something with a sharper edge – metal of some kind.'

'You mean a goddam chopper,' Hugo observed bluntly.

'I don't know,' Jeremy interjected. 'That stick looks pretty murderous to me. You could easily crack a man's head open with that.'

'Evidently,' said Sir Rowland, drily. He turned to Hugo, and handed him the stick. 'Hugo, will you burn this in the kitchen stove, please,' he instructed. 'Warrender, you and I will get the body to the car.'

He and Jeremy bent down on either side of the body. As

they did so, a bell suddenly rang. 'What's that?' Sir Rowland exclaimed, startled.

'It's the front doorbell,' said Clarissa, sounding bewildered. They all stood petrified for a moment. 'Who can it be?' Clarissa wondered aloud. 'It's much too early for Henry and – er – Mr Jones. It must be Sir John.'

'Sir John?' asked Sir Rowland, now sounding even more startled. 'You mean the Prime Minister is expected here this evening?'

'Yes,' Clarissa replied.

'Hm.' Sir Rowland looked momentarily undecided. Then, 'Yes,' he murmured. 'Well, we've got to do something.' The bell rang again, and he stirred into action. 'Clarissa,' he ordered, 'go and answer the door. Use whatever delaying tactics you can think of. In the meantime, we'll clear up in here.'

Clarissa went quickly out to the hall, and Sir Rowland turned to Hugo and Jeremy. 'Now then,' he explained urgently, 'this is what we do. We'll get him into that recess. Later, when everyone's in this room having their pow-wow, we can take him out through the library.'

'Good idea,' Jeremy agreed, as he helped Sir Rowland lift the body.

'Want me to give you a hand?' asked Hugo.

'No, it's all right,' Jeremy replied. He and Sir Rowland supported Costello's body under the armpits and carried it into the recess, while Hugo picked up the torch. A moment or two later, Sir Rowland emerged and pressed the lever as Jeremy hastened out behind him. Hugo quickly slipped under Jeremy's arm into the recess with the torch and stick. The panel then closed.

Sir Rowland, after examining his jacket for signs of blood, murmured, 'Gloves,' removed the gloves he was wearing, and put them under a cushion on the sofa. Jeremy removed his gloves and did likewise. Then, 'Bridge,' Sir Rowland reminded himself, as he hastened to the bridge table and sat.

Jeremy followed him and picked up his cards. 'Come along, Hugo, make haste,' Sir Rowland urged as he picked up his own cards.

He was answered by a knock from inside the recess. Suddenly realizing that Hugo was not in the room, Sir Rowland and Jeremy looked at each other in alarm. Jeremy got up, rushed to the switch and opened the panel. 'Come along, Hugo,' Sir Rowland repeated urgently, as Hugo emerged. 'Quickly, Hugo,' Jeremy muttered impatiently, closing the panel again.

Sir Rowland took Hugo's gloves from him, and put them under the cushion. The three men took their seats quickly at the bridge table and picked up their cards, just as Clarissa came back into the room from the hall, followed by two men in uniform.

In a tone of innocent surprise, Clarissa announced, 'It's the police, Uncle Roly.'

The older of the two police officers, a stocky, grey-haired man, followed Clarissa into the room, while his colleague remained standing by the hall door. 'This is Inspector Lord,' Clarissa declared. 'And –' she turned back to the younger officer, a dark-haired man in his twenties with the build of a footballer. 'I'm sorry, what did you say your name was?' she asked.

The Inspector answered for him. 'That's Constable Jones,' he announced. Addressing the three men, he continued, 'I'm sorry to intrude, gentlemen, but we have received information that a murder has been committed here.'

Clarissa and her friends all spoke simultaneously. 'What?' Hugo shouted. 'A murder!' Jeremy exclaimed. 'Good heavens,' Sir Rowland cried, as Clarissa said, 'Isn't it extraordinary?' They all sounded completely astonished.

'Yes, we had a telephone call at the station,' the Inspector told them. Nodding to Hugo, he added, 'Good evening, Mr Birch.'

'Er – good evening, Inspector,' Hugo mumbled.

'It looks as though somebody's been hoaxing you, Inspector,' Sir Rowland suggested.

'Yes,' Clarissa agreed. 'We've been playing bridge here all evening.'

The others nodded in support, and Clarissa asked, 'Who did they say had been murdered?'

'No names were mentioned,' the Inspector informed them. 'The caller just said that a man had been murdered at Copplestone Court, and would we come along immediately. They rang off before any additional information could be obtained.'

'It must have been a hoax,' Clarissa declared, adding virtuously, 'What a wicked thing to do.'

Hugo tut-tutted, and the Inspector replied, 'You'd be surprised, madam, at the potty things people do.'

He paused, glancing at each of them in turn, and then continued, addressing Clarissa. 'Well now, according to you, nothing out of the ordinary has happened here this evening?' Without waiting for an answer, he added, 'Perhaps I'd better see Mr Hailsham-Brown as well.'

'He's not here,' Clarissa told the Inspector. 'I don't expect him back until late tonight.'

'I see,' he replied. 'Who is staying in the house at present?'

'Sir Rowland Delahaye, and Mr Warrender,' said Clarissa, indicating them in turn. She added, 'And Mr Birch, whom you already know, is here for the evening.'

Sir Rowland and Jeremy murmured acknowledgements. 'Oh, and yes,' Clarissa went on as though she had just remembered, 'my little stepdaughter.' She emphasized 'little'. 'She's in bed and asleep.'

'What about servants?' the Inspector wanted to know.

'There are two of them. A married couple. But it's their night out, and they've gone to the cinema in Maidstone.'

'I see,' said the Inspector, nodding his head gravely.

Just at that moment, Elgin came into the room from the hall, almost colliding with the Constable who was still keeping guard there. After a quick questioning look at the Inspector, Elgin addressed Clarissa. 'Would you be wanting anything, madam?' he asked.

Clarissa looked startled. 'I thought you were at the pictures, Elgin,' she exclaimed, as the Inspector gave her a sharp glance.

'We returned almost immediately, madam,' Elgin explained. 'My wife was not feeling well.' Sounding embarrassed, he added, delicately, 'Er – gastric trouble. It must have been something she ate.' Looking from the Inspector to the Constable, he asked, 'Is anything – wrong?'

'What's your name?' the Inspector asked him.

'Elgin, sir,' the butler replied. 'I'm sure I hope there's nothing –'

He was interrupted by the Inspector. 'Someone rang up the police station and said that a murder had been committed here.'

'A murder?' Elgin gasped.

'What do you know about that?'

'Nothing. Nothing at all, sir.'

'It wasn't you who rang up, then?' the Inspector asked him.

'No, indeed not.'

'When you returned to the house, you came in by the back door – at least I suppose you did?'

'Yes, sir,' Elgin replied, nervousness now making him rather more deferential in manner.

'Did you notice anything unusual?'

The butler thought for a moment, and then replied, 'Now I come to think of it, there was a strange car standing near the stables.'

'A strange car? What do you mean?'

'I wondered at the time whose it might be,' Elgin recalled. 'It seemed a curious place to leave it.'

'Was there anybody in it?'

'Not so far as I could see, sir.'

'Go and take a look at it, Jones,' the Inspector ordered his Constable.

'Jones!' Clarissa exclaimed involuntarily, with a start.

'I beg your pardon?' said the Inspector, turning to her.

Clarissa recovered herself quickly. Smiling at him, she murmured, 'It's nothing – just – I didn't think he looked very Welsh.'

The Inspector gestured to Constable Jones and to Elgin, indicating that they should go. They left the room together, and a silence ensued. After a moment, Jeremy moved to sit on the sofa and began to eat the sandwiches. The Inspector put his hat and gloves on the armchair, and then, taking a deep breath, addressed the assembled company.

'It seems,' he declared, speaking slowly and deliberately, 'that someone came here tonight who is unaccounted for.' He looked at Clarissa. 'You're sure you weren't expecting anyone?' he asked her.

'Oh, no – no,' Clarissa replied. 'We didn't want anyone to turn up. You see, we were just the four of us for bridge.'

'Really?' said the Inspector. 'I'm fond of a game of bridge myself.'

'Oh, are you?' Clarissa replied. 'Do you play Blackwood?'

'I just like a common-sense game,' the Inspector told her.

'Tell me, Mrs Hailsham-Brown,' he continued, 'you haven't lived here for very long, have you?'

'No,' she told him. 'About six weeks.'

The Inspector regarded her steadily. 'And there's been no funny business of any kind since you've been living here?' he asked.

Before Clarissa could answer, Sir Rowland interjected. 'What exactly do you mean by funny business, Inspector?'

The Inspector turned to address him. 'Well, it's rather a curious story, sir,' he informed Sir Rowland. 'This house used to belong to Mr Sellon, the antique dealer. He died six months ago.'

'Yes,' Clarissa remembered. 'He had some kind of accident, didn't he?'

'That's right,' said the Inspector. 'He fell downstairs, pitched on his head.' He looked around at Jeremy and Hugo, and added, 'Accidental death, they brought in. It might have been that, but it might not.'

'Do you mean,' Clarissa asked, 'that somebody might have pushed him?'

The Inspector turned to her. 'That,' he agreed, 'or else somebody hit him a crack on the head –'

He paused, and the tension among his hearers was palpable. Into the silence the Inspector went on. 'Someone could have arranged Sellon's body to look right, at the bottom of the stairs.'

'The staircase here in this house?' Clarissa asked nervously.

'No, it happened at his shop,' the Inspector informed her. 'There was no conclusive evidence, of course – but he was rather a dark horse, Mr Sellon.'

'In what way, Inspector?' Sir Rowland asked him.

'Well,' the Inspector replied, 'once or twice there were a couple of things he had to explain to us, as you might say. And the Narcotics Squad came down from London and had a word with him on one occasion . . .' He paused before continuing, 'but it was all no more than suspicion.'

'Officially, that is to say,' Sir Rowland observed.

The Inspector turned to him. 'That's right, sir,' he said meaningfully. 'Officially.'

'Whereas, unofficially –?' Sir Rowland prompted him.

'I'm afraid we can't go into that,' the Inspector replied. He went on, 'There was, however, one rather curious circumstance. There was an unfinished letter on Mr Sellon's desk, in which he mentioned that he'd come into possession of something which he described as an unparalleled rarity, which he would –' Here the Inspector paused, as if recollecting the exact words, '– would guarantee wasn't a forgery, and he was asking fourteen thousand pounds for it.'

Sir Rowland looked thoughtful. 'Fourteen thousand pounds,' he murmured. In a louder voice he continued, 'Yes, that's a lot of money indeed. Now, I wonder what it could be? Jewellery, I suppose, but the word forgery suggests – I don't know, a picture, perhaps?'

Jeremy continued to munch at the sandwiches, as the Inspector replied, 'Yes, perhaps. There was nothing in the shop worth such a large sum of money. The insurance inventory made that clear. Mr Sellon's partner was a woman who has a business of her own in London, and she wrote and said she couldn't give us any help or information.'

Sir Rowland nodded his head slowly. 'So he might have been murdered, and the article, whatever it was, stolen,' he suggested.

'It's quite possible, sir,' the Inspector agreed, 'but again, the would-be thief may not have been able to find it.'

'Now, why do you think that?' Sir Rowland asked.

'Because,' the Inspector replied, 'the shop has been broken into twice since then. Broken into and ransacked.'

Clarissa looked puzzled. 'Why are you telling us all this, Inspector?' she wanted to know.

'Because, Mrs Hailsham-Brown,' said the Inspector, turning to her, 'it's occurred to me that whatever was hidden away by Mr Sellon may have been hidden here in this house, and not at his shop in Maidstone. That's why I asked you if anything peculiar had come to your notice.'

Holding up a hand as though she had suddenly remembered, Clarissa said excitedly, 'Somebody rang up only today and asked to speak to me, and when I came to the phone whoever it was had just hung up. In a way, that's rather odd, isn't it?' She turned to Jeremy, adding, 'Oh yes, of course. You know, that man who came the other day and wanted to buy things – a horsey sort of man in a check suit. He wanted to buy that desk.'

The Inspector crossed the room to look at the desk. 'This one here?' he asked.

'Yes,' Clarissa replied. 'I told him, of course, that it wasn't ours to sell, but he didn't seem to believe me. He offered me a large sum, far more than it's worth.'

'That's very interesting,' the Inspector commented as he studied the desk. 'These things often have a secret drawer, you know.'

'Yes, this one has,' Clarissa told him. 'But there was nothing very exciting in it. Only some old autographs.'

The Inspector looked interested. 'Old autographs can be

immensely valuable, I understand,' he said. 'Whose were they?'

'I can assure you, Inspector,' Sir Rowland informed him, 'that these weren't anything rare enough to be worth more than a pound or two.'

The door to the hall opened, and Constable Jones entered, carrying a small booklet and a pair of gloves.

'Yes, Jones? What is it?' the Inspector asked him.

'I've examined the car, sir,' he replied. 'Just a pair of gloves on the driving seat. But I found this registration book in the side pocket.' He handed the book to the Inspector, and Clarissa exchanged a smile with Jeremy as they heard the Constable's strong Welsh accent.

The Inspector examined the registration book. '"Oliver Costello, 27 Morgan Mansions, London SW3",' he read aloud. Then, turning to Clarissa, he asked sharply, 'Has a man called Costello been here today?'

CHAPTER 11

The four friends exchanged guiltily furtive glances. Clarissa and Sir Rowland both looked as though they were about to attempt an answer, but it was Clarissa who actually spoke. 'Yes,' she admitted. 'He was here about –' She paused, and then, 'let me see,' she continued. 'Yes, it was about half past six.'

'Is he a friend of yours?' the Inspector asked her.

'No, I wouldn't call him a friend,' Clarissa replied. 'I had met him only once or twice.' She deliberately assumed an embarrassed look, and then said, hesitantly, 'It's – a little awkward, really –' She looked appealingly at Sir Rowland, as though passing the ball to him.

That gentleman was quick to respond to her unspoken request. 'Perhaps, Inspector,' he said, 'it would be better if I explained the situation.'

'Please do, sir,' the Inspector responded somewhat tersely.

'Well,' Sir Rowland continued, 'it concerns the first Mrs Hailsham-Brown. She and Hailsham-Brown were divorced just over a year ago, and recently she married Mr Oliver Costello.'

'I see,' observed the Inspector. 'And Mr Costello came here today.' He turned to Clarissa. 'Why was that?' he asked. 'Did he come by appointment?'

'Oh no,' Clarissa replied glibly. 'As a matter of fact, when Miranda and my husband divorced, she took with her one or two things that weren't really hers. Oliver Costello happened to be in this part of the world, and he just looked in to return them to Henry.'

'What kind of things?' the Inspector asked quickly.

Clarissa was ready for this question. 'Nothing very important,' she said with a smile. Picking up the small silver cigarette-box from a table by the sofa, she held it out to the Inspector. 'This was one of them,' she told him. 'It belonged to my husband's mother, and he values it for sentimental reasons.'

The Inspector looked at Clarissa reflectively for a moment, before asking her, 'How long did Mr Costello remain here when he came at six-thirty?'

'Oh, a very short time,' she replied as she replaced the cigarette box on the table. 'He said he was in a hurry. About ten minutes, I should think. No longer than that.'

'And your interview was quite amicable?' the Inspector enquired.

'Oh, yes,' Clarissa assured him. 'I thought it was very kind of him to take the trouble to return the things.'

The Inspector thought for a moment, before asking, 'Did he mention where he was going when he left here?'

'No,' Clarissa replied. 'Actually, he went out by that window,' she continued, gesturing towards the French windows. 'As a matter of fact, my lady gardener, Miss Peake, was here, and she offered to show him out through the garden.'

'Your gardener – does she live on the premises?' the Inspector wanted to know.

'Well, yes. But not in the house. She lives in the cottage.'

'I think I should like a word with her,' the Inspector decided. He turned to the Constable. 'Jones, go and get her.'

'There's a telephone connection through to the cottage. Shall I call her for you, Inspector?' Clarissa offered.

'If you would be so kind, Mrs Hailsham-Brown,' the Inspector replied.

'Not at all. I don't suppose she'll have gone to bed yet,' Clarissa said, pressing a button on the telephone. She flashed a smile at the Inspector, who responded by looking bashful. Jeremy smiled to himself and took another sandwich.

Clarissa spoke into the telephone. 'Hello, Miss Peake. This is Mrs Hailsham-Brown . . . I wonder, would you mind coming over? Something rather important has happened . . . Oh yes, of course that will be all right. Thank you.'

She replaced the receiver and turned to the Inspector. 'Miss Peake has been washing her hair, but she'll get dressed and come right over.'

'Thank you,' said the Inspector. 'After all, Costello may have mentioned to her where he was going.'

'Yes, indeed, he may have,' Clarissa agreed.

The Inspector looked puzzled. 'The question that bothers me,' he announced to the room in general, 'is why Mr Costello's car is still here, and where is Mr Costello?'

Clarissa gave an involuntary glance towards the bookshelves and the panel, then walked across to the French windows to watch for Miss Peake. Jeremy, noticing her glance, sat back innocently and crossed his legs as the Inspector continued, 'Apparently this Miss Peake was the last person to see him. He left, you say, by that window. Did you lock it after him?'

'No,' Clarissa replied, standing at the window with her back to the Inspector.

'Oh?' the Inspector queried.

Something in his tone made Clarissa turn to face him. 'Well, I – I don't think so,' she said, hesitantly.

'So he might have re-entered that way,' the Inspector observed. He took a deep breath and announced importantly, 'I think, Mrs Hailsham-Brown, that, with your permission, I should like to search the house.'

'Of course,' Clarissa replied with a friendly smile. 'Well, you've seen this room. Nobody could be hidden here.' She held the window curtains open for a moment, as though awaiting Miss Peake, and then exclaimed, 'Look! Through here is the library.' Going to the library door and opening it, she suggested, 'Would you like to go in there?'

'Thank you,' said the Inspector. 'Jones!' As the two police officers went into the library, the Inspector added, 'Just see where that door leads to, Jones,' gesturing towards another door immediately inside the library.

'Very good, sir,' the Constable replied, as he went through the door indicated.

As soon as they were out of earshot, Sir Rowland went to Clarissa. 'What's on the other side?' he asked her quietly, indicating the panel.

'Bookshelves,' she replied tersely.

He nodded and strolled nonchalantly across to the sofa, as the Constable's voice was heard calling, 'Just another door through to the hall, sir.'

The two officers returned from the library. 'Right,' said the

Inspector. He looked at Sir Rowland, apparently taking note of the fact that he had moved. 'Now we'll search the rest of the house,' he announced, going to the hall door.

'I'll come with you, if you don't mind,' Clarissa offered, 'in case my little stepdaughter should wake up and be frightened. Not that I think she will. It's extraordinary how deeply children can sleep. You have to practically shake them awake.'

As the Inspector opened the hall door, she asked him, 'Have you got any children, Inspector?'

'One boy and one girl,' he replied shortly, as he made his way out of the room, crossed the hall, and began to ascend the stairs.

'Isn't that nice?' Clarissa observed. She turned to the Constable. 'Mr Jones,' she invited him with a gesture to precede her. He made his way out of the room and she followed him closely.

As soon as they had gone, the three remaining occupants of the room looked at one another. Hugo wiped his hands and Jeremy mopped his forehead. 'And now what?' Jeremy asked, taking another sandwich.

Sir Rowland shook his head. 'I don't like this,' he told them. 'We're getting in very deep.'

'If you ask me,' Hugo advised him, 'there's only one thing to do. Come clean. Own up now before it's too late.'

'Damn it, we can't do that,' Jeremy exclaimed. 'It would be too unfair to Clarissa.'

'But we'll get her in a worse mess if we keep on with this,' Hugo insisted. 'How are we ever going to get the body away? The police will impound the fellow's car.'

'We could use mine,' Jeremy suggested.

'Well, I don't like it,' Hugo persisted. 'I don't like it at all.

Damn it, I'm a local JP. I've got my reputation with the police here to consider.' He turned to Sir Rowland. 'What do you say, Roly? You've got a good level head.'

Sir Rowland looked grave. 'I admit I don't like it,' he replied, 'but personally I am committed to the enterprise.'

Hugo looked perplexed. 'I don't understand you,' he told his friend.

'Take it on trust, if you will, Hugo,' said Sir Rowland. He looked gravely at both men, and continued, 'We're in a very bad jam, all of us. But if we stick together and have reasonable luck, I think there's a chance we may be able to pull it off.'

Jeremy looked as though he was about to say something, but Sir Rowland held up a hand, and went on, 'Once the police are satisfied that Costello isn't in this house, they'll go off and look elsewhere. After all, there are plenty of reasons why he might have left his car and gone off on foot.' He gestured towards them both and added, 'We're all respectable people – Hugo's a JP, as he's reminded us, and Henry Hailsham-Brown's high up in the Foreign Office –'

'Yes, yes, and you've had a blameless and even distinguished career, we know all that,' Hugo intervened. 'All right then, if you say so, we brazen it out.'

Jeremy rose to his feet and nodded towards the recess. 'Can't we do something about that straightaway?' he asked.

'There's no time now,' Sir Rowland decreed, tersely. 'They'll be back any minute. He's safer where he is.'

Jeremy nodded in reluctant agreement. 'I must say Clarissa's a marvel,' he observed. 'She doesn't turn a hair. She's got that police inspector eating out of her hand.'

The front door bell rang. 'That'll be Miss Peake, I expect,'

Sir Rowland announced. 'Go and let her in, Warrender, would you?'

As soon as Jeremy had left the room, Hugo beckoned to Sir Rowland.

'What's up, Roly?' he asked in an urgent whisper. 'What did Clarissa tell you when she got you to herself?'

Sir Rowland began to speak, but, hearing the voices of Jeremy and Miss Peake exchanging greetings at the front door, he made a gesture indicating 'Not now'.

'I think you'd better come in here,' Jeremy told Miss Peake as he slammed the front door shut. A moment later, the gardener preceded him into the drawing-room, looking as though she had dressed very hastily. She had a towel wrapped around her head.

'What is all this?' she wanted to know. 'Mrs Hailsham-Brown was most mysterious on the phone. Has anything happened?'

Sir Rowland addressed her with the utmost courtesy. 'I'm so sorry you've been routed out like this, Miss Peake,' he apologized. 'Do sit down.' He indicated a chair by the bridge table.

Hugo pulled the chair out for Miss Peake, who thanked him. He then seated himself in a more comfortable easy chair, while Sir Rowland informed the gardener, 'As a matter of fact, we've got the police here, and –'

'The police?' Miss Peake interrupted, looking startled. 'Has there been a burglary?'

'No, not a burglary, but –'

He stopped speaking as Clarissa, the Inspector and the Constable came back into the room. Jeremy sat on the sofa, while Sir Rowland took up a position behind it.

'Inspector,' Clarissa announced, 'this is Miss Peake.'

The Inspector went across to the gardener. His 'Good evening, Miss Peake' was accompanied by a stiff little bow.

'Good evening, Inspector,' Miss Peake replied. 'I was just asking Sir Rowland – has there been a robbery, or what?'

The Inspector regarded her searchingly, allowed a moment or two to elapse, and then spoke. 'We received a rather peculiar telephone call which brought us out here,' he told her. 'And we think that perhaps you might be able to clear up the matter for us.'

CHAPTER 12

The Inspector's announcement was greeted by Miss Peake with a jolly laugh. 'I say, this is mysterious. I *am* enjoying myself,' she exclaimed delightedly.

The Inspector frowned. 'It concerns Mr Costello,' he explained. 'Mr Oliver Costello of 27, Morgan Mansions, London SW3. I believe that's in the Chelsea area.'

'Never heard of him,' was Miss Peake's robustly expressed response.

'He was here this evening, visiting Mrs Hailsham-Brown,' the Inspector reminded her, 'and I believe you showed him out through the garden.'

Miss Peake slapped her thigh. 'Oh, that man,' she recalled. 'Mrs Hailsham-Brown did mention his name.' She looked at the Inspector with a little more interest. 'Yes, what do you want to know?' she asked.

'I should like to know,' the Inspector told her, speaking slowly and deliberately, 'exactly what happened, and when you last saw him.'

Miss Peake thought for a moment before replying. 'Let me see,' she said. 'We went out through the French window, and

I told him there was a short cut if he wanted the bus, and he said no, he'd come in his car, and he'd left it round by the stables.'

She beamed at the Inspector as though she expected to be praised for her succinct recollection of what had occurred, but he merely looked thoughtful as he commented, 'Isn't that rather an odd place to leave a car?'

'That's just what I thought,' Miss Peake agreed, slapping the Inspector's arm as she spoke. He looked surprised at this, but she continued, 'You'd think he'd drive right up to the front door, wouldn't you? But people are so odd. You never know what they're going to do.' She gave a hearty guffaw.

'And then what happened?' the Inspector asked.

Miss Peake shrugged her shoulders. 'Well, he went off to his car, and I suppose he drove away,' she replied.

'You didn't see him do so?'

'No – I was putting my tools away,' was the gardener's reply.

'And that's the last you saw of him?' the Inspector asked, with emphasis.

'Yes, why?'

'Because his car is still here,' the Inspector told her. Speaking slowly and emphatically, he continued, 'A phone-call was put through to the police station at seven forty-nine, saying that a man had been murdered at Copplestone Court.'

Miss Peake looked appalled. 'Murdered?' she exclaimed. 'Here? Ridiculous!'

'That's what everybody seems to think,' the Inspector observed drily, with a significant look at Sir Rowland.

'Of course,' Miss Peake went on, 'I know there are all these maniacs about, attacking women – but you say a man was murdered –'

The Inspector cut her short. 'You didn't hear another car this evening?' he asked brusquely.

'Only Mr Hailsham-Brown's,' she replied.

'Mr Hailsham-Brown?' the Inspector queried with a raise of his eyebrows. 'I thought he wasn't expected home till late.'

His glance swung round to Clarissa, who hastened to explain. 'My husband did come home, but he had to go out again almost immediately.'

The Inspector assumed a deliberately patient expression. 'Oh, is that so?' he commented in a tone of studied politeness. 'Exactly when did he come home?'

'Let me see –' Clarissa began to stammer. 'It must have been about –'

'It was about a quarter of an hour before I went off duty,' Miss Peake interjected. 'I work a lot of overtime, Inspector. I never stick to regulation hours,' she explained. 'Be keen on your job, that's what I say,' she continued, thumping the table as she spoke. 'Yes, it must have been about a quarter past seven when Mr Hailsham-Brown got in.'

'That would have been shortly after Mr Costello left,' the Inspector observed. He moved to the centre of the room, and his manner changed almost imperceptibly as he continued, 'He and Mr Hailsham-Brown probably passed each other.'

'You mean,' Miss Peake said thoughtfully, 'that he may have come back again to see Mr Hailsham-Brown.'

'Oliver Costello definitely didn't come back to the house,' Clarissa cut in sharply.

'But you can't be sure of that, Mrs Hailsham-Brown,' the gardener contradicted her. 'He might have got in by that window without your knowing anything about it.' She paused, and then exclaimed, 'Golly! You don't think he murdered Mr Hailsham-Brown, do you? I say, I am sorry.'

'Of course he didn't murder Henry,' Clarissa snapped irritably.

'Where did your husband go when he left here?' the Inspector asked her.

'I've no idea,' Clarissa replied shortly.

'Doesn't he usually tell you where he's going?' the Inspector persisted.

'I never ask questions,' Clarissa told him. 'I think it must be so boring for a man if his wife is always asking questions.'

Miss Peake gave a sudden squeal. 'But how stupid of me,' she shouted. 'Of course, if that man's car is still here, then he must be the one who's been murdered.' She roared with laughter.

Sir Rowland rose to his feet. 'We've no reason to believe anyone has been murdered, Miss Peake,' he admonished her with dignity. 'In fact, the Inspector believes it was all some silly hoax.'

Miss Peake was clearly not of the same opinion. 'But the car,' she insisted. 'I do think that car still being here is very suspicious.' She got up and approached the Inspector. 'Have you looked about for the body, Inspector?' she asked him eagerly.

'The Inspector has already searched the house,' Sir Rowland answered before the police officer had a chance to speak. He was rewarded by a sharp glance from the Inspector, whom Miss Peake was now tapping on the shoulder as she continued to air her views.

'I'm sure those Elgins have something to do with it – the

butler and that wife of his who calls herself a cook,' the gardener assured the Inspector confidently. 'I've had my suspicions of them for quite some time. I saw a light in their bedroom window as I came along here just now. And that in itself is suspicious. It's their night out, and they usually don't return until well after eleven.' She gripped the Inspector's arm. 'Have you searched their quarters?' she asked him urgently.

The Inspector opened his mouth to speak, but she interrupted him with another tap on the shoulder. 'Now listen,' she began. 'Suppose this Mr Costello recognized Elgin as a man with a criminal record. Costello might have decided to come back and warn Mrs Hailsham-Brown about the man, and Elgin assaulted him.'

Looking immensely pleased with herself, she flashed a glance around the room, and continued. 'Then, of course, Elgin would have to hide the body somewhere quickly, so that he could dispose of it later in the night. Now, where would he hide it, I wonder?' she asked rhetorically, warming to her thesis. With a gesture towards the French windows, she began, 'Behind a curtain or –'

She was cut short by Clarissa who interrupted angrily. 'Oh, really, Miss Peake. There isn't anybody hidden behind any of the curtains. And I'm sure Elgin would never murder anybody. It's quite ridiculous.'

Miss Peake turned. 'You're so trusting, Mrs Hailsham-Brown,' she admonished her employer. 'When you get to my age, you'll realize how very often people are simply not quite what they seem.' She laughed heartily as she turned back to the Inspector.

When he opened his mouth to speak, she gave him yet another tap on the shoulder. 'Now then,' she continued, 'where would a man like Elgin hide the body? There's that cupboard place between here and the library. You've looked there, I suppose?'

Sir Rowland intervened hastily. 'Miss Peake, the Inspector has looked both here *and* in the library,' he insisted.

The Inspector, however, after a meaning look at Sir Rowland, turned to the gardener. 'What exactly do you mean by "that cupboard place", Miss Peake?' he enquired.

The others in the room all looked more than somewhat tense as Miss Peake replied, 'Oh, it's a wonderful place when you're playing hide-and-seek. You'd really never dream it was there. Let me show it to you.'

She walked over to the panel, followed by the Inspector. Jeremy got to his feet at the same moment that Clarissa exclaimed forcefully, 'No.'

The Inspector and Miss Peake both turned to look at her. 'There's nothing there now,' Clarissa informed them. 'I know because I went that way, through to the library, just now.'

Her voice trailed off. Miss Peake, sounding disappointed, murmured, 'Oh well, in that case, then –' and turned away from the panel. The Inspector, however, called her back. 'Just show me all the same, Miss Peake,' he ordered. 'I'd like to see.'

Miss Peake went to the bookshelves. 'It was a door originally,' she explained. 'It matched the one over there.' She activated the lever, explaining as she did so, 'You pull this catch back, and the door comes open. See?'

The panel opened, and the body of Oliver Costello slumped down and fell forward. Miss Peake screamed.

'So,' the Inspector observed, looking grimly at Clarissa,

'You were mistaken, Mrs Hailsham-Brown. It appears that there was a murder here tonight.'

Miss Peake's scream rose to a crescendo.

Ten minutes later, things were somewhat quieter, for Miss Peake was no longer in the room. Nor, for that matter, were Hugo and Jeremy. The body of Oliver Costello, however, was still lying collapsed in the recess, the panel of which was open. Clarissa was stretched out on the sofa, with Sir Rowland sitting by her and holding a glass of brandy which he was attempting to make her sip. The Inspector was talking on the telephone, and Constable Jones continued to stand guard.

'Yes, yes –' the Inspector was saying. 'What's that? – Hit and run? – Where? – Oh, I see – Yes, well, send them along as soon as you can – Yes, we'll want photographs – Yes, the whole bag of tricks.'

He replaced the receiver, and went over to the Constable. 'Everything comes at once,' he complained to his colleague. 'Weeks go by and nothing happens, and now the Divisional Surgeon's out at a bad car accident – a smash on the London road. It'll all mean quite a bit of delay. However, we'll get on as well as we can until the M.O. arrives.' He gestured towards the corpse. 'We'd better not move him until they've taken the photographs,' he suggested. 'Not that it will tell us anything. He wasn't killed there, he was put there afterwards.'

'How can you be sure, sir?' the Constable asked.

The Inspector looked down at the carpet. 'You can see where his feet have dragged,' he pointed out, crouching down behind the sofa. The Constable knelt beside him.

Sir Rowland peered over the back of the sofa, and then turned to Clarissa to ask, 'How are you feeling now?'

'Better, thanks, Roly,' she replied, faintly.

The two police officers got to their feet. 'It might be as well to close that book-case door,' the Inspector instructed his colleague. 'We don't want any more hysterics.'

'Right, sir,' the Constable replied. He closed the panel so that the body could no longer be seen. As he did so, Sir Rowland rose from the sofa to address the Inspector. 'Mrs Hailsham-Brown has had a bad shock,' he told the policeman. 'I think she ought to go to her room and lie down.'

Politely, but with a certain reserve, the Inspector replied, 'Certainly, sir, but not for a moment or two just yet. I'd like to ask her a few questions first.'

Sir Rowland tried to persist. 'She's really not fit to be questioned at present.'

'I'm all right, Roly,' Clarissa interjected, faintly. 'Really, I am.'

Sir Rowland addressed her, adopting a warning tone. 'It's very brave of you, my dear,' he said, 'but I really think it would be wiser of you to go and rest for a while.'

'Dear Uncle Roly,' Clarissa responded with a smile. To the Inspector she said, 'I sometimes call him Uncle Roly, though he's my guardian, not my uncle. But he's so sweet to me always.'

'Yes, I can see that,' was the dry response.

'Do ask me anything you want to, Inspector,' Clarissa continued graciously. 'Though actually I don't think I can help you very much, I'm afraid, because I just don't know anything at all about any of this.'

Sir Rowland sighed, shook his head slightly, and turned away.

'We shan't worry you for long, madam,' the Inspector assured her. Going to the library door, he held it open, and turned to address Sir Rowland. 'Will you join the other gentlemen in the library, sir?' he suggested.

'I think I'd better remain here, in case –' Sir Rowland began, only to be interrupted by the Inspector whose tone had now become firmer. 'I'll call you if it should be necessary, sir. In the library, please.'

After a short duel of eyes, Sir Rowland conceded defeat and went into the library. The Inspector closed the door after him, and indicated silently to the Constable that he should sit and take notes. Clarissa swung her feet off the sofa and sat up, as Jones got out his notebook and pencil.

'Now, Mrs Hailsham-Brown,' the Inspector began, 'if you're ready, let's make a start.' He picked up the cigarette box from the table by the sofa, turned it over, opened it, and looked at the cigarettes in it.

'Dear Uncle Roly, he always wants to spare me everything,' Clarissa told the Inspector with an enchanting smile. Then, seeing him handling the cigarette box, she became anxious. 'This isn't going to be the third degree or anything, is it?' she asked, trying to make her question sound like a joke.

'Nothing of that kind, madam, I assure you,' said the Inspector. 'Just a few simple questions.' He turned to the

Constable. 'Are you ready, Jones?' he asked, as he pulled out a chair from the bridge table, turned it around, and sat facing Clarissa.

'All ready, sir,' Constable Jones replied.

'Good. Now, Mrs Hailsham-Brown,' the Inspector began. 'Do you say that you had no idea there was a body concealed in that recess?'

The Constable began his note-taking as Clarissa answered, wide-eyed, 'No, of course not. It's horrible.' She shivered. 'Quite horrible.'

The Inspector looked at her enquiringly. 'When we were searching this room,' he asked, 'why didn't you call our attention to that recess?'

Clarissa met his gaze with a look of wide-eyed innocence. 'Do you know,' she said, 'the thought never struck me. You see, we never use the recess, so it just didn't come into my head.'

The Inspector pounced. 'But you said,' he reminded her, 'that you had just been through there into the library.'

'Oh no,' Clarissa exclaimed quickly. 'You must have mis-understood me.' She pointed to the library door. 'What I meant was that we had gone through that door into the library.'

'Yes, I certainly must have misunderstood you,' the Inspector observed grimly. 'Now, let me at least be clear about this. You say you have no idea when Mr Costello came back to this house, or what he might have come for?'

'No, I simply can't imagine,' Clarissa replied, her voice dripping with innocent candour.

'But the fact remains that he did come back,' the Inspector persisted.

'Yes, of course. We know that now.'

'Well, he must have had some reason,' the Inspector pointed out.

'I suppose so,' Clarissa agreed. 'But I've no idea what it could have been.'

The Inspector thought for a moment, and then tried another line of approach. 'Do you think that perhaps he wanted to see your husband?' he suggested.

'Oh, no,' Clarissa replied quickly, 'I'm quite sure he didn't. Henry and he never liked each other.'

'Oh!' the Inspector exclaimed. 'They never liked each other. I didn't realize that. Had there been a quarrel between them?'

Again Clarissa spoke quickly to forestall a new and potentially dangerous line of enquiry. 'Oh no,' she assured the Inspector, 'no, they hadn't quarrelled. Henry just thought he wore the wrong shoes.' She smiled engagingly. 'You know how odd men can be.'

The Inspector's look suggested that this was something of which he was personally ignorant. 'You're absolutely certain that Costello wouldn't have come back here to see you?' he asked again.

'Me?' Clarissa echoed innocently. 'Oh no, I'm sure he didn't. What reason could he possibly have?'

The Inspector took a deep breath. Then, speaking slowly and deliberately, he asked her, 'Is there anybody else in the house he might have wanted to see? Now please think carefully before you answer.'

Again, Clarissa gave him her look of bland innocence. 'I can't think who,' she insisted. 'I mean, who else is there?'

The Inspector rose, turned his chair around and put it back against the bridge table. Then, pacing slowly about the room, he began to muse. 'Mr Costello comes here,' he began slowly, 'and returns the articles which the first Mrs Hailsham-Brown had taken from your husband by mistake. Then he says good-bye. But then he comes back to the house.'

He went across to the French windows. 'Presumably he effects an entrance through these windows,' he continued, gesturing at them. 'He is killed – and his body is pushed into that recess – all in a space of about ten to twenty minutes.'

He turned back to face Clarissa. 'And nobody hears anything?' he ended, on a rising inflection. 'I find that very difficult to believe.'

'I know,' Clarissa agreed. 'I find it just as difficult to believe. It's really extraordinary, isn't it?'

'It certainly is,' the Inspector agreed, his tone distinctly ironical. He tried one last time. 'Mrs Hailsham-Brown, are you absolutely sure that you didn't hear anything?' he asked her pointedly.

'I heard nothing at all,' she answered. 'It really is fantastic.'

'Almost too fantastic,' the Inspector commented grimly. He paused, then went over to the hall door and held it open. 'Well, that's all for the present, Mrs Hailsham-Brown.'

Clarissa rose and walked rather quickly towards the library door, only to be intercepted by the Inspector. 'Not that way, please,' he instructed her, and led her over to the hall door.

'But I think, really, I'd rather join the others,' she protested.

'Later, if you don't mind,' said the Inspector tersely.

Very reluctantly, Clarissa went out through the hall door.

The Inspector closed the hall door behind Clarissa, then went over to Constable Jones who was still writing in his notebook. 'Where's the other woman? The gardener. Miss – er – Peake?' the Inspector asked.

'I put her on the bed in the spare room,' the Constable told his superior. 'After she came out of the hysterics, that is. A terrible time I had with her, laughing and crying something terrible, she was.'

'It doesn't matter if Mrs Hailsham-Brown goes and talks to her,' the Inspector told him. 'But she's not to talk to those three men. We'll have no comparing of stories, and no prompting. I hope you locked the door from the library to the hall?'

'Yes, sir,' the Constable assured him. 'I've got the key here.'

'I don't know what to make of them at all,' the Inspector confessed to his colleague. 'They're all highly respectable people. Hailsham-Brown's a Foreign Office diplomat, Hugo Birch is a JP whom we know, and Hailsham-Brown's other two guests seem decent upper-class types – well, you know what I mean . . . But there's something funny going on. None of them are being straightforward with us – and that includes Mrs Hailsham-Brown. They're hiding something, and I'm determined to find out what it is, whether it's got anything to do with this murder or not.'

He stretched his arms above his head as though seeking inspiration from on high, and then addressed the Constable again. 'Well, we'd better get on with it,' he said. 'Let's take them one at a time.'

As the Constable got to his feet, the Inspector changed his mind. 'No. Just a moment. First I'll have a word with that butler chap,' he decided.

'Elgin?'

'Yes, Elgin. Call him in. I've got an idea he knows something.'

'Certainly, sir,' the Constable replied.

Leaving the room, he found Elgin hovering near the sitting-room door. The butler made a tentative pretence of heading for the stairs, but stopped when the Constable called him and came into the room rather nervously.

The Constable closed the hall door and resumed his place for note-taking, while the Inspector indicated the chair near the bridge table.

Elgin sat down, and the Inspector began his interrogation. 'Now, you started off for the pictures this evening,' he reminded the butler, 'but you came back. Why was that?'

'I've told you, sir,' Elgin replied. 'My wife wasn't feeling well.'

The Inspector regarded him steadily. 'It was you who let Mr Costello into the house when he called here this evening, was it not?' he asked.

'Yes, sir.'

The Inspector took a few paces away from Elgin, and then turned back suddenly. 'Why didn't you tell us at once that it was Mr Costello's car outside?' he asked.

'I didn't know whose car it was, sir. Mr Costello didn't drive up to the front door. I didn't even know he'd come in a car.'

'Wasn't that rather peculiar? Leaving his car around by the stables?' the Inspector suggested.

'Well, yes, sir, I suppose it was,' the butler replied. 'But I expect he had his reasons.'

'Just what do you mean by that?' the Inspector asked quickly.

'Nothing, sir,' Elgin answered. He sounded almost smug. 'Nothing at all.'

'Had you ever seen Mr Costello before?' The Inspector's voice was sharp as he asked this.

'Never, sir,' Elgin assured him.

The Inspector adopted a meaning tone to enquire, 'It wasn't because of Mr Costello that you came back this evening?'

'I've told you, sir,' said Elgin. 'My wife –'

'I don't want to hear any more about your wife,' the Inspector interrupted. Moving away from Elgin, he continued, 'How long have you been with Mrs Hailsham-Brown?'

'Six weeks, sir,' was the reply.

The Inspector turned back to face Elgin. 'And before that?'

'I'd – I'd been having a little rest,' the butler replied uneasily.

'A rest?' the Inspector echoed, in a tone of suspicion. He paused and then added, 'You do realize that, in a case like this, your references will have to be looked into very carefully.'

Elgin began to get to his feet. 'Will that be all –' he started to say, and then stopped and resumed his seat. 'I – I wouldn't wish to deceive you, sir,' he continued. 'It wasn't anything really wrong. What I mean is – the original reference having got torn – I couldn't quite remember the wording –'

'So you wrote your own references,' the Inspector interrupted. 'That's what it comes to, doesn't it?'

'I didn't mean any harm,' Elgin protested. 'I've got my living to earn –'

The Inspector interrupted him again. 'At the moment, I'm not interested in fake references,' he told the butler. 'I want to know what happened here tonight, and what you know about Mr Costello.'

'I'd never set eyes on him before,' Elgin insisted. Looking around at the hall door, he continued, 'But I've got a good idea of why he came here.'

'Oh, and what is that?' the Inspector wanted to know.

'Blackmail,' Elgin told him. 'He had something on her.'

'By "her",' said the Inspector, 'I assume you mean Mrs Hailsham-Brown.'

'Yes,' Elgin continued eagerly. 'I came in to ask if there was anything more she wanted, and I heard them talking.'

'What did you hear exactly?'

'I heard her say "But that's blackmail. I won't submit to it".' Elgin adopted a highly dramatic tone as he quoted Clarissa's words.

'Hm!' the Inspector responded a little doubtfully. 'Anything more?'

'No,' Elgin admitted. 'They stopped when I came in, and when I went out they dropped their voices.'

'I see,' the Inspector commented. He looked intently at the butler, waiting for him to speak again.

Elgin got up from his chair. His voice was almost a whine as he pleaded, 'You won't be hard on me, sir, will you? I've had a lot of trouble one way and another.'

The Inspector regarded him for a moment longer, and then said dismissively, 'Oh, that will do. Get out.'

'Yes, sir. Thank you, sir,' Elgin responded quickly as he made a hasty exit into the hall.

The Inspector watched him go, and then turned to the Constable. 'Blackmail, eh?' he murmured, exchanging glances with his colleague.

'And Mrs Hailsham-Brown such a nice seeming lady,' Constable Jones observed with a somewhat prim look.

'Yes, well one never can tell,' the Inspector observed. He paused, and then ordered curtly, 'I'll see Mr Birch now.' The Constable went to the library door. 'Mr Birch, please.'

Hugo came through the library door, looking dogged and rather defiant. The Constable closed the door behind him and took a seat at the table, while the Inspector greeted Hugo pleasantly. 'Come in, Mr Birch,' he invited. 'Sit down here, please.'

Hugo sat, and the Inspector continued, 'This is a very unpleasant business, I'm afraid, sir. What have you to tell us about it?'

Slapping his spectacle case on the table, Hugo replied defiantly, 'Absolutely nothing.'

'Nothing?' queried the Inspector, sounding surprised.

'What do you expect me to say?' Hugo expostulated. 'The blinking woman snaps open the blinking cupboard, and out falls a blinking corpse.' He gave a snort of impatience. 'Took my breath away,' he declared. 'I've not got over it yet.' He glared at the Inspector. 'It's no good asking me anything,' he said firmly, 'because I don't know anything about it.'

The Inspector regarded Hugo steadily for a moment before asking, 'That's your statement, is it? Just that you know nothing at all about it?'

'I'm telling you,' Hugo repeated. 'I didn't kill the fellow.' Again he glared defiantly. 'I didn't even know him.'

'You didn't know him,' the Inspector repeated. 'Very well. I'm not suggesting that you did know him. I'm certainly not suggesting that you murdered him. But I can't believe that you "know nothing", as you put it. So let's collaborate to find out what you do know. To begin with, you'd heard of him, hadn't you?'

'Yes,' snapped Hugo, 'and I'd heard he was a nasty bit of goods.'

'In what way?' the Inspector asked calmly.

'Oh, I don't know,' Hugo blustered. 'He was the sort of fellow that women liked and men had no use for. That sort of thing.'

The Inspector paused before asking carefully, 'You've no idea why he should come back to this house a second time this evening?'

'Not a clue,' replied Hugo dismissively.

The Inspector took a few steps around the room, then turned abruptly to face Hugo. 'Was there anything between him and the present Mrs Hailsham-Brown, do you think?' he asked.

Hugo looked shocked. 'Clarissa? Good Lord, no! Nice girl, Clarissa. Got a lot of sense. She wouldn't look twice at a fellow like that.'

The Inspector paused again, and then said, finally, 'So you can't help us.'

'Sorry. But there it is,' replied Hugo with an attempt at nonchalance.

Making one last effort to extract at least a crumb of information from Hugo, the Inspector asked, 'Had you really no idea that the body was in that recess?'

'Of course not,' replied Hugo, now sounding offended.

'Thank you, sir,' said the Inspector, turning away from him.

'What?' queried Hugo vaguely.

'That's all, thank you, sir,' the Inspector repeated. He went to the desk and picked up a red book that lay on it.

Hugo rose, picked up his spectacle case, and was about to go across to the library door when the Constable got up and barred his way. Hugo then turned towards the French windows, but the Constable said, 'This way, Mr Birch, please,' and opened the hall door. Giving up, Hugo went out and the policeman closed the door behind him.

The Inspector carried his huge red book over to the bridge table, and sat consulting it, as Constable Jones commented satirically, 'Mr Birch was a mine of information, wasn't he? Mind you, it's not very nice for a JP to be mixed up in a murder.'

The Inspector began to read aloud. '"Delahaye, Sir Rowland Edward Mark, KCB, MVO –"'

'What have you got there?' the Constable asked. He peered over the Inspector's shoulder. 'Oh, *Who's Who.*'

The Inspector went on reading. '"Educated Eton – Trinity College –" Um! "Attached Foreign Office – second Secretary – Madrid – Plenipotentiary".'

'Ooh!' the Constable exclaimed at this last word.

The Inspector gave him an exasperated look, and continued, '"Constantinople, Foreign Office – special commission rendered – Clubs – Boodles – Whites".'

'Do you want him next, sir?' the Constable asked.

The Inspector thought for a moment. 'No,' he decided. 'He's the most interesting of the lot, so I'll leave him till the last. Let's have young Warrender in now.'

CHAPTER 15

Constable Jones, standing at the library door, called, 'Mr Warrender, please.'

Jeremy came in, attempting rather unsuccessfully to look completely at his ease. The Constable closed the door and resumed his seat at the table, while the Inspector half rose and pulled out a chair from the bridge table for Jeremy.

'Sit down,' he ordered somewhat brusquely as he resumed his seat. Jeremy sat, and the Inspector asked formally, 'Your name?'

'Jeremy Warrender.'

'Address?'

'Three hundred and forty, Broad Street, and thirty-four Grosvenor Square,' Jeremy told him, trying to sound nonchalant. He glanced across at the Constable who was writing all this down, and added, 'Country address, Hepplestone, Wiltshire.'

'That sounds as though you're a gentleman of independent means,' the Inspector commented.

'I'm afraid not,' Jeremy admitted, with a smile. 'I'm private secretary to Sir Kenneth Thomson, the Chairman of Saxon-Arabian Oil. Those are his addresses.'

The Inspector nodded. 'I see. How long have you been with him?'

'About a year. Before that, I was personal assistant to Mr Scott Agius for four years.'

'Ah, yes,' said the Inspector. 'He's that wealthy businessman in the City, isn't he?' He thought for a moment before going on to ask, 'Did you know this man, Oliver Costello?'

'No, I'd never heard of him till tonight,' Jeremy told him.

'And you didn't see him when he came to the house earlier this evening?' the Inspector continued.

'No,' Jeremy replied. 'I'd gone over to the golf club with the others. We were dining there, you see. It was the servants' night out, and Mr Birch had asked us to dine with him at the club.'

The Inspector nodded his head. After a pause, he asked, 'Was Mrs Hailsham-Brown invited, too?'

'No, she wasn't,' said Jeremy.

The Inspector raised his eyebrows, and Jeremy hurried on. 'That is,' he explained, 'she could have come if she'd liked.'

'Do you mean,' the Inspector asked him, 'that she was asked, then? And she refused?'

'No, no,' Jeremy replied hurriedly, sounding as though he was getting rattled. 'What I mean is – well, Hailsham-Brown is usually quite tired by the time he gets down here, and Clarissa said they'd just have a scratch meal here, as usual.'

The Inspector looked confused. 'Let me get this clear,' he said rather snappily. 'Mrs Hailsham-Brown expected her husband to dine here? She didn't expect him to go out again as soon as he came in?'

Jeremy was now quite definitely flustered. 'I – er – well

– er – really, I don't know,' he stammered. 'No – Now that you mention it, I believe she did say he was going to be out this evening.'

The Inspector rose and took a few paces away from Jeremy. 'It seems odd, then,' he observed, 'that Mrs Hailsham-Brown should not have come out to the club with the three of you, instead of remaining here to dine all by herself.'

Jeremy turned on his chair to face the Inspector. 'Well – er – well –' he began, and then, gaining confidence, continued quickly, 'I mean, it was the kid – Pippa, you know. Clarissa wouldn't have liked to go out and leave the kid all by herself in the house.'

'Or perhaps,' the Inspector suggested, speaking with heavy significance, 'perhaps she was making plans to receive a visitor of her own?'

Jeremy rose to his feet. 'I say, that's a rotten thing to suggest,' he exclaimed hotly. 'And it isn't true. I'm sure she never planned anything of the kind.'

'Yet Oliver Costello came here to meet someone,' the Inspector pointed out. 'The two servants had the night off. Miss Peake has her own cottage. There was really no one he could have come to the house to meet except Mrs Hailsham-Brown.'

'All I can say is –' Jeremy began. Then, turning away, he added limply, 'Well, you'd better ask her.'

'I have asked her,' the Inspector informed him.

'What did she say?' asked Jeremy, turning back to face the police officer.

'Just what you say,' the Inspector replied suavely.

Jeremy sat down again at the bridge table. 'There you are, then,' he observed.

The Inspector took a few steps around the room, his eyes on the floor as though deep in thought. Then he turned back to face Jeremy. 'Now tell me,' he queried, 'just how you all happened to come back here from the club. Was that your original plan?'

'Yes,' Jeremy replied, but then quickly changed his answer. 'I mean, no.'

'Which do you mean, sir?' the Inspector queried smoothly.

Jeremy took a deep breath. 'Well,' he began, 'it was like this. We all went over to the club. Sir Rowland and old Hugo went straight into the dining-room and I came in a bit later. It's all a cold buffet, you know. I'd been knocking balls about until it got dark, and then – well, somebody said "Bridge, anyone?", and I said, "Well, why don't we go back to the Hailsham-Browns' where it's more cosy, and play there?" So we did.'

'I see,' observed the Inspector. 'So it was your idea?'

Jeremy shrugged his shoulders. 'I really don't remember who suggested it first,' he admitted. 'It may have been Hugo Birch, I think.'

'And you arrived back here – when?'

Jeremy thought for a moment, and then shook his head. 'I can't say exactly,' he murmured. 'We probably left the club house just a bit before eight.'

'And it's – what?' the Inspector wondered. 'Five minutes' walk?'

'Yes, just about that. The golf course adjoins this garden,' Jeremy answered, glancing out of the window.

The Inspector went across to the bridge table, and looked down at its surface. 'And then you played bridge?'

'Yes,' Jeremy confirmed.

The Inspector nodded his head slowly. 'That must have

been about twenty minutes before my arrival here,' he calcu-
lated. He began to walk slowly around the table. 'Surely you
didn't have time to complete two rubbers and start –' he held
up Clarissa's marker so that Jeremy could see it – 'a third?'

'What?' Jeremy looked confused for a moment, but then
said quickly, 'Oh, no. No. That first rubber must have been
yesterday's score.'

Indicating the other markers, the Inspector remarked thoughtfully, 'Only one person seems to have scored.'

'Yes,' Jeremy agreed. 'I'm afraid we're all a bit lazy about
scoring. We left it to Clarissa.'

The Inspector walked across to the sofa. 'Did you know
about the passage-way between this room and the library?'
he asked.

'You mean the place where the body was found?'

'That's what I mean.'

'No. No, I'd no idea,' Jeremy asserted. 'Wonderful bit of
camouflage, isn't it? You'd never guess it was there.'

The Inspector sat on an arm of the sofa, leaning back and
dislodging a cushion. He noticed the gloves that had been
lying under the cushion. His face wore a serious expression
as he said quietly, 'Consequently, Mr Warrender, you couldn't
know there was a body in that passage-way. Could you?'

Jeremy turned away. 'You could have knocked me over with
a feather, as the saying goes,' he replied. 'Absolute blood and
thunder melodrama. Couldn't believe my eyes.'

While Jeremy was speaking, the Inspector had been sorting
out the gloves on the sofa. He now held up one pair of
them, rather in the manner of a conjuror. 'By the way, are
these your gloves, Mr Warrender?' he asked, trying to sound
off-handed.

Jeremy turned back to him. 'No. I mean, yes,' he replied confusedly.

'Again, which do you mean, sir?'

'Yes, they are mine, I think.'

'Were you wearing them when you came back here from the golf club?'

'Yes,' Jeremy recalled. 'I remember now. Yes, I was wearing them. There's a bit of a nip in the air this evening.'

The Inspector got up from the arm of the sofa, and approached Jeremy. 'I think you're mistaken, sir.' Indicating the initials in the gloves, he pointed out, 'These have Mr Hailsham-Brown's initials inside them.'

Returning his gaze calmly, Jeremy replied, 'Oh, that's funny. I've got a pair just the same.'

The Inspector returned to the sofa, sat on the arm again and, leaning over, produced the second pair of gloves. 'Perhaps these are yours?' he suggested.

Jeremy laughed. 'You don't catch me a second time,' he replied. 'After all, one pair of gloves looks exactly like another.'

The Inspector produced the third pair of gloves. 'Three pairs of gloves,' he murmured, examining them. 'All with Hailsham-Brown's initials inside. Curious.'

'Well, it is his house, after all,' Jeremy pointed out. 'Why shouldn't he have three pairs of gloves lying about?'

'The only interesting thing,' the Inspector replied, 'is that you thought one of them might have been yours. And I think that your gloves are just sticking out of your pocket, now.'

Jeremy put his hand in his right-hand pocket. 'No, the other one,' the Inspector told him.

Removing the gloves from his left-hand pocket, Jeremy exclaimed, 'Oh yes. Yes, so they are.'

'They're not really very like these. Are they?' the Inspector asked, pointedly.

'Actually, these are my golfing gloves,' Jeremy replied with a smile.

'Thank you, Mr Warrender,' the Inspector said abruptly and dismissively, patting the cushion back into place on the sofa. 'That will be all for now.'

Jeremy rose, looking upset. 'Look here,' he exclaimed, 'you don't think –' He paused.

'I don't think what, sir?' asked the Inspector.

'Nothing,' Jeremy replied uncertainly. He paused, and then made for the library door, only to be intercepted by the Constable. Turning back to the Inspector, Jeremy pointed mutely and enquiringly at the hall door. The Inspector nodded, and Jeremy made his way out of the room, closing the hall door behind him.

Leaving the gloves on the sofa, the Inspector went across to the bridge table, sat, and consulted *Who's Who* again. 'Here we are,' he murmured, and began to read aloud, '"Thomson, Sir Kenneth. Chairman of Saxon-Arabian Oil Company, Gulf Petroleum Company." Hmm! Impressive. "Recreations: Philately, golf, fishing. Address, three hundred and forty Broad Street, thirty-four Grosvenor Square".'

While the Inspector was reading, Constable Jones went across to the table by the sofa and began to sharpen his pencil into the ashtray. Stooping to pick up some shavings from the floor, he saw a playing-card lying there and brought it to the bridge table, throwing it down in front of his superior.

'What have you got there?' the Inspector asked.

'Just a card, sir. Found it over there, under the sofa.'

The Inspector picked up the card. 'The ace of spades,'

he noted. 'A very interesting card. Here, wait a minute.' He turned the card over. 'Red. It's the same pack.' He picked up the red pack of cards from the table, and spread them out.

The Constable helped him sort through the cards. 'Well, well, no ace of spades,' the Inspector exclaimed. He rose from his chair. 'Now, that's very remarkable, don't you think, Jones?' he asked, putting the card in his pocket and going across to the sofa. 'They managed to play bridge without missing the ace of spades.'

'Very remarkable indeed, sir,' Constable Jones agreed, as he tidied the cards on the table.

The Inspector collected the three pairs of gloves from the sofa. 'Now I think we'll have Sir Rowland Delahaye,' he instructed the Constable, as he took the gloves to the bridge table and spread them out in pairs.

CHAPTER 16

The Constable opened the library door, calling, 'Sir Rowland Delahaye.'

As Sir Rowland paused in the doorway, the Inspector called, 'Do come in, sir, and sit down here, please.'

Sir Rowland approached the bridge table, paused for a moment as he noticed the gloves spread out on it, and then sat.

'You are Sir Rowland Delahaye?' the Inspector asked him formally. Receiving a grave, affirmative nod, he next asked, 'What is your address?'

'Long Paddock, Littlewich Green, Lincolnshire,' Sir Rowland replied. Tapping a finger on the copy of *Who's Who*, he added, 'Couldn't you find it, Inspector?'

The Inspector chose to ignore this. 'Now, if you please,' he said, 'I'd like your account of the evening, after you left here shortly before seven.'

Sir Rowland had obviously already given some thought to this. 'It had been raining all day,' he began smoothly, 'and then it suddenly cleared up. We had already arranged to go to the golf club for dinner, as it is the servants' night out. So we did that.' He glanced across at the Constable, as though to make sure he was keeping up, then continued, 'As we were finishing dinner, Mrs Hailsham-Brown rang up and suggested that, as her husband had unexpectedly had to go out, we three should return here and make up a four for bridge. We did so. About twenty minutes after we'd started playing, you arrived, Inspector. The rest – you know.'

The Inspector looked thoughtful. 'That's not quite Mr Warrender's account of the matter,' he observed.

'Indeed?' said Sir Rowland. 'And how did he put it?'

'He said that the suggestion to come back here and play bridge came from one of you. But he thought it was probably Mr Birch.'

'Ah,' replied Sir Rowland easily, 'but you see Warrender came into the dining-room at the club rather late. He did not realize that Mrs Hailsham-Brown had rung up.'

Sir Rowland and the Inspector looked at each other, as though trying to stare each other out. Then Sir Rowland continued, 'You must know better than I do, Inspector, how very rarely two people's accounts of the same thing agree. In fact, if the three of us were to agree exactly, I should regard it as suspicious. Very suspicious indeed.'

The Inspector chose not to comment on this observation. Drawing a chair up close to Sir Rowland, he sat down. 'I'd like to discuss the case with you, sir, if I may,' he suggested.

'How very agreeable of you, Inspector,' Sir Rowland replied.

After looking thoughtfully at the table-top for a few seconds, the Inspector began the discussion. 'The dead man, Mr Oliver Costello, came to this house with some particular object in view.' He paused. 'Do you agree that that is what must have happened, sir?'

'My understanding is that he came to return to Henry Hailsham-Brown certain objects which Mrs Miranda Hailsham-Brown, as she then was, had taken away in error,' Sir Rowland replied.

'That may have been his excuse, sir,' the Inspector pointed out, 'though I'm not even sure of that. But I'm certain it wasn't the real reason that brought him here.'

Sir Rowland shrugged his shoulders. 'You may be right,' he observed. 'I can't say.'

The Inspector pressed on. 'He came, perhaps, to see a particular person. It may have been you, it may have been Mr Warrender, or it may have been Mr Birch.'

'If he had wanted to see Mr Birch, who lives locally,' Sir Rowland pointed out, 'he would have gone to his house. He wouldn't have come here.'

'That is probably so,' the Inspector agreed. 'Therefore that leaves us with the choice of four people. You, Mr Warrender, Mr Hailsham-Brown and Mrs Hailsham-Brown.' He paused and gave Sir Rowland a searching glance before asking, 'Now, sir, how well did you know Oliver Costello?'

'Hardly at all. I've met him once or twice, that's all.'

'Where did you meet him?' asked the Inspector.

Sir Rowland reflected. 'Twice at the Hailsham-Browns' in London, over a year ago, and once in a restaurant, I believe.'

'But you had no reason for wishing to murder him?'

'Is that an accusation, Inspector?' Sir Rowland asked with a smile.

The Inspector shook his head. 'No, Sir Rowland,' he replied. 'I should call it more an elimination. I don't think you have any motive for doing away with Oliver Costello. So that leaves just three people.'

'This is beginning to sound like a variant of "Ten Little Indians",' Sir Rowland observed with a smile.

The Inspector smiled back. 'We'll take Mr Warrender next,' he proposed. 'Now, how well do you know him?'

'I met him here for the first time two days ago,' Sir Rowland replied. 'He appears to be an agreeable young man, well bred, and well educated. He's a friend of Clarissa's. I know nothing about him, but I should say he's an unlikely murderer.'

'So much for Mr Warrender,' the Inspector noted. 'That brings me to my next question.'

Anticipating him, Sir Rowland nodded. 'How well do I know Henry Hailsham-Brown, and how well do I know Mrs Hailsham-Brown? That's what you want to know, isn't it?' he asked. 'Actually, I know Henry Hailsham-Brown very well indeed. He is an old friend. As for Clarissa, I know all there is to know about her. She is my ward, and inexpressibly dear to me.'

'Yes, sir,' said the Inspector. 'I think that answer makes certain things very clear.'

'Does it, indeed?'

The Inspector rose and took a few paces about the room before turning back to face Sir Rowland. 'Why did you three change your plans this evening?' he asked. 'Why did you come back here and pretend to play bridge?'

'Pretend?' Sir Rowland exclaimed sharply.

The Inspector took the playing card from his pocket. 'This card,' he said, 'was found on the other side of the room under the sofa. I can hardly believe that you would have played two rubbers of bridge and started a third with a pack of fifty-one cards, and the ace of spades missing.'

Sir Rowland took the card from the Inspector, looked at the

back of it, and then returned it. 'Yes,' he admitted. 'Perhaps that is a little difficult to believe.'

The Inspector cast his eyes despairingly upwards before adding, 'I also think that three pairs of Mr Hailsham-Brown's gloves need a certain amount of explanation.'

After a moment's pause, Sir Rowland replied, 'I'm afraid, Inspector, you won't get any explanation from me.'

'No, sir,' the Inspector agreed. 'I take it that you are out to do your best for a certain lady. But it's not a bit of good, sir. The truth will out.'

'I wonder if it will,' was Sir Rowland's only response to this observation.

The Inspector went across to the panel. 'Mrs Hailsham-Brown knew that Costello's body was in the recess,' he insisted. 'Whether she dragged it there herself, or whether you helped her, I don't know. But I'm convinced that she knew.' He came back to face Sir Rowland. 'I suggest,' he continued, 'that Oliver Costello came here to see Mrs Hailsham-Brown and to obtain money from her by threats.'

'Threats?' Sir Rowland asked. 'Threats of what?'

'That will all come out in due course, I have no doubt,' the Inspector assured him. 'Mrs Hailsham-Brown is young and attractive. This Mr Costello was a great man for the ladies, they say. Now, Mrs Hailsham-Brown is newly married and –'

'Stop!' Sir Rowland interrupted peremptorily. 'I must put you right on certain matters. You can confirm what I tell you easily enough. Henry Hailsham-Brown's first marriage was unfortunate. His wife, Miranda, was a beautiful woman, but unbalanced and neurotic. Her health and disposition had degenerated to such an alarming state that her little daughter had to be removed to a nursing home.'

He paused in reflection. Then, 'Yes, a really shocking state of affairs,' he continued. 'It seemed that Miranda had become a drug addict. How she obtained these drugs was not found out, but it was a very fair guess that she had been supplied with them by this man, Oliver Costello. She was infatuated with him, and finally ran away with him.'

After another pause and a glance across at the Constable, to see if he was keeping up, Sir Rowland resumed his story. 'Henry Hailsham-Brown, who is old-fashioned in his views, allowed Miranda to divorce him,' he explained. 'Henry has now found happiness and peace in his marriage with Clarissa, and I can assure you, Inspector, that there are no guilty secrets in Clarissa's life. There is nothing, I can swear, with which Costello could possibly threaten her.'

The Inspector said nothing, but merely looked thoughtful.

Sir Rowland stood up, tucked his chair under the table, and walked over to the sofa. Then, turning to address the police officer again, he suggested, 'Don't you think, Inspector, that you're on the wrong track altogether? Why should you be so certain that it was a person Costello came here to see? Why couldn't it have been a place?'

The Inspector now looked perplexed. 'What do you mean, sir?' he asked.

'When you were talking to us about the late Mr Sellon,' Sir Rowland reminded him, 'you mentioned that the Narcotics Squad took an interest in him. Isn't there a possible link there? Drugs – Sellon – Sellon's house?'

He paused but, receiving no reaction from the Inspector, continued, 'Costello has been here once before, I understand, ostensibly to look at Sellon's antiques. Supposing Oliver

Costello wanted something in this house. In that desk, perhaps.'

The Inspector glanced at the desk, and Sir Rowland expanded on his theory. 'There is the curious incident of a man who came here and offered an exorbitant price for that desk. Supposing it was that desk that Oliver Costello wanted to examine – wanted to search, if you like. Supposing that he was followed here by someone. And that that someone struck him down, there by the desk.'

The Inspector did not seem impressed. 'There's a good deal of supposition –' he began, only to be interrupted by Sir Rowland who insisted, 'It's a very reasonable hypothesis.'

'The hypothesis being,' the Inspector queried, 'that this somebody put the body in the recess?'

'Exactly.'

'That would have to be somebody who knew about the recess,' the Inspector observed.

'It could be someone who knew the house in Sellon's time,' Sir Rowland pointed out.

'Yes, that's all very well, sir,' the Inspector replied impatiently, 'but it still doesn't explain one thing –'

'What is that?' asked Sir Rowland.

The Inspector looked at him steadily. 'Mrs Hailsham-Brown knew the body was in that recess. She tried to prevent us looking there.'

Sir Rowland opened his mouth to speak, but the Inspector held up a hand and continued, 'It's no good trying to convince me otherwise. She knew.'

For a few moments, a tense silence prevailed. Then Sir Rowland said, 'Inspector, will you allow me to speak to my ward?'

'Only in my presence, sir,' was the prompt reply.

'That will do.'

The Inspector nodded. 'Jones!' The Constable, understanding what was required, left the room.

'We are very much in your hands, Inspector,' Sir Rowland told the police officer. 'I will ask you to make what allowances you can.'

'My one concern is to get at the truth, sir, and to find out who killed Oliver Costello,' the Inspector replied.

CHAPTER 17

The Constable came back into the room, holding the door open for Clarissa.

'Come in here, please, Mrs Hailsham-Brown,' the Inspector called. As Clarissa entered, Sir Rowland went over to her. He spoke very solemnly. 'Clarissa, my dear,' he said. 'Will you do what I ask you? I want you to tell the Inspector the truth.'

'The truth?' Clarissa echoed, sounding very doubtful.

'The truth,' Sir Rowland repeated with emphasis. 'It's the only thing to do. I mean it. Seriously.' He looked at her steadily and indeed seriously for a moment, and then left the room. The Constable closed the door after him and resumed his seat for note-taking.

'Do sit down, Mrs Hailsham-Brown,' the Inspector invited her, this time indicating the sofa.

Clarissa smiled at him, but the look he returned was a stern one. She moved slowly to the sofa, sat, and waited for a moment before speaking. Then, 'I'm sorry,' she told him. 'I'm terribly sorry I told you all those lies. I didn't mean to.' She did indeed sound rueful as she continued, 'One gets into things, if you know what I mean?'

'I can't say that I do know,' the Inspector replied coldly. 'Now, please just give me the facts.'

'Well, it's really all quite simple,' she explained, ticking off the facts on her fingers as she spoke. 'First, Oliver Costello left. Then, Henry came home. Then, I saw him off again in the car. Then, I came in here with the sandwiches.'

'Sandwiches?' the Inspector queried.

'Yes. You see, my husband is bringing home a very important delegate from abroad.'

The Inspector looked interested. 'Oh, who is this delegate?'

'A Mr Jones,' Clarissa told him.

'I beg your pardon?' said the Inspector, with a look at Constable Jones.

'Mr Jones. That's not his real name, but that's what we have to call him. It's all very hush-hush.' Clarissa went on speaking. 'They were going to have the sandwiches while they talked, and I was going to have mousse in the schoolroom.'

The Inspector was looking perplexed. 'Mousse in the – yes, I see,' he murmured, sounding as though he did not see at all.

'I put the sandwiches down there,' Clarissa told him, pointing to the stool, 'and then I began tidying up, and I went to put a book back on the bookshelf and – then – and then I practically fell over it.'

'You fell over the body?' the Inspector asked.

'Yes. It was here, behind the sofa. And I looked to see if it – if he was dead, and he was. It was Oliver Costello, and I didn't know what to do. In the end, I rang up the golf club, and I asked Sir Rowland, Mr Birch and Jeremy Warrender to come back right away.'

Leaning over the sofa, the Inspector asked coldly, 'It didn't occur to you to ring up the police?'

'Well, it occurred to me, yes,' Clarissa answered, 'but then – well –' She smiled at him again. 'Well, I didn't.'

'You didn't,' the Inspector murmured to himself. He walked away, looked at the Constable, lifted his hands despairingly, and then turned back to face Clarissa. 'Why didn't you ring the police?' he asked her.

Clarissa was prepared for this. 'Well, I didn't think it would be nice for my husband,' she replied. 'I don't know whether you know many people in the Foreign Office, Inspector, but they're frightfully unassuming. They like everything very quiet, not noticeable. You must admit that murders are rather noticeable.'

'Quite so,' was all that the Inspector could think of in response to this.

'I'm so glad you understand,' Clarissa told him warmly and almost gushingly. She went on with her story, but her delivery became more and more unconvincing as she began to feel that she was not making headway. 'I mean,' she said, 'he was quite dead, because I felt his pulse, so we couldn't do anything for him.'

The Inspector walked about, without replying. Following him with her eyes, Clarissa continued, 'What I mean is, he might just as well be dead in Marsden Wood as in our drawing-room.'

The Inspector turned sharply to face her. 'Marsden Wood?' he asked abruptly. 'How does Marsden Wood come into it?'

'That's where I was thinking of putting him,' Clarissa replied.

The Inspector put a hand to the back of his head, and looked at the floor as though seeking inspiration there. Then, shaking his head to clear it, he said firmly, 'Mrs Hailsham-Brown, have you never heard that a dead body, if there's any suggestion of foul play, should never be moved?'

'Of course I know that,' Clarissa retorted. 'It says so in all the detective stories. But, you see, this is real life.'

The Inspector lifted his hands in despair.

'I mean,' she continued, 'real life's quite different.'

The Inspector looked at Clarissa in incredulous silence for a moment, before asking her, 'Do you realize the seriousness of what you're saying?'

'Of course I do,' she replied, 'and I'm telling you the truth. So, you see, in the end, I rang up the club and they all came back here.'

'And you persuaded them to hide the body in that recess.'

'No,' Clarissa corrected him. 'That came later. My plan, as I told you, was that they should take Oliver's body away in his car and leave the car in Marsden Wood.'

'And they agreed?' The Inspector's tone was distinctly unbelieving.

'Yes, they agreed,' said Clarissa, smiling at him.

'Frankly, Mrs Hailsham-Brown,' the Inspector told her brusquely, 'I don't believe a word of it. I don't believe that three responsible men would agree to obstruct the course of justice in such a manner for such a paltry cause.'

Clarissa rose to her feet. Walking away from the Inspector, she said more to herself than to him, 'I knew you wouldn't believe me if I told you the truth.' She turned to face him. 'What *do* you believe, then?' she asked him.

Watching Clarissa closely as he spoke, the Inspector replied,

'I can see only one reason why those three men should agree to lie.'

'Oh? What do you mean? What other reason would they have?'

'They would agree to lie,' the Inspector continued, 'if they believed, or, even more so, if they actually knew – that you had killed him.'

Clarissa stared at him. 'But I had no *reason* for killing him,' she protested. 'Absolutely no reason.' She flung away from him. 'Oh, I knew you'd react like this,' she exclaimed. 'That's why –'

She broke off suddenly, and the Inspector turned to her. 'That's why what?' he asked abruptly.

Clarissa stood thinking. Some moments passed, and then her manner appeared to change. She began to speak more convincingly. 'All right, then,' she announced, with the air of one who is making a clean breast of things. 'I'll tell you why.'

'I think that would be wiser,' the Inspector said.

'Yes,' she agreed, turning to face him squarely. 'I suppose I'd better tell you the *truth*.' She emphasized the word.

The Inspector smiled. 'I can assure you,' he advised her, 'that telling the police a pack of lies will do you very little good, Mrs Hailsham-Brown. You'd better tell me the real story. And from the beginning.'

'I will,' Clarissa promised. She sat down in a chair by the bridge table. 'Oh dear,' she sighed, 'I thought I was being so clever.'

'It's much better not to try to be clever,' the Inspector told her. He seated himself facing Clarissa. 'Now then,' he asked, 'what really did happen this evening?'

Clarissa was silent for a few moments. Then, looking the Inspector steadily in the eye, she began to speak. 'It all started as I've already explained to you. I said good-bye to Oliver Costello, and he'd gone off with Miss Peake. I had no idea he would come back again, and I still can't understand why he did.'

She paused, and seemed to be trying to recall what had happened next. 'Oh, yes,' she continued. 'Then my husband came home, explaining that he would have to go out again immediately. He went off in the car, and it was just after I had shut the front door, and made sure that it was latched and bolted, that I suddenly began to feel nervous.'

'Nervous?' asked the Inspector, looking puzzled. 'Why?'

'Well, I'm not usually nervous,' she told him, speaking with great feeling, 'but it occurred to me that I'd never been alone in the house at night.'

She paused. 'Yes, go on,' the Inspector encouraged her.

'I told myself not to be so silly. I said to myself, "You've got the phone, haven't you? You can always ring for help." I said to myself, "Burglars don't come at this time of the evening. They come in the middle of the night." But I still kept thinking I heard a door shutting somewhere, or footsteps up in my bedroom. So I thought I'd better do something.'

She paused again, and again the Inspector prompted her. 'Yes?'

'I went into the kitchen,' Clarissa said, 'and made the sandwiches for Henry and Mr Jones to have when they got back. I got them all ready on a plate, with a napkin around them to keep them soft, and I was just coming across the hall to put them in here, when –' she paused dramatically – 'I really heard something.'

'Where?' the Inspector asked.

'In this room,' she told him. 'I knew that, this time, I wasn't imagining it. I heard drawers being pulled open and shut, and then I suddenly remembered that the French windows in here weren't locked. We never do lock them. Somebody had come in that way.'

Again she paused. 'Go on, Mrs Hailsham-Brown,' said the Inspector impassively.

Clarissa made a gesture of helplessness. 'I didn't know what to do. I was petrified. Then I thought, "What if I'm just being a fool? What if it's Henry come back for something – or even Sir Rowland or one of the others? A nice fool you'll look if you go upstairs and ring the police on the extension." So then I thought of a plan.'

She paused once more, and the Inspector's 'Yes?' this time sounded a trifle impatient.

'I went to the hall stand,' Clarissa said slowly, 'and I took the heaviest stick I could find. Then I went into the library. I didn't turn the light on. I felt my way across the room to that recess. I opened it very gently and slipped inside. I thought I could ease the door into here and see who it was.' She pointed to the panel. 'Unless anyone knew about it, you'd never dream there was a door just there.'

'No,' the Inspector agreed, 'you certainly wouldn't.'

Clarissa seemed now to be almost enjoying her narrative. 'I eased the catch open,' she continued, 'and then my fingers slipped, and the door swung right open and hit against a chair. A man who was standing by the desk straightened up. I saw something bright and shining in his hand. I thought it was a revolver. I was terrified. I thought he was going to shoot me. I hit out at him with the stick with all my might, and he fell.'

She collapsed and leant on the table with her face in her hands. 'Could I – could I have a little brandy, please?' she asked the Inspector.

'Yes, of course.' The Inspector got to his feet. 'Jones!' he called. The Constable poured some brandy into a glass and handed it to the Inspector. Clarissa had lifted her face, but quickly covered it with her hands again and held out her hand as the Inspector brought her the brandy. She drank, coughed, and returned the glass. Constable Jones replaced it on a table and resumed his seat and his note-taking.

The Inspector looked at Clarissa. 'Do you feel able to continue, Mrs Hailsham-Brown?' he asked sympathetically.

'Yes,' Clarissa replied, glancing up at him. 'You're very kind.' She took a breath and continued her story. 'The man just lay there. He didn't move. I switched on the light and I saw then that it was Oliver Costello. He was dead. It was terrible. I – I couldn't understand it.'

She gestured towards the desk. 'I couldn't understand what he was doing there, tampering with the desk. It was all like some ghastly nightmare. I was so frightened that I rang the golf club. I wanted my guardian to be with me. They all came over. I begged them to help me, to take the body away – somewhere.'

The Inspector stared at her intently. 'But why?' he asked.

Clarissa turned away from him. 'Because I was a coward,' she said. 'A miserable coward. I was frightened of the publicity, of having to go to a police court. And it would be so bad for my husband and for his career.'

She turned back to the Inspector. 'If it had really been a burglar, perhaps I could have gone through with it, but being someone we actually knew, someone who is married to Henry's first wife – Oh, I just felt I couldn't go through with it.'

'Perhaps,' the Inspector suggested, 'because the dead man had, a short while before, attempted to blackmail you?'

'Blackmail me? Oh, that's nonsense!' Clarissa replied with complete confidence. 'That's just silly. There's nothing any-one could blackmail me about.'

'Elgin, your butler, overheard a mention of blackmail,' the Inspector told her.

'I don't believe he heard anything of the kind,' replied Clarissa. 'He couldn't. If you ask me, he's making the whole thing up.'

'Come now, Mrs Hailsham-Brown,' the Inspector insisted, 'are you deliberately telling me that the word blackmail was never mentioned? Why would your butler make it up?'

'I swear there was no mention of blackmail,' Clarissa exclaimed, banging the table with her hand. 'I assure you –' Her hand stopped in mid-air, and she suddenly laughed. 'Oh, how silly. Of course. That was it.'

'You've remembered?' the Inspector asked calmly.

'It was nothing, really,' Clarissa assured him. 'It was just that Oliver was saying something about the rent of furnished houses being absurdly high, and I said we'd been amazingly lucky and were only paying four guineas a week for this. And he said, "I can hardly believe it, Clarissa. What's your pull? It must be blackmail." And I laughed and said, "That's it. Blackmail."'

She laughed now, apparently recalling the exchange. 'Just a silly, joking way of talking. Why, I didn't even remember it.'

'I'm sorry, Mrs Hailsham-Brown,' said the Inspector, 'but I really can't believe that.'

Clarissa looked astonished. 'Can't believe what?'

'That you're only paying four guineas a week for this house, furnished.'

'Honestly! You really are the most unbelieving man I've ever met,' Clarissa told him as she rose and went to the desk. 'You don't seem to believe a single thing I've said to you this evening. Most things I can't prove, but this one I can. And this time I'm going to show you.'

She opened a drawer of the desk and searched through the papers in it. 'Here it is,' she exclaimed. 'No, it isn't. Ah! Here we are.' She took a document from the drawer and showed it to the Inspector. 'Here's the agreement for our tenancy of this house, furnished. It's made out by a firm of solicitors acting for the executors and, look – four guineas per week.'

The Inspector looked jolted. 'Well, I'm blessed! It's extra-ordinary. Quite extraordinary. I'd have thought it was worth much more than that.'

Clarissa gave him one of her most charming smiles. 'Don't you think, Inspector, that you ought to beg my pardon?' she suggested.

The Inspector injected a certain amount of charm into his voice as he responded. 'I do apologize, Mrs Hailsham-Brown,' he said, 'but it really is extremely odd, you know.'

'Why? What do you mean?' Clarissa asked, as she replaced the document in the drawer.

'Well, it so happens,' the Inspector replied, 'that a lady and a gentleman were down in this area with orders to view this house, and the lady happened to lose a very valuable brooch somewhere in the vicinity. She called in at the police station to give particulars, and she happened to mention this house. She said the owners were asking an absurd price. She thought eighteen guineas a week for a house out in the country and miles from anywhere was ridiculous. I thought so too.'

'Yes, that is extraordinary, very extraordinary,' Clarissa agreed, with a friendly smile. 'I understand why you were sceptical. But perhaps now you'll believe some of the other things I said.'

'I'm not doubting your final story, Mrs Hailsham-Brown,' the Inspector assured her. 'We usually know the truth when we hear it. I knew, too, that there would have to be some serious reason for those three gentlemen to cook up this harebrained scheme of concealment.'

'You mustn't blame them too much, Inspector,' Clarissa pleaded. 'It was my fault. I went on and on at them.'

All too aware of her charm, the Inspector replied, 'Ah, I've no doubt you did. But what I still don't understand is, who telephoned the police in the first place and reported the murder?'

'Yes, that is extraordinary!' said Clarissa, sounding startled. 'I'd completely forgotten that.'

'It clearly wasn't you,' the Inspector pointed out, 'and it wouldn't have been any of the three gentlemen –'

Clarissa shook her head. 'Could it have been Elgin?' she wondered. 'Or perhaps Miss Peake?'

'I don't think it could possibly have been Miss Peake,' said the Inspector. 'She clearly didn't know Costello's body was there.'

'I wonder if that's so,' said Clarissa thoughtfully.

'After all, when the body was discovered, she had hysterics,' the Inspector reminded her.

'Oh, that's nothing. Anyone can have hysterics,' Clarissa remarked incautiously. The Inspector shot her a suspicious glance, at which she felt it expedient to give him as innocent a smile as she could manage.

'Anyway, Miss Peake doesn't live in the house,' the Inspector observed. 'She has her own cottage in the grounds.'

'But she could have been in the house,' said Clarissa. 'You know, she has keys to all the doors.'

The Inspector shook his head. 'No, it looks to me more like Elgin who must have called us,' he said.

Clarissa moved closer to him, and flashed him a somewhat anxious smile. 'You're not going to send me to prison, are you?' she asked. 'Uncle Roly said he was sure you wouldn't.'

The Inspector gave her an austere look. 'It's a good thing you changed your story in time, and told us the truth, madam,' he advised her sternly. 'But, if I may say so, Mrs Hailsham-Brown, I think you should get in touch with your solicitor as soon as possible and give him all the relevant facts. In the meantime, I'll get your statement typed out and read over to you, and perhaps you will be good enough to sign it.'

Clarissa was about to reply when the hall door opened and

Sir Rowland entered. 'I couldn't keep away any longer,' he explained. 'Is it all right now, Inspector? Do you understand what our dilemma was?'

Clarissa went across to her guardian before he could say any more. 'Roly, darling,' she greeted him, taking his hand. 'I've made a statement, and the police – or rather Mr Jones here – is going to type it out. Then I've got to sign it, and I've told them everything.'

The Inspector went over to confer with the Constable, and Clarissa continued speaking quietly to Sir Rowland. 'I told them how I thought it was a burglar,' she said with emphasis, 'and hit him on the head –'

When Sir Rowland looked at her in alarm and opened his mouth to speak, she quickly covered his mouth with her hands so that he could not get the words out. She continued hurriedly, 'Then I told them how it turned out to be Oliver Costello, and how I got in a terrible flap and rang you, and how I begged and begged and at last you all gave in. I see now how wrong of me it was –'

The Inspector turned back to them, and Clarissa removed her hand from Sir Rowland's mouth just in time. 'But when it happened,' she was saying, 'I was just scared stiff, and I thought it would be cosier for everybody – me, Henry and even Miranda – if Oliver was found in Marsden Wood.'

Sir Rowland looked aghast. 'Clarissa! What on earth have you been saying?' he gasped.

'Mrs Hailsham-Brown has made a very full statement, sir,' the Inspector said complacently.

Recovering himself somewhat, Sir Rowland replied drily, 'So it seems.'

'It's the best thing to do,' said Clarissa. 'In fact, it was the only thing to do. The Inspector made me see that. And I'm truly sorry to have told all those silly lies.'

'It will lead to far less trouble in the end,' the Inspector assured her. 'Now, Mrs Hailsham-Brown,' he went on, 'I shan't ask you to go into the recess while the body is still there, but I'd like you to show me exactly where the man was standing when you came through that way into this room.'

'Oh – yes – well – he was –' Clarissa began hesitantly. She went across to the desk. 'No,' she continued, 'I remember now. He was standing here like this.' She stood at one end of the desk, and leaned over it.

'Be ready to open the panel when I give you the word, Jones,' said the Inspector, motioning to the Constable, who rose and put his hand on the panel switch.

'I see,' the Inspector said to Clarissa. 'That's where he was standing. And then the door opened and you came out. All right, I don't want you to have to look in there at the body now, so just stand in front of the panel when it opens. Now – Jones.'

The Constable activated the switch, and the panel opened. The recess was empty except for a small piece of paper on the floor which Constable Jones retrieved, while the Inspector looked accusingly at Clarissa and Sir Rowland.

The Constable read out what was on the slip of paper. 'Sucks to you!' As the Inspector snatched the paper from him, Clarissa and Sir Rowland looked at each other in astonishment.

A loud ring from the front-door bell broke the silence.

A few moments later Elgin came into the drawing-room to announce that the Divisional Surgeon had arrived. The Inspector and Constable Jones immediately accompanied the butler to the front door, where the Inspector had the unenviable task of confessing to the Divisional Surgeon that, as it turned out, there was at present no body to examine.

'Really, Inspector Lord,' the Divisional Surgeon said irritably. 'Do you realize how infuriating it is to have brought me all this way on a wild-goose chase?'

'But I assure you, Doctor,' the Inspector attempted to explain, 'we did have a body.'

'The Inspector's right, Doctor,' Constable Jones added his voice. 'We certainly did have a body. It just happens to have disappeared.'

The sound of their voices had brought Hugo and Jeremy out from the dining-room on the other side of the hall. They could not refrain from making unhelpful comments. 'I can't think how you policemen ever get anything done – losing bodies indeed,' Hugo expostulated, while Jeremy exclaimed, 'I don't understand why a guard wasn't put on the body.'

'Well, whatever has happened, if there's no body for me to examine, I'm not wasting any more time here,' the Divisional Surgeon snapped at the Inspector. 'I can assure you that you'll hear more about this, Inspector Lord.'

'Yes, Doctor. I've no doubt of that. Goodnight, Doctor,' the Inspector replied wearily.

The Divisional Surgeon left, slamming the front door behind him, and the Inspector turned to Elgin, who forestalled him by saying quickly, 'I know nothing about it, I assure you, sir, nothing at all.'

Meanwhile, in the drawing-room, Clarissa and Sir Rowland were enjoying overhearing the discomfiture of the police officers. 'Rather a bad moment for the police reinforcements to arrive,' Sir Rowland chuckled. 'The Divisional Surgeon seems very annoyed at finding no corpse to examine.'

Clarissa giggled. 'But who can have spirited it away?' she asked. 'Do you think Jeremy managed it somehow?'

'I don't see how he could have done,' Sir Rowland replied. 'They didn't let anyone back into the library, and the door from the library to the hall was locked. Pippa's "Sucks to you" was the last straw.'

Clarissa laughed, and Sir Rowland continued, 'Still, it shows us one thing. Costello had managed to open the secret drawer.' He paused, and his manner changed. 'Clarissa,' he said in a serious tone, 'why on earth didn't you tell the truth to the Inspector when I begged you to?'

'I did,' Clarissa protested, 'except for the part about Pippa. But he just didn't believe me.'

'But, for Heaven's sake, why did you have to stuff him with all that nonsense?' Sir Rowland insisted on knowing.

'Well,' Clarissa replied with a helpless gesture, 'it seemed to me the most likely thing he would believe. And,' she ended triumphantly, 'he does believe me now.'

'And a nice mess you're in as a result,' Sir Rowland pointed out. 'You'll be up on a charge of manslaughter, for all you know.'

'I shall claim it was self-defence,' Clarissa said confidently.

Before Sir Rowland had a chance to reply, Hugo and Jeremy entered from the hall, and Hugo walked over to the bridge table, grumbling. 'Wretched police, pushing us around here and there. Now it seems they've gone and lost the body.'

Jeremy closed the door behind him, then went over to the stool and took a sandwich. 'Damn peculiar, I call it,' he announced.

'It's fantastic,' said Clarissa. 'The whole thing's fantastic. The body's gone, and we still don't know who rang up the police in the first place and said there'd been a murder here.'

'Well, that was Elgin, surely,' Jeremy suggested, as he sat on an arm of the sofa and began to eat his sandwich.

'No, no,' Hugo disagreed. 'I'd say it was that Peake woman.'

'But why?' Clarissa asked. 'Why would either of them do that, and not tell us? It doesn't make sense.'

Miss Peake put her head in at the hall door and looked around with a conspiratorial air. 'Hello, is the coast clear?' she asked. Closing the door, she strode confidently into the room. 'No bobbies about? They seem to be swarming all over the place.'

'They're busy searching the house and grounds now,' Sir Rowland informed her.

'What for?' asked Miss Peake.

'The body,' Sir Rowland replied. 'It's gone.'

Miss Peake gave her usual hearty laugh. 'What a lark!' she boomed. 'The disappearing body, eh?'

Hugo sat at the bridge table. Looking around the room, he observed to no one in particular, 'It's a nightmare. The whole thing's a damn nightmare.'

'Quite like the movies, eh, Mrs Hailsham-Brown?' Miss Peake suggested with another hoot of laughter.

Sir Rowland smiled at the gardener. 'I hope you are feeling better now, Miss Peake?' he asked her courteously.

'Oh, I'm all right,' she replied. 'I'm pretty tough really, you know. I was just a bit bowled over by opening that door and finding a corpse. Turned me up for the moment, I must admit.'

'I wondered, perhaps,' said Clarissa quietly, 'if you already knew it was there.'

The gardener stared at her. 'Who? Me?'

'Yes. You.'

Again seeming to be addressing the entire universe, Hugo said, 'It doesn't make sense. Why take the body away? We all know there is a body. We know his identity and everything. No point in it. Why not leave the wretched thing where it was?'

'Oh, I wouldn't say there was no point in it, Mr Birch,' Miss Peake corrected Hugo, leaning across the bridge table to address him. 'You've got to have a body, you know. Habeas corpus and all that. Remember? You've got to have a body before you can bring a charge of murder against anybody.' She turned around to Clarissa. 'So don't you worry, Mrs Hailsham-Brown,' she assured her. 'Everything's going to be all right.'

Clarissa stared at her. 'What do you mean?'

'I've kept my ears open this evening,' the gardener told her. 'I haven't spent all my time lying on the bed in the spare room.' She looked around at everyone. 'I never liked that man Elgin, or his wife,' she continued. 'Listening at doors, and running to the police with stories about blackmail.'

'So you heard that?' Clarissa asked, wonderingly.

'What I always say is, stand by your own sex,' Miss Peake declared. She looked at Hugo. 'Men!' she snorted. 'I don't hold with them.' She sat down next to Clarissa on the sofa. 'If they can't find the body, my dear,' she explained, 'they can't bring a charge against you. And what I say is, if that brute was blackmailing you, you did quite right to crack him over the head and good riddance.'

'But I didn't –' Clarissa began faintly, only to be interrupted by Miss Peake.

'I heard you tell that Inspector all about it,' the gardener informed her. 'And if it wasn't for that eavesdropping skulking fellow Elgin, your story would sound quite all right. Perfectly believable.'

'Which story do you mean?' Clarissa wondered aloud.

'About mistaking him for a burglar. It's the blackmail angle that puts a different complexion on it all. So I thought there was only one thing to do,' the gardener continued. 'Get rid of the body and let the police chase their tails looking for it.'

Sir Rowland took a few steps backward, staggering in disbelief, as Miss Peake looked complacently around the room. 'Pretty smart work, even if I do say so myself,' she boasted.

Jeremy rose, fascinated. 'Do you mean to say that it was you who moved the body?' he asked, incredulously.

Everyone was now staring at Miss Peake. 'We're all friends here, aren't we?' she asked, looking around at them. 'So I may as well spill the beans. Yes,' she admitted, 'I moved the body.' She tapped her pocket. 'And I locked the door. I've got keys to all the doors in this house, so that was no problem.'

Open-mouthed, Clarissa gazed at her in wonderment. 'But how? Where – where did you put the body?' she gasped.

Miss Peake leaned forward and spoke in a conspiratorial whisper. 'The bed in the spare room. You know, that big four-poster. Right across the head of the bed, under the bolster. Then I remade the bed and lay down on top of it.'

Sir Rowland, flabbergasted, sat down at the bridge table.

'But how did you get the body up to the spare room?' Clarissa asked. 'You couldn't manage it all by yourself.'

'You'd be surprised,' said Miss Peake jovially. 'Good old fireman's lift. Slung it over my shoulder.' With a gesture, she demonstrated how it was done.

'But what if you had met someone on the stairs?' Sir Rowland asked her.

'Ah, but I didn't,' replied Miss Peake. 'The police were in here with Mrs Hailsham-Brown. You three chaps were being kept in the dining-room by then. So I grabbed my chance, and of course grabbed the body too, took it through the hall, locked the library door again, and carried it up the stairs to the spare room.'

'Well, upon my soul!' Sir Rowland gasped.

Clarissa got to her feet. 'But he can't stay under the bolster for ever,' she pointed out.

Miss Peake turned to her. 'No, not for ever, of course, Mrs Hailsham-Brown,' she admitted. 'But he'll be all right for twenty-four hours. By that time, the police will have finished with the house and grounds. They'll be searching further afield.'

She looked around at her enthralled audience. 'Now, I've been thinking about how to get rid of him,' she went on. 'I happened to dig out a nice deep trench in the garden this morning – for the sweet peas. Well, we'll bury the body there and plant a nice double row of sweet peas all along it.'

Completely at a loss for words, Clarissa collapsed onto the sofa.

'I'm afraid, Miss Peake,' said Sir Rowland, 'grave-digging is no longer a matter for private enterprise.'

The gardener laughed merrily at this. 'Oh, you men!' she exclaimed, wagging her finger at Sir Rowland. 'Always such sticklers for propriety. We women have got more common sense.' She turned to address Clarissa. 'We can even take murder in our stride. Eh, Mrs Hailsham-Brown?'

Hugo suddenly leapt to his feet. 'This is absurd!' he shouted. 'Clarissa didn't kill him. I don't believe a word of it.'

'Well, if she didn't kill him,' Miss Peake asked breezily, 'who did?'

At that moment, Pippa entered the room from the hall, wearing a dressing-gown, walking in a very sleepy manner, yawning, and carrying a glass dish containing chocolate mousse with a teaspoon in it. Everyone turned and looked at her.

Startled, Clarissa jumped to her feet. 'Pippa!' she cried. 'What are you doing out of bed?'

'I woke up, so I came down,' said Pippa between yawns.

Clarissa led her to the sofa. 'I'm so frightfully hungry,' Pippa complained, yawning again. She sat, then looked up at Clarissa and said, reproachfully, 'You said you'd bring this up to me.'

Clarissa took the dish of chocolate mousse from Pippa, placed it on the stool, and then sat on the sofa next to the child. 'I thought you were still asleep, Pippa,' she explained.

'I was asleep,' Pippa told her, with another enormous yawn. 'Then I thought a policeman came in and looked at me. I'd been having an awful dream, and then I half woke up. Then I was hungry, so I thought I'd come down.'

She shivered, looked around at everyone, and continued, 'Besides, I thought it might be true.'

Sir Rowland came and sat on the sofa on Pippa's other side. 'What might be true, Pippa?' he asked her.

'That horrible dream I had about Oliver,' Pippa replied, shuddering as she recollected it.

'What was your dream about Oliver, Pippa?' Sir Rowland asked quietly. 'Tell me.'

Pippa looked nervous as she took a small piece of moulded wax from a pocket of her dressing-gown. 'I made this earlier tonight,' she said. 'I melted down a wax candle, then I made a pin red hot, and I stuck the pin through it.'

As she handed the small wax figure to Sir Rowland, Jeremy suddenly gave a startled exclamation of 'Good Lord!' He leapt up and began to look around the room, searching for the book Pippa had tried to show him earlier.

'I said the right words and everything,' Pippa was explaining to Sir Rowland, 'but I couldn't do it quite the way the book said.'

'What book?' Clarissa asked. 'I don't understand.'

Jeremy, who had been looking along the bookshelves, now found what he was seeking. 'Here it is,' he exclaimed, handing the book to Clarissa over the back of the sofa. 'Pippa got it in the market today. She called it a recipe book.'

Pippa suddenly laughed. 'And you said to me, "Can you eat it?"' she reminded Jeremy.

Clarissa examined the book. '*A Hundred Well-tried and Trusty Spells*,' she read on the cover. She opened the book, and read on. '"How to cure warts. How to get your heart's desire. How to destroy your enemy." Oh, Pippa – is that what you did?'

Pippa looked at her stepmother solemnly. 'Yes,' she answered.

As Clarissa handed the book back to Jeremy, Pippa looked at the wax figure Sir Rowland was still holding. 'It isn't very like Oliver,' she admitted, 'and I couldn't get any clippings of his hair. But it was as much like him as I could make it – and then – then – I dreamed, I thought –' She pushed her hair back from her face as she spoke. 'I thought I came down here and he was there.' She pointed behind the sofa. 'And it was all true.'

Sir Rowland put the wax figure down on the stool quietly, as Pippa continued, 'He was there, dead. I had killed him.' She looked around at them all, and began to shake. 'Is it true?' she asked. 'Did I kill him?'

'No, darling. No,' said Clarissa tearfully, putting an arm around Pippa.

'But he was there,' Pippa insisted.

'I know, Pippa,' Sir Rowland told her. 'But you didn't kill him. When you stuck the pin through that wax figure, it was your hate and your fear of him that you killed in that way. You're not afraid of him and you don't hate him any longer. Isn't that true?'

Pippa turned to him. 'Yes, it's true,' she admitted. 'But I did see him.' She glanced over the back of the sofa. 'I came down here and I saw him lying there, dead.' She leaned her head on Sir Rowland's chest. 'I did see him, Uncle Roly.'

'Yes, dear, you did see him,' Sir Rowland told her gently. 'But it wasn't you who killed him.' She looked up at him anxiously, and he continued, 'Now, listen to me, Pippa. Somebody hit him over the head with a big stick. You didn't do that, did you?'

'Oh, no,' said Pippa, shaking her head vigorously. 'No, not a stick.' She turned to Clarissa. 'You mean a golf stick like Jeremy had?'

Jeremy laughed. 'No, not a golf club, Pippa,' he explained. 'Something like that big stick that's kept in the hall stand.'

'You mean the one that used to belong to Mr Sellon, the one Miss Peake calls a knobkerry?' Pippa asked.

Jeremy nodded.

'Oh, no,' Pippa told him. 'I wouldn't do anything like that. I couldn't.' She turned back to Sir Rowland. 'Oh, Uncle Roly, I wouldn't have killed him really.'

'Of course you wouldn't,' Clarissa intervened in a voice of calm common-sense. 'Now come along, darling, you eat up your chocolate mousse and forget all about it.' She picked up the dish and offered it, but Pippa refused with a shake of her head, and Clarissa replaced the dish on the stool. She and Sir Rowland helped Pippa to lie down on the sofa, Clarissa took Pippa's hand, and Sir Rowland stroked the child's hair affectionately.

'I don't understand a word of all this,' Miss Peake announced. 'What is that book, anyway?' she asked Jeremy who was now glancing through it.

'"How to bring a murrain on your neighbour's cattle." Does that attract you, Miss Peake?' he replied. 'I daresay with a little adjusting you could bring black spot to your neighbour's roses.'

'I don't know what you're talking about,' the gardener said brusquely.

'Black magic,' Jeremy explained.

'I'm not superstitious, thank goodness,' she snorted dismissively, moving away from him.

Hugo, who had been attempting to follow the train of events, now confessed, 'I'm in a complete fog.'

'Me, too,' Miss Peake agreed, tapping him on the shoulder. 'So I'll just have a peep and see how the boys in blue are getting on.' With another of her boisterous laughs, she went out into the hall.

Sir Rowland looked around at Clarissa, Hugo and Jeremy.

'Now where does that leave us?' he wondered aloud.

Clarissa was still recovering from the revelations of the previous few minutes.

'What a fool I've been,' she exclaimed, confusedly. 'I should have known Pippa couldn't possibly – I didn't know anything about this book. Pippa said she killed him and I – I thought it was true.'

Hugo got to his feet. 'Oh, you mean that you thought Pippa –'

'Yes, darling,' Clarissa interrupted him urgently and emphatically to stop him from saying any more. But Pippa, fortunately, was now sleeping peacefully on the sofa.

'Oh, I see,' said Hugo. 'That explains it. Good God!'

'Well, we'd better go to the police now, and tell them the truth at last,' Jeremy suggested.

Sir Rowland shook his head thoughtfully. 'I don't know,' he murmured. 'Clarissa has already told them three different stories –'

'No. Wait,' Clarissa interrupted suddenly. 'I've just had an idea. Hugo, what was the name of Mr Sellon's shop?'

'It was just an antique shop,' Hugo replied, vaguely.

'Yes, I know that,' Clarissa exclaimed impatiently. 'But what was it called?'

'What do you mean – "what was it called"?'

'Oh, dear, you are being difficult,' Clarissa told him. 'You said it earlier, and I want you to say it again. But I don't want to tell you to say it, or say it for you.'

Hugo, Jeremy and Sir Rowland all looked at one another. 'Do you know what the blazes the girl is getting at, Roly?' Hugo asked plaintively.

'I've no idea,' replied Sir Rowland. 'Try us again, Clarissa.'

Clarissa looked exasperated. 'It's perfectly simple,' she insisted. 'What was the name of the antique shop in Maidstone?'

'It hadn't got a name,' Hugo replied. 'I mean, antique shops aren't called "Seaview" or anything.'

'Heaven give me patience,' Clarissa muttered between clenched teeth. Speaking slowly and distinctly, and pausing after each word, she asked him again, 'What – was – written – up – over – the – door?'

'Written up? Nothing,' said Hugo. 'What should be written up? Only the names of the owners, "Sellon and Brown", of course.'

'At last,' Clarissa cried jubilantly. 'I thought that was what you said before, but I wasn't sure. Sellon and Brown. My name is Hailsham-Brown.' She looked at the three men in turn, but they merely stared back at her with total incomprehension written on their faces.

'We got this house dirt cheap,' Clarissa continued. 'Other people who came to see it before us were asked such an exorbitant rent that they went away in disgust. Now have you got it?'

Hugo looked at her blankly before replying, 'No.'

Jeremy shook his head. 'Not yet, my love.'

Sir Rowland looked at her keenly. 'In a glass darkly,' he said thoughtfully.

Clarissa's face wore a look of intense excitement. 'Mr Sellon's partner who lives in London is a woman,' she explained to her friends. 'Today, someone rang up here and asked to speak to Mrs Brown. Not Mrs Hailsham-Brown, just Mrs Brown.'

'I see what you're getting at,' Sir Rowland said, nodding his head slowly.

Hugo shook his head. 'I don't,' he admitted.

Clarissa looked at him. 'A horse chestnut or a chestnut horse – one of them makes all the difference,' she observed inscrutably.

'You're not delirious or anything, are you, Clarissa?' Hugo asked her anxiously.

'Somebody killed Oliver,' Clarissa reminded them. 'It wasn't any of you three. It wasn't me or Henry.' She paused, before continuing, 'And it wasn't Pippa, thank God. Then who was it?'

'Surely it's as I said to the Inspector,' Sir Rowland suggested. 'An outside job. Someone followed Oliver here.'

'Yes, but why did they?' Clarissa asked meaningfully. Getting no reply from anyone, she continued with her speculation. 'When I left you all at the gate today,' she reminded her three friends, 'I came back in through the French windows, and Oliver was standing here. He was very surprised to see me. He said, "What are you doing here, Clarissa?" I just thought it was an elaborate way of annoying me. But suppose it was just what it seemed?'

Her hearers looked attentive, but said nothing. Clarissa continued, 'Just suppose that he was surprised to see me. He thought the house belonged to someone else. He thought the person he'd find here would be the Mrs Brown who was Mr Sellon's partner.'

Sir Rowland shook his head. 'Wouldn't he know that you and Henry had this house?' he asked her. 'Wouldn't Miranda know?'

'When Miranda has to communicate, she always does it through her lawyers. Neither she nor Oliver necessarily knew that we lived in this house,' Clarissa explained. 'I tell you, I'm sure Oliver Costello had no idea he was going to see me. Oh, he recovered pretty quickly and made the excuse that he'd come to talk about Pippa. Then he pretended to go away, but he came back because –'

She broke off as Miss Peake came in through the hall door. 'The hunt's still on,' the gardener announced briskly. 'They've looked under all the beds, I gather, and now they're out in the grounds.' She gave her familiar hearty laugh.

Clarissa looked at her keenly. Then, 'Miss Peake,' she said, 'do you remember what Mr Costello said just before he left? Do you?'

Miss Peake looked blank. 'Haven't the foggiest idea,' she admitted.

'He said, didn't he, "I came to see Mrs Brown"?' Clarissa reminded her.

Miss Peake thought for a moment, and then answered, 'I believe he did. Yes. Why?'

'But it wasn't me he came to see,' Clarissa insisted.

'Well, if it wasn't you, then I don't know who it could have been,' Miss Peake replied with another of her jovial laughs.

Clarissa spoke with emphasis. 'It was you,' she said to the gardener. '*You* are Mrs Brown, aren't you?'

CHAPTER 21

Miss Peake, looking extremely startled at Clarissa's accusation, seemed for a moment unsure how to act. When she did reply, her manner had changed. Dropping her usual jolly, hearty tone, she spoke gravely. 'That's very bright of you,' she said. 'Yes, I'm Mrs Brown.'

Clarissa had been doing some quick thinking. 'You're Mr Sellon's partner,' she said. 'You own this house. You inherited it from Sellon with the business. For some reason, you had the idea of finding a tenant for it whose name was Brown. In fact, you were determined to have a Mrs Brown in residence here. You thought that wouldn't be too difficult, since it's such a common name. But in the end you had to compromise on Hailsham-Brown. I don't know exactly why you wanted me to be in the limelight whilst you watched. I don't understand the ins and outs –'

Mrs Brown, alias Miss Peake, interrupted her. 'Charles Sellon was murdered,' she told Clarissa. 'There's no doubt of that. He'd got hold of something that was very valuable. I don't know how – I don't even know what it was. He wasn't always very –' she hesitated '– scrupulous.'

'So we have heard,' Sir Rowland observed drily.

'Whatever it was,' Mrs Brown continued, 'he was killed for it. And whoever killed him didn't find the thing. That was probably because it wasn't in the shop, it was here. I thought that whoever it was who killed him would come here sooner or later, looking for it. I wanted to be on the watch, therefore I needed a dummy Mrs Brown. A substitute.'

Sir Rowland made an exclamation of annoyance. 'It didn't worry you,' he asked the gardener, speaking with feeling, 'that Mrs Hailsham-Brown, a perfectly innocent woman who had done you no harm, would be in danger?'

'I've kept an eye on her, haven't I?' Mrs Brown replied defensively. 'So much so that it annoyed you all sometimes. The other day, when a man came along and offered her a ridiculous price for that desk, I was sure I was on the right track. Yet I'll swear there was nothing in that desk that meant anything at all.'

'Did you examine the secret drawer?' Sir Rowland asked her.

Mrs Brown looked surprised. 'A secret drawer, is there?' she exclaimed, moving towards the desk.

Clarissa intercepted her. 'There's nothing there now,' she assured her. 'Pippa found the drawer, but there were only some old autographs in it.'

'Clarissa, I'd rather like to see those autographs again,' Sir Rowland requested.

Clarissa went to the sofa. 'Pippa,' she called, 'where did you put – ? Oh, she's asleep.'

Mrs Brown moved to the sofa and looked down at the child. 'Fast asleep,' she confirmed. 'It's all the excitement that's done that.' She looked at Clarissa. 'I'll tell you what,' she said, 'I'll carry her up and dump her on her bed.'

'No,' said Sir Rowland, sharply.

Everyone looked at him. 'She's no weight at all,' Mrs Brown pointed out. 'Not a quarter as heavy as the late Mr Costello.'

'All the same,' Sir Rowland insisted, 'I think she'll be safer here.'

The others now all looked at Miss Peake/Mrs Brown, who took a step backwards, looked around her, and exclaimed indignantly, 'Safer?'

'That's what I said,' Sir Rowland told her. He glanced around the room, and continued, 'That child said a very significant thing just now.'

He sat down at the bridge table, watched by all. There was a pause, and then Hugo, moving to sit opposite Sir Rowland at the bridge table, asked, 'What did she say, Roly?'

'If you all think back,' Sir Rowland suggested, 'perhaps you'll realize what it was.'

His hearers looked at one another, while Sir Rowland picked up the copy of *Who's Who* and began to consult it.

'I don't get it,' Hugo admitted, shaking his head.

'What did Pippa say?' Jeremy wondered aloud.

'I can't imagine,' said Clarissa. She tried to cast her mind back. 'Something about the policeman? Or dreaming? Coming down here? Half awake?'

'Come on, Roly,' Hugo urged his friend. 'Don't be so damned mysterious. What's this all about?'

Sir Rowland looked up. 'What?' he asked, absent-mindedly. 'Oh, yes. Those autographs. Where are they?'

Hugo snapped his fingers. 'I believe I remember Pippa putting them in that shell box over there,' he recalled.

Jeremy went over to the bookshelves. 'Up here?' he asked. Locating the shell box, he took out the envelope. 'Yes, quite right. Here we are,' he confirmed as he took the autographs from the envelope and handed them to Sir Rowland, who had now closed *Who's Who*. Jeremy put the empty envelope in his pocket while Sir Rowland examined the autographs with his eyeglass.

'Victoria Regina, God bless her,' murmured Sir Rowland, looking at the first of the autographs. 'Queen Victoria. Faded brown ink. Now, what's this one? John Ruskin – yes, that's authentic, I should say. And this one? Robert Browning – Hm – the paper's not as old as it ought to be.'

'Roly! What do you mean?' Clarissa asked excitedly.

'I had some experience of invisible inks and that sort of thing, during the war,' Sir Rowland explained. 'If you wanted to make a secret note of something, it wouldn't be a bad idea to write it in invisible ink on a sheet of paper, and then fake an autograph. Put that autograph with other genuine autographs and nobody would notice it or look at it twice, probably. Any more than we did.'

Mrs Brown looked puzzled. 'But what could Charles Sellon have written which would be worth fourteen thousand pounds?' she wanted to know.

'Nothing at all, dear lady,' Sir Rowland replied. 'But it occurs to me, you know, that it might have been a question of safety.'

'Safety?' Mrs Brown queried.

'Oliver Costello,' Sir Rowland explained, 'is suspected of supplying drugs. Sellon, so the Inspector tells us, was questioned once or twice by the Narcotics Squad. There's a connection there, don't you think?'

When Mrs Brown merely looked blank, he continued, 'Of course, it might be just a foolish idea of mine.' He looked down at the autograph he was holding. 'I don't think it would be anything elaborate on Sellon's part. Lemon juice, perhaps, or a solution of barium chloride. Gentle heat might do the trick. We can always try iodine vapour later. Yes, let's try a little gentle heat first.'

He rose to his feet. 'Shall we attempt the experiment?'

'There's an electric fire in the library,' Clarissa remembered. 'Jeremy, will you get it?'

Hugo rose and tucked in his chair, while Jeremy went off to the library.

'We can plug it in here,' Clarissa pointed out, indicating a socket in the skirting-board running around the drawing-room.

'The whole thing's ridiculous,' Mrs Brown snorted. 'It's too far-fetched for words.'

Clarissa disagreed. 'No, it isn't. I think it's a wonderful idea,' she declared, as Jeremy returned from the library carrying a small electric radiator. 'Got it?' she asked him.

'Here it is,' he replied. 'Where's the plug?'

'Down there,' Clarissa told him, pointing. She held the radiator while Jeremy plugged its lead into the socket, and then she put it down on the floor.

Sir Rowland took the Robert Browning autograph and stood close to the radiator. Jeremy knelt by it, and the others stood as close as possible to observe the result.

'We mustn't hope for too much,' Sir Rowland warned them. 'After all, it's only an idea of mine, but there must have been some very good reason why Sellon kept these bits of paper in such a secret place.'

'This takes me back years,' Hugo recalled. 'I remember writing secret messages with lemon juice when I was a kid.'

'Which one shall we start with?' Jeremy asked enthusiastically.

'I say Queen Victoria,' said Clarissa.

'No, six to one on Ruskin,' was Jeremy's guess.

'Well, I'm putting my money on Robert Browning,' Sir Rowland decided, bending over and holding the paper in front of the radiator.

'Ruskin? Most obscure chap. I never could understand a word of his poetry,' Hugo felt moved to comment.

'Exactly,' Sir Rowland agreed. 'It's full of hidden meaning.'

They all craned over Sir Rowland. 'I can't bear it if nothing happens,' Clarissa exclaimed.

'I believe – yes, there's something there,' Sir Rowland murmured.

'Yes, there is something coming up,' Jeremy noticed.

'Is there? Let me see,' said Clarissa excitedly.

Hugo pushed between Clarissa and Jeremy. 'Out of the way, young man.'

'Steady,' Sir Rowland complained. 'Don't joggle me – yes – there is writing.' He paused for a moment, and then straightened up with a cry of, 'We've got it!'

'What have you got?' Mrs Brown wanted to know.

'A list of six names and addresses,' Sir Rowland told them. 'Distributors in the drug racket, I should say. And one of those names is Oliver Costello.'

There were exclamations all around. 'Oliver!' said Clarissa. 'So that's why he came, and someone must have followed him and – Oh, Uncle Roly, we must tell the police. Come along, Hugo.'

Clarissa rushed to the hall door followed by Hugo who, as he went, was muttering, 'Most extraordinary thing I ever heard of.' Sir Rowland picked up the other autographs, while Jeremy unplugged the radiator and took it back into the library.

About to follow Clarissa and Hugo out, Sir Rowland paused in the doorway. 'Coming, Miss Peake?' he asked.

'You don't need me, do you?'

'I think we do. You were Sellon's partner.'

'I've never had anything to do with the drug business,' Mrs Brown insisted. 'I just ran the antique side. I did all the London buying and selling.'

'I see,' Sir Rowland replied non-committally as he held the hall door open for her.

Jeremy returned from the library, closing the door carefully behind him. He went over to the hall door and listened for a moment. After a glance at Pippa, he went over to the easy chair, picked up the cushion from it, and moved slowly back towards the sofa where Pippa lay sleeping.

Pippa stirred in her sleep. Jeremy stood frozen for a moment, but when he was certain she was still asleep, he continued towards the sofa until he stood behind Pippa's head. Then, slowly, he began to lower the cushion over her face.

At that moment, Clarissa re-entered the room from the hall. Hearing the door, Jeremy carefully placed the cushion over Pippa's feet. 'I remembered what Sir Rowland said,' he explained to Clarissa, 'so I thought perhaps we oughtn't to leave Pippa all alone. Her feet seemed a bit cold, so I was just covering them up.'

Clarissa went across to the stool. 'All this excitement has made me feel terribly hungry,' she declared. She looked down at the plate of sandwiches, and then continued in a tone of great disappointment, 'Oh, Jeremy, you've eaten them all.'

'Sorry, but I was starving,' he said, sounding not at all sorry.

'I don't see why you should be,' she reprimanded him. 'You've had dinner. I haven't.'

Jeremy perched on the back of the sofa. 'No, I haven't had any dinner either,' he told her. 'I was practising approach shots. I only came into the dining-room just after your telephone call came.'

'Oh, I see,' Clarissa replied nonchalantly. She bent over the back of the sofa to pat the cushion. Suddenly her eyes widened. In a deeply moved voice she repeated, 'I see. You – it was you.'

'What do you mean?'

'You!' Clarissa repeated, almost to herself.

'What do you mean?'

Clarissa looked him in the eye. 'What were you doing with that cushion when I came into the room?' she asked.

He laughed. 'I told you. I was covering up Pippa's feet. They were cold.'

'Were you? Is that really what you were going to do? Or were you going to put that cushion over her mouth?'

'Clarissa!' he exclaimed indignantly. 'What a ridiculous thing to say!'

'I was certain that none of us could have killed Oliver Costello. I said so to everyone,' Clarissa recalled. 'But one of us could have killed him. You. You were out on the golf course alone. You could have come back to the house, got in through the library window which you'd left open, and you had your golf club still in your hand. Of course. That's what Pippa saw. That's what she meant when she said, "A golf stick like Jeremy had". She saw you.'

'That's absolute nonsense, Clarissa,' Jeremy objected, with a poor attempt at a laugh.

'No, it isn't,' she insisted. 'Then, after you'd killed Oliver you went back to the club and rang the police so that they would come here, find the body, and think it was Henry or I who had killed him.'

Jeremy leaped to his feet. 'What bloody rubbish!' he declared.

'It's not rubbish. It's true. I know it's true,' Clarissa exclaimed. 'But why? That's what I don't understand. Why?'

They stood facing each other in tense silence for a few moments. Then Jeremy gave a deep sigh. He took from his pocket the envelope that had contained the autographs. He held it out to Clarissa, but did not let her take it. 'This is what it's all about,' he told her.

Clarissa glanced at it. 'That's the envelope the autographs were kept in,' she said.

'There's a stamp on it,' Jeremy explained quietly. 'It's what's known as an error stamp. Printed in the wrong colour. One from Sweden sold last year for fourteen thousand three hundred pounds.'

'So that's it,' Clarissa gasped, stepping backwards.

'This stamp came into Sellon's possession,' Jeremy continued. 'He wrote to my boss Sir Kenneth about it. But it was I who opened the letter. I came down here and visited Sellon –'

He paused, and Clarissa completed his sentence for him: '– and killed him.'

Jeremy nodded without saying anything.

'But you couldn't find the stamp,' Clarissa guessed aloud, backing away from him.

'You're right again,' Jeremy admitted. 'It wasn't in the shop, so I felt sure it must be here, in his house.'

He began to move towards Clarissa, as she continued to back away. 'Tonight I thought Costello had beaten me to it.'

'And so you killed him, too,' said Clarissa.

Jeremy nodded again.

'And just now, you would have killed Pippa?' she gasped.

'Why not?' he replied blandly.

'I can't believe it,' Clarissa told him.

'My dear Clarissa, fourteen thousand pounds is a great deal of money,' he observed with a smile that contrived to be both apologetic and sinister.

'But why are you telling me this?' she asked, sounding both perplexed and anxious. 'Do you imagine for one moment that I shan't go to the police?'

'You've told them so many lies, they'll never believe you,' he replied off-handedly.

'Oh yes, they will.'

'Besides,' Jeremy continued, advancing upon her, 'you're not going to get the chance. Do you think that when I've killed two people I shall worry about killing a third?'

He gripped Clarissa by the throat, and she screamed.

CHAPTER 22

Clarissa's scream was answered immediately. Sir Rowland came in swiftly from the hall, switching on the wall-brackets as he did so, while Constable Jones rushed into the room through the French windows, and the Inspector hurried in from the library.

The Inspector grabbed Jeremy. 'All right, Warrender. We've heard it all, thank you,' he announced. 'And that's just the evidence we need,' he added. 'Give me that envelope.'

Clarissa backed behind the sofa, holding her throat, and Jeremy handed the envelope to the Inspector, observing coolly, 'So it was a trap, was it? Very clever.'

'Jeremy Warrender,' said the Inspector, 'I arrest you for the murder of Oliver Costello, and I must warn you that anything you say may be taken down and given in evidence.'

'You can save your breath, Inspector,' was Jeremy's smoothly uttered reply. 'I'm not saying anything. It was a good gamble, but it just didn't work.'

'Take him away,' the Inspector instructed Constable Jones, who took Jeremy by the arm.

'What's the matter, Mr Jones? Forgotten your handcuffs?'

Jeremy asked coldly as his right arm was twisted behind his back and he was marched off through the French windows.

Shaking his head sadly, Sir Rowland watched him go, and then turned to Clarissa. 'Are you all right, my dear?' he asked her anxiously.

'Yes, yes, I'm all right,' Clarissa replied somewhat breathlessly.

'I never meant to expose you to this,' Sir Rowland said apologetically.

She looked at him shrewdly. 'You knew it was Jeremy, didn't you?' she asked.

The Inspector added his voice. 'But what made you think of the stamp, sir?'

Sir Rowland approached Inspector Lord and took the envelope from him. 'Well, Inspector,' he began, 'it rang a bell when Pippa gave me the envelope this evening. Then, when I found from *Who's Who* that young Warrender's employer, Sir Kenneth Thomson, was a stamp collector, my suspicion developed, and just now, when he had the impertinence to pocket the envelope under my nose, I felt it was a certainty.'

He returned the envelope to the Inspector. 'Take great care of this, Inspector. You'll probably find it's extremely valuable, besides being evidence.'

'It's evidence, all right,' replied the Inspector. 'A particularly vicious young criminal is going to get his deserts.' Walking across to the hall door, he continued, 'However, we've still got to find the body.'

'Oh, that's easy, Inspector,' Clarissa assured him. 'Look in the bed in the spare room.'

The Inspector turned and regarded her disapprovingly. 'Now, really, Mrs Hailsham-Brown –' he began.

He was interrupted by Clarissa. 'Why does nobody ever believe me?' she cried plaintively. 'It is in the spare room bed. You go and look, Inspector. Across the bed, under the bolster. Miss Peake put it there, trying to be kind.'

'Trying to be –?' The Inspector broke off, clearly at a loss for words. He went to the door, turned, and said reproachfully, 'You know, Mrs Hailsham-Brown, you haven't made things easier for us tonight, telling us all these tall stories. I suppose you thought your husband had done it, and were lying to cover up for him. But you shouldn't do it, madam. You really shouldn't do it.' With a final shake of his head, he left the room.

'Well!' Clarissa exclaimed indignantly. She turned towards the sofa. 'Oh, Pippa –' she remembered.

'Better get her up to bed,' Sir Rowland advised. 'She'll be safe now.'

Gently shaking the child, Clarissa said softly, 'Come on, Pippa. Ups-a-daisy. Time you were in bed.'

Pippa got up, waveringly. 'I'm hungry,' she murmured.

'Yes, yes, I'm sure you are,' Clarissa assured her as she led her to the hall door. 'Come on, we'll see what we can find.'

'Good night, Pippa,' Sir Rowland called to her, and was rewarded with a yawned 'Goo' night' as Clarissa and Pippa left the room. He sat down at the bridge table and had begun to put the playing cards in their boxes when Hugo came in from the hall.

'God bless my soul,' Hugo exclaimed. 'I'd never have believed it. Young Warrender, of all people. He seemed a decent enough young fellow. Been to a good school. Knew all the right people.'

'But was quite willing to commit murder for the sake of fourteen thousand pounds,' Sir Rowland observed suavely. 'It happens now and then, Hugo, in every class of society. An attractive personality, and no moral sense.'

Mrs Brown, the erstwhile Miss Peake, stuck her head around the hall door. 'I thought I'd just tell you, Sir Rowland,' she announced, reverting to her familiar booming voice, 'I've got to go along to the police station. They want me to make a statement. They're not too pleased at the trick I played on them. I'm in for a wigging, I'm afraid.' She roared with laughter, withdrew, and slammed the door shut.

Hugo watched her go, then went over to join Sir Rowland at the bridge table. 'You know, Roly, I still don't quite get it,' he admitted. 'Was Miss Peake Mrs Sellon, or was Mr Sellon Mr Brown? Or the other way round?'

Sir Rowland was saved from having to reply by the return of the Inspector who came into the room to pick up his cap and gloves. 'We're removing the body now, gentlemen,' he informed them both. He paused momentarily before adding, 'Sir Rowland, would you mind advising Mrs Hailsham-Brown that, if she tells these fancy stories to the police, one day she'll get into real trouble.'

'She did actually tell you the truth once, you know, Inspector,' Sir Rowland reminded him gently, 'but on that occasion you simply wouldn't believe her.'

The Inspector looked a trifle embarrassed. 'Yes – hmmm – well,' he began. Then, pulling himself together, he said, 'Frankly, sir, it was a bit difficult to swallow, you'll admit.'

'Oh, I admit that, certainly,' Sir Rowland assured him.

'Not that I blame you, sir,' the Inspector went on in a confidential tone. 'Mrs Hailsham-Brown is a lady who has a very taking way with her.' He shook his head reflectively, then, 'Well, good night, sir,' he said.

'Good night, Inspector,' Sir Rowland replied amiably.

'Good night, Mr Birch,' the Inspector called, backing towards the hall door.

'Good night, Inspector, and well done,' Hugo responded, coming over to him and shaking hands.

'Thank you, sir,' said the Inspector.

He left, and Hugo yawned. 'Oh, well, I suppose I'd better be going home to bed,' he announced to Sir Rowland. 'Some evening, eh?'

'As you say, Hugo, some evening,' Sir Rowland replied, tidying the bridge table as he spoke. 'Good night.'

'Good night,' Hugo responded, and made his way out into the hall.

Sir Rowland left the cards and markers in a neat pile on the table, then picked up *Who's Who* and replaced it on the bookshelves. Clarissa came in from the hall, went over to him and put her hands on his arms. 'Darling Roly,' she addressed him. 'What would we have done without you? You are so clever.'

'And you are a very lucky young woman,' he told her. 'It's a good thing you didn't lose your heart to that young villain, Warrender.'

Clarissa shuddered. 'There was no danger of that,' she replied. Then, smiling tenderly, 'If I lost my heart to anybody, darling, it would be to you,' she assured him.

'Now, now, none of your tricks with me,' Sir Rowland warned her, laughing. 'If you –'

He stopped short as Henry Hailsham-Brown came in through the French windows, and Clarissa gave a startled exclamation. 'Henry!'

'Hello, Roly,' Henry greeted his friend. 'I thought you were going to the club tonight.'

'Well – er – I thought I'd turn in early,' was all that Sir Rowland felt capable of saying at that moment. 'It's been rather a strenuous evening.'

Henry looked at the bridge table. 'What? Strenuous bridge?' he inquired playfully.

Sir Rowland smiled. 'Bridge and – er – other things,' he replied as he went to the hall door. 'Good night, all.'

Clarissa blew him a kiss and he blew one to her in return as he left the room. Then Clarissa turned to Henry. 'Where's Kalendorff – I mean, where's Mr Jones?' she asked urgently.

Henry put his briefcase on the sofa. In a voice of weary frustration he muttered, 'It's absolutely infuriating. He didn't come.'

'What?' Clarissa could hardly believe her ears.

'The plane arrived with nothing but a half-baked aide-de-camp in it,' Henry told her, unbuttoning his overcoat as he spoke.

Clarissa helped him off with the coat, and Henry continued, 'The first thing he did was to turn round and fly back again where he'd come from.'

'What on earth for?'

'How do I know?' Understandably, Henry sounded some-what on edge. 'He was suspicious, it seems. Suspicious of what? Who knows?'

'But what about Sir John?' Clarissa asked as she removed Henry's hat from his head.

'That's the worst of it,' he groaned. 'I was too late to stop him, and he'll be arriving down here any minute now, I expect.' Henry consulted his watch. 'Of course, I rang up Downing Street at once from the aerodrome, but he'd already started out. Oh, the whole thing's a most ghastly fiasco.'

Henry sank on to the sofa with an exhausted sigh, and as he did so the telephone rang. 'I'll answer it,' Clarissa said, crossing the room to do so. 'It may be the police.' She lifted the receiver.

Henry looked at her questioningly. 'The police?'

'Yes, this is Copplestone Court,' Clarissa was saying into the telephone. 'Yes – yes, he's here.' She looked across at Henry. 'It's for you, darling,' she told him. 'It's Bindley Heath aerodrome.'

Henry rose and began to rush across to the phone, but stopped half-way and proceeded at a dignified walk. 'Hello,' he said into the receiver.

Clarissa took Henry's hat and coat to the hall but returned immediately and stood behind him.

'Yes – speaking,' Henry announced. 'What? – Ten minutes later? – Shall I? – Yes – Yes, yes – No – No, no – You have? – I see – Yes – Right.'

He replaced the receiver, shouted 'Clarissa!', and then turned to find that she was right behind him. 'Oh! There you are. Apparently another plane came in just ten minutes after the first, and Kalendorff was on it.'

'Mr Jones, you mean,' Clarissa reminded him.

'Quite right, darling. One can't be too careful,' he acknowledged. 'Yes, it seems that the first plane was a kind of security precaution. Really, one can't fathom how these people's minds work. Well, anyway, they're sending – er – Mr Jones over here now with an escort. He'll be here in about a quarter of an hour. Now then, is everything all right? Everything in order?' He looked at the bridge table. 'Do get rid of those cards, will you, darling?'

Clarissa hurriedly collected the cards and markers and put them out of sight, while Henry went to the stool and picked up the sandwich plate and mousse dish with an air of great surprise. 'What's on earth's this?' he wanted to know.

Rushing over to him, Clarissa seized the plate and dish. 'Pippa was eating it,' she explained. 'I'll take it away. And I'd better go and make some more ham sandwiches.'

'Not yet – these chairs are all over the place.' Henry's tone was slightly reproachful. 'I thought you were going to have everything ready, Clarissa.'

He began to fold the legs of the bridge table. 'What have you been doing all the evening?' he asked her as he carried the bridge table off to the library.

Clarissa was now busy pushing chairs around. 'Oh, Henry,' she exclaimed, 'it's been the most terribly exciting evening. You see, I came in here with some sandwiches soon after you left, and the first thing that happened was I fell over a body. There.' She pointed. 'Behind the sofa.'

'Yes, yes, darling,' Henry muttered absent-mindedly, as he helped her push the easy chair into its usual position. 'Your stories are always enchanting, but really there isn't time now.'

'But, Henry, it's true,' she insisted. 'And that's only the beginning. The police came, and it was just one thing after another.' She was beginning to babble. 'There was a narcotic ring, and Miss Peake isn't Miss Peake, she's really Mrs Brown, and Jeremy turned out to be the murderer and he was trying to steal a stamp worth fourteen thousand pounds.'

'Hmm! Must have been a second Swedish yellow,' Henry commented. His tone was indulgent, but he was not really listening.

'I believe that's just what it was!' Clarissa exclaimed delightedly.

'Really, the things you imagine, Clarissa,' said Henry affectionately. He moved the small table, set it between the armchair and the easy chair, and flicked the crumbs off it with his handkerchief.

'But, darling, I didn't imagine it,' Clarissa went on. 'I couldn't have imagined half as much.'

Henry put his briefcase behind a cushion on the sofa, plumped up another cushion, then made his way with a third cushion to the easy chair. Meanwhile, Clarissa continued her attempts to engage his attention. 'How extraordinary it is,' she observed. 'All my life nothing has really happened to me, and tonight I've had the lot. Murder, police, drug addicts, invisible ink, secret writing, almost arrested for manslaughter, and very nearly murdered.' She paused and looked at Henry. 'You know, darling, in a way it's almost too much all in one evening.'

'Do go and make that coffee, darling,' Henry replied. 'You can tell me all your lovely rigmarole tomorrow.'

Clarissa looked exasperated. 'But don't you realize, Henry,' she asked him, 'that I was nearly murdered this evening?'

Henry looked at his watch. 'Either Sir John or Mr Jones might arrive at any minute,' he said anxiously.

'What I've been through this evening,' Clarissa continued. 'Oh dear, it reminds me of Sir Walter Scott.'

'What does?' Henry asked vaguely as he looked around the room to make sure that everything was now in its proper place.

'My aunt made me learn it by heart,' Clarissa recalled.

Henry looked at her questioningly, and she recited, 'O what a tangled web we weave, when first we practise to deceive.'

Suddenly conscious of her, Henry leaned over the armchair and put his arms around her. 'My adorable spider!' he said.

Clarissa put her arms around his shoulders. 'Do you know the facts of life about spiders?' she asked him. 'They eat their husbands.' She scratched his neck with her fingers.

'I'm more likely to eat you,' Henry replied passionately, as he kissed her.

The front door bell suddenly rang. 'Sir John!' gasped Clarissa, starting away from Henry who exclaimed at the same time, 'Mr Jones!'

Clarissa pushed Henry towards the hall door. 'You go out and answer the front door,' she ordered. 'I'll put coffee and sandwiches in the hall, and you can bring them in here when you're ready for them. High level talks will now begin.' She kissed her hand, then put it to his mouth. 'Good luck, darling.'

'Good luck,' Henry replied. He turned away, then turned back again. 'I mean, thanks. I wonder which one of them has got here first.' Hastily buttoning his jacket and straightening his tie, he rushed off to the front door.

Clarissa picked up the plate and dish, began to go to the hall door, but stopped when she heard Henry's voice saying heartily, 'Good evening, Sir John.' She hesitated briefly, then quickly went over to the bookshelves and activated the panel switch. The panel opened, and she backed into it. 'Exit Clarissa mysteriously,' she declaimed in a dramatic stage whisper as she disappeared into the recess, a split second before Henry ushered the Prime Minister into the drawing-room.

THE UNEXPECTED QUEST

•

THE UNEXPECTED GUEST

•

THE UNEXPECTED GUEST

CHAPTER I

It was shortly before midnight on a chilly November evening, and swirls of mist obscured parts of the dark, narrow, tree-lined country road in South Wales, not far from the Bristol Channel whence a foghorn sounded its melancholy boom automatically every few moments. Occasionally, the distant barking of a dog could be heard, and the melancholy call of a night-bird. What few houses there were along the road, which was little better than a lane, were about a half-mile apart. On one of its darkest stretches the road turned, passing a handsome, three-storey house standing well back from its spacious garden, and it was at this spot that a car sat, its front wheels caught in the ditch at the side of the road. After two or three attempts to accelerate out of the ditch, the driver of the car must have decided it was no use persevering, and the engine fell silent.

A minute or two passed before the driver emerged from the vehicle, slamming the door behind him. He was a somewhat thick-set, sandy-haired man of about thirty-five, with an out-door look about him, dressed in a rough tweed suit and dark overcoat and wearing a hat. Using a torch to find his way, he began to walk cautiously across the lawn towards the house, stopping halfway to survey the eighteenth-century building's elegant façade. The house appeared to be in total darkness as he approached the french windows on that side of the edifice which faced him. After turning to look back at the lawn he had crossed, and the road beyond it, he walked right up to the french windows, ran his hands over the glass, and peered in. Unable to discern any movement within, he knocked on the window. There was no response, and after a pause he knocked again much louder. When he realized that his knocking was not having any effect, he tried the handle. Immediately, the window opened and he stumbled into a room that was in darkness.

Inside the room, he paused again, as though attempting to discern any sound or movement. Then, 'Hello,' he called. 'Is anyone there?' Flashing his torch around the room which revealed itself to be a well-furnished study, its walls lined with books, he saw in the centre of the room a handsome middle-aged man sitting in a wheelchair facing the french windows, with a rug over his knees. The man appeared to have fallen asleep in his chair. 'Oh, hello,' said the intruder. 'I didn't mean to startle you. So sorry. It's this confounded fog. I've just run my car off the road into a ditch, and I haven't the faintest idea where I am. Oh, and I've left the window open. I'm so sorry.' Continuing to speak apologetically as he moved, he turned back to the french windows, shut them, and closed the curtains. 'Must have run off the main road somewhere,' he explained. 'I've been driving round these topsy-turvy lanes for an hour or more.'

There was no reply. 'Are you asleep?' the intruder asked, as he faced the man in the wheelchair again. Still receiving no answer, he shone his torch on the face of the chair's

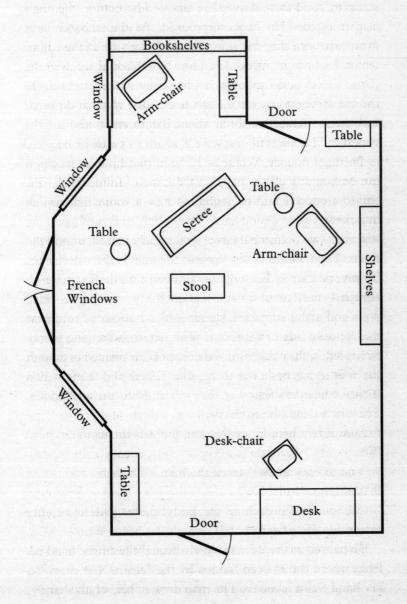

occupant, and then stopped abruptly. The man in the chair neither opened his eyes nor moved. As the intruder bent over him, touching his shoulder as though to awaken him, the man's body slumped down into a huddled position in the chair. 'Good God!' the man holding the torch exclaimed. He paused momentarily, as though undecided what to do next, and then, shining his torch about the room, found a light switch by a door, and crossed the room to switch it on.

The light on a desk came on. The intruder put his torch on the desk and, looking intently at the man in the wheelchair, circled around him. Noticing another door with a light switch by it, he went across and flicked the switch, thus turning on the lamps on two occasional tables strategically placed around the room. Then, taking a step towards the man in the wheelchair, he gave a start as he suddenly noticed for the first time an attractive, fair-haired woman of about thirty, wearing a cocktail dress and matching jacket, standing by a book-lined recess on the opposite side of the room. With her arms hanging limply by her sides, she neither moved nor spoke. It seemed as though she was trying not even to breathe. There was a moment's silence while they stared at each other. Then the man spoke. 'He – he's dead!' he exclaimed.

Completely without expression, the woman answered him. 'Yes.'

'You already knew?' asked the man.

'Yes.'

Cautiously approaching the body in the wheelchair, the man said, 'He's been shot. Through the head. Who – ?'

He paused as the woman slowly brought her right hand up from where it had been hidden by the folds of her dress. In her hand was a revolver. The man drew in his breath sharply.

When it seemed that she was not threatening him with it, he approached her, and gently took the gun from her. 'You shot him?' he asked.

'Yes,' the woman replied, after a pause.

The man moved away from her, and put the gun on a table by the wheelchair. For a moment he stood looking at the dead body, and then gazed uncertainly around the room.

'The telephone is over there,' said the woman, nodding towards the desk.

'Telephone?' the man echoed. He sounded startled.

'If you want to ring up the police,' the woman continued, still speaking in the same detached, expressionless manner.

The stranger stared at her as though unable to make her out. Then, 'A few minutes one way or the other won't make any difference,' he said. 'They'll have a bit of a job getting here in this fog anyway. I'd like to know a little more –' He broke off and looked at the body. 'Who is he?'

'My husband,' replied the woman. She paused, and then continued, 'His name is Richard Warwick. I am Laura Warwick.'

The man continued to stare at her. 'I see,' he murmured finally. 'Hadn't you better – sit down?'

Laura Warwick moved slowly and somewhat unsteadily to a sofa. Looking around the room, the man asked, 'Can I get you a – drink – or something? It must have been a shock.'

'Shooting my husband?' Her tone was drily ironic.

Appearing to regain his poise somewhat, the man attempted to match her expression. 'I should imagine so, yes. Or was it just fun and games?'

'It was fun and games,' replied Laura Warwick inscrutably as she sat down on the sofa. The man frowned, looking puzzled. 'But I would like – that drink,' she continued.

The man took off his hat and threw it onto an armchair, then poured brandy from a decanter on the table close to the wheelchair and handed her the glass. She drank and, after a pause, the man said, 'Now, suppose you tell me all about it.'

Laura Warwick looked up at him. 'Hadn't you better ring the police?' she asked.

'All in good time. Nothing wrong with having a cosy little chat first, is there?' He took off his gloves, stuffed them into his overcoat pocket, and started unbuttoning his coat.

Laura Warwick's poise began to break. 'I don't –' she began. She paused and then continued, 'Who are you? How did you happen to come here tonight?' Without giving him time to answer, she went on, her voice now almost a shout, 'For God's sake, tell me who you are!'

CHAPTER 2

'By all means,' the man replied. He ran a hand through his hair, looked around the room for a moment as though wondering where or how to begin, and then continued, 'My name's Michael Starkwedder. I know it's an unusual name.' He spelt it out for her. 'I'm an engineer. I work for Anglo-Iranian, and I'm just back in this country from a term in the Persian Gulf.' He paused, seeming briefly to be remembering the Middle East, or perhaps trying to decide how much detail to go into, then shrugged his shoulders. 'I've been down here in Wales for a couple of days, looking up old landmarks. My mother's family came from this part of the world and I thought I might buy a little house.'

He shook his head, smiling. 'The last two hours – more like three, I should think – I've been hopelessly lost. Driving round all the twisting lanes in South Wales, and ending up in a ditch! Thick fog everywhere. I found a gate, groped my way to this house, hoping to get hold of a telephone or perhaps, if I was lucky, get put up for the night. I tried the handle of the french window there, found it wasn't locked, so I walked in. Whereupon I find –' He gestured towards the wheelchair, indicating the body slumped in it.

Laura Warwick looked up at him, her eyes expression-less. 'You knocked on the window first – several times,' she murmured.

'Yes, I did. Nobody answered.'

Laura caught her breath. 'No, I didn't answer.' Her voice was now almost a whisper.

Starkwedder looked at her, as though trying to make her out. He took a step towards the body in the wheelchair, then turned back to the woman on the sofa. To encourage her into speaking again, he repeated, 'As I say, I tried the handle, the window wasn't locked, so I came in.'

Laura stared down into her brandy glass. She spoke as though she were quoting. '"The door opens and the unexpected guest comes in."' She shivered slightly. 'That saying always frightened me when I was a child. "The unexpected guest".' Throwing her head back she stared up at her unexpected visitor, and exclaimed with sudden intensity, 'Oh, why don't you ring up the police and get it over?'

Starkwedder walked over to the body in the chair. 'Not yet,' he said. 'In a moment, perhaps. Can you tell me why you shot him?'

The note of irony returned to Laura's voice as she answered him. 'I can give you some excellent reasons. For one thing, he drank. He drank excessively. For another, he was cruel. Unbearably cruel. I've hated him for years.' Catching the sharp look Starkwedder gave her at this, she continued angrily, 'Oh, what do you expect me to say?'

'You've hated him for years?', Starkwedder murmured as though to himself. He looked thoughtfully at the body. 'But something – something special – happened tonight, didn't it?' he asked.

'You're quite right,' Laura replied emphatically. 'Something special indeed happened tonight. And so – I took the gun off the table from where it was lying beside him, and – and I shot him. It was as simple as that.' She threw an impatient glance at Starkwedder as she continued, 'Oh, what's the good of talking about it? You'll only have to ring up the police in the end. There's no way out.' Her voice dropped as she repeated, 'No way out!'

Starkwedder looked at her from across the room. 'It's not quite as simple as you think,' he observed.

'Why isn't it simple?' asked Laura. Her voice sounded weary.

Approaching her, Starkwedder spoke slowly and deliberately. 'It isn't so easy to do what you're urging me to do,' he said. 'You're a woman. A very attractive woman.'

Laura looked up at him sharply. 'Does that make a difference?' she asked.

Starkwedder's voice sounded almost cheerful as he replied, 'Theoretically, certainly not. But in practical terms, yes.' He took his overcoat over to the recess, put it on the armchair, and returned to stand looking down at the body of Richard Warwick.

'Oh, you're talking about chivalry,' Laura observed listlessly.

'Well, call it curiosity if you prefer,' said Starkwedder. 'I'd like to know what this is all about.'

Laura paused before replying. Then, 'I've told you,' was all she said.

Starkwedder walked slowly around the wheelchair containing the body of Laura's husband, as though fascinated by it. 'You've told me the bare facts, perhaps,' he admitted. 'But nothing *more* than the bare facts.'

'And I've given you my excellent motive,' Laura replied. 'There's nothing more to tell. In any case, why should you believe what I tell you? I could make up any story I liked. You've only got my word for it that Richard was a cruel beast and that he drank and that he made life miserable for me – and that I hated him.'

'I can accept the last statement without question, I think,' said Starkwedder. 'After all, there's a certain amount of evidence to support it.' Approaching the sofa again, he looked down at Laura. 'All the same, it's a bit drastic, don't you think? You say you've hated him for years.Why didn't you leave him? Surely that would have been much simpler.'

Laura's voice was hesitant as she replied, 'I've – I've no money of my own.'

'My dear girl,' said Starkwedder, 'if you could have proved cruelty and habitual drunkenness and all the rest of it, you could have got a divorce – or separation – and then you'd get alimony or whatever it is they call it.' He paused, waiting for an answer.

Finding it difficult to reply, Laura rose and, keeping her back to him, went across to the table to put her glass down.

'Have you got children?' Starkwedder asked her.

'No – no, thank God,' Laura replied.

'Well, then, why didn't you leave him?'

Confused, Laura turned to face her questioner. 'Well –' she said finally, 'well – you see – now I shall inherit all his money.'

'Oh, no, you won't,' Starkwedder informed her. 'The law won't allow you to profit as the result of a crime.' Taking a step towards Laura, he asked, 'Or did you think that – ?' He hesitated, and then continued, 'What *did* you think?'

'I don't know what you mean,' Laura told him.

'You're not a stupid woman,' Starkwedder said, looking at her. 'Even if you did inherit his money, it wouldn't be much good to you if you were going to be imprisoned for life.' Settling himself comfortably in the armchair, he added, 'Supposing that I hadn't come knocking at the window just now? What were you going to do?'

'Does it matter?'

'Perhaps not – but I'm interested. What was your story going to be, if I hadn't come barging in and caught you here red-handed? Were you going to say it was an accident? Or suicide?'

'I don't *know*,' Laura exclaimed. She sounded distraught. Crossing to the sofa, she sat facing away from Starkwedder. 'I've no idea,' she added. 'I tell you I – I haven't had time to think.'

'No,' he agreed. 'No, perhaps not – I don't think it was a premeditated affair. I think it was an impulse. In fact, I think it was probably something your husband said. Was that it?'

'It doesn't matter, I tell you,' Laura replied.

'What *did* he say?' Starkwedder insisted. 'What was it?'

Laura gazed at him steadily. 'That is something I shall never tell anybody,' she exclaimed.

Starkwedder went over to the sofa and stood behind her. 'You'll be asked it in court,' he informed her.

Her expression was grim as she replied, 'I shan't answer. They can't make me answer.'

'But your counsel will have to know,' said Starkwedder. Leaning over the sofa and looking at her earnestly, he continued, 'It might make all the difference.'

Laura turned to face him. 'Oh, don't you see?' she exclaimed.

'Don't you understand? I've no hope. I'm prepared for the worst.'

'What, just because I came in through that window? If I hadn't —'

'But you did!' Laura interrupted him.

'Yes, I did,' he agreed. 'And consequently you're for it. Is that what you think?'

She made no reply. 'Here,' he said as he handed her a cigarette and took one himself. 'Now, let's go back a little. You've hated your husband for a long time, and tonight he said something that just pushed you over the edge. You snatched up the gun that was lying beside —' He stopped suddenly, staring at the gun on the table. 'Why was he sitting here with a gun beside him, anyway? It's hardly usual.'

'Oh, that,' said Laura. 'He used to shoot at cats.'

Starkwedder looked at her, surprised. 'Cats?' he asked.

'Oh, I suppose I shall have to do some explaining,' said Laura resignedly.

Starkwedder looked at her with a somewhat bemused expression. 'Well?' he prompted.

Laura took a deep breath. Then, staring straight ahead of her, she began to speak. 'Richard used to be a big-game hunter,' she said. 'That was where we first met – in Kenya. He was a different sort of person then. Or perhaps his good qualities showed, and not his bad ones. He did have good qualities, you know. Generosity and courage. Supreme courage. He was a very attractive man to women.'

She looked up suddenly, seeming to be aware of Starkwedder for the first time. Returning her gaze, he lit her cigarette with his lighter, and then his own. 'Go on,' he urged her.

'We married soon after we met,' Laura continued. 'Then, two years later, he had a terrible accident – he was mauled by a lion. He was lucky to escape alive, but he's been a semi-cripple ever since, unable to walk properly.' She leaned back, apparently more relaxed, and Starkwedder moved to a footstool, facing her.

Laura took a puff at her cigarette and then exhaled the smoke. 'They say misfortune improves your character,' she said. 'It didn't improve his. Instead, it developed all his bad points. Vindictiveness, a streak of sadism, drinking too much. He made life pretty impossible for everyone in this house, and we all put up with it because – oh, you know what one says. "So sad for poor Richard being an invalid." We shouldn't have put up with it, of course. I see that, now. It simply encouraged him to feel that he was different from other people, and that he could do as he chose without being called to account for it.'

She rose and went across to the table by the armchair to flick ash in the ashtray. 'All his life,' she continued, 'shooting had been the thing Richard liked doing best. So, when we came to live in this house, every night after everyone else had gone to bed, he'd sit here' – she gestured towards the wheelchair – 'and Angell, his – well, valet and general factotum I suppose you'd call him – Angell would bring the brandy and one of Richard's guns, and put them beside him. Then he'd have the french windows wide open, and he'd sit in here looking out, watching for the gleam of a cat's eyes, or a stray rabbit, or a dog for that matter. Of course, there haven't been so many rabbits lately. That disease – what d'you call it? – mixymatosis or whatever – has been killing them off. But he shot quite a lot of cats.' She took a drag on her cigarette. 'He shot them in the daytime, too. And birds.'

'Didn't the neighbours ever complain?' Starkwedder asked her.

'Oh, of couse they did,' Laura replied as she returned to sit on the sofa. 'We've only lived here for a couple of years, you know. Before that, we lived on the east coast, in Norfolk. One or two household pets were victims of Richard's there, and we had a lot of complaints. That's really why we came to live here. It's very isolated, this house. We've only got one neighbour for miles around. But there are plenty of squirrels and birds and stray cats.'

She paused for a moment, and then continued. 'The main trouble in Norfolk was really because a woman came to call at the house one day, collecting subscriptions for the village fête. Richard sent shots to the right and left of her as she was going away, walking down the drive. She bolted like a hare, he said. He roared with laughter when he told us about it. I remember him saying her fat backside was quivering like a jelly. But she went to the police about it, and there was a terrible row.'

'I can well imagine that,' was Starkwedder's dry comment.

'But Richard got away with it all right,' Laura told him. 'He had a permit for all his firearms, of course, and he assured the police that he only used them to shoot rabbits. He explained away poor Miss Butterfield by claiming that she was just a nervous old maid who imagined he was shooting at her, which he swore he would never have done. Richard was always plausible. He had no trouble making the police believe him.'

Starkwedder got up from his footstool and went across to Richard Warwick's body. 'Your husband seems to have had a rather perverted sense of humour,' he observed tartly. He looked down at the table beside the wheelchair. 'I see what you mean,' he continued. 'So a gun by his side was a nightly routine. But surely he couldn't have expected to shoot anything tonight. Not in this fog.'

'Oh, he always had a gun put there,' replied Laura. 'Every night. It was like a child's toy. Sometimes he used to shoot into the wall, making patterns. Over there, if you look.' She indicated the french windows. 'Down there to the left, behind the curtain.'

Starkwedder went across and lifted the curtain on the left-hand side, revealing a pattern of bullet holes in the panelling. 'Good heavens, he's picked out his own initials in the wall. "R.W", done in bullet holes. Remarkable.' He replaced the curtain, and turned back to Laura. 'I must admit that's damned good shooting. Hm, yes. He must have been pretty frightening to live with.'

'He was,' Laura replied emphatically. With almost hysterical vehemence, she rose from the sofa and approached her uninvited guest. 'Must we go on talking and talking about all this?' she asked in exasperation. 'It's only putting off what's got to happen in the end. Can't you realize that you've *got* to ring up the police? You've no option. Don't you see it would be far kinder to just do it now? Or is it that you want me to do it? Is that it? All right, I will.'

She moved quickly to the phone, but Starkwedder came up to her as she was lifting the receiver, and put his hand over hers. 'We've got to talk first,' he told her.

'We've been talking,' said Laura. 'And anyway, there's nothing to talk about.'

'Yes, there is,' he insisted. 'I'm a fool, I dare say. But we've got to find some way out.'

'Some way out? For me?' asked Laura. She sounded incredulous.

'Yes. For you.' He took a few steps away from her, and then turned back to face her. 'How much courage have you got?' he asked. 'Can you lie if necessary – and lie convincingly?'

Laura stared at him. 'You're crazy,' was all she said.

'Probably,' Starkwedder agreed.

She shook her head in perplexity. 'You don't know what you're doing,' she told him.

'I know very well what I'm doing,' he answered. 'I'm making myself an accessory after the fact.'

'But why?' asked Laura. 'Why?'

Starkwedder looked at her for a moment before replying. Then, 'Yes, why?' he repeated. Speaking slowly and deliberately, he said, 'For the simple reason, I suppose, that you're a very attractive woman, and I don't like to think of you being shut up in prison for all the best years of your life. Just as horrible as being hanged by the neck until you are dead, in my view. And the situation looks far from promising for you. Your husband was an invalid and a cripple. Any evidence there might be of provocation would rest entirely on your word, a word which you seem extremely unwilling to give. Therefore it seems highly unlikely that a jury would acquit you.'

Laura looked steadily at him. 'You don't know me,' she said. 'Everything I've told you may have been lies.'

'It may,' Starkwedder agreed cheerfully. 'And perhaps I'm a sucker. But I'm believing you.'

Laura looked away, then sank down on the footstool with her back to him. For a few moments nothing was said. Then, turning to face him, her eyes suddenly alight with hope, she looked at him questioningly, and then nodded almost imperceptibly. 'Yes,' she told him, 'I can lie if I have to.'

'Good,' Starkwedder exclaimed with determination. 'Now, talk and talk fast.' He walked over to the table by the wheelchair, flicking ash in the ashtray. 'In the first place, who exactly is there in this house? Who lives here?'

After a moment's hesitation, Laura began to speak, almost mechanically. 'There's Richard's mother,' she told him. 'And there's Benny – Miss Bennett, but we call her Benny – she's a sort of combined housekeeper and secretary. An ex-hospital nurse. She's been here for ages, and she's devoted to Richard. And then there's Angell. I mentioned him, I think. He's a male nurse-attendant, and – well, valet, I suppose. He looks after Richard generally.'

'Are there servants who live in the house as well?'

'No, there are no live-in servants, only dailies who come in.' She paused. 'Oh – and I almost forgot,' she continued. 'There's Jan, of course.'

'Jan?' Starkwedder asked, sharply. 'Who's Jan?'

Laura gave him an embarrassed look before replying. Then, with an air of reluctance, she said, 'He's Richard's young half-brother. He – he lives with us.'

Starkwedder moved over to the stool where she still sat. 'Come clean, now,' he insisted. 'What is there about Jan that you don't want to tell me?'

After a moment's hesitation, Laura spoke, though she still sounded guarded. 'Jan is a dear,' she said. 'Very affectionate and sweet. But – but he isn't quite like other people. I mean he's – he's what they call retarded.'

'I see,' Starkwedder murmured sympathetically. 'But you're fond of him, aren't you?'

'Yes,' Laura admitted. 'Yes – I'm very fond of him. That's – that's really why I couldn't just go away and leave Richard. Because of Jan. You see, if Richard had had his own way, he would have sent Jan to an institution. A place for the mentally retarded.'

Starkwedder slowly circled the wheelchair, looking down at Richard Warwick's body, and pondering. Then, 'I see,' he murmured. 'Is that the threat he held over you? That, if you left him, he'd send the boy to an institution?'

'Yes,' replied Laura. 'If I – if I believed that I could have earned enough to keep Jan and myself – but I don't know that I could. And anyway, Richard was the boy's legal guardian of course.'

'Was Richard kind to him?' Starkwedder asked.

'Sometimes,' she replied.

'And at other times?'

'He'd – he'd quite frequently talk about sending Jan away,' Laura told him. 'He'd say to Jan, "They'll be quite kind to you, boy. You'll be well looked after. And Laura, I'm sure, would come and see you once or twice a year." He'd get Jan all worked up, terrified, begging, pleading, stammering. And then Richard would lean back in his chair and roar with laughter. Throw back his head and laugh, laugh, laugh.'

'I see,' said Starkwedder, watching her carefully. After a pause, he repeated thoughtfully, 'I see.'

Laura rose quickly, and went to the table by the armchair to stub out her cigarette. 'You needn't believe me,' she exclaimed. 'You needn't believe a word I say. For all you know, I might be making it all up.'

'I've told you I'll risk it,' Starkwedder replied. 'Now then,' he continued, 'what's this, what's-her-name, Bennett – Benny – like? Is she sharp? Bright?'

'She's very efficient and capable,' Laura assured him.

Starkwedder snapped his fingers. 'Something's just occurred to me,' he said. 'How is it that nobody in the house heard the shot tonight?'

'Well, Richard's mother is quite old, and she's rather deaf,' Laura replied. 'Benny's room is over on the other side of the house, and Angell's quarters are quite separate, shut off by a baize door. There's young Jan, of course. He sleeps in the room over this. But he goes to bed early, and he sleeps very heavily.'

'That all seems extremely fortunate,' Starkwedder observed.

Laura looked puzzled. 'But what are you suggesting?' she asked him. 'That we could make it look like suicide?'

He turned to look at the body again. 'No,' he said, shaking his head. 'There's no hope of suicide, I'm afraid.' He walked over to the wheelchair and looked down at the corpse of Richard Warwick for a moment, before asking, 'He was right-handed, I assume?'

'Yes,' replied Laura.

'Yes, I was afraid so. In which case he couldn't possibly have shot himself at that angle,' he declared, pointing to Warwick's left temple. 'Besides, there's no mark of scorching.' He considered for a few seconds and then added, 'No, the gun must have been fired from a certain distance away. Suicide is certainly out.' He paused again before continuing. 'But there's accident, of course. After all, it could have been an accident.'

After a longer pause, he began to act out what he had in mind. 'Now, say for instance that I came here this evening. Just as I did, in fact. Blundered in through this window.' He went to the french windows, and mimed the act of stumbling into the room. 'Richard thought I was a burglar, and took a pot shot at me. Well, that's quite likely, from all you've been telling me about his exploits. Well, then, I come up to him' – and Starkwedder hastened to the body in the wheelchair – 'I get the gun away from him –'

Laura interrupted eagerly. 'And it went off in the struggle – yes?'

'Yes,' Starkwedder agreed, but immediately corrected himself. 'No, that won't do. As I say, the police would spot at once that the gun wasn't fired at such close quarters.' He took a few more moments to reconsider, and then continued. 'Well now, say I got the gun right away from him.' He shook his head, and waved his arms in a gesture of frustration. 'No, that's no good. Once I'd done that, why the hell should I shoot him? No, I'm afraid it's tricky.'

He sighed. 'All right,' he decided, 'let's leave it at murder. Murder pure and simple. But murder by someone from outside. Murder by person or persons unknown.' He crossed to the french windows, held back a curtain, and peered out as though seeking inspiration.

'A real burglar, perhaps?' Laura suggested helpfully.

Starkwedder thought for a moment, and then said, 'Well, I suppose it *could* be a burglar, but it seems a bit bogus.' He paused, then added, 'What about an enemy? That sounds melodramatic perhaps, but from what you've told me about your husband it seems he was the sort who might have had enemies. Am I right?'

'Well, yes,' Laura replied, speaking slowly and uncertainly, 'I suppose Richard had enemies, but –'

'Never mind the buts for the time being,' Starkwedder interrupted her, stubbing out his cigarette at the table by the wheelchair, and moving to stand over her as she sat on the sofa. 'Tell me all you can about Richard's enemies. Number One, I suppose, would be Miss – you know, Miss quivering backside – the woman he took pot shots at. But I don't suppose she's a likely murderer. Anyway, I imagine she still lives in Norfolk, and it would be a bit far-fetched to imagine her taking a cheap day return to Wales to bump him off. Who else?' he urged. 'Who else is there who had a grudge against him?'

Laura looked doubtful. She got up, moved about, and began

to unbutton her jacket. 'Well,' she began cautiously, 'there was a gardener, about a year ago. Richard sacked him and wouldn't give him a reference. The man was very abusive about it and made a lot of threats.'

'Who was he?' Starkwedder asked. 'A local chap?'

'Yes,' Laura replied. 'He came from Llanfechan, about four miles away.' She took off her jacket and laid it across an arm of the sofa.

Starkwedder frowned. 'I don't think much of your gardener,' he told her. 'You can bet he's got a nice, stay-at-home alibi. And if he hasn't got an alibi, or it's an alibi that only his wife can confirm or support, we might end up getting the poor chap convicted for something he hasn't done. No, that's no good. What we want is some enemy out of the past, who wouldn't be so easy to track down.'

Laura moved slowly around the room, trying to think, as Starkwedder continued, 'How about someone from Richard's tiger- and lion-shooting days? Someone in Kenya, or South Africa, or India? Some place where the police can't check up on him very easily.'

'If I could only think,' said Laura, despairingly. 'If I could only remember. If I could remember some of the stories about those days that Richard told us at one time or another.'

'It isn't even as though we'd got any nice props handy,' Starkwedder muttered. 'You know, a Sikh turban carelessly draped over the decanter, or a Mau Mau knife, or a poisoned arrow.' He pressed his hands to his forehead in concentration. 'Damn it all,' he went on, 'what we want is someone with a grudge, someone who'd been kicked around by Richard.' Approaching Laura, he urged her, 'Think, woman. Think. Think!'

'I – I *can't* think,' replied Laura, her voice almost breaking with frustration.

'You've told me the kind of man your husband was. There must have been incidents, people. Heavens above, there must have been *something*,' he exclaimed.

Laura paced about the room, trying desperately to remember.

'Someone who made threats. Justifiable threats, perhaps,' Starkwedder encouraged her.

Laura stopped her pacing, and turned to face him. 'There was – I've just remembered,' she said. She spoke slowly. 'There was a man whose child Richard ran over.'

Starkwedder stared at Laura. 'Richard ran over a child?' he asked excitedly. 'When was this?'

'It was about two years ago,' Laura told him. 'When we were living in Norfolk. The child's father certainly made threats at the time.'

Starkwedder sat down on the footstool. 'Now, that sounds like a possibility,' he said. 'Anyway, tell me all you can remember about him.'

Laura thought for a moment, and then began to speak. 'Richard was driving back from Cromer,' she said. 'He'd had far too much to drink, which was by no means unusual. He drove through a little village at about sixty miles an hour, apparently zig-zagging quite a bit. The child – a little boy – ran out into the road from the inn there – Richard knocked him down and he was killed instantly.'

'Do you mean,' Starkwedder asked her, 'that your husband could drive a car, despite his disability?'

'Yes, he could. Oh, it had to be specially built, with special controls that he could manage, but, yes, he was able to drive that vehicle.'

'I see,' said Starkwedder. 'What happened about the child? Surely the police could have got Richard for manslaughter?'

'There was an inquest, of course,' Laura explained. A bitter note crept into her voice as she added, 'Richard was exonerated completely.'

'Were there any witnesses?' Starkwedder asked her.

'Well,' Laura replied, 'there was the child's father. He saw it happen. But there was also a hospital nurse – Nurse Warburton – who was in the car with Richard. She gave evidence, of course. And according to her, the car was going under thirty miles an hour and Richard had had only one glass of sherry. She said that the accident was quite unavoidable – the little boy just suddenly rushed out, straight in front of the car. They believed *her*, and not the child's father who said that the car was being driven erratically and at a very high speed. I understand the poor man was – rather over-violent in expressing his feelings.' Laura moved to the armchair, adding, 'You see, anyone *would* believe Nurse Warburton. She seemed the very essence of honesty and reliability and accuracy and careful understatement and all that.'

'You weren't in the car yourself?' Starkwedder asked.

'No, I wasn't,' Laura replied. 'I was at home.'

'Then how do you know that what Nurse what's-her-name said mightn't have been the truth?'

'Oh, the whole thing was very freely discussed by Richard,' she said bitterly. 'After they came back from the inquest, I remember very clearly. He said, "Bravo, Warby, jolly good show. You've probably got me off quite a stiff jail sentence." And she said, "You don't deserve to have got off, Mr Warwick. You know you were driving much too fast. It's a shame about that poor child." And then Richard said, "Oh, forget it! I've made it worth your while. Anyway, what's one brat more or less in this overcrowded world? He's just as well out of it all. It's not going to spoil *my* sleep, I assure you.'''

Starkwedder rose from the stool and, glancing over his shoulder at Richard Warwick's body, said grimly, 'The more I hear about your husband, the more I'm willing to believe that what happened tonight was justifiable homicide rather than murder.' Approaching Laura, he continued, 'Now then. This man whose child was run over. The boy's father. What's his name?'

'A Scottish name, I think,' Laura replied. 'Mac – Mac something – MacLeod? MacCrae? – I can't remember.'

'But you've got to try to remember,' Starkwedder insisted. 'Come on, you must. Is he still living in Norfolk?'

'No, no,' said Laura. 'He was only over here for a visit. To his wife's relations, I think. I seem to remember he came from Canada.'

'Canada – that's a nice long way away,' Starkwedder observed. 'It would take time to chase up. Yes,' he continued, moving to behind the sofa, 'yes, I think there are possibilities there. But for God's sake try to remember the man's name.' He went across to his overcoat on the armchair in the recess, took his gloves from a pocket, and put them on. Then, looking searchingly around the room, he asked, 'Got any newspapers about?'

'Newspapers?' Laura asked, surprised.

'Not today's,' he explained. 'Yesterday's or the day before would do better.'

Rising from the sofa, Laura went to a cupboard behind the armchair. 'There are some old ones in the cupboard here. We keep them for lighting fires,' she told him.

Starkwedder joined her, opened the cupboard door, and took out a newspaper. After checking the date, he announced, 'This is fine. Just what we want.' He closed the cupboard door, took the newspaper to the desk, and from a pigeon-hole on the desk extracted a pair of scissors.

'What are you going to do?' asked Laura.

'We're going to manufacture some evidence.' He clicked the scissors as though to demonstrate.

Laura stared at him, perplexed. 'But suppose the police succeed in finding this man,' she asked. 'What happens then?'

Starkwedder beamed at her. 'If he still lives in Canada, it'll take a bit of doing,' he announced with an air of smugness. 'And by the time they do find him, he'll no doubt have an alibi for tonight. Being a few thousand miles away ought to be satisfactory enough. And by then it will be a bit late for them to check up on things here. Anyway, it's the best we can do. It'll give us breathing space at all events.'

Laura looked worried. 'I don't like it,' she complained.

Starkwedder gave her a somewhat exasperated look. 'My dear girl,' he admonished her, 'you can't afford to be choosy. But you must try to remember that man's name.'

'I can't, I tell you, I can't,' Laura insisted.

'Was it MacDougall, perhaps? Or Mackintosh?' he suggested helpfully.

Laura took a few steps away from him, putting her hands to her ears. 'Do stop,' she cried. 'You're only making it worse. I'm not sure now that it was Mac anything.'

'Well, if you can't remember, you can't,' Starkwedder conceded. 'We shall have to manage without. You don't remember the date, by any chance, or anything useful like that?'

'Oh, I can tell you the date, all right,' said Laura. 'It was May the fifteenth.'

Surprised, Starkwedder asked, 'Now, how on earth can you remember that?'

There was bitterness in Laura's voice as she replied, 'Because it happened on my birthday.'

'Ah, I see – yes – well, that solves one little problem,' observed Starkwedder. 'And we've also got one little piece of luck. This paper is dated the fifteenth.' He cut the date out carefully from the newspaper.

Joining him at the desk and looking over his shoulder, Laura pointed out that the date on the newspaper was November the fifteenth, not May. 'Yes,' he admitted, 'but it's the numbers that are the more awkward. Now, May. May's a short word – ah, yes, here's an M. Now an A, and a Y.'

'What in heaven's name are you doing?' Laura asked.

Starkwedder's only response, as he seated himself in the desk chair, was, 'Got any paste?'

Laura was about to take a pot of paste from a pigeon-hole, but he stopped her. 'No, don't touch,' he instructed. 'We don't want your fingerprints on it.' He took the pot of paste in his gloved hands, and removed the lid. 'How to be a criminal in one easy lesson,' he continued. 'And, yes, here's a plain block of writing paper – the kind sold all over the British Isles.' Taking a notepad from the pigeon-hole, he proceeded to paste words and letters onto a sheet of notepaper. 'Now, watch this, one – two – three – a bit tricky with gloves. But there we are. "May fifteen. Paid in full." Oh, the "in" has come off.' He pasted it back on again. 'There, now. How do you like that?'

He tore the sheet off the pad and showed it to her, then

went across to Richard Warwick's body in its wheelchair. 'We'll tuck it neatly into his jacket pocket, like that.' As he did so, he dislodged a pocket lighter, which fell to the floor. 'Hello, what's this?'

Laura gave a sharp exclamation and tried to snatch the lighter up, but Starkwedder had already done so, and was examining it. 'Give it to me,' cried Laura breathlessly. 'Give it to me!'

Looking faintly surprised, Starkwedder handed it to her. 'It's – it's my lighter,' she explained, unnecessarily.

'All right, so it's your lighter,' he agreed. 'That's nothing to get upset about.' He looked at her curiously. 'You're not losing your nerve, are you?'

She walked away from him to the sofa. As she did so, she rubbed the lighter on her skirt as though to remove possible fingerprints, taking care to ensure that Starkwedder did not observe her doing so. 'No, of course I'm not losing my nerve,' she assured him.

Having made certain that the pasted-up message from the newspaper in Richard Warwick's breast pocket was tucked securely under the lapel, Starkwedder went over to the desk, replaced the lid of the paste-pot, removed his gloves, took out a handkerchief, and looked at Laura. 'There we are!' he announced. 'All ready for the next step. Where's that glass you were drinking out of just now?'

Laura retrieved the glass from the table where she had deposited it. Leaving her lighter on the table, she returned with the glass to Starkwedder. He took it from her, and was about to wipe off her fingerprints, but then stopped. 'No,' he murmured. 'No, that would be stupid.'

'Why?' asked Laura.

'Well, there ought to be fingerprints,' he explained, 'both on the glass and on the decanter. This valet fellow's, for one, and probably your husband's as well. No fingerprints at all would look very fishy to the police.' He took a sip from the glass he was holding. 'Now I must think of a way to explain mine,' he added. 'Crime isn't easy, is it?'

With sudden passion, Laura exclaimed, 'Oh, don't! Don't get mixed up in this. They might suspect *you*.'

Amused, Starkwedder replied, 'Oh, I'm a very respectable chap – quite above suspicion. But, in a sense I *am* mixed up in it already. After all, my car's out there, stuck fast in the ditch. But don't worry, just a spot of perjury and a little tinkering with the time element – that's the worst they'd be able to bring against me. And they won't, if you play your part properly.'

Frightened, Laura sat on the footstool, with her back to him. He came round to face her. 'Now then,' he said, 'are you ready?'

'Ready – for what?' asked Laura.

'Come on, you must pull yourself together,' he urged her.

Sounding dazed, she murmured, 'I feel – stupid – I – I can't think.'

'You don't have to think,' Starkwedder told her. 'You've just got to obey orders. Now then, here's the blueprint. First, have you got a furnace of any kind in the house?'

'A furnace?' Laura thought, and then replied, 'Well, there's the water boiler.'

'Good.' He went to the desk, took the newspaper, and rolled up the scraps of paper in it. Returning to Laura, he handed her the bundle. 'Now then,' he instructed her, 'the first thing you do is to go into the kitchen and put this in the boiler. Then you go upstairs, get out of your clothes and into a dressing-gown

– or negligée, or what-have-you.' He paused. 'Have you got any aspirin?'

Puzzled, Laura replied, 'Yes.'

As though thinking and planning as he spoke, Starkwedder continued, 'Well – empty the bottle down the loo. Then go along to someone – your mother-in-law, or Miss – what is it – Bennett? – and say you've got a headache and want some aspirin. Then, while you're with whoever it is – leave the door open, by the way – you'll hear the shot.'

'What shot?' asked Laura, staring at him.

Without replying, Starkwedder crossed to the table by the wheelchair and picked up the gun. 'Yes, yes,' he murmured absently, 'I'll attend to that.' He examined the gun. 'Hm. Looks foreign to me – war souvenir, is it?'

Laura rose from the stool. 'I don't know,' she told him. 'Richard had several foreign makes of pistol.'

'I wonder if it's registered,' Starkwedder said, almost to himself, still holding the gun.

Laura sat on the sofa. 'Richard had a licence – if that's what you call it – a permit for his collection,' she said.

'Yes, I suppose he would have. But that doesn't mean that they would all be registered in his name. In practice, people are often rather careless about that kind of thing. Is there anyone who'd be likely to know definitely?'

'Angell might,' said Laura. 'Does it matter?'

Starkwedder moved about the room as he replied. 'Well, the way we're building this up, old MacThing – the father of the child Richard ran over – is more likely to come bursting in, breathing blood and thunder and revenge, with his own weapon at the ready. But one could, after all, make out quite a plausible case the other way. This man – whoever he is –

bursts in. Richard, only half awake, snatches up his gun. The other fellow wrenches it away from him, and shoots. I admit it sounds a bit far-fetched, but it'll have to do. We've got to take some risks, it just can't be avoided.'

He placed the gun on the table by the wheelchair, and approached her. 'Now then,' he continued, 'have we thought of everything? I hope so. The fact that he was shot a quarter of an hour or twenty minutes earlier won't be apparent by the time the police get here. Driving along these roads in this fog won't be easy for them.' He went over to the curtain by the french windows, lifted it, and looked at the bullet holes in the wall. '"R.W". Very nice. I'll try to add a full stop.'

Replacing the curtain, he came back to her. 'When you hear the shot,' he instructed Laura, 'what you do is register alarm, and bring Miss Bennett – or anyone else you can collect – down here. Your story is that you don't know anything. You went to bed, you woke up with a violent headache, you went along to look for aspirin – and that's *all* you know. Understand?'

Laura nodded.

'Good,' said Starkwedder. 'All the rest you leave to me. Are you feeling all right now?'

'Yes, I think so,' Laura whispered.

'Then go along and do your stuff,' he ordered her.

Laura hesitated. 'You – you oughtn't to do this,' she urged him again. 'You oughtn't. You shouldn't get involved.'

'Now, don't let's have any more of that,' Starkwedder insisted. 'Everyone has their own form of – what did we call it just now? – fun and games. You had your fun and games shooting your husband. I'm having my fun and games now. Let's just say I've always had a secret longing to see how I could get on with a detective story in real life.' He gave her a quick, reassuring smile. 'Now, can you do what I've told you?'

Laura nodded. 'Yes.'

'Right. Oh, I see you've got a watch. Good. What time do you make it?'

Laura showed him her wristwatch, and he set his accordingly. 'Just after ten minutes to,' he observed. 'I'll allow you three – no, four – minutes. Four minutes to go along to the kitchen, pop that paper in the boiler, go upstairs, get out of your things and into a dressing-gown, and along to Miss Bennett or whoever. Do you think you can do that, Laura?' He smiled at her reassuringly.

Laura nodded.

'Now then,' he continued, 'at five minutes to midnight exactly, you'll hear the shot. Off you go.'

Moving to the door, she turned and looked at him, uncertain of herself. Starkwedder went across to open the door for her. 'You're not going to let me down, are you?' he asked.

'No,' replied Laura faintly.

'Good.'

Laura was about to leave the room when Starkwedder noticed her jacket lying on the arm of the sofa. Calling her back, he gave it to her, smiling. She went out, and he closed the door behind her.

CHAPTER 5

After closing the door behind Laura, Starkwedder paused, working out in his mind what was to be done. After a moment, he glanced at his watch, then took out a cigarette. He moved to the table by the armchair and was about to pick up the lighter when he noticed a photograph of Laura on one of the bookshelves. He picked it up, looked at it, smiled, replaced it, and lit a cigarette, leaving the lighter on the table. Taking out his handkerchief, he rubbed any fingerprints off the arms of the armchair and the photograph, and then pushed the chair back to its original position. He took Laura's cigarette from the ashtray, then went to the table by the wheelchair and took his own stub from the ashtray. Crossing to the desk, he next rubbed any fingerprints from it, replaced the scissors and notepad, and adjusted the blotter. He looked around him on the floor for any scrap of paper that might have been missed, found one near the desk, screwed it up and put it in his trousers pocket. He rubbed fingerprints off the light switch by the door and off the desk chair, picked up his torch from the desk, went over to the french windows, drew the curtain back slightly, and shone the torch through the window onto the path outside.

'Too hard for footprints,' he murmured to himself. He put the torch on the table by the wheelchair and picked up the gun. Making sure that it was sufficiently loaded, he polished it for fingerprints, then went to the stool and put the gun down on it. After glancing again at his watch, he went to the armchair in the recess and put on his hat, scarf and gloves. With his overcoat on his arm, he crossed to the door. He was about to switch off the lights when he remembered to remove the fingerprints from the door-plate and handle. He then switched off the lights, and came back to the stool, putting his coat on. He picked up the gun, and was about to fire it at the initials on the wall when he realized that they were hidden by the curtain.

'Damn!' he muttered. Quickly taking the desk chair, he used it to hold the curtain back. He returned to his position by the stool, fired the gun, and then quickly went back to the wall to examine the result. 'Not bad!' he congratulated himself.

As he replaced the desk chair in its proper position, Starkwedder could hear voices in the hall. He rushed off through the french windows, taking the gun with him. A moment later he reappeared, snatched up the torch, and dashed out again.

From various parts of the house, four people hurried towards the study. Richard Warwick's mother, a tall, commanding old lady, was in her dressing-gown. She looked pallid and walked with the aid of a stick. 'What is it, Jan?' she asked the teenage boy in pyjamas with the strange, rather innocent, faun-like face, who was close behind her on the landing. 'Why is everybody wandering about in the middle of the night?' she exclaimed as they were joined by a grey-haired, middle-aged woman, wearing a sensible flannel dressing-gown. 'Benny,' she ordered the woman, 'tell me what's going on.'

Laura was close behind, and Mrs Warwick continued, 'Have you all taken leave of your senses? Laura, what's happened? Jan – Jan – will someone tell me what is going on in this house?'

'I'll bet it's Richard,' said the boy, who looked about nineteen, though his voice and manner were those of a younger child. 'He's shooting at the fog again.' There was a note of petulance in his voice as he added, 'Tell him he's not to shoot and wake us all up out of our beauty sleep. I was deep asleep, and so was Benny. Weren't you, Benny? Be careful, Laura, Richard's dangerous. He's dangerous, Benny, be careful.'

'There's thick fog outside,' said Laura, looking through the landing window. 'You can barely make out the path. I can't imagine what he can be shooting at in this mist. It's absurd. Besides, I thought I heard a cry.'

Miss Bennett – Benny – an alert, brisk woman who looked like the ex-hospital nurse that she was, spoke somewhat officiously. 'I really can't see why you're so upset, Laura. It's just Richard amusing himself as usual. But I didn't hear any shooting. I'm sure there's nothing wrong. I think you're imagining things. But he's certainly very selfish and I shall tell him so. Richard,' she called as she entered the study, 'really, Richard, it's too bad at this time of night. You frightened us – Richard!'

Laura, wearing her dressing-gown, followed Miss Bennett into the room. As she switched on the lights and moved to the sofa, the boy Jan followed her. He looked at Miss Bennett who stood staring at Richard Warwick in his wheelchair. 'What is it, Benny?' asked Jan. 'What's the matter?'

'It's Richard,' said Miss Bennett, her voice strangely calm. 'He's killed himself.'

'Look,' cried young Jan excitedly, pointing at the table. 'Richard's revolver's gone.'

A voice from outside in the garden called, 'What's going on in there? Is anything wrong?' Looking through the small window in the recess, Jan shouted, 'Listen! There's someone outside!'

'Outside?' said Miss Bennett. 'Who?' She turned to the french windows and was about to draw back the curtain when Starkwedder suddenly appeared. Miss Bennett stepped back in alarm as Starkwedder came forward, asking urgently, 'What's happened here? What's the matter?' His glance fell on Richard Warwick in the wheelchair. 'This man's dead!' he exclaimed. 'Shot.' He looked around the room suspiciously, taking them all in.

'Who are you?' asked Miss Bennett. 'Where do you come from?'

'Just run my car into a ditch,' replied Starkwedder. 'I've been lost for hours. Found some gates and came up to the house to try to get some help and telephone. Heard a shot, and someone came rushing out of the windows and collided with me.' Holding out the gun, Starkwedder added, 'He dropped this.'

'Where did this man go?' Miss Bennett asked him.

'How the hell should I know in this fog?' Starkwedder replied.

Jan stood in front of Richard's body, staring excitedly at it. 'Somebody's shot Richard,' he shouted.

'Looks like it,' Starkwedder agreed. 'You'd better get in touch with the police.' He placed the gun on the table by the wheelchair, picked up the decanter, and poured brandy into a glass. 'Who is he?'

'My husband,' said Laura, expressionlessly, as she went to sit on the sofa.

With what sounded a slightly forced concern, Starkwedder said to her, 'Here – drink this.' Laura looked up at him. 'You've had a shock,' he added emphatically. As she took the glass, with his back turned to the others Starkwedder gave her a conspiratorial grin, to call her attention to his solution of the fingerprint problem. Turning away, he threw his hat on the armchair, and then, suddenly noticing that Miss Bennett was about to bend over Richard Warwick's body, he swung quickly round. 'No, don't touch anything, madam,' he implored her. 'This looks like murder, and if it is then nothing must be touched.'

Straightening up, Miss Bennett backed away from the body in the chair, looking appalled. 'Murder?' she exclaimed. 'It can't be murder!'

Mrs Warwick, the mother of the dead man, had stopped just inside the door of the study. She came forward now, asking, 'What has happened?'

'Richard's been shot! Richard's been shot!' Jan told her. He sounded more excited than concerned.

'Quiet, Jan,' ordered Miss Bennett.

'What did I hear you say?' asked Mrs Warwick, quietly.

'*He* said – murder,' Benny told her, indicating Starkwedder.

'Richard,' Mrs Warwick whispered, as Jan leaned over the body, calling, 'Look – look – there's something on his chest – a paper – with writing on it.' His hand went out to it, but he was stopped by Starkwedder's command: 'Don't touch – whatever you do, don't touch.' Then he read aloud, slowly, '"May – fifteen – paid in full".'

'Good Lord! MacGregor,' Miss Bennett exclaimed, moving behind the sofa.

Laura rose. Mrs Warwick frowned. 'You mean,' she said, '– that man – the father – the child that was run over – ?'

'Of course, MacGregor,' Laura murmured to herself as she sat in the armchair.

Jan went up to the body. 'Look – it's all newspaper – cut up,' he said in excitement. Starkwedder again restrained him. 'No, don't touch it,' he ordered. 'It's got to be left for the police.' He stepped towards the telephone. 'Shall I – ?'

'No,' said Mrs Warwick firmly. 'I will.' Taking charge of the situation, and summoning her courage, she went to the desk and started to dial. Jan moved excitedly to the stool and knelt upon it. 'The man that ran away,' he asked Miss Bennett. 'Do you think he – ?'

'Ssh, Jan,' Miss Bennett said to him firmly, while Mrs Warwick spoke quietly but in a clear, authoritative voice on the telephone. 'Is that the police station? This is Llangelert House. Mr Richard Warwick's house. Mr Warwick has just been found – shot dead.'

She went on speaking into the phone. Her voice remained low, but the others in the room listened intently. 'No, he was found by a stranger,' they heard her say. 'A man whose car had broken down near the house, I believe . . . Yes, I'll tell him. I'll phone the inn. Will one of your cars be able to take him there when you've finished here? . . . Very well.'

Turning to face the company, Mrs Warwick announced, 'The police will be here as soon as they can in this fog. They'll have two cars, one of which will return right away to take this gentleman' – she gestured at Starkwedder – 'to the inn in the village. They want him to stay overnight and be available to talk to them tomorrow.'

'Well, since I can't leave with my car still in the ditch, that's fine with me,' Starkwedder exclaimed. As he spoke, the door to the corridor opened, and a dark-haired man of medium height in his mid-forties entered the room, tying the cord of his dressing-gown. He suddenly stopped short just inside the door. 'Is something the matter, madam?' he asked, addressing Mrs Warwick. Then, glancing past her, he saw the body of Richard Warwick. 'Oh, my God,' he exclaimed.

'I'm afraid there's been a terrible tragedy, Angell,' Mrs Warwick replied. 'Mr Richard has been shot, and the police are on their way here.' Turning to Starkwedder, she said, 'This is Angell. He's – he was Richard's valet.'

The valet acknowledged Starkwedder's presence wth a slight, absent-minded bow. 'Oh, my God,' he repeated, as he continued to stare at the body of his late employer.

At eleven the following morning, Richard Warwick's study looked somewhat more inviting than it had on the previous foggy evening. For one thing, the sun was shining on a cold, clear, bright day, and the french windows were wide open. The body had been removed overnight, and the wheelchair had been pushed into the recess, its former central place in the room now occupied by the armchair. The small table had been cleared of everything except decanter and ashtray. A good-looking young man in his twenties with short dark hair, dressed in a tweed sports jacket and navy-blue trousers, was sitting in the wheelchair, reading a book of poems. After a few moments, he got up. 'Beautiful,' he said to himself. 'Apposite and beautiful.' His voice was soft and musical, with a pronounced Welsh accent.

The young man closed the book he had been reading, and replaced it on the bookshelves in the recess. Then, after surveying the room for a minute or two, he walked across to the open french windows, and went out onto the terrace. Almost immediately, a middle-aged, thick-set, somewhat poker-faced man carrying a briefcase entered the room from the hallway.

Going to the armchair which faced out onto the terrace, he put his briefcase on it, and looked out of the windows. 'Sergeant Cadwallader!' he called sharply.

The younger man turned back into the room. 'Good morning, Inspector Thomas,' he said, and then continued, with a lilt in his voice, '"Season of mists and mellow fruitfulness, close bosom friend of the maturing sun".'

The inspector, who had begun to unbutton his overcoat, stopped and looked intently at the young sergeant. 'I beg your pardon?' he asked, with a distinct note of sarcasm in his voice.

'That's Keats,' the sergeant informed him, sounding quite pleased with himself. The inspector responded with a baleful look at him, then shrugged, took off his coat, placed it on the wheelchair in the recess, and came back for his briefcase.

'You'd hardly credit the fine day it is,' Sergeant Cadwallader went on. 'When you think of the terrible time we had getting here last night. The worst fog I've known in years. "The yellow fog that rubs its back upon the window-panes". That's T.S. Eliot.' He waited for a reaction to his quotation from the inspector, but got none, so continued, 'It's no wonder the accidents piled up the way they did on the Cardiff road.'

'Might have been worse,' was his inspector's uninterested comment.

'I don't know about that,' said the sergeant, warming to his subject. 'At Porthcawl, that was a nasty smash. One killed and two children badly injured. And the mother crying her heart out there on the road. "The pretty wretch left crying" –'

The inspector interrupted him. 'Have the fingerprint boys finished their job yet?' he asked.

Suddenly realizing that he had better get back to the business in hand, Sergeant Cadwallader replied, 'Yes, sir. I've got them all ready here for you.' He picked up a folder from the desk and opened it. The inspector sat in the desk chair and started to examine the first sheet of fingerprints in the folder. 'No trouble from the household about taking their prints?' he asked the sergeant casually.

'No trouble whatever,' the sergeant told him. 'Most obliging they were – anxious to help, as you might say. And that is only to be expected.'

'I don't know about that,' the inspector observed. 'I've usually found most people kick up no end of a fuss. Seem to think their prints are going to be filed in the Rogues' Gallery.' He took a deep breath, stretching his arms, and continued to study the prints. 'Now, let's see. Mr Warwick – that's the deceased. Mrs Laura Warwick, his wife. Mrs Warwick senior, that's his mother. Young Jan Warwick, Miss Bennett and – who's this? Angle? Oh, Angell. Ah yes, that's his nurse-attendant, isn't it? And two other sets of prints. Let's see now – Hm. On outside of window, on decanter, on brandy glass overlaying prints of Richard Warwick and Angell and Mrs Laura Warwick, on cigarette lighter – and on the revolver. That will be that chap Michael Starkwedder. He gave Mrs Warwick brandy, and of course it was he who carried the gun in from the garden.'

Sergeant Cadwallader nodded slowly. 'Mr Starkwedder,' he growled, in a voice of deep suspicion.

The inspector, sounding amused, asked, 'You don't like him?'

'What's he doing here? That's what I'd like to know,' the sergeant replied. 'Running his car into a ditch and coming up to a house where there's been a murder done?'

The inspector turned in his chair to face his young colleague. 'You nearly ran *our* car into the ditch last night, coming up to a house where there'd been a murder done. And as to what he's doing here, he's been here – in this vicinity – for the last week, looking around for a small house or cottage.'

The sergeant looked unconvinced, and the inspector turned back to the desk, adding wryly, 'It seems he had a Welsh grandmother and he used to come here for holidays when he was a boy.'

Mollified, the sergeant conceded, 'Ah, well now, if he had a Welsh grandmother, that's a different matter, isn't it?' He raised his right arm and declaimed, '"One road leads to London, One road leads to Wales. My road leads me seawards, To the white dipping sails." He was a fine poet, John Masefield. Very underrated.'

The inspector opened his mouth to complain, but then thought better of it and grinned instead. 'We ought to get the report on Starkwedder from Abadan any moment now,' he told the young sergeant. 'Have you got his prints for comparison?'

'I sent Jones round to the inn where he stayed last night,' Cadwallader informed his superior, 'but he'd gone out to the garage to see about getting his car salvaged. Jones rang the garage and spoke to him while he was there. He's been told to report at the station as soon as possible.'

'Right. Now, about this second set of unidentified prints. The print of a man's hand flat on the table by the body, and blurred impressions on both the outside and the inside of the french windows.'

'I'll bet that's MacGregor,' the sergeant exclaimed, snapping his fingers.

'Ye-es. Could be,' the inspector admitted reluctantly. 'But they weren't on the revolver. And you would think any man using a revolver to kill someone would have the sense enough to wear gloves, surely.'

'I don't know,' the sergeant observed. 'An unbalanced fellow like this MacGregor, deranged after the death of his child, he wouldn't think of that.'

'Well, we ought to get a description of MacGregor through from Norwich soon,' the inspector said.

The sergeant settled himself on the footstool. 'It's a sad story, whichever way you look at it,' he suggested. 'A man, his wife but lately dead, and his only child killed by furious driving.'

'If there'd been what you call furious driving,' the inspector corrected him impatiently, 'Richard Warwick would have got a sentence for manslaughter, or at any rate for the driving offence. In point of fact, his licence wasn't even endorsed.' He reached down to his briefcase, and took out the murder weapon.

'There is some fearful lying goes on sometimes,' Sergeant Cadwallader muttered darkly. '"Lord, Lord, how this world is given to lying." That's Shakespeare.'

His superior officer merely rose from the desk and looked at him. After a moment, the sergeant pulled himself together and rose to his feet. 'A man's hand flat on the table,' murmured the inspector as he went across to the table, taking the gun with him, and looking down at the table-top. 'I wonder.'

'Perhaps that could have been a guest in the house,' Sergeant Cadwallader suggested helpfully.

'Perhaps,' the inspector agreed. 'But I understand from Mrs

Warwick that there were no visitors to the house yesterday. That manservant – Angell – might be able to tell us more. Go and fetch him, would you?'

'Yes, sir,' said Cadwallader as he went out. Left alone, the inspector spread out his own left hand on the table, and bent over the chair as if looking down at an invisible occupant. Then he went to the window and stepped outside, glancing both to left and right. He examined the lock of the french windows, and was turning back into the room when the sergeant returned, bringing with him Richard Warwick's valet-attendant, Angell, who was wearing a grey alpaca jacket, white shirt, dark tie and striped trousers.

'You're Henry Angell?' the inspector asked him.

'Yes, sir,' Angell replied.

'Sit down there, will you?' said the inspector.

Angell moved to sit on the sofa. 'Now then,' the inspector continued, 'you've been nurse-attendant and valet to Mr Richard Warwick – for how long?'

'For three and a half years, sir,' replied Angell. His manner was correct, but there was a shifty look in his eyes.

'Did you like the job?'

'I found it quite satisfactory, sir,' was Angell's reply.

'What was Mr Warwick like to work for?' the inspector asked him.

'Well, he was difficult.'

'But there were advantages, were there?'

'Yes, sir,' Angell admitted. 'I was extremely well paid.'

'And that made up for the other disadvantages, did it?' the inspector persisted.

'Yes, sir. I am trying to accumulate a little nest-egg.'

The inspector seated himself in the armchair, placing the

gun on the table beside him. 'What were you doing before you came to Mr Warwick?' he asked Angell.

'The same sort of job, sir. I can show you my references,' the valet replied. 'I've always given satisfaction, I hope. I've had some rather difficult employers – or patients, really. Sir James Walliston, for example. He is now a voluntary patient in a mental home. A *very* difficult person, sir.' He lowered his voice slightly before adding, 'Drugs!'

'Quite,' said the inspector. 'There was no question of drugs with Mr Warwick, I suppose?'

'No, sir. Brandy was what Mr Warwick liked to resort to.'

'Drank a lot of it, did he?' the inspector asked.

'Yes, sir,' Angell replied. 'He was a heavy drinker, but not an alcoholic, if you understand me. He never showed any ill-effects.'

The inspector paused before asking, 'Now, what's all this about guns and revolvers and – shooting at animals?'

'Well, it was his hobby, sir,' Angell told him. 'What we call in the profession a compensation. He'd been a big-game hunter in his day, I understand. Quite a little arsenal he's got in his bedroom there.' He nodded over his shoulder to indicate a room elsewhere in the house. 'Rifles, shotguns, air-guns, pistols and revolvers.'

'I see,' said the inspector. 'Well, now, just take a look at this gun here.'

Angell rose and stepped towards the table, then hesitated. 'It's all right,' the inspector told him, 'you needn't mind handling it.'

Angell picked up the gun, gingerly. 'Do you recognize it?' the inspector asked him.

'It's difficult to say, sir,' the valet replied. 'It looks like one of Mr Warwick's, but I don't really know very much about firearms. I can't say for certain which gun he had on the table beside him last night.'

'Didn't he have the same one every night?' asked the inspector.

'Oh, no, he had his fancies, sir,' said Angell. 'He kept using different ones.' The valet offered the gun back to the inspector, who took it.

'What was the good of his having a gun last night with all that fog?' queried the inspector.

'It was just a habit, sir,' Angell replied. 'He was used to it, as you might say.'

'All right, sit down again, would you?'

Angell sat again at one end of the sofa. The inspector examined the barrel of the gun before asking, 'When did you see Mr Warwick last?'

'About a quarter to ten last night, sir,' Angell told him. 'He had a bottle of brandy and a glass by his side, and the pistol he'd chosen. I arranged his rug for him, and wished him good-night.'

'Didn't he ever go to bed?' the inspector asked.

'No, sir,' replied the valet. 'At least, not in the usual sense of the term. He always slept in his chair. At six in the morning I would bring him tea, then I would wheel him into his bedroom, which had its own bathroom, where he'd bath and shave and so on, and then he'd usually sleep until lunch-time. I understand that he suffered from insomnia at night, and so he preferred to remain in his chair then. He was rather an eccentric gentleman.'

'And the window was shut when you left him?'

'Yes, sir,' Angell replied. 'There was a lot of fog about last night, and he didn't want it seeping into the house.'

'All right. The window was shut. Was it locked?'

'No, sir. That window was never locked.'

'So he could open it if he wanted to?'

'Oh, yes, sir. He had his wheelchair, you see. He could wheel himself over to the window and open it if the night should clear up.'

'I see.' The inspector thought for a moment, and then asked, 'You didn't hear a shot last night?'

'No, sir,' Angell replied.

The inspector walked across to the sofa and looked down at Angell. 'Isn't that rather remarkable?' he asked.

'No, not really, sir,' was the reply. 'You see, my room is some distance away. Along a passage and through a baize door on the other side of the house.'

'Wasn't that rather awkward, in case your master wanted to summon you?'

'Oh no, sir,' said Angell. 'He had a bell that rang in my room.'

'But he didn't press that bell last night at all?'

'Oh no, sir,' Angell repeated. 'If he had done so, I would have woken up at once. It is, if I may say so, a very loud bell, sir.'

Inspector Thomas leaned forward on the arm of the sofa to approach Angell in another way.

'Did you –' he began in a voice of controlled impatience, only to be interrupted by the shrill ring of the telephone. He waited for Sergeant Cadwallader to answer it, but the sergeant appeared to be dreaming with his eyes open and his lips moving soundlessly, perhaps immersed in some poetic reflection. After a moment, he realized that the inspector was staring at him, and that the phone was ringing. 'Sorry, sir, but a poem is on the way,' he explained as he went to the desk to answer the phone. 'Sergeant Cadwallader speaking,' he said. There was a pause, and then he added, 'Ah yes, indeed.' After another pause, he turned to the inspector. 'It's the police at Norwich, sir.'

Inspector Thomas took the phone from Cadwallader, and sat at the desk. 'Is that you, Edmundson?' he asked. 'Thomas here . . . Got it, right . . . Yes . . . Calgary, yes . . . Yes . . . Yes, the aunt, when did she die? . . . Oh, two months ago . . . Yes, I see . . . Eighteen, Thirty-fourth Street, Calgary.' He looked up impatiently at Cadwallader, and gestured to him to take a note of the address. 'Yes . . . Oh, it was, was it? . . . Yes, slowly please.' He looked meaningfully again at his sergeant. 'Medium height,' he repeated. 'Blue eyes, dark hair and beard . . . Yes, as you say, you remember the case . . . Ah, he did, did he? . . . Violent sort of fellow? . . . Yes . . . You're sending it along? Yes . . . Well, thank you, Edmundson. Tell me, what do you think, yourself? . . . Yes, yes, I know what the findings were, but what did *you* think yourself? . . . Ah, he had, had he? . . . Once or twice before . . . Yes, of course, you'd make some allowances . . . All right. Thanks.'

He replaced the receiver and said to the sergeant, 'Well, we've got some of the dope on MacGregor. It seems that, when his wife died, he travelled back to England from Canada to leave the child with an aunt of his wife's who lived in North Walsham, because he had just got himself a job in Alaska and couldn't take the boy with him. Apparently he was terribly cut up at the child's death, and went about swearing revenge on Warwick. That's not uncommon after one of these accidents.

Anyway, he went off back to Canada. They've got his address, and they'll send a cable off to Calgary. The aunt he was going to leave the child with died about two months ago.' He turned suddenly to Angell. 'You were there at the time, I suppose, Angell? Motor accident in North Walsham, running over a boy.'

'Oh yes, sir,' Angell replied. 'I remember it quite well.'

The inspector got up from the desk and went across to the valet. Seeing the desk chair empty, Sergeant Cadwallader promptly took the opportunity to sit down. 'What happened?' the inspector asked Angell. 'Tell me about the accident.'

'Mr Warwick was driving along the main street, and a little boy ran out of a house there,' Angell told him. 'Or it might have been the inn. I think it was. There was no chance of stopping. Mr Warwick ran over him before he could do a thing about it.'

'He was speeding, was he?' asked the inspector.

'Oh no, sir. That was brought out very clearly at the inquest. Mr Warwick was well within the speed limit.'

'I know that's what he said,' the inspector commented.

'It was quite true, sir,' Angell insisted. 'Nurse Warburton – a nurse Mr Warwick employed at the time – she was in the car, too, and she agreed.'

The inspector walked across to one end of the sofa. 'Did she happen to look at the speedometer at the time?' he queried.

'I believe Nurse Warburton did happen to see the speedometer,' Angell replied smoothly. 'She estimated that they were going at between twenty and twenty-five miles an hour. Mr Warwick was completely exonerated.'

'But the boy's father didn't agree?' the inspector asked.

'Perhaps that's only natural, sir,' was Angell's comment.

'Had Mr Warwick been drinking?'

Angell's reply was evasive. 'I believe he had had a glass of sherry, sir.' He and Inspector Thomas exchanged glances. Then the inspector crossed to the french windows, taking out his handkerchief and blowing his nose. 'Well, I think that'll do for now,' he told the valet.

Angell rose and went to the door. After a moment's hesitation, he turned back into the room. 'Excuse me, sir,' he said. 'But was Mr Warwick shot with his own gun?'

The inspector turned to him. 'That remains to be seen,' he observed. 'Whoever it was who shot him collided with Mr Starkwedder, who was coming up to the house to try to get help for his stranded vehicle. In the collision, the man dropped a gun. Mr Starkwedder picked it up – this gun.' He pointed to the gun on the table.

'I see, sir. Thank you, sir,' said Angell as he turned to the door again.

'By the way,' added the inspector, 'were there any visitors to the house yesterday? Yesterday evening in particular?'

Angell paused for just a moment, then eyed the inspector shiftily. 'Not that I can recall, sir – at present,' he replied. He left the room, closing the door behind him.

Inspector Thomas went back to the desk. 'If you ask me,' he said quietly to the sergeant, 'that fellow's a nasty bit of goods. Nothing you can put your finger on, but I don't like him.'

'I'm of the same opinion as you, regarding that,' Cadwallader replied. 'He's not a man I would trust, and what's more, I'd say there may have been something fishy about that accident.' Suddenly realizing that the inspector was standing over him, he got up quickly from his chair. The inspector took the notes Cadwallader had been making, and began to peruse them.

'Now I wonder if Angell knows something he hasn't told us about last night,' he began, and then broke off. 'Hello, what's this? "'Tis misty in November, But seldom in December." That's not Keats, I hope?'

'No,' said Sergeant Cadwallader proudly. 'That's Cadwallader.'

The inspector thrust Cadwallader's notebook back at him roughly, as the door opened and Miss Bennett came in, closing the door carefully behind her. 'Inspector,' she said, 'Mrs Warwick is very anxious to see you. She is fussing a little.' She added quickly, 'I mean Mrs Warwick senior, Richard's mother. She doesn't admit it, but I don't think she's in the best of health, so please be gentle with her. Will you see her now?'

'Oh, certainly,' replied the inspector. 'Ask her to come in.'

Miss Bennett opened the door, beckoning, and Mrs Warwick came in. 'It's all right, Mrs Warwick,' the housekeeper assured her, leaving the room and shutting the door behind her.

'Good morning, madam,' the inspector said. Mrs Warwick did not return his greeting, but came directly to the point. 'Tell me, Inspector,' she ordered, 'what progress are you making?'

'It's rather early to say that, madam,' he replied, 'but you can rest assured that we're doing everything we can.'

Mrs Warwick sat on the sofa, placing her stick against the

arm. 'This man MacGregor,' she asked. 'Has he been seen hanging about locally? Has anyone noticed him?'

'Enquiries have gone out about that,' the inspector informed her. 'But so far there's been no record of a stranger being seen in the locality.'

'That poor little boy,' Mrs Warwick continued. 'The one Richard ran over, I mean. I suppose it must have unhinged the father's brain. I know they told me he was very violent and abusive at the time. Perhaps that was only natural. But after two years! It seems incredible.'

'Yes,' the inspector agreed, 'it seems a long time to wait.'

'But he was a Scot, of course,' Mrs Warwick recalled. 'A MacGregor. A patient, dogged people, the Scots.'

'Indeed they are,' exclaimed Sergeant Cadwallader, forgetting himself and thinking out loud. '"There are few more impressive sights in the world than a Scotsman on the make,"' he continued, but the inspector immediately gave him a sharp look of disapproval, which quietened him.

'Your son had no preliminary warning?' Inspector Thomas asked Mrs Warwick. 'No threatening letter? Anything of that kind?'

'No, I'm sure he hadn't,' she replied quite firmly. 'Richard would have said so. He would have laughed about it.'

'He wouldn't have taken it seriously at all?' the inspector suggested.

'Richard always laughed at danger,' said Mrs Warwick. She sounded proud of her son.

'After the accident,' the inspector continued, 'did your son offer any compensation to the child's father?'

'Naturally,' Mrs Warwick replied. 'Richard was not a mean man. But it was refused. Indignantly refused, I may say.'

'Quite so,' murmured the inspector.

'I understand MacGregor's wife was dead,' Mrs Warwick recalled. 'The boy was all he had in the world. It was a tragedy, really.'

'But in your opinion it was not your son's fault?' the inspector asked. When Mrs Warwick did not answer, he repeated his question. 'I said – it was not your son's fault?'

She remained silent a moment longer before replying, 'I heard you.'

'Perhaps you don't agree?' the inspector persisted.

Mrs Warwick turned away on the sofa, embarrassed, fingering a cushion. 'Richard drank too much,' she said finally. 'And of course he'd been drinking that day.'

'A glass of sherry?' the inspector prompted her.

'A glass of sherry!' Mrs Warwick repeated with a bitter laugh. 'He'd been drinking pretty heavily. He did drink – very heavily. That decanter there –' She indicated the decanter on the table near the armchair in the french windows. 'That decanter was filled every evening, and it was always practically empty in the morning.'

Sitting on the stool and facing Mrs Warwick, the inspector said to her, quietly, 'So you think that your son was to blame for the accident?'

'Of course he was to blame,' she replied. 'I've never had the least doubt of it.'

'But he was exonerated,' the inspector reminded her.

Mrs Warwick laughed. 'That nurse who was in the car with him? That Warburton woman?' she snorted. 'She was a fool, and she was devoted to Richard. I expect he paid her pretty handsomely for her evidence, too.'

'Do you actually know that?' the inspector asked, sharply.

Mrs Warwick's tone was equally sharp as she replied, 'I don't know anything, but I arrive at my own conclusions.'

The inspector went across to Sergeant Cadwallader and took his notes from him, while Mrs Warwick continued. 'I'm telling you all this now,' she said, 'because what you want is the truth, isn't it? You want to be sure there's sufficient incentive for murder on the part of that little boy's father. Well, in my opinion, there was. Only, I didn't think that after all this time –' Her voice trailed away into silence.

The inspector looked up from the notes he had been consulting. 'You didn't hear anything last night?' he asked her.

'I'm a little deaf, you know,' Mrs Warwick replied quickly. 'I didn't know anything was wrong until I heard people talking and passing my door. I came down, and young Jan said, "Richard's been shot. Richard's been shot." I thought at first –' She passed her hand over her eyes. 'I thought it was a joke of some kind.'

'Jan is your younger son?' the inspector asked her.

'He's not *my* son,' Mrs Warwick replied. The inspector looked at her quickly as she went on, 'I divorced my husband many years ago. He remarried. Jan is the son of the second marriage.' She paused, then continued. 'It sounds more complicated than it is, really. When both his parents died, the boy came here. Richard and Laura had just been married then. Laura has always been very kind to Richard's half-brother. She's been like an elder sister to him, really.'

She paused, and the inspector took the opportunity to lead her back to talking about Richard Warwick. 'Yes, I see,' he said, 'but now, about your son Richard –'

'I loved my son, Inspector,' Mrs Warwick said, 'but I was not blind to his faults, and they were very largely due to the accident that made him a cripple. He was a proud man, an outdoor man, and to have to live the life of an invalid and a semi-cripple was very galling to him. It did not, shall we say, improve his character.'

'Yes, I see,' observed the inspector. 'Would you say his married life was happy?'

'I haven't the least idea.' Mrs Warwick clearly had no intention of saying any more on the subject. 'Is there anything else you wish to know, Inspector?' she asked.

'No thank you, Mrs Warwick,' Inspector Thomas replied. 'But I should like to talk to Miss Bennett now, if I may.'

Mrs Warwick rose, and Sergeant Cadwallader went to open the door for her. 'Yes, of course,' she said. 'Miss Bennett. Benny, we call her. She's the person who can help you most. She's so practical and efficient.'

'She's been with you for a long time?' the inspector asked.

'Oh yes, for years and years. She looked after Jan when he was little, and before that she helped with Richard, too. Oh, yes, she's looked after all of us. A very faithful person, Benny.' Acknowledging the sergeant at the door with a nod, she left the room.

CHAPTER 8

Sergeant Cadwallader closed the door and stood with his back against it, looking at the inspector. 'So Richard Warwick was a drinking man, eh?' he commented. 'You know, I've heard that said of him before. And all those pistols and air-guns and rifles. A little queer in the head, if you ask me.'

'Could be,' Inspector Thomas replied laconically.

The telephone rang. Expecting his sergeant to answer it, the inspector looked meaningfully at him, but Cadwallader had become immersed in his notes as he strolled across to the armchair and sat, completely oblivious of the phone. After a while, realizing that the sergeant's mind was elsewhere, no doubt in the process of composing a poem, the inspector sighed, crossed to the desk, and picked up the receiver.

'Hello,' he said. 'Yes, speaking . . . Starkwedder, he came in? He gave you his prints? . . . Good . . . yes – well, ask him to wait . . . yes, I shall be back in half an hour or so . . . yes, I want to ask him some more questions . . . Yes, goodbye.'

Towards the end of this conversation, Miss Bennett had entered the room, and was standing by the door. Noticing her, Sergeant Cadwallader rose from his armchair and took up a position behind it. 'Yes?' said Miss Bennett with an interrogative inflection. She addressed the inspector. 'You want to ask me some questions? I've got a good deal to do this morning.'

'Yes, Miss Bennett,' the inspector replied. 'I want to hear your account of the car accident with the child in Norfolk.'

'The MacGregor child?'

'Yes, the MacGregor child. You remembered his name very quickly last night, I hear.'

Miss Bennett turned to close the door behind her. 'Yes,' she agreed. 'I have a very good memory for names.'

'And no doubt,' the inspector continued, 'the occurrence made some impression on you. But you weren't in the car yourself, were you?'

Miss Bennett seated herself on the sofa. 'No, no, I wasn't in the car,' she told him. 'It was the hospital nurse Mr Warwick had at the time. A Nurse Warburton.'

'Did you go to the inquest?' the inspector asked.

'No,' she replied. 'But Richard told us about it when he came back. He said the boy's father had threatened him, had said he'd get even with him. We didn't take it seriously, of course.'

Inspector Thomas came closer to her. 'Had you formed any particular impression about the accident?' he asked.

'I don't know what you mean.'

The inspector regarded Miss Bennett for a moment, and then said, 'I mean do you think it happened because Mr Warwick had been drinking?'

She made a dismissive gesture. 'Oh, I suppose his mother told you that,' she snorted. 'Well, you mustn't go by all she says. She's got a prejudice against drink. Her husband – Richard's father – drank.'

'You think, then,' the inspector suggested to her, 'that Richard Warwick's account was true, that he was driving well within the speed limit, and that the accident could not have been avoided?'

'I don't see why it shouldn't have been the truth,' Miss Bennett insisted. 'Nurse Warburton corroborated his evidence.'

'And her word was to be relied upon?'

Clearly taking exception to what she seemed to regard as an aspersion on her profession, Miss Bennett said with some asperity, 'I should hope so. After all, people don't go around telling lies – not about that sort of thing. Do they?'

Sergeant Cadwallader, who had been following the questioning, now broke in. 'Oh, do they not, indeed!' he exclaimed. 'The way they talk sometimes, you'd think that not only were they within the speed limit, but that they'd managed to get into reverse at the same time!'

Annoyed at this latest interruption, the inspector turned slowly and looked at the sergeant. Miss Bennett also regarded the young man in some surprise. Embarrassed, Sergeant Cadwallader looked down at his notes, and the inspector turned again to Miss Bennett. 'What I'm getting at is this,' he told her. 'In the grief and stress of the moment, a man might easily threaten revenge for an accident that had killed his child. But on reflection, if things were as stated, he would surely have realized that the accident was not Richard Warwick's fault.'

'Oh,' said Miss Bennett. 'Yes, I see what you mean.'

The inspector paced slowly about the room as he continued, 'If, on the other hand, the car had been driven erratically and at excessive speed – if the car had been, shall we say, out of control –'

'Did Laura tell you that?' Miss Bennett interrupted him.

The inspector turned to look at her, surprised at her mention of the murdered man's wife. 'What makes you think she told me?' he asked.

'I don't know,' Miss Bennett replied. 'I just wondered.' Looking confused, she glanced at her watch. 'Is that all?' she asked. 'I'm very busy this morning.' She walked to the door, opened it, and was about to leave when the inspector said, 'I'd like to have a word with young Jan next, if I may.'

Miss Bennett turned in the doorway. 'Oh, he's rather excited this morning,' she said, sounding somewhat truculent. 'I'd really be much obliged if you wouldn't talk to him – raking it all up. I've just got him calmed down.'

'I'm sorry, but I'm afraid we must ask him a few questions,' the inspector insisted.

Miss Bennett closed the door firmly and came back into the room. 'Why can't you just find this man MacGregor, and question him?' she suggested. 'He can't have got far away.'

'We'll find him. Don't you worry,' the inspector assured her.

'I hope you will,' Miss Bennett retorted. 'Revenge, indeed! Why, it's not Christian.'

'Of course,' the inspector agreed, adding meaningfully, 'especially when the accident was not Mr Warwick's fault and could not have been avoided.'

Miss Bennett gave him a sharp look. There was a pause, and then the inspector repeated, 'I'd like to speak to Jan, please.'

'I don't know if I can find him,' said Miss Bennett. 'He may have gone out.' She left the room quickly. The inspector looked at Sergeant Cadwallader, nodding his head towards the door, and the sergeant followed her out. In the corridor, Miss Bennett admonished Cadwallader. 'You're not to worry him,' she said. She came back into the room. 'You're not to worry the boy,' she ordered the inspector. 'He's very easily – unsettled. He gets excited, temperamental.'

The inspector regarded her silently for a moment, and then asked, 'Is he ever violent?'

'No, of course not. He's a very sweet boy, very gentle. Docile, really. I simply meant that you might upset him. It's not good for children, things like murder. And that's all he is, really. A child.'

The inspector sat in the chair at the desk. 'You needn't worry, Miss Bennett, I assure you,' he told her. 'We quite understand the position.'

....

Just then, Sergeant Cadwallader ushered in Jan, who rushed up to the inspector. 'Do you want me?' he cried excitedly. 'Have you caught him yet? Will there be blood on his clothes?'

'Now, Jan,' Miss Bennett cautioned him, 'you must behave yourself. Just answer any questions the gentleman asks you.'

Jan turned happily to Miss Bennett, and then back to the inspector. 'Oh, yes, I will,' he promised. 'But can't I ask any questions?'

'Of course you can ask questions,' the inspector assured him kindly.

Miss Bennett sat on the sofa. 'I'll wait while you're talking to him,' she said.

The inspector got up quickly, went to the door and opened it invitingly. 'No thank you, Miss Bennett,' he said firmly. 'We shan't need you. And didn't you say you're rather busy this morning?'

'I'd rather stay,' she insisted.

'I'm sorry.' The inspector's voice was sharp. 'We always like to talk to people one at a time.'

Miss Bennett looked at the inspector and then at Sergeant

Cadwallader. Realizing that she was defeated, she gave a snort of annoyance and swept out of the room, the inspector closing the door after her. The sergeant moved to the alcove, preparing to take more notes, while Inspector Thomas sat on the sofa. 'I don't suppose,' he said amiably to Jan, 'that you've ever been in close contact with a murder before, have you?'

'No, no, I haven't,' Jan replied eagerly. 'It's very exciting, isn't it?' He knelt on the footstool. 'Have you got any clues – fingerprints or bloodstains or anything?'

'You seem very interested in blood,' the inspector observed with a friendly smile.

'Oh, I am,' Jan replied, quietly and seriously. 'I like blood. It's a beautiful colour, isn't it? That nice clear red.' He too sat down on the sofa, laughing nervously. 'Richard shot things, you know, and then they used to bleed. It's really very funny, isn't it? I mean it's funny that Richard, who was always shooting things, should have been shot himself. Don't you think that's funny?'

The inspector's voice was quiet, his inflection rather dry, as he replied, 'I suppose it has its humorous side.' He paused. 'Are you very upset that your brother – your half-brother, I mean – is dead?'

'Upset?' Jan sounded surprised. 'That Richard is dead? No, why should I be?'

'Well, I thought perhaps you were – very fond of him,' the inspector suggested.

'Fond of him!' exclaimed Jan in what sounded like genuine astonishment. 'Fond of Richard? Oh, no, nobody could be *fond* of Richard.'

'I suppose his wife was fond of him, though,' the inspector urged.

A look of surprise passed across Jan's face. 'Laura?' he exclaimed. 'No, I don't think so. She was always on *my* side.'

'On your side?' the inspector asked. 'What does that mean, exactly?'

Jan suddenly looked scared. 'Yes. Yes,' he almost shouted, hurriedly. 'When Richard wanted to have me sent away.'

'Sent away?' the inspector prompted him gently.

'To one of those places,' the youngster explained. 'You know, where they send you, and you're locked up, and you can't get out. He said Laura would come and see me, perhaps, sometimes.' Jan shook a little, then rose, backed away from the inspector, and looked across at Sergeant Cadwallader. 'I wouldn't like to be locked up,' he continued, his voice now tremulous. 'I'd hate to be locked up.'

He stood at the french windows, looking out onto the terrace. 'I like things open, always,' he called out to them. 'I like my window open, and my door, so that I can be sure I can get out.' He turned back into the room. 'But nobody can lock me up *now*, can they?'

'No, lad,' the inspector assured him. 'I shouldn't think so.'

'Not now that Richard's dead,' Jan added. Momentarily, he sounded almost smug.

The inspector got up and moved round the sofa. 'So Richard wanted you locked up?' he asked.

'Laura says he only said it to tease me,' Jan told him. 'She said that was all it was, and she said it was all right, and that as long as she was here she'd make quite sure that I would never be locked up.' He went to perch on one arm of the armchair. 'I love Laura,' he continued, speaking with a nervous excitement. 'I love Laura a terrible lot. We have wonderful times together, you know. We look for butterflies and birds' eggs, and we play games together. Bezique. Do you know that game? It's a clever one. And Beggar-my-neighbour. Oh, it's great fun doing things with Laura.'

The inspector went across to lean on the other arm of the chair. His voice had a kindly tone to it as he asked, 'I don't suppose you remember anything about this accident that happened when you were living in Norfolk, do you? When a little boy got run over?'

'Oh, yes, I remember that,' Jan replied quite cheerfully. 'Richard went to the inquest.'

'Yes, that's right. What else do you remember?' the inspector encouraged him.

'We had salmon for lunch that day,' Jan said immediately. 'Richard and Warby came back together. Warby was a bit flustered, but Richard was laughing.'

'Warby?' the inspector queried. 'Is that Nurse Warburton?'

'Yes, Warby. I didn't like her much. But Richard was so pleased with her that day that he kept saying, "Jolly good show, Warby."'

The door suddenly opened, and Laura Warwick appeared. Sergeant Cadwallader went across to her, and Jan called out, 'Hello, Laura.'

'Am I interrupting?' Laura asked the inspector.

'No, of course not, Mrs Warwick,' he replied. 'Do sit down, won't you?'

Laura came further into the room, and the sergeant shut the door behind her. 'Is – is Jan – ?' Laura began. She paused.

'I'm just asking him,' the inspector explained, 'if he remembers anything about that accident to the boy in Norfolk. The MacGregor boy.'

Laura sat at the end of the sofa. 'Do you remember, Jan?' she asked him.

'Of course I remember,' the lad replied, eagerly. 'I remember everything.' He turned to the inspector. 'I've told you, haven't I?' he asked.

The inspector did not reply to him directly. Instead, he moved slowly to the sofa and, addressing Laura Warwick, asked, 'What do you know about the accident, Mrs Warwick? Was it discussed at luncheon that day, when your husband came back from the inquest?'

'I don't remember,' Laura replied immediately.

Jan rose quickly and moved towards her. 'Oh, yes, you do, Laura, surely,' he reminded her. 'Don't you remember Richard saying that one brat more or less in the world didn't make any difference?'

Laura rose. 'Please –' she implored the inspector.

'It's quite all right, Mrs Warwick,' Inspector Thomas assured her gently. 'It's important, you know, that we get at the truth of that accident. After all, presumably it's the motive for what happened here last night.'

'Oh yes,' she sighed. 'I know. I know.'

'According to your mother-in-law,' the inspector continued, 'your husband had been drinking that day.'

'I expect he had,' Laura admitted. 'It – it wouldn't surprise me.'

The inspector moved to sit at the end of the sofa. 'Did you actually see or meet this man, MacGregor?' he asked her.

'No,' said Laura. 'No, I didn't go to the inquest.'

'He seems to have felt very revengeful,' the inspector commented.

Laura gave a sad smile. 'It must have affected his brain, I think,' she agreed.

Jan, who had gradually been getting very excited, came up to them. 'If I had an enemy,' he exclaimed aggressively, 'that's what I'd do. I'd wait a long time, and then I'd come creeping along in the dark with my gun. Then –' He shot at the armchair with an imaginary gun. 'Bang, bang, bang.'

'Be quiet, Jan,' Laura ordered him, sharply.

Jan suddenly looked upset. 'Are you angry with me, Laura?' he asked her, childishly.

'No, darling,' Laura reassured him, 'I'm not angry. But try not to get too excited.'

'I'm not excited,' Jan insisted.

CHAPTER 10

Crossing the front hall, Miss Bennett paused to admit Starkwedder and a police constable who seemed to have arrived on the doorstep together.

'Good morning, Miss Bennett,' Starkwedder greeted her. 'I'm here to see Inspector Thomas.'

Miss Bennett nodded. 'Good morning – oh, good morning, Constable. They're in the study, both of them – I don't know what's going on.'

'Good morning, madam,' the police constable replied. 'I've brought these for the inspector. Perhaps Sergeant Cadwallader could take them.'

'What's this?' Laura asked, over the rumble of voices outside.

The inspector rose and moved towards the door. 'It sounds as if Mr Starkwedder is back.'

As Starkwedder entered the room, Sergeant Cadwallader went out into the hall to deal with the constable. Meanwhile, young Jan sank into the armchair, and observed the proceedings eagerly.

'Look here,' exclaimed Starkwedder as he came into the

room. 'I can't spend all day kicking my heels at the police station. I've given you my fingerprints, and then I insisted that they bring me along here. I've got things to do. I've got two appointments with a house agent today.' He suddenly noticed Laura. 'Oh – good morning, Mrs Warwick,' he greeted her. 'I'm terribly sorry about what has happened.'

'Good morning,' Laura replied, distantly.

The inspector went across to the table by the armchair. 'Last night, Mr Starkwedder,' he asked, 'did you by any chance lay your hand on this table, and subsequently push the window open?'

Starkwedder joined him at the table. 'I don't know,' he admitted. 'I could have done. Is it important? I can't remember.'

Sergeant Cadwallader came back into the room, carrying a file. After shutting the door behind him, he walked across to the inspector. 'Here are Mr Starkwedder's prints, sir,' he reported. 'The constable brought them. And the ballistics report.'

'Ah, let's see,' said the inspector. 'The bullet that killed Richard Warwick definitely came from this gun. As for the fingerprints, well, we'll soon see.' He went to the chair by the desk, sat, and began to study the documents, while the sergeant moved into the alcove.

After a pause, Jan, who had been staring intently at Starkwedder, asked him, 'You've just come back from Abadan, haven't you? What's Abadan like?'

'It's hot,' was the only response he got from Starkwedder, who then turned to Laura. 'How are you today, Mrs Warwick?' he asked. ' Are you feeling better?'

'Oh yes, thank you,' Laura replied. 'I've got over the shock now.'

'Good,' said Starkwedder.

The inspector had risen, and now approached Starkwedder on the sofa. 'Your prints,' he announced, 'are on the window, decanter, glass and cigarette lighter. The prints on the table are not yours. They're a completely unidentified set of prints.' He looked around the room. 'That settles it, then,' he continued. 'Since there were no visitors here –' he paused and looked at Laura – 'last night – ?'

'No,' Laura assured him.

'Then they must be MacGregor's,' continued the inspector.

'MacGregor's?' asked Starkwedder, looking at Laura.

'You sound surprised,' said the inspector.

'Yes – I am, rather,' Starkwedder admitted. 'I mean, I should have expected him to have worn gloves.'

The inspector nodded. 'You're right,' he agreed. 'He handled the revolver with gloves.'

'Was there any quarrel?' Starkwedder asked, addressing his question to Laura Warwick. 'Or was nothing heard but the shot?'

It was with an effort that Laura replied, 'I – we – Benny and I, that is – we just heard the shot. But then, we wouldn't have heard anything from upstairs.'

Sergeant Cadwallader had been gazing out at the garden through the small window in the alcove. Now, seeing someone approaching across the lawn, he moved to one side of the french windows. In through the windows there entered a handsome man in his mid-thirties, above medium height, with fair hair, blue eyes and a somewhat military aspect. He paused at the entrance, looking very worried. Jan, the first of the others in the room to notice him, squealed excitedly, 'Julian! Julian!'

The newcomer looked at Jan and then turned to Laura Warwick. 'Laura!' he exclaimed. 'I've just heard. I'm – I'm most terribly sorry.'

'Good morning, Major Farrar,' Inspector Thomas greeted him.

Julian Farrar turned to the inspector. 'This is an extraordinary business.' he said. 'Poor Richard.'

'He was lying here in his wheelchair,' Jan told Farrar excitedly. 'He was all crumpled up. And there was a piece of paper on his chest. Do you know what it said? It said "Paid in full".'

'Yes. There, there, Jan,' Julian Farrar murmured, patting the boy's shoulder.

'It *is* exciting, isn't it?' Jan continued, looking eagerly at him.

Farrar moved past him. 'Yes. Yes, of course it's exciting,' he assured Jan, looking enquiringly towards Starkwedder as he spoke.

The inspector introduced the two men to each other. 'This is Mr Starkwedder – Major Farrar, who may be our next Member of Parliament. He's contesting the by-election.'

Starkwedder and Julian Farrar shook hands, politely murmuring, 'How do you do?' The inspector moved away, beckoning to the sergeant who joined him. They conferred, as Starkwedder explained to Major Farrar, 'I'd run my car into a ditch, and I was coming up to the house to see if I could telephone and get some help. A man dashed out of the house, almost knocking me over.'

'But which way did this man go?' Farrar asked.

'No idea,' Starkwedder replied. 'He vanished into the mist like a conjuring trick.' He turned away, while Jan, kneeling in the armchair and looking expectantly at Farrar, said, 'You told Richard someone would shoot him one day, didn't you, Julian?'

There was a pause. Everyone in the room looked at Julian Farrar.

Farrar thought for a moment. Then, 'Did I? I don't remember,' he said brusquely.

'Oh, yes, you did,' Jan insisted. 'At dinner one night. You know, you and Richard were having a sort of argument, and you said, "One of these days, Richard, somebody'll put a bullet through your head."'

'A remarkable prophecy,' the inspector commented.

Julian Farrar moved to sit on one end of the footstool. 'Oh well,' he said, 'Richard and his guns were pretty fair nuisance value, you know. People didn't like it. Why, there was that fellow – you remember, Laura? Your gardener, Griffiths. You know – the one Richard sacked. Griffiths certainly said to me – and on more than one occasion – "One of these days, look you, I shall come with my gun and I shall shoot Mr Warwick."'

'Oh, Griffiths wouldn't do a thing like that,' Laura exclaimed quickly.

Farrar looked contrite. 'No, no, of course not,' he admitted. 'I – I didn't mean that. I mean that it was the sort of thing that – er – people said about Richard.'

To cover his embarrassment, he took out his cigarette-case and extracted a cigarette.

The inspector sat in the desk chair, looking thoughtful. Starkwedder stood in a corner near the alcove, close to Jan who gazed at him with interest.

'I wish I'd come over here last night,' Julian Farrar announced, addressing no one in particular. 'I meant to.'

'But that awful fog,' Laura said quietly. 'You couldn't come out in that.'

'No,' Farrar replied. 'I had my committee members over to dine with me. When they found the fog coming on, they went home rather early. I thought then of coming along to see you, but I decided against it.' Searching in his pockets, he asked, 'Has anyone got a match? I seem to have mislaid my lighter.'

He looked around, and suddenly noticed the lighter on the table where Laura had left it the night before. Rising, he went across to pick it up, observed by Starkwedder. 'Oh, here it is,' said Farrar. 'Couldn't imagine where I'd left it.'

'Julian –' Laura began.

'Yes?' Farrar offered her a cigarette, and she took one. 'I'm most awfully sorry about all this, Laura,' he said. 'If there's anything I can do –' His voice trailed off indecisively.

'Yes. Yes, I know,' Laura replied, as Farrar lit their cigarettes.

Jan suddenly spoke, addressing Starkwedder. 'Can you shoot, Mr Starkwedder?' he asked. 'I can, you know. Richard used to let me try, sometimes. Of course, I wasn't as good as he was.'

'Did he, indeed?' said Starkwedder, turning to Jan. 'What sort of gun did he let you use?'

As Jan engaged Starkwedder's attention, Laura took the opportunity of speaking quickly to Julian Farrar.

'Julian, I must talk to you. I must,' she murmured softly.

Farrar's voice was equally low. 'Careful,' he warned her.

'It was a .22,' Jan was telling Starkwedder. 'I'm quite good at shooting, aren't I, Julian?' He went across to Julian Farrar. 'Do you remember the time you took me to the fair? I knocked two of the bottles down, didn't I?'

'You did indeed, my lad,' Farrar assured him. 'You've got a good eye, that's what counts. Good eye for a cricket ball, too. That was quite a sensational game, that match we had last summer,' he added.

Jan smiled at him happily, and then sat on the footstool, looking across at the inspector who was now examining documents on the desk. There was a pause. Then Starkwedder, as he took out a cigarette, asked Laura, 'Do you mind if I smoke?'

'Of course not,' replied Laura.

Starkwedder turned to Julian Farrar. 'May I borrow your lighter?'

'Of course,' said Farrar. 'Here it is.'

'Ah, a nice lighter, this,' Starkwedder commented, lighting his cigarette.

Laura made a sudden movement, and then stopped herself. 'Yes,' Farrar said carelessly. 'It works better than most.'

'Rather – distinctive,' Starkwedder observed. He gave a quick glance at Laura, and then returned the lighter to Julian Farrar with a murmured word of thanks.

Jan left his footstool, and stood behind the inspector's chair. 'Richard has lots of guns,' he confided. 'Air-guns, too. And he's got one gun that he used to use in Africa to shoot elephants. Would you like to see them? They're in Richard's bedroom through there.' He pointed the way.

'All right,' said the inspector, rising. 'You show them to us.' He smiled at Jan, adding genially, 'You know, you're being very helpful to us. Helping us quite a lot. We ought to take you into the police force.'

Putting a hand on the boy's shoulder, he steered him towards the door, which the sergeant opened for them. 'We don't need to keep you, Mr Starkwedder,' the inspector called from the door. 'You can go about your business now. Just keep in touch with us, that's all.'

'All right,' replied Starkwedder, as Jan, the inspector and the sergeant left the room, the sergeant closing the door behind them.

CHAPTER 11

There was an awkward pause after the police officers had left the room with Jan. Then Starkwedder remarked, 'Well, I suppose I'd better go and see whether they've managed to get my car out of the ditch yet. We didn't seem to pass it on the way here.'

'No,' Laura explained. 'The drive comes up from the other road.'

'Yes, I see,' Starkwedder answered, as he walked across to the french windows. He turned. 'How different things look in the daylight,' he observed as he stepped out onto the terrace.

As soon as he had gone, Laura and Julian Farrar turned to each other. 'Julian!' Laura exclaimed. 'That lighter! I said it was *mine*.'

'You said it was yours? To the inspector?' Farrar asked.

'No. To *him*.'

'To – to this fellow –' Farrar began, and then stopped as they both noticed Starkwedder walking along the terrace outside the windows. 'Laura –' he began again.

'Be careful,' said Laura, going across to the little window in the alcove and looking out. 'He may be listening to us.'

'Who is he?' asked Farrar. 'Do you know him?'

Laura came back to the centre of the room. 'No. No, I don't know him,' she told Farrar. 'He – he had an accident with his car, and he came here last night. Just after –'

Julian Farrar touched her hand which rested on the back of the sofa. 'It's all right, Laura. You know that I'll do everything I can.'

'Julian – *fingerprints*,' Laura gasped.

'What fingerprints?'

'On that table. On that table there, and on the pane of glass. Are they – yours?'

Farrar removed his hand from hers, indicating that Stark-wedder was again walking along the terrace outside. Without turning to the window, Laura moved away from him, saying loudly, 'It's very kind of you, Julian, and I'm sure there will be a lot of business things you can help us with.'

Starkwedder was pacing about, outside on the terrace. When he had moved out of sight, Laura turned to face Julian Farrar again. 'Are those fingerprints yours, Julian? Think.'

Farrar considered for a moment. Then, 'On the table – yes – they might have been.'

'Oh God!' Laura cried. 'What shall we do?'

Starkwedder could now be glimpsed again, walking back and forth along the terrace just outside the windows. Laura puffed at her cigarette. 'The police think it's a man called MacGregor –' she told Julian. She gave him a desperate look, pausing to allow him an opportunity to make some comment.

'Well, that's all right, then,' he replied. 'They'll probably go on thinking so.'

'But suppose –' Laura began.

Farrar interrupted her. 'I must go,' he said. 'I've got an appointment.' He rose. 'It's all right, Laura,' he said, patting her shoulder. 'Don't worry. I'll see that you're all right.'

The look on Laura's face was one of an incomprehension verging on desperation. Apparently oblivious of it, Farrar walked across to the french windows. As he pushed a window open, Starkwedder was approaching with the obvious intention of entering the room. Farrar politely moved aside, to avoid colliding with him.

'Oh, are you off now?' Starkwedder asked him.

'Yes,' said Farrar. 'Things are rather busy these days. Election coming on, you know, in a week's time.'

'Oh, I see,' Starkwedder replied. 'Excuse my ignorance, but what are you? Tory?'

'I'm a Liberal,' said Farrar. He sounded slightly indignant.

'Oh, are they still at it?' Starkwedder asked, brightly.

Julian Farrar drew a sharp breath, and left the room without another word. When he had gone, not quite slamming the door behind him, Starkwedder looked at Laura almost fiercely. Then, 'I see,' he said, his anger rising. 'Or at least I'm beginning to see.'

'What do you mean?' Laura asked him.

'That's the boyfriend, isn't it?' He came closer to her. 'Well, come on now, is it?'

'Since you ask,' Laura replied, defiantly, 'yes, it is!'

Starkwedder looked at her for a moment without speaking. Then, 'There are quite a few things you didn't tell me last night, aren't there?' he said angrily. 'That's why you snatched up his lighter in such a hurry and said it was yours.' He walked away a few paces and then turned to face her again. 'And how long has this been going on between you and him?'

'For quite some time now,' Laura said quietly.

'But you didn't ever decide to leave Warwick and go away together?'

'No,' Laura answered. 'There's Julian's career, for one thing. It might ruin him politically.'

Starkwedder sat himself down ill-temperedly at one end of the sofa. 'Oh, surely not, these days,' he snapped. 'Don't they all take adultery in their stride?'

'These would have been special circumstances,' Laura tried to explain. 'He was a friend of Richard's, and with Richard being a cripple –'

'Oh yes, I see. It certainly wouldn't have been good publicity!' Starkwedder retorted.

Laura came over to the sofa and stood looking down at him. 'I suppose you think I ought to have told you this last night?' she observed, icily.

Starkwedder looked away from her. 'You were under no obligation,' he muttered.

Laura seemed to relent. 'I didn't think it mattered –' she began. 'I mean – all I could think of was my having shot Richard.'

Starkwedder seemed to warm to her again, as he murmured, 'Yes, yes, I see.' After a pause, he added, '*I* couldn't think of anything else, either.' He paused again, and then looked up at her. 'Do you want to try a little experiment?' he asked. 'Where were you standing when you shot Richard?'

'Where was I standing?' Laura echoed. She sounded perplexed.

'That's what I said.'

After a moment's thought, Laura replied, 'Oh – over there.' She nodded vaguely towards the french windows.

'Go and stand where you were standing,' Starkwedder instructed her.

Laura rose and began to move nervously about the room. 'I – I can't remember,' she told him. 'Don't ask me to remember.' She sounded scared now. 'I – I was upset. I –'

Starkwedder interrupted her. 'Your husband said something to you,' he reminded her. 'Something that made you snatch up the gun.'

Rising from the sofa, he went to the table by the armchair and put his cigarette out. 'Well, come on, let's act it out,' he continued. 'There's the table, there's the gun.' He took Laura's cigarette from her, and put it in the ashtray. 'Now then, you were quarrelling. You picked up the gun – pick it up –'

'I don't want to!' Laura cried.

'Don't be a little fool,' Starkwedder growled. 'It's not loaded. Come on, pick it up. Pick it up.'

Laura picked up the gun, hesitantly.

'You snatched it up,' he reminded her. 'You didn't pick it up gingerly like that. You snatched it up, and you shot him. Show me how you did it.'

Holding the gun awkwardly, Laura backed away from him. 'I – I –' she began.

'Go on. Show me,' Starkwedder shouted at her.

Laura tried to aim the gun. 'Go on, shoot!' he repeated, still shouting. 'It isn't loaded.'

When she still hesitated, he snatched the gun from her in triumph. 'I thought so,' he exclaimed. 'You've never fired a revolver in your life. You don't know how to do it.' Looking at the gun, he continued, 'You don't even know enough to release the safety catch.'

He dropped the gun on the footstool, then walked to the back of the sofa, and turned to face her. After a pause, he said quietly, 'You didn't shoot your husband.'

'I did,' Laura insisted.

'Oh no, you didn't,' Starkwedder repeated with conviction.

Sounding frightened, Laura asked, 'Then why should I say I did?'

Starkwedder took a deep breath and then exhaled. Coming round the sofa, he threw himself down on it heavily. 'The answer to that seems pretty obvious to me. Because it was Julian Farrar who shot him,' he retorted.

'No!' Laura exclaimed, almost shouting.

'Yes!'

'No!' she repeated.

'I say yes,' he insisted.

'If it was Julian,' Laura asked him, 'why on earth should I say *I* did it?'

Starkwedder looked at her levelly. 'Because,' he said, 'you thought – and thought quite rightly – that I'd cover up for *you*. Oh yes, you were certainly right about that.' He lounged back into the sofa before continuing, 'Yes, you played me along very prettily. But I'm through, do you hear? I'm through. I'm damned if I'm going to tell a pack of lies to save Major Julian Farrar's skin.'

There was a pause. For a few moments Laura said nothing. Then she smiled and calmly walked over to the table by the armchair to pick up her cigarette. Turning back to Starkwedder, she said, 'Oh yes, you are! You'll have to! You can't back out now! You've told your story to the police. You can't change it.'

'What?' Starkwedder gasped, taken aback.

Laura sat in the armchair. 'Whatever you know, or think you know,' she pointed out to him, 'you've got to stick to your story. You're an accessory after the fact – you said so yourself.' She drew on her cigarette.

Starkwedder rose and faced her. Dumbfounded, he exclaimed, 'Well, I'm damned! You little bitch!' He glared at her for a few moments without saying anything further, then suddenly turned on his heel, went swiftly to the french windows, and left. Laura watched him striding across the garden. She made a movement as though to follow and call him back, but then apparently thought better of it. With a troubled look on her face, she slowly turned away from the windows.

CHAPTER 12

Later that day, towards the end of the afternoon, Julian Farrar paced nervously up and down in the study. The french windows to the terrace were open, and the sun was about to set, throwing a golden light onto the lawn outside. Farrar had been summoned by Laura Warwick, who apparently needed to see him urgently. He kept glancing at his watch as he awaited her.

Farrar seemed very upset and distraught. He looked out onto the terrace, turned back into the room again, and glanced at his watch. Then, noticing a newspaper on the table by the armchair, he picked it up. It was a local paper, *The Western Echo*, with a news story on the front page reporting Richard Warwick's death. 'PROMINENT LOCAL RESIDENT MURDERED BY MYSTERIOUS ASSAILANT,' the headline announced. Farrar sat in the armchair and began nervously to read the report. After a moment, he flung the paper aside, and strode over to the french windows. With a final glance back into the room, he set off across the lawn. He was halfway across the garden, when he heard a sound behind him. Turning, he called, 'Laura, I'm sorry I –' and then stopped, disappointed, as he saw that the person coming towards him was not Laura Warwick, but Angell, the late Richard Warwick's valet and attendant.

'Mrs Warwick asked me to say she will be down in a moment, sir,' said Angell as he approached Farrar. 'But I wondered if I might have a brief word with you?'

'Yes, yes. What is it?'

Angell came up to Julian Farrar, and walked on for a pace or two further away from the house, as if anxious that their talk should not be overheard. 'Well?' said Farrar, following him.

'I am rather worried, sir,' Angell began, 'about my own position in the house, and I felt I would like to consult you on the matter.'

His mind full of his own affairs, Julian Farrar was not really interested. 'Well, what's the trouble?' he asked.

Angell thought for a moment before replying. Then, 'Mr Warwick's death, sir,' he said, 'it puts me out of a job.'

'Yes. Yes, I suppose it does,' Farrar responded. 'But I imagine you will easily get another, won't you?'

'I hope so, sir,' Angell replied.

'You're a qualified man, aren't you?' Farrar asked him.

'Oh, yes, sir. I'm qualified,' Angell replied, 'and there is always either hospital work or private work to be obtained. I know that.'

'Then what's troubling you?'

'Well, sir,' Angell told him, 'the circumstances in which this job came to an end are very distasteful to me.'

'In plain English,' Farrar remarked, 'you don't like having been mixed up with murder. Is that it?'

'You could put it that way, sir,' the valet confirmed.

'Well,' said Farrar, 'I'm afraid there is nothing anyone

can do about that. Presumably you'll get a satisfactory reference from Mrs Warwick.' He took out his cigarette-case and opened it.

'I don't think there will be any difficulty about that, sir,' Angell responded. 'Mrs Warwick is a very nice lady – a very charming lady, if I may say so.' There was a faint insinuation in his tone.

Julian Farrar, having decided to await Laura after all, was about to go back into the house. However, he turned, struck by something in the valet's manner. 'What do you mean?' he asked quietly.

'I shouldn't like to inconvenience Mrs Warwick in any way,' Angell replied, unctuously.

Before speaking, Farrar took a cigarette from his case, and then returned the case to his pocket. 'You mean,' he said, 'you're – stopping on a bit to oblige her?'

'That is quite true, sir,' Angell affirmed. 'I am helping out in the house. But that is not exactly what I meant.' He paused, and then continued, 'It's a matter, really – of my conscience, sir.'

'What in hell do you mean – your conscience?' Farrar asked sharply.

Angell looked uncomfortable, but his voice was quite confident as he continued, 'I don't think you quite appreciate my difficulties, sir. In the matter of giving my evidence to the police, that is. It is my duty as a citizen to assist the police in any manner possible. At the same time, I wish to remain loyal to my employers.'

Julian Farrar turned away to light his cigarette. 'You speak as though there was a conflict,' he said quietly.

'If you think about it, sir,' Angell remarked, 'you will realize that there is bound to be a conflict – a conflict of loyalties if I may so put it.'

Farrar looked directly at the valet. 'Just exactly what are you getting at, Angell?' he asked.

'The police, sir, are not in a position to appreciate the background,' Angell replied. 'The background might – I just say *might* – be very important in a case like this. Also, of late I have been suffering rather severely from insomnia.'

'Do your ailments have to come into this?' Farrar asked him sharply.

'Unfortunately they do, sir,' was the valet's smooth reply. 'I retired early last night, but I was unable to get to sleep.'

'I'm sorry about that,' Farrar commiserated drily, 'but really –'

'You see, sir,' Angell continued, ignoring the interruption, 'owing to the position of my bedroom in this house, I have become aware of certain matters of which perhaps the police are not fully cognizant.'

'Just what are you trying to say?' Farrar asked, coldly.

'The late Mr Warwick, sir,' Angell replied, 'was a sick man and a cripple. It's really only to be expected under those sad circumstances that an attractive lady like Mrs Warwick might – how shall I put it? – form an attachment elsewhere.'

'So that's it, is it?' said Farrar. 'I don't think I like your tone, Angell.'

'No, sir,' Angell murmured. 'But please don't be too precipitate in your judgement. Just think it over, sir. You will perhaps realize my difficulty. Here I am, in possession of knowledge which I have not, so far, communicated to the police – but knowledge which, perhaps, it is my duty to communicate to them.'

Julian Farrar stared at Angell coldly. 'I think,' he said, 'that this story of going to the police with your information is all ballyhoo. What you're really doing is suggesting that you're in a position to stir up dirt unless –' he paused, and then completed his sentence: '– unless what?'

Angell shrugged his shoulders. 'I am, of course, as you have just pointed out,' he observed, 'a fully qualified nurse-attendant. But there are times, Major Farrar, when I feel I would like to set up on my own. A small – not a nursing-home, exactly – but an establishment where I could take on perhaps five or six patients. With an assistant, of course. The patients would probably include gentlemen who are alcoholically difficult to manage at home. That sort of thing. Unfortunately, although I have accumulated a certain amount of savings, they are not enough. I wondered –' His voice trailed off suggestively.

Julian Farrar completed his thought for him. 'You wondered,' he said, 'if I – or I and Mrs Warwick together – could come to your assistance in this project, no doubt.'

'I just wondered, sir,' Angell replied meekly.'It would be a great kindness on your part.'

'Yes, it would, wouldn't it?' Farrar observed sarcastically.

'You suggested rather harshly,' Angell went on, 'that I'm threatening to stir up dirt. Meaning, I take it, scandal. But it's not that at all, sir. I wouldn't dream of doing such a thing.'

'What exactly is it you are driving at, Angell?' Farrar sounded as though he were beginning to lose his patience. 'You're certainly driving at something.'

Angell gave a self-deprecating smile before replying. Then he spoke quietly but with emphasis. 'As I say, sir, last night I couldn't sleep very well. I was lying awake, listening to the booming of the foghorn. An extremely depressing sound I always find it, sir. Then it seemed to me that I heard a shutter banging. A very irritating noise when you're trying to get to sleep. I got up and leaned out of my window. It seemed to be the shutter of the pantry window, almost immediately below me.'

'Well?' asked Farrar, sharply.

'I decided, sir, to go down and attend to the shutter,' Angell continued. 'As I was on my way downstairs, I heard a shot.' He paused briefly. 'I didn't think anything of it at the time. "Mr Warwick at it again," I thought. "But surely he can't see what he's shooting at in a mist like this." I went to the pantry, sir, and fastened back the shutter securely. But, as I was standing there, feeling a bit uneasy for some reason, I heard footsteps coming along the path outside the window –'

'You mean,' Farrar interrupted, 'the path that –' His eyes went towards it.

'Yes, sir,' Angell agreed. 'The path that leads from the terrace, around the corner of the house, that way – past the domestic offices. A path that's not used very much, except of course by you, sir, when you come over here, seeing as it's a short cut from your house to this one.'

He stopped speaking, and looked intently at Julian Farrar, who merely said icily, 'Go on.'

'I was feeling, as I said, a bit uneasy,' Angell continued, 'thinking there might be a prowler about. I can't tell you how relieved I was, sir, to see *you* pass the pantry window, walking quickly – hurrying on your way back home.'

After a pause, Farrar said, 'I can't really see any point in what you're telling me. Is there supposed to be one?'

With an apologetic cough, Angell answered him. 'I just

wondered, sir, whether you have mentioned to the police that you came over here last night to see Mr Warwick. In case you have not done so, and supposing that they should question me further as to the events of last night –'

Farrar interrupted him. 'You do realize, don't you,' he asked tersely, 'that the penalty for blackmail is severe?'

'Blackmail, sir?' responded Angell, sounding shocked. 'I don't know what you mean. It's just a question, as I said, of deciding where my duty lies. The police –'

'The police,' Farrar interrupted him sharply, 'are perfectly satisfied as to who killed Mr Warwick. The fellow practically signed his name to the crime. They're not likely to come asking you any more questions.'

'I assure you, sir,' Angell interjected, with alarm in his voice, 'I only meant –'

'You know perfectly well,' Farrar interrupted again, 'that you couldn't have recognized anybody in that thick fog last night. You've simply invented this story in order to –' He broke off, as he saw Laura Warwick emerging from the house into the garden.

'I'm sorry I've kept you waiting, Julian,' Laura called as she approached them. She looked surprised to see Angell and Julian Farrar apparently in conversation.

'Perhaps I may speak to you later, sir, about this little matter,' the valet murmured to Farrar. He moved away, half bowing to Laura, then walked quickly across the garden and around a corner of the house.

Laura watched him go, and then spoke urgently. 'Julian,' she said, 'I must –'

Farrar interrupted her. 'Why did you send for me, Laura?' he asked, sounding annoyed.

'I've been expecting you all day,' Laura replied, surprised.

'Well, I've been up to my ears ever since this morning,' Farrar exclaimed. 'Committees, and more meetings this afternoon. I can't just drop any of these things so soon before the election. And in any case, don't you see, Laura, that it's much better that we shouldn't meet at present?'

'But there are things we've got to discuss,' Laura told him.

Taking her arm briefly, Farrar led her further away from

the house. 'Do you know that Angell is setting out to blackmail me?' he asked her.

'Angell?' cried Laura, incredulously. 'Angell is?'

'Yes. He obviously knows about us – and he also knows, or at any rate pretends to know, that I was here last night.'

Laura gasped. 'Do you mean he saw you?'

'He *says* he saw me,' Farrar retorted.

'But he couldn't have seen you in that fog,' Laura insisted.

'He's got some story,' Farrar told her, 'about coming down to the pantry and doing something to the shutter outside the window, and seeing me pass on my way home. He also says he heard a shot, not long before that, but didn't think anything of it.'

'Oh my God!' Laura gasped. 'How awful! What are we going to do?'

Farrar made an involuntary gesture as though he were about to comfort Laura with an embrace, but then, glancing towards the house, thought better of it. He gazed at her steadily. 'I don't know yet what we're going to do,' he told her. 'We'll have to think.'

'You're not going to pay him, surely?'

'No, no,' Farrar assured her. 'If one starts doing that, it's the beginning of the end. And yet, what is one to do?' He passed a hand across his brow. 'I didn't think anyone knew I came over yesterday evening,' he continued. 'I'm certain my housekeeper didn't. The point is, did Angell really see me, or is he pretending he did?'

'Supposing he does go to the police?' Laura asked, tremulously.

'I know,' murmured Farrar. Again, he ran his hand across his brow. 'One's got to think – think carefully.' He began to walk to and fro. 'Either bluff it out – say he's lying, that I never left home yesterday evening –'

'But there are the fingerprints,' Laura told him.

'What fingerprints?' asked Farrar, startled.

'You've forgotten,' Laura reminded him. 'The fingerprints on the table. The police have been thinking that they're MacGregor's, but if Angell goes to them with this story, then they'll ask to take your fingerprints, and then –'

She broke off. Julian Farrar now looked very worried. 'Yes, yes, I see,' he muttered. 'All right, then. I'll have to admit that I came over here and – tell some story. I came over to see Richard about something, and we talked –'

'You can say he was perfectly all right when you left him,' Laura suggested, speaking quickly.

There was little trace of affection in Farrar's eyes as he looked at her. 'How easy you make it sound!' he retorted, hotly. 'Can I really say that?' he added sarcastically.

'One has to say something!' she told him, sounding defensive.

'Yes, I must have put my hand there as I bent over to see –' He swallowed, as the scene came back to him.

'So long as they believe the prints are MacGregor's,' said Laura, eagerly.

'MacGregor! MacGregor!' Farrar exclaimed angrily. He was almost shouting now. 'What on earth made you think of cooking up that message from the newspaper and putting it on Richard's body? Weren't you taking a terrific chance?'

'Yes – no – I don't know,' Laura cried in confusion.

Farrar looked at her with silent revulsion. 'So damned cold-blooded,' he muttered.

'We had to think of something,' Laura sighed. 'I – I just couldn't think. It was really Michael's idea.'

'Michael?'

'Michael – Starkwedder,' Laura told him.

'You mean he helped you?' Farrar asked. He sounded incredulous.

'Yes, yes, yes!' Laura cried impatiently. 'That's why I wanted to see you – to explain to you –'

Farrar came up close to her. His tone was icily jealous as he asked, firmly, 'What's *Michael*' – he emphasized Starkwedder's Christian name with a cold anger – 'what's Michael Starkwedder doing in all this?'

'He came in and – and found me there,' Laura told him. 'I'd – I'd got the gun in my hand and –'

'Good God!' Farrar exclaimed with distaste, moving away from her. 'And somehow you persuaded him –'

'I think he persuaded me,' Laura murmured sadly. She moved closer to him. 'Oh, Julian –' she began.

Her arms were about to go around his neck, but he pushed her away slightly. 'I've told you, I'll do anything I can,' he assured her. 'Don't think I won't – but –'

Laura looked at him steadily. 'You've changed,' she said quietly.

'I'm sorry, but I can't feel the same,' Farrar admitted desperately. 'After what's happened – I just can't feel the same.'

'I can,' Laura assured him. 'At least, I think I can. No matter what you'd done, Julian, I'd always feel the same.'

'Never mind our feelings for the moment,' said Farrar. 'We've got to get down to facts.'

Laura looked at him. 'I know,' she said. 'I – I told Starkwedder that *I'd* – you know, that I'd done it.'

Farrar looked at her incredulously. 'You told Starkwedder that?'

'Yes.'

'And he agreed to help you? He – a stranger? The man must be mad!'

Stung, Laura retorted, 'I think perhaps he *is* a little mad. But he was very comforting.'

'So! No man can resist you,' Farrar exclaimed angrily. 'Is that it?' He took a step away from her, and then turned to face her again. 'All the same, Laura, murder –' His voice died away and he shook his head.

'I shall try never to think of it,' Laura answered. 'And it wasn't premeditated, Julian. It *was* just an impulse.' She spoke almost pleadingly.

'There's no need to go back over it all,' Farrar told her. 'We've got to think now what we're going to do.'

'I know,' she replied. 'There are the fingerprints and your lighter.'

'Yes,' he recalled. 'I must have dropped it as I leaned over his body.'

'Starkwedder knows it's yours,' Laura told him. 'But he can't do anything about it. He's committed himself. He can't change his story now.'

Julian Farrar looked at her for a moment. When he spoke, his voice had a slightly heroic tone. 'If it comes to it, Laura, I'll take the blame,' he assured her.

'No, I don't want you to,' Laura cried. She clasped his arm, and then released him quickly with a nervous glance towards the house. 'I don't want you to!' she repeated urgently.

'You mustn't think that I don't understand – how it happened,' said Farrar, speaking with an effort. 'You picked up the gun, shot him without really knowing what you were doing, and –'

Laura gave a gasp of surprise. 'What? Are you trying to make me say *I* killed him?' she cried.

'Not at all,' Farrar responded. He sounded embarrassed. 'I've told you I'm perfectly prepared to take the blame if it comes to it.'

Laura shook her head in confusion. 'But – you said –' she began. 'You said you knew how it happened.'

He looked at her steadily. 'Listen, Laura,' he said. 'I don't think you did it deliberately. I don't think it was premeditated. I know it wasn't. I know quite well that you only shot him because –'

Laura interrupted quickly. '*I* shot him?' she gasped. 'Are you really pretending to believe that *I* shot him?'

Turning his back on her, Farrar exclaimed angrily, 'For God's sake, this is impossible if we're not going to be honest with each other!'

Laura sounded desperate as, trying not to shout, she announced clearly and emphatically, 'I didn't shoot him, and you know it!'

There was a pause. Julian Farrar slowly turned to face her. 'Then who did?' he asked. Suddenly realizing, he added, 'Laura! Are you trying to say that *I* shot him?'

They stood facing each other, neither of them speaking for a moment. Then Laura said, 'I heard the shot, Julian.' She took a deep breath before continuing. 'I heard the shot, and your footsteps on the path going away. I came down, and there he was – dead.'

After a pause Farrar said quietly, 'Laura, I didn't shoot him.' He gazed up at the sky as though seeking help or inspiration, and then looked at her intently. 'I came over here to see Richard,' he explained, 'to tell him that after the election we'd got to come to some arrangement about a divorce. I heard a shot just before I got here. I just thought it was Richard up to his tricks as usual. I came in here, and there he was. Dead. He was still warm.'

Laura was now very perplexed. 'Warm?' she echoed.

'He hadn't been dead more than a minute or two,' said Farrar. 'Of course I believed you'd shot him. Who else could have shot him?'

'I don't understand,' Laura murmured.

'I suppose – I suppose it could have been suicide,' Farrar began, but Laura interrupted him. 'No, it couldn't, because –'

She broke off, as they both heard Jan's voice inside the house, shouting excitedly.

Julian Farrar and Laura ran towards the house, almost colliding with Jan as he emerged through the french windows. 'Laura,' Jan cried as she gently but firmly propelled him back into the study. 'Laura, now that Richard's dead, all of his pistols and guns and things belong to me, don't they? I mean, I'm his brother, I'm the next man in the family.'

Julian Farrar followed them into the room and wandered distractedly across to the armchair, sitting on an arm of it as Laura attempted to pacify Jan who was now complaining petulantly, 'Benny won't let me have his guns. She's locked them up in the cupboard in there.' He waved vaguely towards the door. 'But they're mine. I've got a right to them. Make her give me the key.'

'Now listen, Jan darling,' Laura began, but Jan would not be interrupted. He went quickly to the door, and then turned back to her, exclaiming, 'She treats me like a child. Benny, I mean. Everyone treats me like a child. But I'm not a child, I'm a man. I'm nineteen. I'm nearly of age.' He stretched his arms across the door as though protecting his guns. 'All of Richard's sporting things belong to me. I'm going to do what

Richard did. I'm going to shoot squirrels and birds and cats.' He laughed hysterically. 'I might shoot people, too, if I don't like them.'

'You mustn't get too excited, Jan,' Laura warned him.

'I'm not excited,' Jan cried petulantly. 'But I'm not going to be – what's it called? – I'm not going to be victimized.' He came back into the centre of the room, and faced Laura squarely. 'I'm master here now. I'm the master of this house. Everybody's got to do as I say.' He paused, then turned and addressed Julian Farrar. 'I could be a JP if I wanted to, couldn't I, Julian?'

'I think you're a little young for that yet,' Farrar told him.

Jan shrugged, and turned back to Laura. 'You all treat me like a child,' he complained again. 'But you can't do it any longer – not now that Richard's dead.' He flung himself onto the sofa, legs sprawling. 'I expect I'm rich, too, aren't I?' he added. 'This house belongs to me. Nobody can push me around any longer. I can push *them* around. I'm not going to be dictated to by silly old Benny. If Benny tries ordering me about, I shall –' He paused, then added childishly, 'I know what I shall do!'

Laura approached him. 'Listen, Jan darling,' she murmured gently. 'It's a very worrying time for all of us, and Richard's things don't belong to anybody until the lawyers have come and read his will and granted what they call probate. That's what happens when anyone dies. Until then, we all have to wait and see. Do you understand?'

Laura's tone had a calming and quietening effect on Jan. He looked up at her, then put his arms around her waist, nestling close to her. 'I understand what you tell me, Laura,' he said. 'I love you, Laura. I love you very much.'

'Yes, darling,' Laura murmured soothingly. 'I love you, too.'

'You're glad Richard's dead, aren't you?' Jan asked her suddenly.

Slightly startled, Laura replied hurriedly, 'No, of course I'm not glad.'

'Oh yes, you are,' said Jan, slyly. 'Now you can marry Julian.'

Laura looked quickly at Julian Farrar, who rose to his feet as Jan continued, 'You've wanted to marry Julian for a long time, haven't you? *I* know. They think I don't notice or know things. But I do. And so it's all right for both of you now. It's been made all right for you, and you're both pleased. You're pleased, because –'

He broke off, hearing Miss Bennett out in the corridor calling, 'Jan!', and laughed. 'Silly old Benny!' he shouted, bouncing up and down on the sofa.

'Now, do be nice to Benny,' Laura cautioned Jan, as she pulled him to his feet. 'She's having such a lot of trouble and worry over all this.' Guiding Jan to the door, Laura continued gently, 'You must help Benny, Jan, because you're the man of the family now.'

Jan opened the door, then looked from Laura to Julian. 'All right, all right,' he promised, with a smile. 'I will.' He left the room, shutting the door behind him and calling 'Benny!' as he went.

Laura turned to Julian Farrar who had risen from his armchair and walked over to her. 'I'd no idea he knew about us,' she exclaimed.

'That's the trouble with people like Jan,' Farrar retorted. 'You never know how much or how little they do know.

He's very – well, he gets rather easily out of hand, doesn't he?'

'Yes, he does get easily excited,' Laura admitted. 'But now that Richard isn't here to tease him, he'll calm down. He'll get to be more normal. I'm sure he will.'

Julian Farrar looked doubtful. 'Well, I don't know about that,' he began, but broke off as Starkwedder suddenly appeared at the french windows.

'Hello – good evening,' Starkwedder called, sounding quite happy.

'Oh – er – good evening,' Farrar replied, hesitantly.

'How's everything? Bright and cheerful?' Starkwedder enquired, looking from one to the other. He suddenly grinned. 'I see,' he observed. 'Two's company and three's none.' He stepped into the room. 'Shouldn't have come in by the window this way. A gentleman would have gone to the front door and rung the bell. Is that it? But then, you see, I'm no gentleman.'

'Oh, please –' Laura began, but Starkwedder interrupted her. 'As a matter of fact,' he explained, 'I've come for two reasons. First, to say goodbye. My character's been cleared. High-level cables from Abadan saying what a fine, upright fellow I am. So I'm free to depart.'

'I'm so sorry you're going – so soon,' Laura told him, with genuine feeling in her voice.

'That's nice of you,' Starkwedder responded with a touch of bitterness, 'considering the way I butted in on your family murder.' He looked at her for a moment, then moved across to the desk chair. 'But I came in by the window for another reason,' he went on. 'The police brought me up in their car. And, although they're being very tight-lipped about it, it's my belief there's something up!'

Dismayed, Laura gasped, 'The police have come back?'

'Yes,' Starkwedder affirmed, decisively.

'But I thought they'd finished this morning,' said Laura.

Starkwedder gave her a shrewd look. 'That's why I say –
something's up!' he exclaimed.

There were voices in the corridor outside. Laura and
Julian Farrar drew together as the door opened, and Richard
Warwick's mother came in, looking very upright and self-
possessed, though still walking with the aid of a cane.

'Benny!' Mrs Warwick called over her shoulder, and then
addressed Laura. 'Oh, there you are, Laura. We've been
looking for you.'

Julian Farrar went to Mrs Warwick and helped her into the
armchair. 'How kind you are to come over again, Julian,' the
old lady exclaimed, 'when we all know how busy you are.'

'I would have come before, Mrs Warwick,' Farrar told her,
as he settled her in the chair, 'but it's been a particularly
hectic day. Anything that I can possibly do to help –' He
stopped speaking as Miss Bennett entered followed by Inspector Thomas. Carrying a briefcase, the inspector moved to take
up a central position. Starkwedder went to sit in the desk chair,
and lit a cigarette as Sergeant Cadwallader came in with Angell,
who closed the door and stood with his back to it.

'I can't find young Mr Warwick, sir,' the sergeant reported,
crossing to the french windows.

'He's out somewhere. Gone for a walk,' Miss Bennett
announced.

'It doesn't matter,' said the inspector. There was a momentary pause as he surveyed the occupants of the room. His
manner had changed, for it now had a grimness it did not
have before.

After waiting a moment for him to speak, Mrs Warwick asked coldly, 'Do I understand that you have further questions to ask us, Inspector Thomas?'

'Yes, Mrs Warwick,' he replied, 'I'm afraid I have.'

Mrs Warwick's voice sounded weary as she asked, 'You still have no news of this man MacGregor?'

'On the contrary.'

'He's been found?' Mrs Warwick asked, eagerly.

'Yes,' was the inspector's terse reply.

There was a definite reaction of excitement from the assembled company. Laura and Julian Farrar looked incredulous, and Starkwedder turned in his chair to face the inspector.

Miss Bennett's voice suddenly rang out sharply. 'You've arrested him, then?'

The inspector looked at her for a moment before replying. Then, 'That, I'm afraid, would be impossible, Miss Bennett,' he informed her.

'Impossible?' Mrs Warwick interjected. 'But why?'

'Because he's dead,' the inspector replied, quietly.

CHAPTER 15

A shocked silence greeted Inspector Thomas's announcement. Then, hesitantly and, it seemed, fearfully, Laura whispered, 'Wh– what did you say?'

'I said that this man MacGregor is dead,' the inspector affirmed.

There were gasps from everyone in the room, and the inspector expanded upon his terse announcement. 'John MacGregor,' he told them, 'died in Alaska over two years ago – not very long after he returned to Canada from England.'

'Dead!' Laura exclaimed, incredulously.

Unnoticed by anyone in the room, young Jan passed quickly along the terrace outside the french windows, and disappeared from view.

'That makes a difference, doesn't it?' the inspector continued. 'It wasn't John MacGregor who put that revenge note on the dead body of Mr Warwick. But it's clear, isn't it, that it was put there by someone who knew all about MacGregor and the accident in Norfolk. Which ties it in, very definitely, with someone in this house.'

'No,' Miss Bennett exclaimed sharply. 'No, it could have

been – surely it could have been –' She broke off.

'Yes, Miss Bennett?' the inspector prompted her. He waited for a moment, but Miss Bennett could not continue. Suddenly looking completely broken, she moved away towards the french windows.

The inspector turned his attention to Richard Warwick's mother. 'You'll understand, madam,' he said, attempting to put a note of sympathy into his voice, 'that this alters things.'

'Yes, I see that,' Mrs Warwick replied. She rose. 'Do you need me any further, Inspector?' she asked.

'Not for the moment, Mrs Warwick,' the inspector told her.

'Thank you,' Mrs Warwick murmured as she went to the door, which Angell hastened to open for her. Julian Farrar helped the old lady to the door. As she left the room, he returned and stood behind the armchair, looking pensive. Meanwhile, Inspector Thomas had been opening his briefcase, and was now taking out a gun.

Angell was about to follow Mrs Warwick from the room when the inspector called, peremptorily, 'Angell!'

The valet gave a start, and turned back into the room, closing the door. 'Yes, sir?' he responded quietly.

The inspector approached him, carrying what was clearly the murder weapon. 'About this gun,' he asked the valet. 'You were uncertain this morning. Can you, or can you not, say definitely that it belonged to Mr Warwick?'

'I wouldn't like to be definite, Inspector,' Angell replied. 'He had so many, you see.'

'This one is a continental weapon,' the inspector informed him, holding the gun out in front of him. 'It's a war souvenir of some kind, I'd say.'

As he was speaking, again apparently unnoticed by anyone in the room Jan passed along the terrace outside, going in the opposite direction, and carrying a gun which he seemed to be attempting to conceal.

Angell looked at the weapon. 'Mr Warwick did have some foreign guns, sir,' he stated. 'But he looked after all his shooting equipment himself. He wouldn't let me touch them.'

The inspector went over to Julian Farrar. 'Major Farrar,' he said, 'you probably have war souvenirs. Does this weapon mean anything to you?'

Farrar glanced at the gun casually. 'Not a thing, I'm afraid,' he answered.

Turning away from him, the inspector went to replace the gun in his briefcase. 'Sergeant Cadwallader and I,' he announced, turning to face the assembled company, 'will want to go over Mr Warwick's collection of weapons very carefully. He had permits for most of them, I understand.'

'Oh yes, sir,' Angell assured him. 'The permits are in one of the drawers in his bedroom. And all the guns and other weapons are in the gun cupboard.'

Sergeant Cadwallader went to the door, but was stopped by Miss Bennett before he could leave the room. 'Wait a minute,' she called to him. 'You'll want the key of the gun cupboard.' She took a key from her pocket.

'You locked it up?' the inspector queried, turning sharply to her. 'Why was that?'

Miss Bennett's retort was equally sharp. 'I should hardly think you'd need to ask that,' she snapped. 'All those guns, and ammunition as well. Highly dangerous. Everyone knows that.'

Concealing a grin, the sergeant took the key she offered

him, and went to the door, pausing in the doorway to see whether the inspector wished to accompany him. Sounding distinctly annoyed at Miss Bennett's uncalled-for comment, Inspector Thomas remarked, 'I shall need to talk to you again, Angell,' as he picked up his briefcase and left the room. The sergeant followed him, leaving the door open for Angell.

However, the valet did not leave the room immediately. Instead, after a nervous glance at Laura who now sat staring at the floor, he went up to Julian Farrar, and murmured, 'About that little matter, sir. I am anxious to get something settled soon. If you could see your way, sir –'

Speaking with difficulty, Farrar answered, 'I think – something – could be managed.'

'Thank you, sir,' Angell responded with a faint smile on his face. 'Thank you very much, sir.' He went to the door and was about to leave the room when Farrar stopped him with a peremptory 'No! Wait a moment, Angell.'

As the valet turned to face him, Farrar called loudly, 'Inspector Thomas!'

There was a tense pause. Then, after a moment or two, the inspector appeared in the doorway, with the sergeant behind him. 'Yes, Major Farrar?' the inspector asked, quietly.

Resuming a pleasant, natural manner, Julian Farrar strolled across to the armchair. 'Before you get busy with routine, Inspector,' he remarked, 'there is something I ought to have told you. Really, I suppose, I should have mentioned it this morning. But we were all so upset. Mrs Warwick has just informed me that there are some fingerprints that you are anxious to identify. On the table here, I think you said.' He paused, then added, easily, 'In all probability, Inspector, those are my fingerprints.'

There was a pause. The inspector slowly approached Farrar, and then asked quietly, but with an accusing note in his voice, 'You were over here last night, Major Farrar?'

'Yes,' Farrar replied. 'I came over, as I often do after dinner, to have a chat with Richard.'

'And you found him – ?' the inspector prompted.

'I found him very moody and depressed. So I didn't stay long.'

'At about what time was this, Major Farrar?'

Farrar thought for a moment, and then replied, 'I really can't remember. Perhaps ten o'clock, or ten-thirty. Thereabouts.'

The inspector regarded him steadily. 'Can you get a little closer than that?' he asked.

'I'm sorry. I'm afraid I can't,' was Farrar's immediate answer.

After a somewhat tense pause, the inspector asked, trying to sound casual, 'I don't suppose there would have been any quarrel – or bad words of any kind?'

'No, certainly not,' Farrar retorted indignantly. He looked at his watch. 'I'm late,' he observed. 'I've got to take the chair at a meeting in the Town Hall. I can't keep them waiting.' He turned and walked towards the french windows. 'So, if you don't mind –' He paused on the terrace.

'Mustn't keep the Town Hall waiting,' the inspector agreed, following him. 'But I'm sure you'll understand, Major Farrar, that I should like a full statement from you of your movements last night. Perhaps we could do this tomorrow morning.' He paused, and then continued, 'You realize, of course, that there is no obligation on you to make a statement, that it is purely voluntary on your part – and that you are fully entitled to have your solicitor present, should you so wish.'

Mrs Warwick had re-entered the room. She stood in the doorway, leaving the door open, and listening to the inspector's last few words. Julian Farrar drew in his breath as he grasped the significance of what the inspector had said. 'I understand – perfectly,' he said. 'Shall we say ten o'clock tomorrow morning? And my solicitor will be present.'

Farrar made his exit along the terrace, and the inspector turned to Laura Warwick. 'Did you see Major Farrar when he came here last night?' he asked her.

'I – I –,' Laura began uncertainly, but was interrupted by Starkwedder who suddenly jumped up from his chair and went across to them, interposing himself between the inspector and Laura. 'I don't think Mrs Warwick feels like answering any questions just now,' he said.

Starkwedder and Inspector Thomas faced each other in silence for a moment. Then the inspector spoke. 'What did you say, Mr Starkwedder?' he asked, quietly.

'I said,' Starkwedder replied, 'that I don't think Mrs Warwick feels like any more questions just at the moment.'

'Indeed?' growled the inspector. 'And what business is it of yours, might I ask?'

Mrs Warwick senior joined in the confrontation. 'Mr Starkwedder is quite right,' she announced.

The inspector turned to Laura questioningly. After a pause, she murmured, 'No, I don't want to answer any more questions just now.'

Looking rather smug, Starkwedder smiled at the inspector who turned away angrily and swiftly left the room with the sergeant. Angell followed them, shutting the door behind him. As he did so, Laura burst out, 'But I should speak. I must – I must tell them –'

'Mr Starkwedder is quite right, Laura,' Mrs Warwick interjected forcefully. 'The less you say now, the better.' She took a few paces about the room, leaning heavily on her stick, and then continued. 'We must get in touch with Mr Adams at once.' Turning to Starkwedder, she explained, 'Mr Adams is our solicitor.' She glanced across at Miss Bennett. 'Ring him up now, Benny.'

Miss Bennett nodded and went towards the telephone, but Mrs Warwick stopped her. 'No, use the extension upstairs,' she instructed, adding, 'Laura, go with her.'

Laura rose, and then hesitated, looking confusedly at her mother-in-law, who merely added, 'I want to talk to Mr Starkwedder.'

'But –' Laura began, only to be immediately interrupted by Mrs Warwick. 'Now don't worry, my dear,' the old lady assured her. 'Just do as I say.'

Laura hesitated for a moment, then went out into the hall, followed by Miss Bennett who closed the door. Mrs Warwick immediately went up to Starkwedder. 'I don't know how much time we have,' she said, speaking rapidly and glancing towards the door. 'I want you to help me.'

Starkwedder looked surprised. 'How?' he asked.

After a pause, Mrs Warwick spoke again. 'You're an intelligent man – and you're a stranger. You've come into our lives from outside. We know nothing about you. You've nothing to do with any of us.'

Starkwedder nodded. 'The unexpected guest, eh?' he murmured. He perched on an arm of the sofa. 'That's been said to me already,' he remarked.

'Because you're a stranger,' Mrs Warwick continued, 'there is something I'm going to ask you to do for me.' She moved across to the french windows and stepped out onto the terrace, looking along it in both directions.

After a pause, Starkwedder spoke. 'Yes, Mrs Warwick?'

Coming back into the room, Mrs Warwick began to speak with some urgency. 'Up until this evening,' she told him, 'there was a reasonable explanation for this tragedy. A man whom my son had injured – by accidentally killing his child – came to take his revenge. I know it sounds melodramatic, but, after all, one does read of such things happening.'

'As you say,' Starkwedder remarked, wondering where this conversation was leading.

'But now, I'm afraid that explanation has gone,' Mrs Warwick continued. 'And it brings the murder of my son back into the family.' She took a few steps towards the armchair. 'Now, there are two people who definitely could not have shot my son. And they are his wife and Miss Bennett. They were actually together when the shot was fired.'

Starkwedder gave a quick look at her, but all he said was, 'Quite.'

'However,' Mrs Warwick continued, 'although Laura could not have shot her husband, she could have known who did.'

'That would make her an accessory before the fact,' Starkwedder remarked. 'She and this Julian Farrar chap in it together? Is that what you mean?'

A look of annoyance crossed Mrs Warwick's face. 'That is *not* what I mean,' she told him. She cast another quick glance at the door, and then continued, 'Julian Farrar did not shoot my son.'

Starkwedder rose from the arm of the sofa. 'How can you possibly know that?' he asked her.

'I do know it,' was Mrs Warwick's reply. She looked steadily at him. 'I am going to tell you, a stranger, something that none of my family know,' she stated calmly. 'It is this. I am a woman who has not very long to live.'

'I am sorry –' Starkwedder began, but Mrs Warwick raised her hand to stop him. 'I am not telling you this for sympathy,' she remarked. 'I am telling you in order to explain what otherwise might be difficult of explanation. There are times when you decide on a course of action which you would not decide upon if you had several years of life before you.'

'Such as?' asked Starkwedder quietly.

Mrs Warwick regarded him steadily. 'First, I must tell you something else, Mr Starkwedder,' she said. 'I must tell you something about my son.' She went to the sofa and sat. 'I loved my son very dearly. As a child, and in his young manhood, he had many fine qualities. He was successful, resourceful, brave, sunny-tempered, a delightful companion.' She paused, and seemed to be remembering. Then she continued. 'There were, I must admit, always the defects of those qualities in him. He was impatient of controls, of restraints. He had a cruel streak in him, and he had a kind of fatal arrogance. So long as he was successful, all was well. But he did not have the kind of nature that could deal with adversity, and for some time now I have watched him slowly go downhill.'

Starkwedder quietly seated himself on the stool, facing her.

'If I say that he had become a monster,' Richard Warwick's mother continued, 'it would sound exaggerated. And yet, in some ways he *was* a monster – a monster of egoism, of pride, of cruelty. Because he had been hurt himself, he had an enormous desire to hurt others.' A hard note crept into her voice. 'So others began to suffer because of him. Do you understand me?'

'I think so – yes,' Starkwedder murmured softly.

Mrs Warwick's voice became gentle again as she went

on. 'Now, I am very fond of my daughter-in-law. She has spirit, she is warm-hearted, and she has a very brave power of endurance. Richard swept her off her feet, but I don't know whether she was ever really in love with him. However, I will tell you this – she did everything a wife could do to make Richard's illness and inaction bearable.'

She thought for a moment, and her voice was sad as she continued, 'But he would have none of her help. He rejected it. I think at times he hated her, and perhaps that's more natural than one might suppose. So, when I tell you that the inevitable happened, I think you will understand what I mean. Laura fell in love with another man, and he with her.'

Starkwedder regarded Mrs Warwick thoughtfully. 'Why are you telling me all this?' he asked.

'Because you are a stranger,' she replied, firmly. 'These loves and hates and tribulations mean nothing to you, so you can hear about them unmoved.'

'Possibly.'

As though she had not heard him, Mrs Warwick went on speaking. 'So there came a time,' she said, 'when it seemed that only one thing would solve all the difficulties. Richard's death.'

Starkwedder continued to study her face. 'And so,' he murmured, 'conveniently, Richard died?'

'Yes,' Mrs Warwick answered.

There was a pause. Then Starkwedder rose, moved around the stool, and went to the table to stub out his cigarette. 'Excuse me putting this bluntly, Mrs Warwick,' he said, 'but are you confessing to murder?'

Mrs Warwick was silent for a few moments. Then she said sharply, 'I will ask you a question, Mr Starkwedder. Can you understand that someone who has given life might also feel themselves entitled to take that life?'

Starkwedder paced around the room as he thought about this. Finally, 'Mothers have been known to kill their children, yes,' he admitted. 'But it's usually been for a sordid reason – insurance – or perhaps they have two or three children already and don't want to be bothered with another one.' Turning back suddenly to face her, he asked quickly, 'Does Richard's death benefit you financially?'

'No, it does not,' Mrs Warwick replied firmly.

Starkwedder made a deprecatory gesture. 'You must forgive my frankness –' he began, only to be interrupted by Mrs Warwick, who asked with more than a touch of asperity in her voice, 'Do you understand what I am trying to tell you?'

'Yes, I think I do,' he replied. 'You're telling me that it's possible for a mother to kill her son.' He walked over to the sofa and leaned across it as he continued. 'And you're telling me – specifically – that it's possible that *you* killed *your* son.'

He paused, and looked at her steadily. 'Is that a theory,' he asked, 'or am I to understand it as a fact?'

'I am not confessing to *anything*,' Mrs Warwick answered. 'I am merely putting before you a certain point of view. An emergency might arise at a time when I was no longer here to deal with it. And in the event of such a thing happening, I want you to have this, and to make use of it.' She took an envelope from her pocket and handed it to him.

Starkwedder took the envelope, but remarked, 'That's all very well. However, I shan't be here. I'm going back to Abadan to carry on with my job.'

Mrs Warwick made a gesture of dismissal, clearly regarding the objection as insignificant. 'You won't be out of touch with civilization,' she reminded him. 'There are newspapers, radio and so on in Abadan, presumably.'

'Oh yes,' he agreed. 'We have all the civilized blessings.'

'Then please keep that envelope. You see whom it's addressed to?'

Starkwedder glanced at the envelope. 'The Chief Constable. Yes. But I'm not at all clear what's really in your mind,' he told Mrs Warwick. 'For a woman, you're really remarkably good at keeping a secret. Either you committed this murder yourself, or you know who did commit it. That's right, isn't it?'

She looked away from him as she replied, 'I don't propose to discuss the matter.'

Starkwedder sat in the armchair. 'And yet,' he persisted, 'I'd like very much to know exactly what is in your mind.'

'Then I'm afraid I shan't tell you,' Mrs Warwick retorted. 'As you say, I am a woman who can keep her secrets well.'

Deciding to try a different tack, Starkwedder said, 'This

valet fellow – the chap who looked after your son –' He paused as though trying to remember the valet's name.

'You mean Angell,' Mrs Warwick told him. 'Well, what about Angell?'

'Do you like him?' asked Starkwedder.

'No, I don't, as it happens,' she replied. 'But he was efficient at his job, and Richard was certainly not easy to work for.'

'I imagine not,' Starkwedder remarked. 'But Angell put up with these difficulties, did he?'

'It was made worth his while,' was Mrs Warwick's wry response.

Starkwedder again began to pace about the room. Then he turned to face Mrs Warwick and, trying to draw her out, asked, 'Did Richard have anything on him?'

The old lady looked puzzled for a moment. 'On him?' she repeated. 'What do you mean? Oh, I see. You mean, did Richard know something to Angell's discredit?'

'Yes, that's what I mean,' Starkwedder affirmed. 'Did he have a hold over Angell?'

Mrs Warwick thought for a moment before replying. Then, 'No, I don't think so,' she said.

'I was just wondering –' he began.

'You mean,' Mrs Warwick broke in, impatiently, 'did Angell shoot my son? I doubt it. I doubt that very much.'

'I see. You're not buying that one,' Starkwedder remarked. 'A pity, but there it is.'

Mrs Warwick suddenly got to her feet. 'Thank you, Mr Starkwedder,' she said. 'You have been very kind.'

She gave him her hand. Amused at her abruptness, he shook hands with her, then went to the door and opened it. After a moment she left the room. Starkwedder closed the door after her, smiling. 'Well, I'm damned!' he exclaimed to himself, as he looked again at the envelope. 'What a woman!'

Hurriedly, he put the envelope into his pocket, as Miss Bennett came into the room looking upset and preoccupied. 'What's she been saying to you?' she demanded.

Taken aback, Starkwedder played for time. 'Eh? What's that?' he responded.

'Mrs Warwick – what's she been saying?' Miss Bennett asked again.

Avoiding a direct reply, Starkwedder merely remarked, 'You seem upset.'

'Of course I'm upset,' she replied. 'I know what she's capable of.'

Starkwedder looked at the housekeeper steadily before asking, 'What *is* Mrs Warwick capable of? Murder?'

Miss Bennett took a step towards him. 'Is that what she's been trying to make you believe?' she asked. 'It isn't true, you know. You've got to realize that. It isn't true.'

'Well, one can't be sure. After all, it might be,' he observed judiciously.

'But I tell you it isn't,' she insisted.

'How can you possibly know that?' Starkwedder asked.

'I do know,' Miss Bennett replied. 'Do you think there's anything I don't know about the people in this house? I've been with them for years. Years, I tell you.' She sat in the armchair. 'I care for them very much, all of them.'

'Including the late Richard Warwick?' Starkwedder asked.

Miss Bennett seemed lost in thought for a moment. Then, 'I used to be fond of him – once,' she replied.

There was a pause. Starkwedder sat on the stool and regarded her steadily before murmuring, 'Go on.'

'He changed,' said Miss Bennett. 'He became – warped. His whole mentality became quite different. Sometimes he could be a devil.'

'Yes, everybody seems to agree on that,' Starkwedder observed.

'But if you'd known him as he used to be –' she began.

He interrupted her. 'I don't believe that, you know. I don't think people change.'

'Richard did,' Miss Bennett insisted.

'Oh, no, he didn't,' Starkwedder contradicted her. He resumed his prowling about the room. 'You've got things the wrong way round, I'll bet. I'd say he was always a devil underneath. I'd say he was one of those people who have to be happy and successful – or else! They hide their real selves as long as it gets them what they want. But underneath, the bad streak's always there.'

He turned to face Miss Bennett. 'His cruelty, I bet, was always there. He was probably a bully at school. He was attractive to women, of course. Women are always attracted by bullies. And he took a lot of his sadism out in his big-game hunting, I dare say.' He indicated the hunting trophies on the walls.

'Richard Warwick must have been a monstrous egoist,' he continued. 'That's how he seems to me from the way all you people talk about him. He enjoyed building himself up as a good fellow, generous, successful, lovable and all the rest of it.' Starkwedder was still pacing restlessly. 'But the mean streak was there, all right. And when his accident came, it was just the façade that was torn away, and you all saw him as he really was.'

Miss Bennett rose. 'I don't see that you've got any business to talk,' she exclaimed indignantly. 'You're a stranger, and you know nothing about it.'

'Perhaps not, but I've heard a great deal about it,' Starkwedder retorted. 'Everyone seems to talk to me for some reason.'

'Yes, I suppose they do. Yes, I'm talking to you now, aren't I?' she admitted, as she sat down again. 'That's because we none of us here dare talk to one another.' She looked up at him, appealingly. 'I wish you weren't going away,' she told him.

Starkwedder shook his head. 'I've done nothing to help at all, really,' he said. 'All I've done is blunder in and discover a dead body for you.'

'But it was Laura and I who discovered Richard's body,' Miss Bennett contradicted him. She paused and then suddenly added, 'Or did Laura – did you – ?' Her voice trailed off into silence.

CHAPTER 18

Starkwedder looked at Miss Bennett and smiled. 'You're pretty sharp, aren't you?' he observed.

Miss Bennett stared at him fixedly. 'You helped her, didn't you?' she asked, making it sound like an accusation.

He walked away from her. 'Now you're imagining things,' he told her.

'Oh, no, I'm not,' Miss Bennett retorted. 'I want Laura to be happy. Oh, I so very much want her to be happy!'

Starkwedder turned to her, exclaiming passionately, 'Damn it, so do I!'

Miss Bennett looked at him in surprise. Then she began to speak. 'In that case I – I've got to –' she began, but was interrupted. Gesturing to her to be silent, Starkwedder murmured, 'Just a minute.' He hastened to the french windows, opened a window and called, 'What are you doing?'

Miss Bennett now caught sight of Jan out on the lawn, brandishing a gun. Rising quickly, she too went across to the french windows and called urgently, 'Jan! Jan! Give me that gun.'

Jan, however, was too quick for her. He ran off laughing,

and shouting, 'Come and get it,' as he ran. Miss Bennett followed him, with urgent cries of 'Jan! Jan!'

Starkwedder looked out across the lawn, trying to see what was happening. Then he turned back, and was about to go to the door, when Laura suddenly entered the room.

'Where's the inspector?' she asked him.

Starkwedder made an ineffectual gesture. Laura shut the door behind her, and came over to him. 'Michael, you must listen to me,' she implored him. 'Julian didn't kill Richard.'

'Indeed?' Starkwedder replied coldly. 'He told you so, did he?'

'You don't believe me, but it's true.' Laura sounded desperate.

'You mean you believe it's true,' Starkwedder pointed out to her.

'No, I know it's true,' Laura replied. 'You see, he thought *I'd* killed Richard.'

Starkwedder moved back into the room, away from the french windows. 'That's not exactly surprising,' he said with an acid smile. 'I thought so, too, didn't I?'

Laura's voice sounded even more desperate as she insisted, 'He thought I'd shot Richard. But he couldn't cope with it. It made him feel –' She stopped, embarrassed, then continued, 'It made him feel differently towards me.'

Starkwedder looked at her coldly. 'Whereas,' he pointed out, 'when you thought *he'd* killed Richard, you took it in your stride without turning a hair!' Suddenly relenting a little, he smiled. 'Women are wonderful!' he murmured. He perched on the sofa arm. 'What made Farrar come out with the damaging fact that he was here last night? Don't tell me it was a pure and simple regard for the truth?'

'It was Angell,' Laura replied. 'Angell saw – or says he saw – Julian here.'

'Yes,' Starkwedder remarked with a somewhat bitter laugh. 'I thought I got a whiff of blackmail. Not a nice fellow, Angell.'

'He says he saw Julian just after the – after the shot was fired,' Laura told him. 'Oh, I'm frightened. It's all closing in. I'm so frightened.'

Starkwedder went over to her and took her by the shoulders. 'You needn't be,' he said, reassuringly. 'It's going to be all right.'

Laura shook her head. 'It can't be,' she cried.

'It will be all right, I tell you,' he insisted, shaking her gently.

She looked at him wonderingly. 'Shall we ever know who shot Richard?' she asked him.

Starkwedder looked at her for a moment without replying, and then went to the french windows and gazed out into the garden. 'Your Miss Bennett,' he said, 'seems very positive she knows all the answers.'

'She's always positive,' Laura replied. 'But she's sometimes wrong.'

Apparently glimpsing something outside, Starkwedder suddenly beckoned to Laura to join him. Running across to him, she took his outstretched hand. 'Yes, Laura,' he exclaimed excitedly, still looking out into the garden. 'I thought so!'

'What is it?' she asked.

'Ssh!' he cautioned. At almost the same moment, Miss Bennett came into the room from the hallway. 'Mr Starkwedder,' she said hurriedly. 'Go into the room next door – the inspector's already there. Quickly!'

Starkwedder and Laura crossed the study swiftly, and hurried into the corridor, closing the door behind them. As soon as they had gone, Miss Bennett looked out into the garden, where daylight was beginning to fade. 'Now come in, Jan,' she called to him. 'Don't tease me any more. Come in, come inside.'

CHAPTER 19

Miss Bennett beckoned to Jan, then stepped back into the room and stood to one side of the french windows. Jan suddenly appeared from the terrace, looking half mutinous and half flushed with triumph. He was carrying a gun.

'Now, Jan, how on earth did you get hold of that?' Miss Bennett asked him.

Jan came into the room. 'Thought you were so clever, didn't you, Benny?' he said, quite belligerently. 'Very clever, locking up all Richard's guns in there.' He nodded in the direction of the hallway. 'But I found a key that fitted the gun cupboard. I've got a gun now, just like Richard. I'm going to have lots of guns and pistols. I'm going to shoot things.' He suddenly raised the gun and pointed it at Miss Bennett, who flinched. 'Be careful, Benny,' he went on with a chuckle, 'I might shoot you.'

Miss Bennett tried not to look too alarmed as she said, in as soothing a tone as she could muster, 'Why, you wouldn't do a thing like that, Jan, I know you wouldn't.'

Jan continued to point the gun at Miss Bennett, but after a few moments he lowered it.

Miss Bennett relaxed slightly, and after a pause Jan exclaimed, sweetly and rather eagerly, 'No, I wouldn't. Of course I wouldn't.'

'After all, it's not as though you were just a careless boy,' Miss Bennett told him, reassuringly. 'You're a man now, aren't you?'

Jan beamed. He walked over to the desk and sat in the chair. 'Yes, I'm a man,' he agreed. 'Now that Richard's dead, I'm the only man in the house.'

'That's why I know you wouldn't shoot me,' Miss Bennett said. 'You'd only shoot an enemy.'

'That's right,' Jan exclaimed with delight.

Sounding as though she were choosing her words very carefully, Miss Bennett said, 'During the war, if you were in the Resistance, when you killed an enemy you put a notch on your gun.'

'Is that true?' Jan responded, examining his gun. 'Did they really?' He looked eagerly at Miss Bennett. 'Did some people have a lot of notches?'

'Yes,' she replied, 'some people had quite a lot of notches.'

Jan chortled with glee. 'What fun!' he exclaimed.

'Of course,' Miss Bennett continued, 'some people don't like killing anything – but other people do.'

'Richard did,' Jan reminded her.

'Yes, Richard liked killing things,' Miss Bennett admitted. She turned away from him casually, as she added, 'You like killing things, too, don't you, Jan?'

Unseen by her, Jan took a penknife from his pocket and began to make a notch on his gun. 'It's exciting to kill things,' he observed, a trifle petulantly.

Miss Bennett turned back to face him. 'You didn't want

Richard to have you sent away, did you, Jan?' she asked him quietly.

'He said he would,' Jan retorted with feeling. 'He was a beast!'

Miss Bennett walked around behind the desk chair in which Jan was still sitting. 'You said to Richard once,' she reminded him, 'that you'd kill him if he was going to send you away.'

'Did I?' Jan responded. He sounded nonchalantly offhand.

'But you didn't kill him?' Miss Bennett asked, her intonation making her words into only a half-question.

'Oh, no, I didn't kill him.' Again, Jan sounded unconcerned.

'That was rather weak of you,' Miss Bennett observed.

There was a crafty look in Jan's eyes as he responded, 'Was it?'

'Yes, I think so. To say you'd kill him, and then not to do it.' Miss Bennett moved around the desk, but looked towards the door. 'If anyone was threatening to shut *me* up, I'd want to kill him, and I'd do it, too.'

'Who says someone else did?' Jan retorted swiftly. 'Perhaps it *was* me.'

'Oh, no, it wouldn't be you,' Miss Bennett said, dismissively. 'You were only a boy. You wouldn't have dared.'

Jan jumped up and backed away from her. 'You think I wouldn't have dared?' His voice was almost a squeal. 'Is that what you think?'

'Of course it's what I think.' She seemed now deliberately to be taunting him. 'Of course you wouldn't have dared to kill Richard. You'd have to be very brave and grown-up to do that.'

Jan turned his back on her, and walked away. 'You don't

know everything, Benny,' he said, sounding hurt. 'Oh no, old Benny. You don't know everything.'

'Is there something I don't know?' Miss Bennett asked him. 'Are you laughing at me, Jan?' Seizing her opportunity, she opened the door a little way. Jan stood near the french windows, whence a shaft of light from the setting sun shone across the room.

'Yes, yes, I'm laughing,' Jan suddenly shouted at her. 'I'm laughing because I'm so much cleverer than you are.'

He turned back into the room. Miss Bennett involuntarily gave a start and clutched the door frame. Jan took a step towards her. 'I know things you don't know,' Jan added, speaking more soberly.

'What do you know that I don't know?' Miss Bennett asked. She tried not to sound too anxious.

Jan made no reply, but merely smiled mysteriously. Miss Bennett approached him. 'Aren't you going to tell me?' she asked again, coaxingly. 'Won't you trust me with your secret?'

Jan drew away from her. 'I don't trust anybody,' he said, bitterly.

Miss Bennett changed her tone to one of puzzlement. 'I wonder, now,' she murmured. 'I wonder if perhaps you've been very clever.'

Jan giggled. 'You're beginning to see how clever I can be,' he told her.

She regarded him speculatively. 'Perhaps there are a lot of things I don't know about you,' she agreed.

'Oh, lots and lots,' Jan assured her. 'And I know a lot of things about everybody else, but I don't always tell. I get up sometimes in the night and I creep about the house. I see a lot of things, and I find out a lot of things, but I don't tell.'

Adopting a conspiratorial air, Miss Bennett asked, 'Have you got some big secret now?'

Jan swung one leg over the stool, sitting astride it. 'Big secret! Big secret!' he squealed delightedly. 'You'd be frightened if you knew,' he added, laughing almost hysterically.

Miss Bennett came closer to him. 'Would I? Would I be frightened?' she asked. 'Would I be frightened of *you*, Jan?' Placing herself squarely in front of Jan, she stared intently at him.

Jan looked up at her. The expression of delight left his face, and his voice was very serious as he replied, 'Yes, you'd be very frightened of me.'

She continued to regard him closely. 'I haven't known what you were really like,' she admitted. 'I'm just beginning to understand what you're like, Jan.'

Jan's mood changes were becoming more pronounced. Sounding more and more wild, he exclaimed, 'Nobody knows anything about me really, or the things I can do.' He swung round on the stool, and sat with his back to her. 'Silly old Richard, sitting there and shooting at silly old birds.' He turned back to Miss Bennett, adding intensely, 'He didn't think anyone would shoot *him*, did he?'

'No,' she replied. 'No, that was his mistake.'

Jan rose. 'Yes, that was his mistake,' he agreed. 'He thought he could send me away, didn't he? *I* showed him.'

'Did you?' asked Miss Bennett quickly. 'How did you show him?'

Jan looked at her craftily. He paused, then finally said, 'Shan't tell you.'

'Oh, do tell me, Jan,' she pleaded.

'No,' he retorted, moving away from her. He went to the

armchair and climbed into it, nestling the gun against his cheek. 'No, I shan't tell anyone.'

Miss Bennett went across to him. 'Perhaps you're right,' she told him. 'Perhaps I can guess what you did, but I won't say. It will be just your secret, won't it?'

'Yes, it's my secret,' Jan replied. He began to move restlessly about the room. 'Nobody knows what I'm like,' he exclaimed excitedly. 'I'm dangerous. They'd better be careful. Everybody had better be careful. I'm *dangerous*.'

Miss Bennett looked at him sadly. 'Richard didn't know how dangerous you were,' she said. 'He must have been surprised.'

Jan went back to the armchair, and looked into it. 'He was. He was surprised,' he agreed. 'His face went all silly. And then – and then his head dropped down when it was done, and there was blood, and he didn't move any more. I showed him. I showed him! Richard won't send me away now!'

He perched on one end of the sofa, waving the gun at Miss Bennett who was trying to fight back her tears. 'Look,' Jan ordered her. 'Look. See? I've put a notch on my gun!' He tapped the gun with his knife.

'So you have!' Miss Bennett exclaimed, approaching him. 'Isn't that exciting?' She tried to grab the gun, but he was too quick for her.

'Oh, no, you don't,' he cried, as he danced away from her. 'Nobody's going to take my gun away from me. If the police come and try to arrest me, I shall shoot them.'

'There's no need to do that,' Miss Bennett assured him. 'No need at all. You're clever. You're so clever that they would never suspect you.'

'Silly old police! Silly old police!' Jan shouted jubilantly.

'And silly old Richard.' He brandished the gun at an imaginary Richard, then caught sight of the door opening. With a cry of alarm, he quickly ran off into the garden. Miss Bennett collapsed upon the sofa in tears, as Inspector Thomas hastened into the room followed by Sergeant Cadwallader.

'After him! Quickly!' the inspector shouted to Cadwallader as they ran into the room. The sergeant raced out onto the terrace through the french windows, as Starkwedder rushed into the room from the hallway. He was followed by Laura, who ran to the french windows and looked out. Angell was the next to appear. He, too, went across to the french windows. Mrs Warwick stood, an upright figure, in the doorway.

Inspector Thomas turned to Miss Bennett. 'There, there, dear lady,' he comforted her. 'You mustn't take on so. You did very well.'

In a broken voice, Miss Bennett replied. 'I've known all along,' she told the inspector. 'You see, I know better than anyone else what Jan is like. I knew that Richard was pushing him too far, and I knew – I've known for some time – that Jan was getting dangerous.'

'Jan!' Laura exclaimed. With a sigh of deep distress, she murmured, 'Oh, no, oh, no, not Jan.' She sank into the desk chair. 'I can't believe it,' she gasped.

Mrs Warwick glared at Miss Bennett. 'How could you,

Benny?' she said, accusingly. 'How could you? I thought that at least you would be loyal.'

Miss Bennett's reply was defiant. 'There are times,' she told the old lady, 'when truth is more important than loyalty. You didn't see – any of you – that Jan was becoming dangerous. He's a dear boy – a sweet boy – but –' Overcome with grief, she was unable to continue.

Mrs Warwick moved slowly and sadly across to the armchair and sat, staring into space.

Speaking quietly, the inspector completed Miss Bennett's thought. 'But when they get above a certain age, then they get dangerous, because they don't understand what they're doing any more,' he observed. 'They haven't got a man's judgement or control.' He went across to Mrs Warwick. 'You mustn't grieve, madam. I think I can take it upon myself to say that he'll be treated with humanity and consideration. There's a clear case to be made, I think, for his not being responsible for his actions. It'll mean detention in comfortable surroundings. And that, you know, is what it would have come to soon, in any case.' He turned away, and walked across the room, closing the hall door as he passed it.

'Yes, yes, I know you're right,' Mrs Warwick admitted. Turning to Miss Bennett, she said, 'I'm sorry, Benny. You said that nobody else knew he was dangerous. That's not true. I knew – but I couldn't bring myself to do anything about it.'

'Somebody had to do something!' Benny replied strongly. The room fell silent, but tension mounted as they all waited for Sergeant Cadwallader's return with Jan in custody.

By the side of the road several hundred yards from the house, with a mist beginning to close in, the sergeant had got Jan cornered with a high wall behind him. Jan brandished his gun, shouting, 'Don't come any closer. No one's going to shut me away anywhere. I'll shoot you. I mean it. I'm not frightened of anyone!'

The sergeant stopped a good twenty feet away. 'Now come on, lad,' he called, coaxingly. 'No one's going to hurt you. But guns are dangerous things. Just give it to me, and come back to the house with me. You can talk to your family, and they'll help you.'

He advanced a few steps towards Jan, but stopped when the boy cried hysterically, 'I mean it. I'll shoot you. I don't care about policemen. I'm not frightened of you.'

'Of course you're not,' the sergeant replied. 'You've no reason to be frightened of me. I wouldn't hurt you. But come back into the house with me. Come on, now.' He stepped forward again, but Jan jerked the gun up and fired two shots in quick succession. The first went wide, but the second struck Cadwallader in the left hand. He gave a cry of pain, but rushed at Jan, knocking him to the ground, and attempting to get the gun away from him. As they struggled, the gun suddenly went off again. Jan gave a quick gasp, and lay silent.

Horrified, the sergeant knelt over him, staring at him in disbelief. 'No, oh no,' he murmured. 'Poor, silly boy. No! You can't be dead. Oh, please God –' He checked Jan's pulse, then shook his head slowly. Rising to his feet, he backed slowly away for a few paces, and only then noticed that his hand was bleeding badly. Wrapping a handkerchief around it, he ran back to the house, holding his left arm in the air and gasping with pain.

By the time he got back to the french windows, he was

staggering. 'Sir!' he called, as the inspector and the others ran out onto the terrace.

'What on earth's happened?' the inspector asked.

His breath coming with difficulty, the sergeant replied, 'It's terrible, what I've got to tell you.' Starkwedder helped him into the room and the sergeant staggered to the stool and sank onto it.

The inspector moved quickly to his side. 'Your hand!' he exclaimed.

'I'll see to it,' Starkwedder murmured. Holding Sergeant Cadwallader's arm, he discarded the now heavily bloodstained piece of cloth, took out a handkerchief from his own pocket, and began to tie it around the sergeant's hand.

'The mist coming on, you see,' Cadwallader began to explain. 'It was difficult to see clearly. He shot at me. Up there, along the road, near the edge of the spinney.'

With a look of horror on her face, Laura rose and went across to the french windows.

'He shot at me twice,' the sergeant was saying, 'and the second time he got me in the hand.'

Miss Bennett suddenly rose, and put her hand to her mouth. 'I tried to get the gun away from him,' the sergeant went on, 'but I was hampered with my hand, you see –'

'Yes. What happened?' the inspector prompted him.

'His finger was on the trigger,' the sergeant gasped, 'and it went off. He's shot through the heart. He's dead.'

CHAPTER 21

Sergeant Cadwallader's announcement was greeted with a stunned silence. Laura put her hand to her mouth to stifle a cry, then slowly moved back to the desk chair and sat, staring at the floor. Mrs Warwick lowered her head and leaned on her stick. Starkwedder paced about the room, looking distracted.

'Are you sure he's dead?' the inspector asked.

'I am indeed,' the sergeant replied. 'Poor young lad, shouting defiance at me, loosing off his gun as though he loved the firing of it.'

The inspector walked across to the french windows. 'Where is he?'

'I'll come with you and show you,' the sergeant replied, struggling to his feet.

'No, you'd better stay here.'

'I'm all right now,' the sergeant insisted. 'I'll do all right until we get back to the station.' He walked out onto the terrace, swaying slightly. Looking back at the others, his face filled with misery, he murmured distractedly, '"One would not, sure, be frightful when one's dead." That's Pope.

Alexander Pope.' He shook his head, and then walked slowly away.

The inspector turned back to face Mrs Warwick and the others. 'I'm more sorry than I can say, but perhaps it's the best way out,' he said, then followed the sergeant out into the garden.

Mrs Warwick watched him go. 'The best way out!' she exclaimed, half angrily, half despairingly.

'Yes, yes,' Miss Bennett sighed. 'It is for the best. He's out of it now, poor boy.' She went to help Mrs Warwick up. 'Come, my dear, come, this has been too much for you.'

The old lady looked at her vaguely. 'I – I'll go and lie down,' she murmured, as Miss Bennett supported her to the door. Starkwedder opened it for them, and then took an envelope out of his pocket, holding it out to Mrs Warwick. 'I think you'd better have this back,' he suggested.

She turned in the doorway and took the envelope from him. 'Yes,' she replied. 'Yes, there's no need for that now.'

Mrs Warwick and Miss Bennett left the room. Starkwedder was about to close the door after them when he realized that Angell was moving across to Laura who was still sitting at the desk. She did not turn at his approach.

'May I say, madam,' Angell addressed her, 'how sorry I am. If there is anything I can do, you have only –'

Without looking up, Laura interrupted him. 'We shall need no more help from you, Angell,' she told him coldly. 'You shall have a cheque for your wages, and I should like you out of the house today.'

'Yes, madam. Thank you, madam,' Angell replied, apparently without feeling, then turned away and left the room. Starkwedder closed the door after him. The room was now growing dark, the last rays of the sun throwing shadows on the walls.

Starkwedder looked across at Laura. 'You're not going to prosecute him for blackmail?' he asked.

'No,' Laura replied, listlessly.

'A pity.' He walked over to her. 'Well, I suppose I'd better be going. I'll say goodbye.' He paused. Laura still had not looked at him. 'Don't be too upset,' he added.

'I *am* upset,' Laura responded with feeling.

'Because you loved the boy?' Starkwedder asked.

She turned to him. 'Yes. And because it's my fault. You see, Richard was right. Poor Jan should have been sent away somewhere. He should have been shut up where he couldn't do any harm. It was I who wouldn't have that. So, really, it was my fault that Richard was killed.'

'Come now, Laura, don't let's sentimentalize,' Starkwedder retorted roughly. He came closer to her. 'Richard was killed because he asked for it. He could have shown some ordinary kindness to the boy, couldn't he? Don't you fret yourself. What you've got to do now is to be happy. Happy ever after, as the stories say.'

'Happy? With Julian?' Laura responded with bitterness in her voice. 'I wonder!' She frowned. 'You see, it isn't the same now.'

'You mean between Farrar and you?' he asked.

'Yes. You see, when I thought Julian had killed Richard, it made no difference to me. I loved him just the same.' Laura paused, then continued, 'I was even willing to say I'd done it myself.'

'I know you were,' said Starkwedder. 'More fool you. How women enjoy making martyrs of themselves!'

'But when Julian thought *I* had done it,' Laura continued passionately, 'he changed. He changed towards me completely. Oh, he was willing to try to do the decent thing and not incriminate me. But that was all.' She leaned her chin on her hand, dispirited. 'He didn't feel the same any more.'

Starkwedder shook his head. 'Look here, Laura,' he exclaimed, 'men and women don't react in the same way. What it comes down to is this. Men are really the sensitive sex. Women are tough. Men can't take murder in their stride. Women apparently can. The fact is, if a man's committed a murder for a woman, it probably enhances his value in her eyes. A man feels differently.'

She looked up at him. 'You didn't feel that way,' she observed. 'When *you* thought I had shot Richard, you helped me.'

'That was different,' Starkwedder replied quickly. He sounded slightly taken aback. 'I had to help you.'

'Why did you have to help me?' Laura asked him.

Starkwedder did not reply directly. Then, after a pause, he said quietly, 'I still want to help you.'

'Don't you see,' said Laura, turning away from him, 'we're back where we started. In a way it *was* I who killed Richard because – because I was being so obstinate about Jan.'

Starkwedder drew up the stool and sat down beside her. 'That's what's eating you, really, isn't it?' he declared. 'Finding out that it was Jan who shot Richard. But it needn't be true, you know. You needn't think that unless you like.'

Laura stared at him intently. 'How can you say such a thing?' she asked. 'I heard – we all heard – he admitted it – he boasted of it.'

'Oh, yes,' Starkwedder admitted. 'Yes, I know that. But how

much do you know about the power of suggestion? Your Miss Bennett played Jan very carefully, got him all worked up. And the boy was certainly suggestible. He liked the idea, as many adolescents do, of being thought to have power, of – yes, of being a killer, if you like. Your Benny dangled the bait in front of him, and he took it. He'd shot Richard, and he put a notch on his gun, and he was a hero!' He paused. 'But you don't know – none of us really know – whether what he said was true.'

'But, for heaven's sake, he shot at the sergeant!' Laura expostulated.

'Oh, yes, he was a potential killer all right!' Starkwedder admitted. 'It's quite likely he shot Richard. But you can't say for sure that he did. It might have been –' He hesitated. 'It might have been somebody else.'

Laura stared at him in disbelief. 'But who?' she asked, incredulously.

Starkwedder thought for a moment. Then, 'Miss Bennett, perhaps,' he suggested. 'After all, she's very fond of you all, and she might have thought it was all for the best. Or, for that matter, Mrs Warwick. Or even your boyfriend Julian – afterwards pretending that he thought you'd done it. A clever move which took you in completely.'

Laura turned away. 'You don't believe what you're saying,' she accused him. 'You're only trying to console me.'

Starkwedder looked absolutely exasperated. 'My dear girl,' he expostulated, 'anyone might have shot Richard. Even MacGregor.'

'MacGregor?' she asked, staring at him. 'But MacGregor's dead.'

'Of course he's dead,' Starkwedder replied. 'He'd have to

be.' He rose and moved to the sofa. 'Look here,' he continued, 'I can put up a very pretty case for MacGregor having been the killer. Say he decided to kill Richard as revenge for the accident in which his little boy was killed.' He sat on the sofa arm. 'What does he do? Well, first thing is he has to get rid of his own personality. It wouldn't be difficult to arrange for him to be reported dead in some remote part of Alaska. It would cost a little money and some fake testimony, of course, but these things can be managed. Then he changes his name, and he starts building up a new personality for himself in some other country, some other job.'

Laura stared at him for a moment, then left the desk and went to sit in the armchair. Closing her eyes, she took a deep breath, then opened her eyes and looked at him again.

Starkwedder continued with his speculative narrative. 'He keeps tabs on what's going on over here, and when he knows that you've left Norfolk and come to this part of the world, he makes his plans. He shaves his beard, and dyes his hair, and all that sort of thing, of course. Then, on a misty night, he comes here. Now, let's say it goes like this.' He went and stood by the french windows. 'Let's say MacGregor says to Richard, "I've got a gun, and so have you. I count three, and we both fire. I've come to get you for the death of my boy."'

Laura stared at him, appalled.

'You know,' Starkwedder went on, 'I don't think that your husband was quite the fine sporting fellow you think he was. I have an idea he mightn't have waited for a count of three. You say he was a damn good shot, but this time he missed, and the bullet went out here' – he gestured as he walked out onto the terrace – 'into the garden where there are a good many other bullets. But MacGregor doesn't miss. He shoots and kills.' Starkwedder came back into the room. 'He drops his gun by the body, takes Richard's gun, goes out of the window, and presently he comes back.'

'Comes back?' Laura asked. 'Why does he come back?'

Starkwedder looked at her for a few seconds without speaking. Then, taking a deep breath, he asked, 'Can't you guess?'

Laura looked at him wonderingly. She shook her head. 'No, I've no idea,' she replied.

He continued to regard her steadily. After a pause, he spoke slowly and with an effort. 'Well,' he said, 'suppose MacGregor has an accident with his car and can't get away from here. What else can he do? Only one thing – come up to the house and discover the body!'

'You speak –' Laura gasped, 'you speak as though you know just what happened.'

Starkwedder could no longer restrain himself. 'Of course I know,' he burst out passionately. 'Don't you understand? *I'm* MacGregor!' He leaned back against the curtains, shaking his head desperately.

Laura rose, an incredulous look on her face. She stepped towards him, half raising her arm, unable to grasp the full meaning of his words. 'You –' she murmured. 'You –'

Starkwedder walked slowly towards Laura. 'I never meant any of this to happen,' he told her, his voice husky with emotion. 'I mean – finding you, and finding that I cared about you, and that – Oh, God, it's hopeless. Hopeless.' As she stared at him, dazed, Starkwedder took her hand and kissed the palm. 'Goodbye, Laura,' he said, gruffly.

He went quickly out through the french windows and disappeared into the mist. Laura ran out onto the terrace and called after him, 'Wait – wait. Come back!'

The mist swirled, and the Bristol fog signal began to boom. 'Come back, Michael, come back!' Laura cried. There was no reply. 'Come back, Michael,' she called again. 'Please come back! I care about you too.'

She listened intently, but heard only the sound of a car starting up and moving off. The fog signal continued to sound as she collapsed against the window and burst into a fit of uncontrollable sobbing.

•

THE PLAYS OF AGATHA CHRISTIE

•

Alibi, the earliest Agatha Christie play to reach the stage, opening at the Prince of Wales Theatre, London, in May 1928, was not written by Christie herself. It was an adaptation by Michael Morton of her 1926 crime novel, *The Murder of Roger Ackroyd*, and Hercule Poirot was played by Charles Laughton. Christie disliked both the play and Laughton's performance. It was largely because of her dissatisfaction with *Alibi* that she decided to put Poirot on the stage in a play of her own. The result was *Black Coffee*, which ran for several months at St Martin's Theatre, London, in 1930.

Seven years passed before Agatha Christie wrote her next play, *Akhnaton*. It was not a murder mystery but the story of the ancient Pharaoh who attempted to persuade a polytheistic Egypt to turn to the worship of one deity, the sun-god Aton. *Akhnaton* failed to reach the stage in 1937, and lay forgotten for thirty-five years until, in the course of spring cleaning, its author found the typescript again and had it published.

Although she had disliked *Alibi* in 1928, Agatha Christie gave her permission, over the years, for five more of her works to be adapted for the stage by other hands. The earliest of these was *Love From a Stranger* (1936), which Frank Vosper, a popular leading man in British theatre in the twenties and thirties, adapted from the short story 'Philomel Cottage', writing the leading male role for himself to play. The 1932 Hercule Poirot novel, *Peril at End House*, became a play of the same title in 1940, adapted by Arnold Ridley, who was well known as the author of *The Ghost Train*, a popular play of the time. With *Murder at the Vicarage*, a 1949 dramatization by Moie Charles and Barbara Toy of a 1940 novel of the same title, Agatha Christie's other popular investigator, Miss Marple, made her stage debut.

Disillusioned with one or two of these stage adaptations by other writers, in 1945 Agatha Christie had herself begun to adapt some of her already published novels for the theatre. The 1939 murder mystery *Ten Little Niggers* (a title later changed, for obvious reasons, to *And Then There Were None*) was staged very successfully both in London in 1943 and in New York the following year.

Christie's adaptation of *Appointment with Death*, a crime novel published in 1928, was staged in 1945, and two other novels which she subsequently turned into plays were *Death on the Nile* (1937), performed in 1945 as *Murder on the Nile*, and *The Hollow*, published in 1946 and staged in 1951. These three novels all featured Hercule Poirot as the investigator, but in adapting them for the stage, Christie removed Poirot. 'I had got used to having Poirot in my books,' she said of one of them, 'and so naturally he had come into this one, but he was all wrong there. He did his stuff all right, but how much better, I kept thinking, would the book have been without him. So when I came to sketch out the play, out went Poirot.'

For her next play after *The Hollow*, Agatha Christie turned not to a novel, but to her short story 'Three Blind Mice', which had itself been based on a radio play she wrote in 1947 for one of her greatest fans, Queen Mary, widow of the British monarch George V. The Queen, who was celebrating her eightieth birthday that year, had asked the BBC to commission a radio play from Agatha Christie, and 'Three Blind Mice' was the result. For its transmogrification into a stage play, a new title was found, lifted from Shakespeare's *Hamlet*. During the performance which Hamlet causes to be staged before Claudius and Gertrude, the King asks, 'What do you call the play?' to which Hamlet replies, 'The Mousetrap'. *The Mousetrap* opened in London in November 1952, and its producer, Peter Saunders, told Christie that he had hopes for a long run of a year or even fourteen months. 'It won't run that long,' the playwright replied. 'Eight months, perhaps.' Fifty years later, *The Mousetrap* is still running, and may well go on for ever.

A few weeks into the run of *The Mousetrap*, Saunders suggested to Agatha Christie that she should adapt for the stage another of her short stories, 'Witness for the Prosecution'. But she thought this would prove too difficult, and told Saunders to try it himself. This he proceeded to do, and in due course he delivered the first draft of a play to her. When she had read it, Christie told him she did not think his version good enough, but that he had certainly shown her how it could be done. Six weeks later, she had completed the play that she later considered one of her best. On its first night in October 1953 at the Winter Garden Theatre in Drury Lane, the audience sat spellbound by the ingenuity of the surprise ending. *Witness for the Prosecution* played for 468 performances, and enjoyed an even longer run of 646 performances in New York.

Shortly after *Witness for the Prosecution* was launched, Agatha Christie agreed to write a play for the British film star, Margaret Lockwood, who wanted a role that would exploit her talent for comedy. The result was an enjoyable comedy-thriller, *Spider's Web*, which made satirical use of that creaky old device, the secret passage. In December 1954, it opened at the Savoy Theatre, where it stayed for 774 performances, joining *The Mousetrap* and *Witness for the Prosecution*. Agatha Christie had three successful plays running simultaneously in London.

For the next theatre venture, Christie collaborated with Gerald Verner to adapt *Towards Zero*, a murder mystery she had written ten years previously. Opening at St James's Theatre in September 1956, it had a respectable run of six months. The author was now in her late sixties, but still producing at least one novel a year and several short stories, as well as working on her autobiography. She was to write five more plays, all but one of them original works for the stage and not adaptations of novels. The exception was *Go Back for Murder*, a stage version of her 1943 Hercule Poirot murder mystery, *Five Little Pigs*, and once again she banished Poirot from the plot, making the investigator a personable young solicitor. The play opened at the Duchess Theatre in March 1960, but closed after only thirty-one performances.

Her four remaining plays, all original stage works, were *Verdict*, *The Unexpected Guest* (both first staged in 1958), *Rule of Three* (1962), and *Fiddlers Three* (1972). *Rule of Three* is actually three unconnected one-act plays, the last of which, 'The Patient', is an excellent mystery thriller with an unbeatable final line. However, audiences stayed away from this evening of three separate plays, and *Rule of Three* closed at the Duchess Theatre after ten weeks.

Christie's final work for the theatre, *Fiddlers Three*, did not even reach London. It toured the English provinces in 1971 as *Fiddlers Five*, was withdrawn to be rewritten, and reopened at the Yvonne Arnaud Theatre, Guildford, in August 1972. After touring quite successfully for several weeks, it failed to find a suitable London theatre and closed out-of-town.

Verdict, which opened at London's Strand Theatre in May 1958, is unusual in that, although a murder does occur in the play, there is no mystery attached to it, for it is committed in full view of the audience. It closed after a month, but its resilient author murmured, 'At least I am glad *The Times* liked it,' immediately set to work to write another play, and completed it within four weeks. This was *The Unexpected Guest*, which, after a week in Bristol, moved to the Duchess Theatre, London, where it opened in August 1958 and had a satisfactory run of eighteen months. One of the best of Agatha Christie's plays, its dialogue is taut and effective, and its plot full of surprises, despite being economical and not over-complex. Reviews were uniformly enthusiastic, and now, more than forty years later, it has begun a new lease of life as a novel.

A few months before her death in 1976, Agatha Christie gave her consent for a stage adaptation to be made by Leslie Darbon of her 1950 novel, *A Murder is Announced*, which featured Miss Marple. When the play reached the stage posthumously in 1977, the critic of *The Financial Times* predicted that it would run as long as *The Mousetrap*. It did not.

In 1981, Leslie Darbon adapted one more Christie novel, *Cards on the Table*, a Poirot murder mystery published forty-five years earlier. Taking a leaf from the author's book where Hercule Poirot was concerned, Darbon removed him from the cast of characters. To date, there have been no more stage adaptations of Agatha Christie novels. With *Black Coffee*, *The Unexpected Guest*, and now *Spider's Web*, I have started a trend in the opposite direction.

CHARLES OSBORNE

Agatha Christie

The
MARY WESTMACOTT
Collection

VOLUME ONE

Agatha Christie is known throughout the world as the Queen of Crime. It was her sharp observations of people's ambitions, relationships and conflicts that added life and sparkle to her ingenious detective novels. When she turned this understanding of human nature away from the crime genre, writing anonymously as Mary Westmacott, she created bittersweet novels, love stories with a jagged edge, as compelling and memorable as the best of her work.

GIANT'S BREAD

When a gifted composer returns home after being reported killed in the war, he finds his wife has already remarried...

UNFINISHED PORTRAIT

On the verge of suicide after a marriage break up, a young novelist unburdens herself on an unsuspecting young man...

ABSENT IN THE SPRING

Unexpectedly stranded in Iraq, a loyal wife and mother tries to come to terms with her husband's love for another woman...

'I've not been so emotionally moved by a story since the memorable *Brief Encounter*. *Absent in the Spring* is a *tour de force* which should be recognized as a classic.'   *New York Times*

Agatha Christie

The
MARY WESTMACOTT
Collection

VOLUME TWO

Agatha Christie is known throughout the world as the Queen of Crime. It was her sharp observations of people's ambitions, relationships and conflicts that added life and sparkle to her ingenious detective novels. When she turned this understanding of human nature away from the crime genre, writing anonymously as Mary Westmacott, she created bittersweet novels, love stories with a jagged edge, as compelling and memorable as the best of her work.

THE ROSE AND THE YEW TREE

When an aristocratic young woman falls for a working-class war hero, the price of love proves to be costly for both sides…

A DAUGHTER'S A DAUGHTER

Rejecting personal happiness for the sake of her daughter, a mother later regrets the decision and love turns to bitterness…

THE BURDEN

With childhood jealousy behind them, the growing bond between two sisters becomes dangerously one-sided and destructive…

'Miss Westmacott writes crisply and is always lucid. Much material has been skilfully compressed within little more than 200 pages.'   *Times Literary Supplement*

ALSO AVAILABLE

Agatha Christie

The Complete
PARKER PYNE
Private Eye

'ARE YOU HAPPY? IF NOT, CONSULT MR PARKER PYNE, 17 Richmond Street.'

This advertisement appears in *The Times* every morning. Some readers ignore it. Some chuckle, and read on. And a few, the forlorn, the anxious and the unhappy, make their way to the office of a small, balding ex-civil servant who has set himself up as a private investigator. The cases taken on by this typically (some would say conspicuously) English globe-trotter are rarely concerned with crime in the legal sense of that word, for Christopher Parker Pyne describes himself as a 'heart specialist'.

Agatha Christie is well known for Poirot, Marple and Tommy & Tuppence, but it was always a delight when she created other recurring characters. A particular favourite was the kind-hearted yet businesslike Parker Pyne, inspired by an ebullient old gentleman whose enthusiasm for statistics captivated her one lunchtime.

Now, for the first time, this edition brings together all the stories featuring the rather fat and unconventional Mr Parker Pyne, who looked destined to rival Agatha's famous Belgian detective in popularity when *Parker Pyne Investigates* was first published, yet whose appearances were ultimately confined to these 14 ingenious and affectionate stories.

'Crimes of the heart were his forté.'   *Observer*

Agatha Christie Mallowan

COME, TELL ME
HOW YOU LIVE

Agatha Christie was already well known as a crime writer when she accompanied her husband, Max Mallowan, to Syria and Iraq in the 1930s. She took enormous interest in all his excavations, and when friends asked what her strange life was like, she decided to answer their questions in this delightful book.

First published in 1946, *Come, Tell Me How You Live* gives a charming picture of Agatha Christie herself, while also giving insight into some of her most popular novels, including *Murder in Mesopotamia* and *Appointment with Death*. It is, as Jacquetta Hawkes concludes in her introduction, 'a pure pleasure to read'.

'A pure pleasure to read.'

JACQUETTA HAWKES, *from the Introduction*

'Perfectly delightful … colourful, lively and occasionally touching and thought-provoking.'

CHARLES OSBORNE, *Books & Bookmen*

'Good and enjoyable … she has a delightfully light touch.'

MARGHANITA LASKI, *Country Life*

Agatha Christie

The Complete
QUIN & SATTERTHWAITE
Love Detectives

Agatha Christie is well known for creating Poirot, Marple and Tommy & Tuppence. But she wrote about a number of recurring characters, including the enigmatic Messrs Quin and Satterthwaite.

'Mr Quin stories are my favourite. I wrote one, not very often, at intervals perhaps of three or four months, sometimes longer still. Magazines appeared to like them, and I liked them myself – I didn't want to do a series of Mr Quin: I only wanted to do one when I felt like it.

'Mr Quin was a figure who just entered into a story – a catalyst, no more – his mere presence affected human beings. There would be some little fact, some apparently irrelevant phrase, to point him out for what he was: a man shown in a harlequin-coloured light that fell on him through a glass window; a sudden appearance or disappearance. Always he stood for the same thing: he was a friend of lovers, and connected with death.

'Little Mr Satterthwaite, who was, as you might say, Mr Quin's emissary, also became a favourite character of mine … The gossip, the looker-on at life, the little man who, without ever touching the depths of joy and sorrow himself, recognizes drama when he sees it, and is conscious that he has a part to play.'

For the first time, this edition brings their stories and novels together into one captivating collection, a rare treat for discriminating readers of crime and mystery.

Agatha Christie

Collected SHORT STORIES
30 Thrilling Tales of Mystery and Suspense

Agatha Christie was the woman the *Daily Express* famously christened 'the Queen of Crime' – and in more than 25 years since her death, she has never been succeeded or deposed.

Here, for the first time, 30 of her stories have been collected together, perfectly illustrating the true breadth of her talent. From macabre tales of the supernatural, through suspense-ridden mysteries, to heart-stopping cases of murder, this collection includes some of her very best short stories.

In the celebrated *Philomel Cottage*, the appearance of a newly-wedded woman's old flame heralds disaster – but for whom? In *Wireless*, a dead husband communicates with his wife through a newly-bought radio, whilst *The Lamp* tells the story of a child's playmate – a playmate only the child appears to be able top see. And, most famously of all, *Witness for the Prosecution* is a stunning courtroom drama in which a scheming wife testifies against her husband in a shocking murder trial …

Rivalling even the best of her novels, these 30 stories show why Agatha Christie's reign is sure to be a long one.